A LONG DECEMBER

Richard Chizmar

SUBTERRANEAN PRESS 2016

"Powerful…I love it… Richard Chizmar writes clean, no-nonsense prose… sets his tales in no-nonsense, middle class neighborhoods I can relate to… and writes terrific stories served with a very large slice of Disquiet Pie."

— STEPHEN KING

"Chizmar's stories are hard-hitting, spooky, suspenseful, poignant, harrowing, heartbreaking and most of all very well-written. Excellent work!"

— ROBERT MCCAMMON

"Like Ray Bradbury, Richard Chizmar has a sweet, nostalgic streak. The past in his stories is always a warm, perfect place. The present, however, belongs more to Robert Bloch, as wonder gives way to horror. The twists are worthy of the old *Twilight Zone*. Enjoy."

— STEWART O'NAN

"It's an idyllic little world Richard Chizmar has created. Boys fish in the shallows of a winding creek. A father tosses a baseball with his young son in the fading light of a summer day. There's the smell of fresh-cut grass. And then, well…just beneath the surface? There are those missing pets whose collars turn up in a shoebox. Or the disturbing photos the dead can leave behind. Or the terrible thing you might find yourself doing when a long lost brother suddenly returns, demanding money. Chizmar does a tremendous job of peeling back his world's shiny layers, revealing the rot that lies underneath. His stories feel like so many teeth: short and sharp and ready to draw blood."

— SCOTT SMITH

"Richard Chizmar's voice is authentic and powerful, and the stories he tells in A *Long December* are a joy, by turns dark and darkly funny, always compelling, always evocative. He hooks you fast and his words will linger in your mind long after you've finished reading, the mark of a special talent."

—MICHAEL KORYTA

"Exceptional stories that lay our hearts, lives and fears bare with brutal, beautiful economy."

—MICHAEL MARSHALL SMITH

"Richard Chizmar's talent is a fierce, poignant marvel. His exquisite stories shatter."

—RICHARD CHRISTIAN MATHESON

"Richard Chizmar is the kind of writer I love—his prose is sharp, simple, and to the point. He grabs your attention in the first paragraph, and never lets go, and, even better, his writing never gets in the way of his story. It flows so smoothly it's as if you're experiencing it rather than reading it. Another writer told me years ago that whenever he wrote what he thought was a showstopper of a sentence or paragraph, he would stop writing, admire his work, then immediately cut it. 'The last thing you want the reader to do is stop to admire the writing,' he said. 'All that does is pull them out of the story you're trying to tell.' This, of course, is not advice you'll ever hear from MFA writing programs, but for those of us battling in the trenches every day, it was great advice. Chizmar is a master of this form, and hats off to him!"

—JOHN SAUL

"A wonderful, masterful collection—terrifying stories full of heart and soul...and darkness. Sure to please even the most jaded reader."

—BRIAN KEENE

"Chilling and thought-provoking tales that quietly uncover horror in the most ordinary of lives."

—KELLEY ARMSTRONG

"Richard Chizmar has a very special talent for creating a homely, believable world—the kind of world that you and I live in every day. But he gradually invests that world with a creeping sense of unease, and then he throws open those suburban front doors and brings us face to face with all the unthinkable horrors that have been hiding behind them."

—GRAHAM MASTERTON

"...a highly talented dark suspense writer with a wide range of subject matter and a knack for clear, straightforward, but evocative prose that may remind you of Stephen King, Dean Koontz and Ed Gorman."

— ELLERY QUEEN MYSTERY MAGAZINE

"Richard Chizmar is a master delineator of two phenomena—the human condition and the inhuman condition. Some of his people may be monsters, but Chizmar has the rare talent to make you see his monsters as people. His work eloquently and expertly expands the dimensions of the genre...and should concern anyone interested in exceptional writing talent."

— ROBERT BLOCH

"…a writer of great accomplishment. His work, always effective, is notable for its clarity and originality of concept. Chizmar has a great gift for the sinister."

— PETER STRAUB

"Richard Chizmar will soon distinguish himself as a major writer of American suspense fiction."

— ED GORMAN

"Richard Chizmar is the kind of writer who gives the genre of dark fiction the dignity it deserves. He is not only a superb writer, but a seductive storyteller as well. He dangles hidden secrets in front of our faces, and then dares us not to follow him as he pulls away. We do follow, we *have* to follow. With vivid characters, confident prose, dialogue so realistic that the pages nearly speak it *aloud*, and carefully constructed plots, Chizmar *makes* us follow those hidden secrets he dangles before us, just out of reach, and at the end of the journey, we are always amply rewarded."

—RAY GARTON

....

About the title novella, *A Long December*…

"A fresh, compelling take on the serial killer theme. Suspenseful, well structured, expertly characterized."

—BILL PRONZINI

First Edition

ISBN
978-1-59606-793-6

Subterranean Press
PO Box 190106
Burton, MI 48519

subterraneanpress.com

For Kara,
who saved me.

TABLE OF CONTENTS

15   Blood Brothers

31   The Man with X-Ray Eyes

39   The Box

49   Heroes

57   Ditch Treasures

67   The Silence of Sorrow

75   After the Bombs

95   Last Words

103   Night Call

113   The Lake is Life

135   The Good Old Days

145   Grand Finale

157   The Artist

163   Family Ties

175   Mister Parker

185   Monsters

189   Like Father, Like Son

197   The Tower

211   Brothers

241   Cemetery Dance

245   Blue

255   A Crime of Passion

273   Homesick

279   Devil's Night

305   Bride of Frankenstein: A Love Story

313   The Season of Giving

331   A Capital Cat Crime

341   The Sinner King

357   A Season of Change

375   Midnight Promises

383   The Night Shift

389   Only the Strong Survive

407   The Interview

415   The Poetry of Life

419   A Long December

491   Story Notes

"When you light a candle, you also cast a shadow."

—Ursula K. Le Guin

....

"Everyone is a moon, and has a dark side which he never shows to anybody."

—Mark Twain

....

"Time takes it all whether you want it to or not, time takes it all. Time bears it away, and in the end there is only darkness. Sometimes we find others in that darkness, and sometimes we lose them there again."

—Stephen King

BLOOD
BROTHERS

ONE

I GRABBED THE PHONE ON the second ring and cleared my throat, but before I could wake up my mouth enough to speak, there came a man's voice: *"Hank?"*

"Uh, huh."

"It's me...Bill."

The words hit me like a punch to the gut. I jerked upright in the bed, head dizzy, feet kicking at a tangle of blankets.

"Jesus, Billy, I didn't recog—"

"I know, I know...it's been a long time."

We both knew the harsh truth of that simple statement and we let the next thirty seconds pass in silence. Finally I took a deep breath and said, "So I guess you're out, huh? They let you out early."

I listened as he took a deep breath of his own. Then another. When he finally spoke, he sounded scared: *"Hank, listen...I'm in some trouble. I need you to—"*

"Jesus Christ, Billy! You busted out, didn't you? You fucking-a busted out!"

My voice was louder now, almost hysterical, and Sarah lifted her head from the pillow and mumbled, "What's wrong? Who is it, honey?"

I moved the phone away from my face and whispered, "It's no one, sweetheart. Go back to sleep. I'll tell you in the morning."

She sighed in the darkness and rested her head back on the pillow.

"Hey, you still there? Dammit, Hank, don't hang up!"

"Yeah, yeah, I'm here," I said.

"I really need your help, big brother. You know I never woulda called if—"

"Where are you?"

"Close…real close."

"Jesus."

"Can you come?"

"Jesus, Billy. What am I gonna tell Sarah?"

"Tell her it's work. Tell her it's an old friend. Hell, I don't know, tell her whatever you have to."

"Where?"

"The old wooden bridge at Hanson Creek."

"When?"

"As soon as you can get there."

I looked at the glowing red numbers on the alarm clock—5:37.

"I can be there by six-fifteen."

The line went dead.

TWO

I SLIPPED THE phone back onto its cradle and just sat there for a couple of minutes, rubbing my temple with the palm of my hand. It was a habit I'd picked up from my father, and it was a good thing Sarah was still sleeping; she hated when I did it, said it made me look like a tired old man.

She was like that, always telling me to stay positive, to keep my chin up, not to let life beat me down so much. She was one in a million, that's for damn sure. A hundred smiles a day and not one of them halfway or phony.

Sitting there in the darkness, thinking of her that way, I surprised myself and managed something that almost resembled a smile.

But the thought went away and I closed my eyes and it seemed like a very long time was passing, me just sitting there in the bed like a child afraid of the dark or the boogeyman hiding in the bottom of the closet.

Suddenly—and after all this time—there I was thinking so many of the same old thoughts. Anger, frustration, guilt, fear—all of it rushing back at me in a tornado of red-hot emotion…

So I just sat there and hugged myself and felt miserable and lost and lonely and it seemed like a very long time, but when I opened my eyes and looked up at the clock, I saw that not even five minutes had passed.

I dressed quietly in the cold darkness. Back in the far corner of the bedroom. I didn't dare risk opening the dresser drawers and waking Sarah, so I slipped on a pair of wrinkled jeans and a long sleeve t-shirt from the dirty laundry hamper. The shirt smelled faintly of gasoline and sweat.

After checking on Sarah, I tiptoed down the hallway and poked my head into the girls' room for a quick peek, then went downstairs. I washed my face in the guest bathroom and did my business but didn't flush. For just a second, I thought about coffee—something to help clear my head—but decided against it. Too much hassle. Not enough time.

After several minutes of breathless searching, I found the car keys on the kitchen counter. I slipped on a jacket and headed for the garage.

Upstairs, in the bedroom, Sarah rolled over and began lightly snoring. The alarm clock read 5:49.

THREE

HE SAVED MY life once. A long time ago, back when we were kids.

It was a hot July afternoon—ninety-six in the shade and not a breeze in sight. It happened no more than thirty yards downstream from the old Hanson Bridge, just past the cluster of big weeping willow trees. One minute I was splashing and laughing and fooling around, and the next I was clawing at the muddy creek bottom six, seven feet below the surface. It was the mother of all stomach cramps; the kind your parents always warned you about but you never really believe existed. Hell, when you're a kid, the old "stomach cramp warning" falls into the same dubious category as "never fool around with a rusty nail" and "don't play outside in the rain." To adults, these matters make perfect sense, but to a kid…well, you know what I'm talking about.

Anyway, by the time Billy pulled me to the surface and dragged me ashore, my ears had started to ring something awful and the hell with seeing stars, I was seeing entire solar systems. So, Billy put me over his shoulder and carried me a half-mile into town and Dad had to leave the plant three hours early on a Monday just to pick me up at the Emergency Room.

I survived the day, more embarrassed than anything, and Billy was a reluctant hero, not only in our family but all throughout the neighborhood. Old widow Fletcher across the street even baked a chocolate cake to celebrate the occasion with Billy's name written out in bright pink icing.

I was thirteen, Billy twelve, when all this happened.

Like I said, it was a long time ago, but the whole thing makes for a pretty good story, and I've told it at least a hundred times. In fact, it's the one thing I always tell people when the inevitable moment finally arrives and they say, "Jeez, Hank, I didn't know you had a brother."

I hear those words and I just smile and shrug my shoulders as if to say, "Oh, well, sorry I never mentioned it," and then I slip right into the story.

This usually happens at social gatherings—holiday work parties, neighborhood cook-outs, that sort of thing. Someone from the old neighborhood shows up and mentions Billy's name, asks what he's been up to, and another person overhears the conversation.

And then the questions:

"What's your brother's name? Does he live around here? What's he do for a living? Why haven't you mentioned him before, Hank?"

Happens two, three times a year. And when it does I just grin my stupid grin and tell the drowning story one more time...and then I make my escape before they can ask any more questions. "Excuse me, folks, I have to use the restroom." Or "Hey, isn't that Fred Matthews over there by the pool? Fred, wait up. I've been meaning to ask you..."

It works every time.

BILLY WAS JUST a year behind me, but you never would've guessed it growing up. He looked much younger; two, maybe even three years. He was short for his age and thin. Real thin. Dad always used to say—and at the time we could never figure out just *what the hell* he was talking about— that Billy looked like a boy made out of wire. Little guy is tough as wire, he'd always say, and give Billy a proud smile and a punch on the shoulder.

Despite his physical size, Billy was fast and strong and agile and much more athletic than me. His total lack of fear and dogged determination made him a star; my lack of coordination made me a second-stringer. But we both had fun, and we stuck together for the three years we shared in high school. We played all the same sports—football in the fall, basketball in the winter, baseball in the spring.

Baseball. Now, that's where Billy really shined. All-County second-base as a sophomore. All-County and All-State as a junior, and again as a senior.

A true-blue hometown hero by the time he was old enough to drive a car.

After graduation, I stayed in town and took business classes over at the junior college. Summer before sophomore year, I found an apartment a few miles away from home. Got a part-time job at a local video store. Played a little softball on Thursday nights, some intramural flag football on the weekends. Stopped by and saw the folks two, three times a week. Ran around with a few girlfriends, but nothing serious or lasting. For me, not too much had changed.

Then, Billy graduated and went upstate to college on a baseball scholarship and *everything* seemed to change.

First, there was the suspension. Billy and three other teammates got caught cheating on a mid-term English exam and were placed on academic probation and suspended from the team.

Then, a few months later, in the spring, he was arrested at a local rock concert for possession of marijuana. It shouldn't have been that big a deal, but at the time, he'd been carrying enough weed to warrant a charge for Intent to Distribute. Then, at the court trial, we discovered that this was his second offense and the university kindly asked him to clear out his dorm room and leave campus immediately. His scholarship was revoked.

He was lucky enough to receive a suspended sentence from the judge but instead of moving back home and finding a job—which is what Mom and Dad hoped he would do—Billy decided to stay close to campus and continue working at a local restaurant. He claimed he wanted to make amends with his baseball coach and try to re-enroll after the next semester if the university would allow him. So, he moved in with some friends and for a time it appeared as though he'd cleaned up his act. He kept out of trouble—at least as far as we (and his probation officer) could tell—and he stopped by on a regular basis to see Mom and Dad, and he even came by my place once or twice a month (although usually only when he needed to borrow a couple of bucks).

So, anyway, things went well for awhile…

Until the rainy Sunday midnight the police called and told Mom and Dad they needed to come down to Fallston General right away. Billy had been driven to the Emergency Room by one of his roommates; just an hour earlier he'd been dumped in the street in front of his apartment—a bloody mess. Both hands broken. A couple of ribs. Nose mashed. Left ear shredded. He was lucky to be alive.

We found out the whole story then: it seemed that my baby brother had a problem with gambling. The main problem being that he wasn't very good at it. He owed some very dangerous people some very significant amounts of money. The beating had been a friendly reminder that his last installment payment had been twelve hours late.

Billy came home from the hospital ten days later. Moved into his old room at home. This time, Mom and Dad got their way without much of an argument. A month or so later, when Billy was feeling up to it, Dad got him a job counting boxes over at the plant. Soon after, he started dating Cindy Lester, a girl from the other side of town. A very sweet girl. And pretty, too. She was just a senior over at the high school—barely eighteen years old—but she seemed to be good for Billy. She wanted to be a lawyer one day, and she spent most of her weeknights studying at the library, her weekends at the movies or the shopping mall with Billy.

One evening, sometime late October, the leaves just beginning to change their colors, Billy stopped by my apartment with a pepperoni pizza and a six-pack of Coors. We popped in an old Clint Eastwood movie and stayed up most of the night talking and laughing. There was no mention of gambling or drugs or Emergency Room visits. Instead, Billy talked about settling down, making a future with Cindy. He talked about finding a better job, maybe taking some classes over at the junior college. Accounting and business courses, just like his big brother. Jesus, it was like a dream come true. I could hardly wait until morning to call the folks and tell them all about it.

To this very day, I can remember saying my prayers that night, thanking God for giving my baby brother another chance.

That night was more than eight years ago.

I haven't seen him since.

FOUR

I DROVE SLOWLY across the narrow wooden bridge. Clicked on my high-beams.

There were no other cars in sight.

Just empty road. Dense forest. And a cold December wind.

My foot tapped the brake pedal, and I thought to myself: *Hank Foster, you've lost your mind. This is crazy. Absolutely crazy.*

I reached the far side of the bridge and pulled over to the dirt shoulder. I sat there shivering for a long couple of minutes. Looking up at the rearview mirror. Staring out at the frozen darkness.

I turned the heater up a notch.

Turned off the headlights.

It was 6:17.

I LOOKED AT my watch for the tenth time. 6:21.

Jesus, this really *was* crazy. Waiting in the middle of nowhere for God knows what to happen. Hell, it was more than crazy; it was dangerous. Billy had sounded scared on the phone, maybe even desperate, and he'd said he was in trouble. Those had been his exact words: *I'm in some trouble.* Even after all this time, I knew the kind of trouble my brother was capable of. So, what in the hell was I doing out here? I had Sarah and the girls to think about now, a business to consider...

Or maybe, just maybe, he had changed. Maybe he had left the old Billy behind those iron bars and a better man had emerged. Maybe he had actually learned a thing or two—

—yeah, and maybe Elvis was still alive and catching rays down on some Mexican beach and the Cubs were gonna win the goddamn World Series.

Nice to imagine, one and all, but not real likely, huh?

I was starting to sweat now. *Really* sweat. I felt it on my neck. My face. My hands. And I felt it snaking down from my armpits, dribbling across my ribcage. Sticky. Cold and hot at the same time.

I leaned down and turned off the heat. Cracked the window. Inhaled long and deep. The sharp sting of fresh air caught me by surprise, made me dizzy for a moment, and I realized right then and there what was going on: I was scared. Probably more scared than I had ever been in my entire life.

With the window open, I could hear the wind rattling the trees and the creek moving swiftly in the darkness behind me. In the dry months of summer, Hanson Creek was slow-moving and relatively shallow, maybe eight feet at its deepest point. But in the winter, with all the snow run-off, the creek turned fast and mean and unforgiving. Sometimes, after a storm, the water rose so quickly, the police were forced to close down the bridge and detour traffic up north to Route 24. One winter, years ago, it stayed closed for the entire month of January.

The old house where we grew up—where Mom and Dad still live today—was just a short distance north from here. No more than a five minute drive. Back when we were kids, Billy and I walked down here most every morning during the summer. All the neighborhood kids came here. We brought bag lunches and bottles of pop and hid them in the bushes so no one would steal them. Then we swam all day long and held diving contests down at the rope swing. When the weather was too cool to swim, we played war in the woods and built forts made out of rocks and mud and tree branches. Other times, we fished for catfish and carp and the occasional bass or yellow perch. On *real* lucky days, when it rained hard enough to wear away the soil, we searched for (and usually found) Indian arrowheads wedged in with the tree roots that grew along the creek's steep banks. We called those rainy days *treasure hunts*, and took turns acting as "expedition leader." The creek was a pretty wonderful place.

I thought about all this and wondered if that was the reason Billy had chosen the bridge as a meeting place. Was he feeling sentimental? A little nostalgic, maybe? Probably not; as usual, I was probably giving the bastard too much credit.

LIKE I TOLD you, I haven't seen him in more than eight years. Not since that long ago autumn night we spent together talking at my apartment. One week later, Billy just up and disappeared. No note, no message… nothing. Just an empty closet, a missing suitcase, and eighty dollars gone from Mom's purse.

And to make matters worse, Mr. Lester called the house later that evening and told us that Cindy hadn't been to school that day—was she with Billy by any chance?

The next morning, Dad called Billy's probation officer. He wasn't much help. He told us to sit tight, that maybe Billy would come to his senses. Other than that, there was really nothing we could do but wait.

And so for two weeks, we waited and heard nothing.

Then, on a Sunday afternoon, Mom and Dad sitting out on the front porch reading the newspaper, still dressed in their church clothes, there was a phone call: *I know I know it was a stupid thing to do but you see Cindy's pregnant and scared to death of her father he's a mean sonofabitch real mean and California is the place to be these days heck we already have jobs and a place to stay and there's lots of great people out here we've got some really nice friends already c'mon please don't cry Mom please don't yell Dad we're doing just fine really we are we're so much in love and we're doing just fine…*

Six months later, Cindy Lester came home. Alone. While walking back from work one night, she had been raped and beaten in a Los Angeles alley. She'd spent three days in the hospital with severe cuts and bruises. She'd lost her baby during the first night. Cindy told us that she'd begged him over and over again, but Billy had refused to come home with her. So, she'd left him.

Over the next three years, there were exactly seven more phone calls (two begging for money) and three short handwritten letters. The envelopes were postmarked from California, Arizona, and Oregon.

Then, early in the fourth year, the police called. Billy had been arrested in California for drug trafficking. This time, the heavy stuff: cocaine and heroin. Dad hired Billy a decent lawyer, and both he and Mom flew out to the trial and watched as the judge gave Billy seven years in the state penitentiary.

I never went to see him. Not even once. Not at the trial. Not when Mom and Dad went for their twice-a-year visits. And not when Billy sent the letter asking me to come. I just couldn't do it.

I didn't hate him the way Mom and Dad thought I did. Jesus, he was still my baby brother. But he was locked up back there where he belonged, and I was right here where I belonged. We each had our own lives to live.

So no I didn't hate him. But I couldn't forgive him, either. Not for what he had done to this family—the heartbreak of two wonderful, loving parents; the complete waste of their hard-earned retirement savings; the shame and embarrassment he brought to all of us—

—bare knuckles rapped against the windshield, and I jumped so hard I hit my head. I also screamed.

I could hear laughing from outside the car, faint in the howling wind, but clear enough to instantly recognize.

It was him, all right.

My baby brother.

Suddenly, a face bent down into view. Smiled.

And I couldn't help it—I smiled right back.

FIVE

WE HUGGED FOR a long time. Car door open, engine still running. Both of us standing outside in the cold and the wind. Neither of us saying a word.

We hugged until I could no longer stand the smell of him.

Then, we stopped and sort of stood back and looked at each other.

"Jesus, Billy, I can't believe it," I said.

"I know, I know." He shook his head and smiled. "Neither can I."

"Now, talk to me. What's this all about? What kind of trouble are—"

He held up his hand. "In a minute, okay? Lemme just look at you a while longer."

For the next couple of minutes, we stood there facing each other, shivering in the cold. The Foster boys, together once again.

He was heavier than the last time I'd seen him; maybe fifteen, twenty pounds. And he was shaved bald, a faint shadow of dark stubble showing through. Other than that, he was still the Billy I remembered. Bright blue eyes. Big stupid smile. That rosy-cheeked baby face of his.

"Hey, you like my hair," he asked, reading my thoughts.

"Yeah," I said, "who's your barber?"

"Big black sonofabitch from Texas. Doing life for first-degree murder. Helluva nice guy, though."

He waited for my response and when I didn't say anything, he laughed. This time, it sounded harsh and a little mean.

"How's the folks?" he asked.

I shrugged my shoulders. "You know, pretty much the same. They're doing okay."

"And Sarah and the girls?"

My heart skipped a beat. An invisible hand reached up from the ground and squeezed my balls.

"Mom and Dad told me all about 'em. Sent me pictures in the mail," he said.

I opened my mouth, but couldn't speak. Couldn't breathe.

"They're twins, right? Let's see…four years old…Kacy and Katie, if I remember right."

I sucked in a deep breath. Let it out.

"I bet you didn't know I carry their picture around in my wallet. The one where they're sitting on the swings in those fancy little blue dresses—"

"Five," I said, finally finding my voice.

"Huh?"

"The girls," I said. "They just turned five. Back in October."

"Halloween babies, huh? That's kinda neat. Hey, remember how much fun we used to have trick-or-treatin'? 'Member that time we spent the night out back the old Myer's House? Camped out in Dad's old tent. Man, that was a blast."

I nodded my head. I remembered everything. The costumes we used to make. The scary movies we used to watch, huddled together on the sofa, sharing a glass of soda and a bowl of Mom's buttered popcorn. All the creepy stories we used to tell each other before bedtime.

Suddenly, I felt sorry for him—standing there in his tattered old clothes, that dumb smile refusing to leave his face, smelling for all the world like a dumpster full of food gone to spoil. I suddenly felt very sorry for him and very guilty for me.

"I didn't break out, you know," he said. "They released me two weeks ago. Early parole."

"Jesus, Billy. That's great news."

"I spent a week back in L.A. seeing some friends. Then I hitched a ride back here. Made it all the way to the state line. I walked in from there."

"I still can't goddamn believe it. Wait until Mom and Dad see you."

"That's one of the things I need to talk to you about, Hank. Why don't we take a walk and talk for awhile, okay?"

"Sure, Billy," I said. "Let's do that."

So, that's exactly what we did.

SIX

I STILL MISS him.

It's been four months now since that morning at the bridge—and not a word.

I read the newspaper every day. Watch the news every night.

And still there's been nothing.

I think about him all the time now. Much more often than I ever used to. Once or twice a week, I take a drive down to the old bridge. I stand outside the car and watch the creek rushing by, and I think back to the time when we were kids. Back to a time when things were simple and happy.

God, I miss him.

HE WANTED MONEY. Plain and simple, as always.

First, he tried to lie to me. Said it was for his new "family." Said he had gotten married two days after he got out of prison. Needed my help getting back on his feet.

But I didn't fall for it.

So, then he told me the truth. Or something close to it, anyway. There was this guy, an old friend from up around San Francisco. And Billy owed him some big bucks for an old drug deal gone bad. Right around thirty grand. If he didn't come up with the cash, this old friend was gonna track him down and slit his throat.

So, how about a little help, big brother?

Sorry, I told him. No can do. I'd like to help out, but I've got a family now. A mortgage. My own business barely keeping its head above water. Really sorry. Can't help you.

So, then he started crying—and begging me.

And when that didn't work, he got pissed off.

His eyes went cold and distant; his voice got louder.

He said: "Okay that's fine. I'll just hit up the old man and the old lady. They'll help me out. Damn right they will. And if they don't have enough cash, well, there are always other ways I can *persuade* you to help me, big brother. Yes, sir, I can be mighty *persuasive* when I put my mind to it...

"Let's start by talking about that store of yours, Hank—you're paid up on all your insurance, aren't you? I mean, you got fire coverage and all that stuff, right? Jeez, I'd hate to see something bad happen when you're just starting out. And how about Sarah? She still working over at that bank Mom and Dad told me about? That's a pretty dangerous job, ain't it? Working with all that money. Especially for a woman. And, oh yeah, by the way, what school do the girls go to? Evansville? Or are you busing them over to that private school, what's it called again?"

I stabbed him then.

We were standing near the middle of the bridge. Leaning against the thick wooden railing, looking down at the water.

And when he said those things, I took out the steak knife—which had been sitting on the kitchen counter right next to where I'd found my car keys—I took it out from my coat pocket, and I held it in both of my hands and brought it down hard in the back of his neck.

He cried out once—not very loud—and dropped to his knees.

And then there was only the flash of the blade as I stabbed him over and over again...

LAST NIGHT, IT finally happened. Sarah confronted me.

We were alone in the house. The girls were spending the night at their grandparents'—they do this once a month and absolutely love it.

After dinner, she took me downstairs to the den and closed the door. Sat me down on the sofa and stood right in front of me. She told me I looked a mess. I wasn't sleeping, wasn't eating. Either I tell her right now what was going on or she was leaving.

She was serious, too. I think she was convinced I was having an affair. So, I told her.

Everything—starting with the phone call and ending with me dumping Billy's body into the creek.

When I was finished, she ran from the room crying. She made it upstairs to the bathroom, where she dropped to her knees in front of the toilet and got sick. When she was done, she asked me very calmly to go back downstairs and leave her alone for awhile. I agreed. What else could I do?

An hour or so later, she came down and found me out in the backyard looking up at the moon and the stars. She ran to me and hugged me so tight I could barely breathe and then she started crying again. We hugged for a long time, until the tears finally stopped, and then she held my face in her hands and told me that she understood how difficult it had been for me, how horrible it must have felt, but that it was all over now and that I had done the right thing. No matter what, that was the important thing to remember, she kept saying—I had done the right thing.

Then we were hugging again and both of us were crying.

When we finally went inside, we called the girls and took turns saying goodnight. Then we went to bed and made love until we both fell asleep.

Later that night, the moon shining silver and bright through the bedroom window, Sarah woke from a nightmare, her skin glistening with sweat, her voice soft and frightened. She played with my hair and asked: "What if someone finds him, Hank? A fisherman? Some kids? What if someone finds him and recognizes him?"

I put a finger to her lips and *ssshed* her. Put my arms around her and held her close to me. I told her everything was going to be okay. No one would find him. And even if they did, they would never be able to identify him.

"Are you sure they won't recognize him?" she asked. "Are you sure?"

"Absolutely positive," I said, stroking her neck. "Not after all this time. Not after he's been in the water for this long."

And not after I cut up his face the way I did.

No one could recognize him after all that...not even his own brother.

THE MAN WITH X-RAY EYES

Y FATHER DIED WHEN I was just a boy.

There was an accident at the mill where he worked. One man lost a leg. Another lost the vision in his right eye and most of his scalp. My father got the worst of it, though—he was crushed to death.

We buried him two days later on a sunny June morning. After the service, most of our friends and relatives came back to the house. A somber parade. They stood in the kitchen and sat around the living room and the den, whispering, crying, nibbling on little sandwiches and drinking from paper cups.

I stayed outside mostly, sitting in the shade of the front porch.

Most folks didn't know what to say to an eleven-year old who had just lost his father, so they pretty much left me alone.

After a time, my grandfather came out and sat down next to me on the step. He put his arm around me and we sat there in silence, listening to the grass grow and the birds sing. After a while, I asked him if he felt like crying. He slowly nodded his head and told me what it felt like to bury his only son; how his heart ached with sorrow and swelled with pride all at the same time. He told me that my father dying the way he did was a cruel reminder that life has a way of playing tricks on all of us, that sometimes things aren't the way they seem. And then he told me how much he loved me, how proud he was of me, how much I reminded him of my father.

That was just like Grandpa. He always knew the right thing to say, the right thing to do.

And he was right—life does have a way of playing tricks on all of us.

THAT WAS A long time ago; seems like forever. I'm much older now, just turned forty-two last month. My grandfather is gone, of course, and so is my mother. I stayed with her in the old house until she passed away from ovarian cancer in the autumn of '76, and then I sold out to a young couple from somewhere east of Boston. I left town at the age of twenty-one and spent the next five years at the university.

After graduation, I moved back to Coldwater. Just across town, on the other side of the tracks, right next to where the old Lexington Bed and Breakfast used to be. A nice, little house with a decent yard and a white painted fence.

I've been there ever since.

I DON'T DATE very often. There's just not many opportunities in a small town like Coldwater. At least not for a guy like me. Last time I had a date—six months ago, at least—was with a woman I met at the library one evening. Anne something-or-other. A tall redhead from over in Windhurst. We went to a movie and then out for pizza. She spent most of the night staring at her wristwatch and playing with her hair. We never had a second date.

I'M NOT LONELY, though. I guess I've gotten used to this kind of life. Besides, I always have my kids. I see them at school five days a week and around town most every day. They call my name and wave and sometimes stop to talk. So, it's a rare day that I feel alone or without company.

I teach history over at Coldwater High School. Six classes a day, three with the seniors and three with the sophomores. Been there almost fifteen years now.

My teaching philosophy is simple: work hard and have fun. I try to make all my classes interesting for the kids; plenty of films and graphics and student participation. I think they learn more that way—and that's what's important.

Every year the kids tell me I'm one of their favorites. And every year it means the world to me.

My co-workers don't talk to me much, but that's okay. Sometimes I think they're just jealous.

I'VE NEVER SEEN a UFO.

I've met a few people who claim they have.

Roy Welderman, a gym teacher from the high school, swears he saw one fly directly overhead one night when he was crappie fishing out on the lake. He told me (and this is a direct quote): "Hell, I almost shit my pants right there in the boat. That's how scared I was."

A lady down the street from where I live—an old friend of my mother—told me she was actually abducted by a UFO when she was a teenager. Said it flew down and landed in the field behind her house early one morning and when she walked out there to investigate, she was zapped unconscious and abducted. Said she woke up in bed, naked, all covered in grass and dirt, her feet cut and bleeding. When she checked the alarm clock on her nightstand, four-and-a-half hours had passed.

Weird stuff, huh?

Sure, like most folks, I've seen them on television and in pictures, but I've never seen a UFO up close and personal.

I wish I would.

I'M NOT SURE how the aliens got here, or when they first arrived.

I SAW MY first alien the summer I turned sixteen.

Her name was Jenny Glover, and she was new in Coldwater. The weekend after the Fourth of July, her family moved right across the street, into the old Sumner place. She was fifteen, and just like me, an only child.

God, she was beautiful. Long, shiny hair the color of summer wheat. Eyes like an angel. And she liked me. She actually liked me. She always used to say that I made her laugh.

Those first couple weeks, we spent all our free time together. Showing her around town. Going to the movies. Playing card games in my basement. I can still remember how my heart felt every time she came close to me or brushed against my skin: like it was going to jump right out of my chest. Jesus, she drove me crazy.

But then, one day, everything changed...

We were walking on the dirt path that runs alongside Hanson Creek, taking a short-cut back from the grocery store. About halfway home, we took a break and sat down on an old, fallen log. For a long time, we just sat there, shuffling our feet in the dirt, not looking at each other, talking about nothing. Then she took my hand in her hand, and I knew we were going to kiss. If I didn't faint first.

I looked up into those ice blue eyes, *really* looked for the first time...

...and I saw something that wasn't human.

Somehow I *saw.*

And then in a flash of sudden understanding, a flash of absolute *knowing*, I *knew* what she was, what she intended to do.

And I knew right then and there that I had no other choice.

So I killed her.

THE SECOND ONE was many years later.

I was in college at the time. It was summer break, and I was at Fenway Park, watching the Red Sox and the Mariners. An extra inning game in the middle of a gorgeous August afternoon.

Between the tenth and eleventh innings, I moved down a couple dozen rows to a better seat along the third base line. I excused myself and sat down next to a plump, bald man with a smear of mustard on his chin. The man looked up and smiled at me.

I nodded, but didn't return the smile.

He was one of them.

After the game, I followed him home to the suburbs and killed him in his garage.

I'VE ONLY BEEN wrong once.

And once is enough, believe me.

Happened about a year ago. I was vacationing by myself in Florida. I'd never been to Disney and had always wanted to go.

There was a little girl at the park with her family. Cute as a button, and about that small. Maybe six or seven. She was waiting in line ahead of me with her older sister and brother. She kept looking at me and smiling... looking right into my eyes.

And I knew.

Later on, back at the cabin, I discovered my mistake. And it almost killed me. Honestly it did. I couldn't believe it.

Somehow, I had been wrong.

She wasn't one of them after all.

I had killed a human being.

THE DOCTORS AND the detectives like me. Despite what they suspect, despite where they fear all this is leading, they can't help it. I can tell...I can see it in their eyes.

THEY ASKED ME to write down everything in my own words.

They recorded all of our conversations, but they want something down on paper. Something official, I guess.

First, they want a little history about myself. About my life—past, present, future. That's easy enough.

And, then, about the aliens. They want to know every last detail—starting with the first one I killed out by Hanson Creek when I was sixteen years old and ending with the old lady from just last week.

They want to know how many others I've been able to find over the years. Where? When? How?

They want to know where I've traveled to during my summers off from teaching. Visits with relatives? Vacations? They want to know all of it.

And they want to know about the eyes. The eyes are very important, they tell me. How do I know the things I know? How do I see the things I see?

They're all very nice to deal with. Very pleasant. And they're patient, too; they never rush me with anything.

OF COURSE, I'LL give them all the answers they need. They're on my side now. Or at least, they will be very soon.

EARLIER THIS MORNING, when I finished telling my story, I gave them directions to my grandfather's old cabin in the woods. They left a few hours ago by helicopter, so they should be there by now.

Any time now, I expect a phone to ring somewhere down the hall. Then they'll come for me again. With more questions, I'm sure.

After that, I expect a lot of phones will be ringing. All over the country, probably.

Or maybe not...some things are better kept secret.

I TOOK PRECAUTIONS, of course.

Aliens walking our streets is not a very believable story—*Jesus, don't you think I know that?*—so I took some safety measures, just in case.

I cut off their heads.

Each and every one of them. Cut off their heads and saved them. Took them up to my grandfather's cabin. Took Polaroids. Then stripped the flesh away with chemicals. Then I took more photos. Carefully labeled each one of them—date of death, gender, age and identity (whenever possible).

Inside my grandfather's cabin, I have all the proof anyone will ever need...

Skulls. Hideous looking things.

Skulls of various shapes and sizes—none remotely human, none constructed of anything resembling human bone.

Skulls that will forever change our history.

Over forty of them in all.

THEY'RE BACK FROM the cabin.

About twenty minutes ago.

They haven't been in to speak with me yet, but I can see them talking outside in the hallway. The two detectives and the doctor with the long hair.

They're scared. Real scared.

I can see it in their eyes.

THE BOX

ANNIE GRABBED HER PURSE from the counter, glanced at the kitchen clock and yelled, "Charlie, we're leaving."

A muffled voice—*"Coming, mom"*—followed by a stampede of heavy footsteps crashing down the stairs.

Annie shook her head, holding the door open for her teenaged son. "One of these days you're gonna fall right through those stairs."

Charlie grinned and kissed his mom on the cheek. "Sorry, had to pee. Where's Buttercup?"

Annie closed the door behind them and checked to make sure it was locked. *"Bailey's* waiting in the car. And she's grumpy. Again."

Charlie opened the front passenger door and slid inside. Peeked into the back seat. "Cheer up, Buttercup!"

Twelve-year-old Bailey rolled her eyes and pretended to turn up the volume on her iPod. But Annie noticed a hint of a smile as she did it.

Charlie had that effect on pretty much everyone.

ANNIE WAVED GOODBYE and watched Charlie wade into the crowd of students, backpack slung over his shoulder, stopping every few yards to chat with someone or high-five another boy. She recognized Aaron Parker from across the street and the Apperson twins from next door. Aaron got up from the bench he was sharing with two pretty blonde girls, and he and Charlie walked into the school together.

Annie turned to Bailey in the back seat. "You want to move up front?"

No response.

"Bailey, turn down your music."

Again, no response.

Annie sighed and checked the rearview mirror and pulled away from the curb.

ANNIE SAT AT the traffic light after dropping off Bailey, waiting for the light to turn green.

My little girl's not so little anymore, she thought sadly. *And definitely not acting much like her little girl these days. She hadn't even said goodbye when she'd gotten out of the car.*

Annie noticed a MISSING CAT poster taped to a street sign and snapped a picture of it with her cellphone in case she ran across the kitty later. It was exactly the sort of thing Bailey would have once applauded her for, but now would have poked fun at.

Annie didn't care. They had lost their corgi, Max, three months earlier, and it had been a heartbreaking time for the entire family. One day Max was there, begging for breakfast scraps at the table, and the next day they couldn't find the little guy anywhere. They'd hung posters, called area vets, organized search parties.

But they'd never found him. The not knowing had been the worst.

Wouldn't it be wonderful if she somehow found and returned—she checked the photo on her phone—*Sparkles* the cat?

That would show Bailey, wouldn't it?

The light turned green and Annie headed for home.

ANNIE PULLED INTO the driveway, turned off the engine and sat for a moment with three very clear thoughts swirling in her head:

I can't forget to make cookies for Bailey's class tomorrow. I better write myself a note.

I can't forget to pick up Mark's shirts at the drycleaners after lunch.

I can't believe Lisa is having an affair.

It was this last tidbit of gossip that occupied her thoughts as she exited the car and walked into the house.

And that's exactly what it was: *gossip*, because it was all just speculation at this point. Lisa had admitted to nothing. How could she? None of the other neighborhood ladies had confronted her with their suspicions.

Annie didn't know what to think of the whole thing. Yes, Lisa had been acting strangely distant lately. Yes, she had cancelled their last lunch and their last two book club meetings. Yes, she was all of a sudden eating healthier and working out like a madwoman.

But did any of those things really prove anything?

Annie decided she didn't care and was tired of the other women talking about it. It felt…mean. And none of their darn business.

Annie placed her purse back on the counter where she always left it and looked around the kitchen. She glanced through the arched doorway into the living room.

Clean or do laundry?

Some women complained about housework, but Annie actually enjoyed it most days. She believed it was a privilege to stay home and raise the kids. To take care of the household. It was valid and valuable work, she always said.

Annie turned on the radio in the kitchen, adjusted the dial until a Justin Timberlake song came on. She turned up the volume and twirled around the kitchen, singing and giggling.

The song ended, and she started loading the dishwasher.

ANNIE PAUSED AT the bottom of the stairs, adjusting the laundry basket on her hip. It was her second trip upstairs from the basement laundry room, and she was tired and hungry. One more and she would make herself a sandwich for lunch.

She walked into Bailey's room, placed the basket on the bed, and transferred an armload of socks to her sock drawer. The rest of the clothes belonged to Charlie, so she picked up the basket and crossed the hall into his bedroom.

While Bailey's bedroom looked as if a tornado had touched down in the middle of it, Charlie's room was neat and orderly. Football and basketball and soccer trophies lined up just so on his two bookshelves. Books in alphabetical order. Posters hung above his crisply made bed. Framed family and sports photos hanging above a desk that held only a computer and keyboard and a pen and pencil holder.

Thank God Charlie takes after me, Annie thought, starting to hang his t-shirts in the closet. *At least one of them does.*

She started to turn back to the laundry basket for more shirts and almost tripped over the shoe box on the floor.

Charlie had once watched an ESPN interview with a rookie basketball star and they had shown the young man's closet. Row after row of shoe boxes. Stacked high and wide. Each box containing a brand new pair of basketball shoes.

Charlie had been fascinated and shortly thereafter declared that he wanted to do the same thing—on a much smaller scale—in his own closet. So, every time he bought a new pair of shoes, he added the box to his neat little stack at the bottom of his closet.

Except today one of them was sitting out on the floor.

Annie couldn't remember that ever happening before.

She bent down and picked up the box to return it to its proper place…

…and something inside the box *rattled.*

Puzzled, she opened the box and looked inside.

At first she thought it contained nothing but crumpled tissue paper, the kind which stores use to wrap new shoes with. But she gave the box a shake, and it rattled once again.

She walked to Charlie's bed and sat down, the shoe box on her lap. She tossed the lid on the bed beside her and started pulling tissue paper from the box until her hand touched something that felt like leather.

She pulled a dog collar from the box, a heart-shaped tag rattling against the metal buckle.

The collar looked familiar. She quickly read the tag:

MAX
1920 Edgewood Road

Annie sat there, frozen with surprise.

She wouldn't have been more shocked if she had found a live snake inside the shoe box.

What was it doing here? How was it here?

And then it came to her: Charlie had found Max dead somewhere. In the woods beyond the back yard. Alongside a roadway. He had found their sweet Max and kept it to himself, sparing the rest of them the hurt he was experiencing. That would be just like their Charlie.

Annie felt tears come to her eyes. A thickness in her throat. *My poor brave boy.*

She placed the collar back into the box and her hand brushed against something else.

She pulled it out from the box.

A tangle of smaller collars. The kind that cats or small dogs wore.

Again, Annie sat there for a long quiet moment, dumbfounded.

And then her hand started shaking.

It was suddenly hard to breathe.

She started to look at one of the tags—and stopped.

She realized she didn't want to see.

She suddenly felt sick to her stomach.

Don't be ridiculous, she thought. *Of course, there's a good explanation.*

Annie almost screamed when the cell phone in her pocket rang.

She jerked to her feet, spilling the shoebox and Max's collar from her lap to the floor.

She looked at the caller ID on her phone.

Lisa.

She answered without thinking. "Hello."

"Hey, girl, you busy?"

"Ummm…"

"You are. It's okay, we can talk later. Or maybe lunch tomorrow? I have something I want to tell you."

Annie couldn't take her eyes off the collars in her hand.

"Lunch sounds good. Call me…in the morning?"

"Everything okay? You sound funny."

Do I? Annie thought.

She flipped one of the tags over.

"Just…tired. Need to break for lunch."

Annie brought the tag closer and read the tiny print.

"Get some rest, Annie girl. Talk in the morning."

SPARKLES.

Annie didn't hear a word.

She hung up.

THE PHONE SLIPPED from her hand, landed on the floor next to the shoebox.

She stared down at it for a moment. Saw that she was wearing her favorite shoes.

Somewhere, outside in the distance, a lawn mower roared to life. A work truck backed up: BEEP BEEP BEEP. Someone tapped a car horn.

Annie slowly bent down, as if in a dream, picked up her phone and the shoe box with the same trembling hand.

Tissue paper slipped to the floor. She ignored it.

She glanced inside the box and saw that it was empty.

Wait…not quite empty.

There was a key inside. Tucked against the narrow end of the box.

She took the key and let the box fall from her hand.

She didn't have to wonder about the key.

She knew.

IT HAD HAPPENED a few months ago…

She remembered all this as she walked down the stairs, ignoring the voice in the back of her head telling her to call her husband at work, that something was wrong here.

She had gone onto the deck one warm spring evening to read a book and drink a glass of wine and had found Charlie putting a padlock on the old shed in the back corner of the yard. The shed had been battered and leaning even when they'd first moved into the house ten years earlier.

After Mark had assured her it was safe and wasn't going to collapse, the shed had spent most of the years that followed as Charlie's "secret fort." It wasn't much of a fort, and it certainly wasn't a secret, but Charlie had adored it. He had dragged an old card table inside and three folding chairs. Stocked it with books and comics and playing cards. Hung posters of Michael Jordan and Kobe Bryant on the walls.

But Annie hadn't seen him inside or even puttering around the shed for several years until the night of the padlock. She had leaned over the deck railing and yelled down to him that evening.

"What's the lock for, Charlie Brown?"

He looked up, startled, and then that trademark grin of his had come onto his face.

He shrugged. "Figured it was time to lock the old fort up. Lot of little kids running around the neighborhood. Wouldn't want any of them to get hurt in there."

Annie had smiled and sipped her wine and waved down to her beautiful boy. *How thoughtful*, she remembered thinking. *Just like Charlie to do something like that…*

ANNIE NO LONGER felt like she was moving in slow motion, like she was part of some bizarre and confusing dream.

By the time she had made it downstairs and outside, she had convinced herself that she was being ridiculous. That the collars and key meant nothing, certainly nothing dark or dreadful. It was a mystery, but it would all make sense in time.

She crossed the back yard with long, purposeful strides. Didn't hesitate once she reached the shed. She slid the key into the lock, popped it open on the first try and hung the lock on the hinge of the shed door.

She opened the door…

…and the smell hit her.

And still, despite the stench and the return of the voice in the back of her head—*CALL YOUR DAMN HUSBAND, ANNIE!*—she held onto that sliver of new confidence:

Probably just a dead mouse in there.

There was no electricity in the shed, so she swung the door open as wide as she could, jumping when the heavy door banged against the front of the shed.

She stepped into the doorway, the tips of her overpriced shoes toeing the dirt floor inside.

The smell was worse now.

She covered her nose and mouth with her hand and squinted into the darkness.

It was impossible to see.

She stepped inside the shed.

And the inside voice whispered: *that's not a mouse, Annie, and you know it.*

And she did know it…because her eyes had started to adjust to the gloom and she could see them now.

Hanging from nails stuck into the walls.

Cats.

Squirrels.

Rabbits.

Frogs.

Turtles.

Some of them pink and glistening and freshly skinned.

Others dried out and yellowed and rotting with age.

Still others sliced open, insides dripping into wet, ropy piles onto the dirt below.

And then she saw Max.

ANNIE DROPS TO her knees and gets sick right there in the dirt.

She heaves until there is nothing left inside her and when she finally looks up, looks beyond a gutted and crucified Max...she sees the worst of it.

There are dozens of photos on the far wall. Erin Cavanaugh. Their neighbor from down the street. One of the girls Charlie grew up with. The wall looks like a shrine.

Annie struggles to her feet and turns to leave...

...but there is someone standing behind her in the doorway. Silhouetted in the afternoon sunlight.

Annie does scream this time, and the person steps forward.

"Bailey?"

Bailey takes another step, a strange look on her face Annie has never seen before.

She notices that Bailey's hair and shirt are soaked in sweat, as if she had run all the way from school.

"What are you doing home, honey?"

Bailey takes another step and this time Annie notices something else: her little girl's hands are hidden behind her back.

"Bailey, honey..."

The little girl glances at the walls, then back to her mother.

"I remembered in home room...I remembered that I forgot to put it back."

Bailey looks like she wants to cry.

Annie tries to speak, but nothing comes out. She backs up another step.

It's fear she is feeling now. She is more afraid than she has ever felt in her life.

"It was so stupid. I *never* forget."

Bailey takes another step forward.

Annie backs away. *Her baby girl. Big and strong for her age, just like Charlie.*

"I hid them in Charlie's room because you and Dad never snoop around in there. And I wanted them close to me."

Bailey takes another step and starts to move her hands out from behind her back.

"I *needed* them close to me."

Annie backs up another step.

And her back touches the wall.

HEROES

1

I'VE ALWAYS WATCHED him. Secretly. From the time I was a child. Watched the way his eyebrows danced when he laughed. The way he lit his pipe or handled a tool, like a magician wielding a magic wand. The way he walked the family dog; bending to talk with it or ruffle its fur, but only when he was sure no one was watching. The way he read the newspaper or one of his tattered old paperbacks, peering over the worn pages every few minutes to keep me in check. The way his eyes twinkled when he called me "son."

I've always watched him.

2

THE DETECTIVE'S NAME was Crawford and when he disappeared into the crowd, I wondered for what had to be the tenth time tonight if I was truly insane for trusting him.

It was Thursday, December 21, and Baltimore-Washington International Airport was suffering under the strain of thousands of holiday travelers. A river of lonely businessmen and women, sweatshirt-clad college students, and entire families flowed by North Gate 23, blocking my view of the exit tunnel. I remained sitting on one of the orange-padded seats in the waiting area while Crawford tried to get close enough to look out the airport windows. Our man was due on an 8:30 p.m. flight from Paris—a private charter—so the computer screens all around me offered no news of its arrival.

I stared at the clock on the far wall. It was almost time. Months of research and planning were about to come to an end. My stomach felt like it was bubbling over and I was tempted to duck into the bathroom. Instead, afraid to leave my seat, I popped another Tums and waited for it to dissolve under my tongue.

Crawford reappeared, trailing behind an overweight couple who were moving with the grace and speed of a pair of hermit crabs. I could see by the expression on his face that the news was not good. I'd hired Ben Crawford, a Philadelphia-based private detective, two months earlier. He'd been the only one of the half-dozen detectives who'd been recommended to me who was willing to take my case. A fifty-thousand-dollar certified check—half payment in advance—had sealed the deal.

We made an odd pair. I stood over six feet tall but tipped the scales at only one-sixty. Crawford, on the other hand, could best be described as a human stump; only five-four, he weighed in with one hundred and seventy pounds of compressed muscle. His arms and legs strained against his clothing, and like many other muscular men of his size, he more waddled than walked. Despite my edginess, I smiled and almost laughed aloud at the sight before me: the waddling detective and Mr. and Mrs. Hermit Crab.

"What's so damn funny?" he asked, moving his coat from the chair next to me and sitting down.

"What...oh, nothing. Nervous tension, I guess."

He checked his watch. "The plane just landed. It'll be another ten minutes or so."

I nodded, my throat suddenly dry, my stomach tightening another notch.

Now it was Crawford's turn to smirk. "Hey, take it easy, you're white as a sheet. Don't worry, he'll be on that plane." He glanced at his watch again. "Another couple of hours and it'll all be over. Trust me."

I nodded again. I trusted him all right. I had no other choice.

3

TWENTY YEARS AGO, when I was seventeen and still in high school, each student in our senior English class was assigned to write a paper about the person he or she most admired. The class was a large one and the list of heroes was long and impressive: Martin Luther King, Abraham Lincoln, John F. Kennedy, Joe Namath, Willie Mays, John Glenn, and dozens of other famous figures. I was the only student who chose to write about his father. A nine-page tribute. My father cried at the kitchen table when he read it. Stood up and hugged me real close. I'll never forget that day. Never.

4

OUR MAN WAS the only passenger in the tunnel. A shadow. Moving slow. Carrying no luggage.

Even in the dim light, I could see that he was a striking man. Tall. Elegant. Draped in a fine black overcoat, dark slacks, and shiny, zippered boots. His face contrasted sharply with his slicked, black hair and dark apparel. Deathly pale flesh appeared almost luminous in the airport lights, and sharp, high cheekbones seemed to hide his eyes under his forehead. Eyes as dark as midnight.

"Jesus," I whispered.

"Yeah, I know," Crawford said, leaning close enough that I could feel his breath. "He's something, ain't he?"

Before I could answer, the detective stepped past me and met our visitor at the side of the walkway, away from the swelling crowd. I stumbled blindly after him, not wanting to be separated.

"It's a pleasure to see you again, sir," Crawford said.

Neither man offered forth a hand, and I noticed that our visitor's hands were covered by black leather gloves. He nodded and smiled. A quick flash of teeth. Like a shark. A chill swept across my spine.

"As promised, I am here." His voice was mesmerizing; his words soft and melodic like music. I wanted to hear more.

"Yes, you certainly are," Crawford said, sounding infinitely more civilized than I had ever heard him. "I trust your trip was satisfactory."

"Indeed, it was quite comfortable. But, my friend, I long for the journey home, so may we continue on quickly?"

"Yes, yes, of course." Crawford eased me forward, his fingers digging into my arm. "This is—"

"Mr. Francis Wallace," he interrupted, smiling again. I felt a wave of nausea rush forward and began to sway. The detective's fingers tightened on my arm again. "I have crossed an ocean to make your acquaintance."

"I...I really must thank you for coming here," I said. I looked helplessly at Crawford. "I'm not sure I believed him until I saw you walking up the tunnel. I was so terribly afraid that I had been wrong all this time."

"It is not necessary to thank me, Mr. Wallace. I have thought about this moment many times since your friend's visit to my home. I admit, initially, I was wary, hesitant to come. But yours is such a strange story, such a strange reason for my journey. My decision to come here was much easier than your decision to seek me, I trust."

A pack of giggling children skittered past us, brushing the man's coat. He cringed and turned to Crawford. "I am ready to proceed now."

The detective led us through the busy airport, outside into the bitter December air, to his rental car in the upper-level parking lot. The traffic on the interstate was moderate. We drove north in silence.

<u>5</u>

IT WAS MY father who stood at my side on my wedding day, and I by his, eight months later, when Mother passed away. Barely a year later, and it was my father again, his arms around me, who broke the news to me that my precious Jennifer had been killed in an accident. It was the worst of times, but still we had each other.

<u>6</u>

THE HOUSE I grew up in was dark, the street deserted. The rental car was parked in the driveway, its ticking engine the only sound in the night. I sat on the front porch, Crawford on my left side, smoking a cigarette. Snow flurries danced around us, drifting to the ground and melting. I played with the zipper on my coat for a long time before I looked up.

He was staring at me.

"You okay?" he asked, his breath visible in the chill air.

"I don't know." I took a deep breath and looked over my shoulder at the front door, which our visitor had disappeared into just minutes earlier. "I planned this for so long...thought about it for so long, but I don't know. I'm still not sure it's right."

He shook his head. "Listen to me, I gotta admit that I thought you were a genuine nutcase when you hired me. Offered me a hundred thousand to go find this guy and convince him of your little plan. Hell, I only signed on because I was short on cash and long on bills."

He stood up and inhaled on his cigarette. Began pacing the walkway. "I mean, I thought he was a fantasy, something made up for the movies and books. But the more you showed me about this guy—the papers, the files, the photos; all dated over hundreds of years—and the more time I spent around this house, getting to know you and your old man...the more I understood. You've gone to an awful lot of trouble, Wallace, an awful lot. Now, you don't know me very well; not well at all, in fact. But if you're asking for my opinion of all this, I think you did good. I think you did damn good."

A soft thud sounded from inside the house, and I jerked around.

Crawford kneeled at my side, pointed a finger at me. "You did good, Wallace. Trust me."

"Oh, God, I hope so."

7

I DON'T WATCH my father anymore. It hurts too much.

Ten months ago, on a Friday night, he forgot my name. I had just returned from the grocery store with the week's supplies—he was no longer able to drive himself—when he called me into the den. The television was on the wrong channel and he couldn't figure out how to work the remote control. He looked me straight in the eyes and said, "Charlie, could you please turn on HBO?" I laughed, thinking he was acting the smart-ass, one of his favorite pastimes.

But later at dinner, he asked, "Charlie, pass me the salt and pepper."

I looked at him; there was no humor in his voice, no mischief in his eyes. "Dad," I said, scared, "who is Charlie?"

A confused expression creased his face. "What the hell kind of question is that?"

"Just tell me who Charlie is, Dad."

He laughed. "Hell, buddy. Don't you even remember your own name? We served in the war together, Charlie. You were my wing man, for Christsakes."

It came to me then. Charlie Banks—my father's best friend, dead over fifteen years now.

It was a long night, but the next morning, everything was back to normal. I was his son again, Charlie Banks completely forgotten.

But I could see the signs then. No longer able to drive, arthritis, failing eyesight and hearing, advancing stages of senility…the list continued to grow as each month passed.

As did my own depression and anxiety. I remember someone once said that there is nothing sadder, nothing more heartbreaking, than watching your hero die.

They were right.

It was during that time I decided I couldn't let that happen.

8

THE SNOW WAS falling harder now. The narrow streets were covered, neighborhood yards of dead grass just beginning to glisten a beautiful white.

I was standing by the rental car, nervously running my bare hand over the cold metal. The two of them stood huddled together on the porch, Crawford's cigarette aglow. The man had emerged from the house several minutes ago, but the detective had insisted on talking to him first. Alone. I'd trusted him this far, so I'd agreed.

Five minutes later, twenty minutes before midnight, they finished talking and walked to the driveway.

Crawford pulled me aside and said, "Your dad was sleeping like a baby. Just as we planned. There was no pain, no surprise."

I closed my eyes, nodded my head. "Thank you," I whispered. "Thank you so much."

"It's been my pleasure," the detective said, reaching for my hand. "And I mean that. Now, don't worry about anything. I'm going to get our friend back to the airport and back on that plane. You get inside." He waved at me from the car. "I'll be in touch."

Before he joined Crawford, the man laid a hand on each of my shoulders, touched a single gloved finger to my face. "Immortality is a rare and wonderful thing, Mr. Wallace. But it is not without its failings. It will not always be easy. Cherish this gift, protect it, as I know you will, and you and your father will be truly rewarded."

Tears streamed down my cheeks. I opened my mouth to thank him, but the words did not come.

He held a finger to my lips. "Say nothing. I must go." I watched the car back out of the driveway, pull away into the night, its brake lights fading to tiny red sparks in the falling snow. I looked at the second-floor window—my father's bedroom—then at the front door. A snowflake drifted to my lips, and I opened my mouth, tasted it like I had done so many times before as a child. I looked skyward and caught another on my tongue. Then, I started across the lawn, his words still echoing in my head.

Immortality is a rare and wonderful thing.

God, I hoped so.

DITCH TREASURES

1

A TWO-HUNDRED-YEAR-OLD BIBLE.
A brand new pair of Air Jordan sneakers.
An iPhone in a leopard skin case.
A cigar box containing ashes.
An expensive fly fishing rod.
A framed velvet Elvis.
A George Foreman grill still in the box.
A rusty Sucrets tin filled with Buffalo nickels.
Three dead puppies in a burlap bag.
A wallet containing $269 in cash.
A loaded handgun.
A gold Rolex wristwatch, broken but still beautiful.
A ziplock baggie of marijuana.
A powder blue tuxedo balled up in a paper bag.
A battered suitcase full of wind-up monkeys.
A laptop computer with a smiley face sticker.

2

THESE ARE JUST a handful of the more unique items I have found strewn along the grassy shoulder and median strip of I-95 in northern Maryland. For reasons I can't figure out, womens' shoes and compact discs are the most common. I once thought I had found a dead body lying there in the weeds, but it was dusk and the light was bad, and it turned out to be nothing more than a mannequin—incredibly lifelike, nude, with BEAT PENN STATE written across the torso in black magic marker. Some people sure are weird.

3

MY NAME IS Jake Renner, but most everyone calls me Rhino on account of a fight I once got in with a big Mexican. I lowered my head and charged and actually managed to knock the huge bastard off his feet. He still kicked my ass without breaking much of a sweat, but I got his shirt a little dirty, and got a nickname and a little respect out of the deal.

I'm 34 years old and have worked the I-95 grass-cutting crew for going on six years now. Despite the Maryland summer heat and humidity, it's a pretty good gig; we work eight months out of the year and make seventeen dollars an hour. Plus benefits. For a guy with no college, it beats laying asphalt or working construction, that's for sure.

The job is simple, but that's not to say easy. It mainly consists of pushing or riding a mower or working one of those big industrial weed-whackers. The whackers are heavy suckers and can do serious damage in careless hands. That's the first thing we learn around here; those things aren't toys.

The boss only cares about two things: the grass gets cut and the grass gets cut safely. If your crew does those two things, the boss man pretty much leaves you alone.

There are six of us on my crew. Me, three wiry Mexicans we call Huey, Dewey and Louie after the cartoon ducks, a barrel-chested redneck who goes by Tex and doesn't talk all that much, and the only black guy I've ever known named Kyle. Kyle talks enough for all of us. The guy never shuts up, but it's okay; he usually makes us laugh and helps the time pass quicker.

Some days out on the road are a cakewalk. We cut grass and crack jokes and sip lemonade spiked with vodka. Traffic is light and the breeze is cool. Other days are nothing but sunburns and thrown pennies and shouted cuss words from passing cars and nasty surprises run over and shredded by our mower blades. Trust me when I say you have never smelled anything quite as ripe as a loaded diaper—a shit sandwich, we call them—or a rotting, maggot-infested groundhog chewed up and spit out in 90 degree heat. Get some of that juice on your jeans and it'll take three or four washes to erase the stink.

But mostly it's boredom we fight on a daily basis. Cutting grass ain't brain surgery—and I-95 is one long-ass road.

4

WE CALL THEM ditch treasures.

The name came about from a lunch conversation we had one sweltering July afternoon last summer in the shade of a busy underpass.

Between big, sloppy bites of roast beef sandwich, Kyle (of course) expressed his sincere dismay that so few kids today would ever experience the wonder and joy of the rain-soaked and swollen girlie magazine (traditionally fished out of dumpsters or trash cans or ditches, but sometimes—on rare, lucky occasions—found right out in the open).

We all understood where Kyle was coming from and shared in his pain. When I was a kid, every fort and tree house we ever built was stocked with a couple of these puffy, pages-stuck-together treasures. We surely wouldn't have thrown a copy of *Playboy* outta the old treehouse, but we all agreed the nastier the mags the better. Gems like *Swank* and *Penthouse* and *Oui* were especially coveted.

But, nowadays, with all the easily-accessed online porn, these ditch treasures—I'll proudly take credit for that little phrase—had all but become an endangered species. Hell, we didn't even see that many tree houses around anymore.

We all agreed it was a damn shame.

5

THE RULES WERE simple: *finders keepers.*

Any ditch treasures you found, you kept. If you were working by your-self when you stumbled upon it, the treasure was all yours. If you were working with a partner or partners, you split the goodies in equal shares.

Some guys tried to hide their finds if they were working with a partner—if the item was small enough, a stealthy kick of a work boot usually did the trick—so they could sneak back later and pretend to find it when they were alone.

But our crew wasn't like that.

We were all grateful to have the job and liked each others' company. Even Huey, Dewey and Louie. We couldn't understand a damn thing they were saying most days, but that was all right; they worked hard and usually did it with smiles on their faces.

The six of us rooted each other on and were genuinely happy when someone found something tasty.

Kyle's all-time favorite find was a shoebox full of baseball cards. Rare baseball cards.

Tex's was a saddle. A big, leather, scuffed up horse saddle.

Before today, I would have said my favorite ditch treasure was the Rolex—I mean, how else is a guy like me ever gonna hold a genuine Rolex watch?—or maybe the Buffalo Head nickels that reminded me so much of my father.

But all that changed this morning…

6

BEFORE I GET to that, I need to tell you about the ponds.

Although, in reality, very few of them are actually ponds; I think the technical term is run-off collection basin. You've probably seen them your-selves if you've ever driven the interstate. Narrow strips of muddy water sitting just off the shoulder, no more than twenty or thirty yards in length, varying in depth depending on recent rain totals. In mid-Summer, these basins often transform into dried out, sun-cracked depressions in the land-scape, like footprints from a wandering giant.

But every once in awhile, you stumble across an actual real life pond. Complete with plant life and fish and frogs and snakes and even the occasional beaver dam. Our cutting territory on 95 held two such bodies of water, both located flush against exit ramps. The first pond was small and shallow and held little mystery for us. The fact that it was often used as a depository for recent roadkill and smelled pretty rank didn't help matters.

But the second pond was something else entirely. Tucked further back from the road, it sat in the shade of a couple ancient weeping willow trees. The pond itself was bigger and deeper and dappled with lily pads. Water bugs and dragonflies skated across the water's surface. The occasional fish jumped. Turtles sunned themselves on exposed logs and rocks. If it wasn't for the constant hum of traffic, you could stretch out a blanket on the grassy bank and enjoy a picnic lunch and almost forget that thousands of cars were hurtling past you a mere thirty yards away.

Kyle was the fisherman of the group, so the pond was his baby. He would often sneak a fishing rod and tackle box into the work truck on days he knew we'd be cutting nearby. He'd cast a line out during his lunch break, and although on most days he usually only caught a handful of fat sunnies, he once pulled a four pound largemouth bass out of that pond. I still have the picture on my cell phone to prove it.

But Kyle was home sick today. A summer cold, his wife said. Fever and the shakes.

So, I was working alone this morning. Pushing a hand mower in a wide, lazy circle around that pretty little pond. Humming to myself and paying extra attention to the ground in front of me, being especially careful of the weeping willow's thick roots.

7

I THOUGHT IT was a baby doll at first.

Laying half in and half out of the water, face and legs obscured by mud and weeds.

I stopped and stared for a long moment—and my heart skipped a beat.

It looked so *real*.

I switched off the mower and started down the bank. As I did, my mind flashed back to the evening I found the mannequin, and any desire to call out to Tex, who was weed-whacking up on the shoulder, dried up and died in my throat. Better to take a look myself first; I was in no hurry to be the butt of their jokes again.

As I carefully worked my way down to the water, I noticed something distressing: there was a very clear path of broken and pushed-down grass leading to the pond...leading to the *thing* in the pond...as if it had somehow dragged itself there, looking for safety. Or water.

I stopped and picked up a broken tree branch. Eased a little closer. I leaned over and poked at the *thing* on the ground. Once. Twice. It was mushy to the touch, sponge like, and it didn't move.

Holding my breath, I poked it a third time. Harder. Nothing.

I inched closer and used the tip of the stick to flick away the weeds and cattails—and got a much better look at it.

It wasn't a baby doll.

It wasn't a baby.

It wasn't even human.

For a moment, I thought maybe it was some kind of animal. Hairless or even skinned. A species of animal I had never laid eyes on before.

But then I looked closer—at the long, narrow head; the three slanted eyes, wide open and cloudy, lined up *vertically* in the center of the creature's sloping forehead; there was no nose centered below, only a trio of small puckered indentations that could have been nostrils; still lower, a lipless and toothless pink slit for a mouth, stretching grotesquely across the entire length of the thing's lower jaw; no ears; not a wisp of hair; only pale, unlined ivory skin glistening and taut like a rubber wetsuit; and its arms, long, thin, boneless arms, ending in hands that didn't belong to man or beast; the hand-like appendages featuring three slender fingers each, the fingers unmarked by nails or knuckles or blemishes of any kind; and then finally its legs, spindly and spider-like, almost translucent, at least six of them tangled underneath it and submerged in the pond, each leg tapering to tiny claw-like feet.

I stood there for a long time and stared and listened to the cicadas in the trees and my own heavy, quick breathing, my brain still fighting the reality of the situation, even as I put a name to the thing laying in the muddy weeds at my feet.

"*It's a fucking alien,*" I whispered to myself.

A baby alien.

A *dead* baby alien.

I looked around and realized I had dropped the stick and backed away a short distance without even knowing it. I glanced at the stick on the ground, then back to the creature again. I glanced up the hill at Tex, still powering away with his weed whacker, then quickly back to the creature again.

Had it moved?

Had it gotten closer?

I took another step back, then shook my head. *Don't start seeing things now, jackass.*

It hadn't moved. It wasn't breathing. It wasn't alive.

And it definitely wasn't human.

I looked up at Tex again and thought about what he would say. Knowing Tex, probably not a whole helluva lot.

Thought about Huey, Dewey and Louie…what would they say? Probably nothing I could understand.

I wished Kyle wasn't home sick; he would know what to do.

And then I heard my own voice inside my head: *finders keepers.*

It belonged to me, and me alone.

It was my decision.

8

I SAT DOWN on the cool grass in the shade of one of the weeping willows, just staring up at the blue sky above the highway and thinking hard thoughts. Tex and his weed whacker had moved down the road a bit. I could still hear the distant *whir* of the whacker, but could no longer see him. I might as well have been a middle-class suburbanite stretched out on a hammock in his back yard, reading the *Wall Street Journal* and sipping iced tea and listening to a neighbor finish his yard work down the street.

Only I wasn't a suburbanite, had never even been in a hammock before, hated iced tea, and had never laid eyes on a *Wall Street Journal* in my life.

I had a high school education (barely), cut grass eight months out of the year, moved snow the other four months, and lived with my pregnant girlfriend and our baby girl in a two-room apartment above a butcher's shop on Tupelo Street. The shop smelled funny on hot summer days and wasn't exactly located in the best part of town, but rent was cheap and the locks on the doors and windows worked.

I sat there and wondered how much the *National Enquirer* would pay for a story about a real life alien. A story *and* pictures. Hell, a story and pictures *and* the actual body of an alien. We sure could use the money.

Then, I wondered what my boss would say about all this. He was the cantankerous sort and very protective of his little grass-cutting kingdom. Like I said earlier, he mostly left us alone because the grass got cut and the grass got cut safely. What would he think if cops and federal agents (yes, I watch *The X-Files*; who doesn't?) were swarming all over his territory? Searching for evidence. Interviewing his employees. Getting in the way of our grass cutting efficiency? It wasn't a pretty thought.

And, finally, I couldn't help but wonder about those cops and federal agents. Might they be especially interested in the guy who found the alien? Might they even look into that guy's past and find some things that guy didn't want anyone to find, especially that guy's girlfriend and boss? These were troubling thoughts to ponder.

9

I PULLED ON my work gloves and followed the same winding path down to the water's edge. I didn't care about fingerprints; I just didn't want to actually touch the thing.

I walked quickly, any caution from before gone. My mind was made up.

Across the pond, a fish jumped. A gust of wind rippled the surface of the water.

I arrived at the pond and bent down, then decided to take a knee. I reached out with one hand to grab the baby alien—and hesitated, my hand hovering inches away.

What the hell was I doing?

"The only thing I can do," I answered before my mind could waver— and the words gave me courage.

I reached down and took hold of the alien's torso and pulled—but it didn't budge.

It was heavier than its small size indicated, and was stuck in the mud.

I reached down and seized it with both hands and...

...there was a sudden flash of blinding white light behind my eyes...and when my vision cleared I was no longer kneeling by a small pond alongside I-95 in Maryland, but was in a faraway place with a roiling, purplish sky overhead the color of old bruises, jagged lightning strikes etched along the far horizon, and in the foreground, a scattering of strange buildings that almost seemed to be alive and glistening in the flickering purple light, and emerging from these buildings, dozens of skittering creatures, larger versions of the baby alien at my feet, approaching and surrounding me, until a pair of them stand before me, beckoning with their strange hand-like appendages, moist eyes beseeching me, and I suddenly realize what they are and who they are searching for and...

The creature pulled free from the mud with a loud sucking *slurp*, and I tumbled to my ass with it cradled against my chest.

I quickly held it away from my body and got to my feet.

I hurried up the hill, and realized I had tears pouring down my cheeks.

I didn't see anything, I thought to myself, shaking my head.

I reached the mower and said it aloud, "I didn't see anything."

I started to toss the baby alien to the ground, then bent down and gently placed it on the long grass directly in front of the lawn mower.

"I didn't see a fucking thing," I whispered.

And then I started the mower.

THE
SILENCE
OF SORROW

1

E STOOD THERE FOR a long time, just staring out the upstairs bedroom window, listening to the sounds of a lazy spring afternoon. A dog barking somewhere in the distance; a chorus of lawnmowers; the sweet music of a child's laughter; the soft hum of neighborhood traffic.

He stood there, unable to move, unable to breathe, unable to make sense of the thoughts whirling madly within his head. The sheer curtains, nudged by a gentle breeze, fluttered inward and brushed against his arms, and the scent of cut grass and fresh flowers was thick and rich in the air. It filled the room with the promise of summer.

He looked at the photos again, just a quick glance, and suddenly the sun felt unbearably hot on his face; blistering; suffocating. He took a step backward into the room. Closed his eyes. And it was then that his hands began to shake, and he discovered he could not stop them.

The photos slipped from his fingertips, tumbled soundlessly in a stream onto the carpet. Piled there like discards from a poker game. One by one they fell until his hands were empty.

Then he began to weep.

2

HE HADN'T WEPT since the funeral service—a cloudless June morning six days earlier—and now the tears streamed hot and angry down his cheeks. He sobbed with great force, but silently, afraid the others would hear, terrified they would rush to comfort him. He sat down on the edge of the bed and took in deep, whistling gulps of air. After a time, the pressure on his chest eased and he felt less light-headed, but his stomach remained cramped and tight.

He had come here, to this house of death, with a mixture of dread and sorrow. It was such a horrible task—the toughest he had ever faced, in fact—but it was his duty. And he was not the only one. There were eight of them in total. Three (his daughters; all married and living in distant cities) were downstairs talking on the back porch, resting from a long morning of back-breaking work. The others (a son-in-law and three long-time neighbors) had gone downtown twenty minutes earlier in search of drink reinforcements and pizza and sandwiches. And so he was left alone in the house.

3

HE'D FOUND THEM in the bedroom closet. Hidden inside a shoebox, the box carefully tucked away beneath a tangled clutter of clothes hangers and worn-out jogging shoes. There were other things inside the box, but the photos were the worst. And there were dozens of them.

4

THE ACCIDENT HAD made the papers and the television news as far west as Emittsburg and as far east as Baltimore. Yes, sir; it was a pretty big story for a slow week in June. Nine cars and two trucks involved. A series of spectacular explosions. Seven gut-wrenching fatalities, including the owner of the Hagerstown Baysox (a local minor league ballclub; currently four games out of first), a twenty-year veteran of the D.C. police force, a young retarded boy, and a hometown hero.

It was inside this hometown hero's bedroom that Frank Martin sat alone with a pile of photos and his troubled thoughts.

5

FRANK, BACK IN his mid-twenties, had once worked as a maintenance man at an apartment complex just outside of Pittsburgh. During his first month on the job, he'd been forced to help clean out a woman's one-bedroom apartment after she'd committed suicide. The woman had had no family, no friends; no one to carry on her name, much less collect her memories. So the job had fallen to the employees.

Frank had hated it.

All morning and afternoon, while he boxed her personal belongings and piled them in the hallway for the others to carry outside to the truck, he'd felt as if the walls were closing in on him. He'd felt dirty, like a trespasser.

Even then, while he struggled with the cardboard boxes and the packing tape, he'd clearly known that the details of the day would haunt him forever; he would never be able to forget what kind of plates and utensils the woman had in her kitchen, the titles of the books on her shelves, the simple prints and paintings on the walls, her favorite color of shoes, the style of dress she preferred, what her handwriting looked like on a grocery list magneted to the refrigerator door. And so many other little things he had no right to possess knowledge of.

For days after the job, Frank had experienced such a profound feeling of sorrow that he'd broken down in tears several times with the memory, and his nightly routine of seven hours sleep became five hours, then three, then almost nothing. When his appetite began to diminish, Sarah (his wife of just over a year at the time) convinced him to take a weekend off and they'd snuck away to the country for two days of rest, relaxation, and magic.

6

FRANK THOUGHT OF that long-ago day and immediately realized the sad irony. Here he was, after all these years, once again cleaning up after the dead.

His hands still trembled, but just enough now to make picking up the color polaroids a slow process. He crouched to one knee and snatched them up with his right hand and collected them with his left. He did this without looking at the pictures. He had seen enough.

When he was finished he tossed them into the shoebox, which was now resting on the bed, and returned the box to the clutter at the bottom of the closet. He dropped a pair of folded sweaters on top, closed the door, and went downstairs.

7

LUNCH WAS A club sandwich, corn chips, and a frosty can of Coke. They ate outside at the picnic table and Frank forced himself to clean his plate; he knew they were concerned about him and would be watching. In fact, he didn't doubt for a moment that Sarah had asked one—or even all three—of the girls to make sure he didn't skip his lunch. *He'll need the energy*, she probably told them. *So you make certain he eats something, even if it's just a candy bar.*

My God, he thought, watching two squirrels play chase in an ancient weeping willow, he had himself one wonderful old lady.

As they'd done the day before, everyone remained in the backyard sunshine after lunch was finished, planning which area of the house to clear next and discussing which boxes needed to be moved where. Frank said very little. Instead, he found himself studying the faces of his friends and family, listening to each of their voices, watching their gestures and expressions, and he was surprised when he was almost moved to tears. God, how he loved these people. Loved their strengths, their weaknesses. Loved what they stood for after all these long years. He would have gladly faced death for each and every one of them—traded his breath for theirs—and he knew the feeling was mutual…yet at no other time in his life had he felt so utterly helpless.

So completely alone.

8

EVENTUALLY, AS IT had done so many other times during the past week, the conversation turned to fond reminiscing and favorite memories. Frank sat back in the tall grass, stretched his legs, and listened to the familiar stories:

The day when Chuck was six years old and he fell face-first into the wishing fountain at the Gateway Shopping Mall...

The summer day, a year later, when he ran away from home and ended up being sprayed by an angry skunk in the old Hanson woods....

The time he was almost suspended from school for freeing the frogs from the biology lab...

The summer he saved that woman's life at the beach, springing to action and starting CPR when the teenaged lifeguard froze in terror...

The fine spring day he graduated from law school with honors and at the top of his class...

The afternoon he was married to his wonderful Mary Ellen...

The magical night the twins were born...

The day he was elected mayor of their small ("but growing") town, the youngest ever at the age of thirty-three, and a hometown boy to boot...

Despite the midday sun, Frank's hands felt clammy, his chest ice-cold. He listened half-heartedly, nodding when he felt it was appropriate, feigning laughter several times, mainly just smiling sadly.

Soon he found his thoughts drifting away from the conversation to one memory in particular: *It had been Chuck's eleventh birthday, and the two of them had spent the day together. That had been Chuck's only birthday wish that year: to spend the entire day with his Dad; just the two of them. They'd planned the day for weeks, and when it finally arrived, they'd attacked it head-on like a pair of young brothers, instead of a father and son. First thing in the morning, they'd fished for catfish down at the big bend in Hanson's Creek (and been quite lucky with their catch). Next, after a quick shower and a pizza lunch at the mall, they'd watched their Orioles and the Red Sox battle it out in an afternoon double-header at Memorial Stadium. It had been a perfect day, capped off by a post-game photo of father and son and Brooks Robinson, their favorite ball-player...*

Frank, to his amazement and horror, felt a smile forming, and he choked it back in immediately. An enlarged and framed print of the birthday photo hung proudly in his den, a surprise retirement gift from Chuck two years earlier. In his mind's eye, Frank imagined seeing the photo hanging side-by-side next to an enlargement of one of the photos from upstairs—a "that was then, this is now" comparison of his son.

His brain flashed this image in grim detail and, for one frightening moment, he thought he might be sick.

9

THEY WERE PHOTOS of naked children. Glossy, full-color polaroids.
Solo shots. Couples. Group shots.

Frank thought of the photos—images so perverse and unspeakable that nothing in his sixty-four years of life had prepared him for the sight of them—and for a moment he was sure that he had to be dreaming. That the feel of the grass and the sun and the breeze had to be part of the dream. That the faraway voices and faces around him were imagined, not real.

He closed his eyes and rested his head.

Felt the grass tickle the back of his neck.

Listened to the beating of his heart.

But he knew he wasn't dreaming.

And he knew what he had seen: a brown shoebox full of shiny magazines filled with disgusting pictures, a worn datebook full of mysterious addresses and phone numbers and cryptic appointment notes, a pair of unlabeled video cassettes, and dozens and dozens of photos…several of them capturing the smiling image of his only son…

And in these photos Chuck was not alone.

10

FRANK MARTIN STRETCHED out in the cool grass and listened to the silence. The entire neighborhood seemed to be taking a midday break, and he was alone again with his thoughts. The others had all gone back inside, and from time to time, he could hear a muffled voice or the echo of footsteps or the soft thud of a box being moved. But mostly he heard nothing at all.

He sat there, staring up at the bedroom window, and soon his hands began to twitch. He clasped them together and squeezed, and it occurred to him that he was probably losing his mind.

A tornado of thoughts touched down in his head:

He thought of Sarah and the others. What would he—or could he—tell them? That Chuck was not the son, the brother, the friend they all thought him to be?

He thought of Mary Ellen, Chuck's young wife, also lost in the accident. Had she been suspicious? Had she seen the warning signs?

And then he thought of the very worst…the twins. Two bundles of joy and energy and hope, safe at home with their Grandma. What would their futures have held if not for the accident? Would he *(sweet Jesus please please don't let it be true!)* find them upstairs in those photos? On those videos?

He felt smothered by these dark questions, but he ran them through slowly and carefully, a small piece of his heart breaking off and dying with each thought. After a long time, he got up and walked into the house, into a world that suddenly made no sense. No sense at all.

AFTER THE BOMBS

T HE OLD MAN WAS blind and had crumbs in his beard. He sat in a rocking chair with a half eaten biscuit resting on a paper towel in his lap. His left hand was shaking.

But he still felt dangerous.

I sat down in the chair opposite him and watched him and waited.

He took another bite of the biscuit and returned it to the paper towel. I noticed that his right hand was steady. His gun hand, if this was the man I believed him to be.

He chewed slowly and I watched crumbs tumble from his mouth and join the others hiding in his untended whiskers. I could hear men working the field outside the cabin, and farther away, the sound of a child crying.

Finally, after one more bite, he spoke and his voice was that of a man much younger:

"I apologize for not offering you something to eat. We plant these fields but nothing grows now. Like everywhere, the soil is tainted. But we keep trying."

"No apology is necessary. Your daughter kindly gave me water. That is more than enough."

"My daughter is still beautiful, isn't she?"

I hesitated before answering. "Your daughter is very beautiful, yes."

"She had a birthday last week. Do you know how old she is?"

I couldn't even begin to guess his daughter's age; everyone looked older than they were. The "old man" before me was probably only in his fifties. We were all lucky to be alive.

"She is younger than me, that is all I know."

The old man laughed. "A politician's answer. Or maybe just a kind one."

"An honest one."

"My friend told me you were an honest man," he said, nodding. "And a historian."

"Nothing that impressive, I'm afraid. I write down the stories I hear. It is up to those who read them to decide whether they are history or mere campfire tales."

"And today's story...*my* story, for which you have traveled all these miles...which shall it be?"

"I have a feeling it will be a little of both, no?"

The old man slammed his palm down on the rocker's armrest and bellowed laughter. Again, the strength of the sound coming from within did not match the frailness of the body outside.

"I *do* like you, young man. By all appearances, you are every bit as wise as I have heard." He readjusted himself in the chair with a grimace of pain. "Although, I *am* blind, so I am limited in that capacity."

I laughed before I could stop myself. "I have another feeling...that perhaps you *see* things better than most men with healthy, even watchful, eyes."

The old man nodded again, his tired smile fading.

"It wasn't always this way..."

BEFORE THE BOMBS, I was a school teacher. Middle school English. The most "watchful" matters I attended to were keeping my eyes on students passing notes in class or trying to cheat on vocabulary quizzes.

For a time after the war, if you can call what actually happened a war, I was like so many other survivors. Scared. Angry. Confused. But, unlike many others, I was fortunate enough to have family that survived the initial catastrophe. So, despite the hardships, I considered myself doubly blessed. I wasn't alone, and I had something to live for.

We lived in rural West Virginia, far away I suppose from anything of even moderate tactical value, and as a result, we were able to avoid most of the bombs' impact zones and the heaviest radiation levels. As laughable as it now sounds, I once believed our little town to be one of the few safe havens to still exist after the bombs.

Not that our remote location mattered to many of the townspeople. Most of the others chose to leave, and they were never heard from again. Not even a single one of them ever returned.

My wife and daughter and I decided to stay, along with eleven other families, and here we still remain all these years later. A bit the worst for wear, but most of us survived, and that is something I doubt many of the others can lay claim to.

We lived underground in the mines for the first year. Like starving ground hogs. We believed it to be the safest option, and over the course of those first twelve months, we lost only a total of sixteen people and took in strangers totaling twenty-three adults and thirteen children.

We ate canned foods and drank bottled water that we were able to scavenge from abandoned stores and homes in town. Everything was rationed from Day One; we knew what kind of a future we were facing.

Benjamin Travers and Frank Dodd assumed mutual roles of leadership, Benjamin having been a police officer before the bombs dropped and Frank, a retired Master Sergeant in the Marines. They took charge of assigning duties to both men and women. Cooking. Cleaning. Scavenging. Scouting. Weapons collection. Even guard duty.

This hierarchy seemed to work out well, until we were awakened one night by a gunshot near the mouth of the mine. Benjamin had killed himself without warning or explanation. Frank took over after that, and I still remained in the background, doing my daily chores along with the others.

But that all changed in the weeks leading up to the ambush.

"DO YOU MIND if I write some things down?" I asked, reaching for the notebook inside my satchel.

He waved a wrinkled hand. "Just don't expect me to slow down or repeat myself. This story is once for the telling."

IT WAS FIFTEEN months after the bombs dropped, and the main group of us were still living like animals in the mines; but we had recently decided to rotate a group of ten of us above ground. Human guinea pigs to determine how harmful the remaining radiation might be, and what other factors might affect us if we decided to move ourselves back into town.

After much discussion, ten of us—nine men and one woman—had volunteered to take part in the experiment. Two groups of five, alternating for shifts of one month each. I was one of those to volunteer, the first of many decisions that would anger and worry my loving wife. But, after more than a year underground, something had ignited inside of me; a kind of restlessness that could not be quieted regardless of how many tasks I took on or how many miles I traveled. My Annie called it recklessness and a death wish; I called it *living*.

The five of us in my group—all men—lived under one roof during our month spent above ground. The old Tanner cabin on the north side of town. The cabin was perched on a tree-lined ridge and offered a scenic view of the valley below. More importantly, if you didn't know a cabin existed on that ridge, it was nearly impossible to find.

All of us crowded into the same three-room cabin wasn't exactly appealing after living in such close quarters for more than a year; but it was deemed safer this way, and it was also thought to be the best environment in which to observe any subtle changes that might occur amongst ourselves.

As it turned out, radiation didn't end up being much of a short term issue at all.

Other survivors—outsiders—proved much deadlier.

At first, in the months right after the bombs fell, it was mainly groups of men, women, and children, much like those from our own town who had chosen to pack up and move on with the hope of finding something better, perhaps even a government-managed safe haven. There were many such rumors in the early days.

These folks proved to be no trouble at all. They crossed the hills into town in tired, ragged groups, looking like settlers from the Old West. A handful of them chose to remain with us, but most moved on with a friendly handshake and a hopeful promise to send back help if they found it.

Occasionally, a lone man or woman staggered through town, more often than not mad as a hatter and twice as noisy. One time, when Randy Conners and I were moving through town on a scouting patrol, we witnessed a stark naked man zig-zagging his way down main street with a pistol in one hand and what looked like a dead rat in the other. His body was covered with bright red scribbles from what appeared to be a permanent magic marker. We always left those folks alone to their wanderings.

But as time wore on, we noticed something more troubling.

More and more of these roving bands consisted solely of armed men. Usually moving through the valley in rowdy, noisy, and more often than not, drunken disorder. We hid from these men and watched them pass with silent gratitude.

But the day of the ambush was different.

It was two weeks after the five of us had moved into the old Tanner cabin, and Doug Lawrence and I were resting on a boulder the size of a school bus, smoking homemade cigarettes and watching the sun rise over the horizon, when we both spotted them at the same time.

There were eight of them. Moving fast in a staggered line, as one. Using hand signals. They snaked their way through the valley with the discipline, speed, and stealth of a military unit.

We stayed hidden and followed them the best we could and once we observed them crossing the river, we high-tailed it back to the cabin to tell the others, thinking we were safe.

But we were wrong.

We were no more than a half-mile from the cabin when we heard gunfire. The quick, loud bursts of automatic weapons. Maybe thirty seconds, and then silence.

We ran as fast as the ground would allow, but we were too late. We smelled the gunpowder before the cabin came into sight, and then we smelled blood.

Randy was sprawled facedown in the dirt in front of the cabin, his back peppered with bullet holes, and the other two men were crumpled on the blood-splattered porch, no sign of their weapons anywhere.

Once we made sure that our friends were beyond saving and the outsiders were gone, we'd searched the cabin and discovered the food and water missing and the three mens' weapons destroyed. They had somehow been lured outside unarmed, and then ambushed.

Doug and I collected what we could carry and returned to the mines to tell the others. The next morning at dawn, five of us returned to the cabin and buried the dead.

"IS THAT WHEN you decided to go off and help the others?"

The old man shook his head. "That was later…when it became absolutely necessary." He took a deep breath, and I could tell the memories were becoming painful. "We lasted in the mines for another six weeks after the men were killed, but then we had no choice but to move above ground. Food and water were running low, and people were starting to act funny. The crazy kind of funny, if you know what I mean. We needed change. Most of all, we needed *hope*."

"Weren't you worried the outsiders would come back again?"

"Yes, the same men," he nodded. "Or others even worse."

I stared at the old man and realized I was no longer afraid of him. "What did you do?"

"We worked in shifts, constructing bunkers and walls, and turned the town into a fortress. We posted lookouts along the ridgelines to warn us of travelers. We still welcomed anyone with good intentions and helped those we were able to. But we were wary now, even paranoid."

"So why did you decide to leave?"

"I left because my daughter was sick and my friends were starving."

ELIZABETH WAS TWELVE at the time. Even, after the bombs, she was an angel. Unlike many of the other surviving children who passed their days feeling understandably helpless and in tears, Elizabeth spent most of her time reading and helping others. By the time we left the mines and moved into town, she could cook, sew, clean, and administer first aid as well as any adult in camp. All without a word of complaint.

But then she got sick.

At first, we were afraid it was the radiation making her lose her appetite and strength and causing her fever. A handful of us had started to show some minor effects—hair loss, teeth falling out, skin blistering—but the majority of us remained, on the surface at least, unaffected.

It was Gwen Sanderson, the old school nurse, who soon made us realize that it wasn't radiation at all; instead, it was some kind of virus raging inside our little girl's body, as well as the bodies of another dozen or so of the townspeople.

More and more of the others were getting sick.

And we were out of antibiotics.

And running low on pain medication, canned goods, and bottled water.

That evening, we held a town meeting in Memorial Park and took a vote. It was decided that a search party of four armed men would be sent out immediately to look for medicine and supplies.

When the time came for volunteers to step forward, my hand was the first to go up. Annie cried at first, and then later once we returned home, she got angry. When it was apparent that her hard looks and even harsher words weren't going to change my mind, she started crying again.

But I never faltered. Elizabeth was sick and my town was slowing starving to death; someone needed to find help, and fast.

We left at dawn the next morning. The four of us on horseback. Armed with rifles and pistols, lugging mostly empty knapsacks we hoped would be stuffed full upon our return. Despite the early hour, much of the town turned out to wish us luck and say goodbye. Annie blew me kisses, tears streaming down her cheeks, but Elizabeth remained at home in bed.

We waved goodbye and headed east.

···✳···

"EXCUSE THE INTERRUPTION," the old man's daughter said from behind us. "I thought you might both be thirsty." She handed me a plastic glass of water without making eye contact, then placed a second glass on the small table next to her father's chair.

"Thank you," he said, smiling and feeling for the glass.

"Thank you, Elizabeth." I noticed the smile on the old man's face falter and knew it had been unwise to call her by name. He might be old and blind, but there was nothing more dangerous than a protective father.

Elizabeth left the room without another word, and he continued:

"We were gone for nine days…"

THE FIRST FEW days, we searched houses, stores, sheds, schools, even an abandoned police station and came up empty. We were exhausted and dejected and stank worse than any human beings in the history of human beings. We smelled worse than the horses. We decided to give it one more day and then head back.

And then we got lucky.

One of the men spotted a lake in the distance and we all agreed it was time for some rest and a bath. We cut through a meadow and then a thick stand of trees to reach the lake, and it was amidst those trees that we stumbled upon the abandoned camper. The camper was old and covered in Grateful Dead bumper stickers and had four flat tires—it's funny the things you remember—but we searched it anyway, not really expecting to find anything of value.

Boy, were we wrong.

Inside, we found boxes of canned foods and cases of bottled water. More than all of us could possibly carry. We also discovered a mini arsenal of automatic weapons, more than a hundred paperback books, and best of all, two duffle bags full of medical supplies and assorted drugs.

I was the one who found the body curled up in the camper's sleeping bunk. Most of the flesh had decomposed, but we could tell it had once been a man with long gray hair pulled back in a pony tail. His skeletal hands still held a tattered leather Bible.

We buried the man at the edge of the meadow, under an old maple tree, and joined hands in a prayer of gratitude. Then, we skipped our baths in the lake and packed as much as our horses could haul and set off for home. It took us two days of around the clock riding to get there, but we made it in time for the medicine to help Elizabeth and the others.

The food and water were inventoried and organized in the town pantry, and the medical supplies went under lock and key in our makeshift hospital.

Three days later, I led a party of six men back to the camper and we brought all the remaining supplies home with us.

At the time, it felt like a miracle.

"DID YOU SEE anyone else?"

"Not those first two trips, no. We *heard* someone one night. A man screaming in the dark. But he was far away and we never went looking for him."

"During later trips?"

"Later...yes, we did."

"Good guys or bad guys?"

"Both." The old man scratched his whiskers, dislodging a shower of crumbs onto his lap. "We tried to help as many as we could. If we found six cases of water and ran across others in need, we gave them a case with our blessing. The rest went home with us. But many others...we hid from."

"Did you ever see the men from the day of the ambush again?"

Nodding. "We did...but that was years later, and another part of this story."

I itched to ask more but knew it was best to move on for now.

"How often did you leave town on these...missions?"

"At first, only when necessary. When something was needed. But later..." He stopped and reached for the glass of water. Took a drink.

I waited for him to continue. When he didn't, I asked, "Later...what happened?"

He carefully placed the glass back on the table, and then I could feel him staring at me with those sightless eyes.

"A stranger came to town. A nearly-dying man. With a story to tell..."

HIS NAME WAS Joseph, and he was the biggest man I had ever seen. At least six-six and two hundred and seventy pounds. A mountain of thick, black muscle.

And he was bleeding to death from a gunshot wound in his stomach. How he walked the miles he claimed to have walked is beyond me; the pain he must have endured.

At first, we kept him under armed guard as we administered first aid and allowed him to recover in our hospital. His brute size and obvious strength frightened us. But it was something else, too: he was too quiet, too aware. Even in the haze of pain medication, he seemed to be somehow—borrowing your word—*watchful*.

A week later, he was amazingly back on his feet, still weak but able to walk with a cane for short periods of time. We had already decided to ask him to leave once he'd fully recuperated when he found me in the fields one evening and, with great difficulty, told me about Camelot.

At first, I misunderstood, and thought he was telling me a good thing. An entire city protected by concrete walls—with an abundance of food and water and supplies; even luxuries such as real doctors and scientists and rudimentary electrical and irrigation systems—all of it guarded by a private security team armed to the teeth.

It sounded like heaven.

But then he explained in greater detail, and I understood that the news was anything but good. Camelot was controlled by power hungry men and women, whose cunning and ruthlessness were matched only by their cruel ambition. They allowed no strangers inside their precious walls. Any survivors who approached were either killed or captured and turned into slaves to work in their fields or do other manual labor. But that wasn't enough. They sent out search and destroy missions and executed and robbed any other survivors they could find. They burned entire settlements to the ground. Killed men, women, and children without remorse. Anyone living outside of their walls was considered a threat and an enemy.

When I asked him how he had come upon this knowledge, Joseph explained with great shame that he had once been a member of this city. A high-ranking officer in charge of dozens of men, but that as soon as he'd realized the true intent of the city leaders, he'd stolen away in the middle of the night and escaped. He'd been wounded by a sharp-eyed sentry, but had managed to get away on horseback. He had ridden until his horse, also wounded, had died, and then he'd walked the rest of the way.

He estimated Camelot to be located some fifty miles to the Northwest of our town. He believed it was only a matter of time before they found us…and destroyed us.

"SO HE STAYED?" I asked, leaning forward in my chair.

"He never left. In time, Joseph became my best friend, my brother."

"And he did great things?"

The old man slowly nodded, remembering. "Until the day he died."

"How did he die?" I asked.

"I rather tell you how he *lived*…"

I DECIDED TO share the news of Camelot with only a handful of others in town, and Annie wasn't one of them. I felt horrible about this, of course, but I didn't want to cause unnecessary panic or worry. Besides, I had an idea.

While Joseph continued to recuperate, we quietly posted double sentries and did our best to solidify the town's walls. Mostly constructed of dirt and timber, the walls had served well over the years at providing sufficient protection from disorganized stragglers that happened upon our town; but we all knew they would be useless against an army of any size. Still, we did our best.

Each evening after my work duties were completed, I would sit outside and smoke and talk with Joseph. I grew fond of him very quickly, as did my family. He often played cards with Elizabeth and taught her how to read the stars at night. He insisted on helping Annie clear the table after every meal and told her stories about his own mother, a single mom who had raised him and his three brothers while working the day shift at a hospital and the night shift at a Dunkin' Donuts.

Joseph had a contagious laughter and a generous spirit. He didn't talk about a wife or children of his own, and we didn't ask. This was a lesson we learned very quickly after the bombs.

By the time Joseph was strong enough to travel and I told him about my plan, it felt like we had known each other for a lifetime.

Two days later, we rode out alone. The black giant and the school teacher.

"AND THAT'S HOW the raids started?" I asked, scribbling in my notebook.

The old man ignored my question. "My plan was for Joseph to lead us to Camelot, which we would survey from a safe distance. Along the way, we would keep our eyes open for any sign of a Camelot raiding party or—our biggest fear—an advancing army. It was predominately a scouting mission, meant to make us feel more secure in the knowledge that no one was looking in our direction for Joseph. But I had other things in mind, too..."

WE STUMBLED UPON the raiding party at dusk on our third day of riding.

Joseph estimated that we were within fifteen miles of the city by then. His initial guess that Camelot was some fifty miles northwest of our town had now grown to seventy miles; a fact which brought me great relief.

There were six men in the raiding party. Armed and on horseback. Joseph recognized two of the men from Camelot, even from a distance.

We tracked them west for a number of miles and watched them take up positions along a grassy bluff. An hour later, hidden in a treeline, we watched in horror as they swooped down from their hiding place and sur-rounded a group of unsuspecting survivors on foot, most of them women and children.

A pair of survivors—a man and a child—broke free and tried to escape, but they were gunned down in cold blood. Shot in the back.

As the men dismounted and began to ransack the survivors' belong-ings at gunpoint, Joseph and I quietly circled behind them on foot, nothing but shadows now in the moonlight.

We stopped some thirty yards behind them and with guns drawn—a rifle for me, a pistol for Joseph—we looked at each other and nodded. I know it sounds brave; I know it sounds heroic; but it wasn't. I was scared shitless; but more than that, I was angry.

I broke cover first, walking on my heels the way my father had taught me to move in the forest when hunting deer. I hadn't taken but a handful of steps when I sensed Joseph at my side. I stopped and raised my rifle and sighted in one of the men.

"Black hat," I whispered, marking my target.

From the darkness beside me: "Skinny asshole on his left."

Then we both pulled the trigger.

THE OLD MAN started coughing then, a harsh sound that I could feel deep in my own chest. He fumbled for a sip of water, but it seemed to make the coughing worse. I noticed that both of his hands were shaking now and his face had gone pale.

I was just getting up from my chair to call for help when Elizabeth hurried into the room. "Here, try this." She held a baby blue breath-inhaler to his mouth. He immediately closed his lips around it and she pushed the button. There was a hissing sound, and when she pulled the inhaler away from his mouth, the old man's coughing had stopped. He sat in his rocking chair, eyes closed, taking slow and steady breaths. After a moment: "Thank you, darling. I needed that."

"You need to rest. I knew all this would be too much. You need to—"

"You know who you sound like, don't you?"

She smiled in spite of herself, and I think that is the moment I fell in love with her. "I sound like Mom."

"Right as rain. Spitting image."

"Don't try to sweet talk me, mister. It's not going to work this time."

"Ain't sweet talking anyone. Just telling the truth." He turned in my direction. "Right, friend?"

I was still smiling at Elizabeth. I couldn't help it. "Right."

She rolled her eyes at me. "Dad, I really think you should—"

"What I need is for you and my new friend here to help me out onto the porch so I can finish this story and eat me some supper."

So, that's what we did.

IT'S NOT EASY to kill a man. But that's what we did that night. All six of them.

My plan all along had been for Joseph and me to start intercepting their raiding parties and to return what they had stolen to the folks they had taken it from. If those folks couldn't be found, and quickly, then we would bring the supplies back to town for ourselves.

That first time was an accident the way it happened.

The next dozen or so times were not.

We learned how to set up an ambush; how to flank an enemy with superior numbers and firepower; how to booby trap a trail; how to strike fast and disappear into the wilderness without leaving a trace of our passage.

And we learned how to kill without mercy when necessary. It never got easier and I never learned to like it, like some men did, but for a school teacher, I found that I was extraordinarily good at it. I had a steady hand and a true aim.

Joseph and I learned to trust each other with our lives—and to believe that what we were doing had purpose and meaning.

We took back food and water. We took back weapons and ammunition. We took back *hope*. And, all of this, we either gave to others in need or we hauled it back to town for our own.

It was months before the higher powers at Camelot figured out what was happening, and by then, it was too late.

…⁂…

"SO THAT'S WHEN the stories started? That's when they started calling you Robin Hood?"

There was a nice breeze on the porch. The setting sun felt warm on my face.

"Some folks started with that nonsense, yes. But that's all it was."

The old man was propped up on a straight back chair, ankles crossed on the ground, a thick blanket thrown over his lap. Most of the color had returned to his face.

"'Course, the fact that it was nonsense didn't stop me from calling Joseph 'Little John'; just to get a rise outta him. It worked, too."

"The two of you became legends…"

He scowled at that. "For a lot of survivors, we represented hope and maybe some goodness left in this world. But that's all it was. Yes, we took from the haves and gave to the have-nots. But that's where any comparison stopped."

"What do you mean?" I asked, looking up from my notebook.

"The Robin Hood in the movies and books never did much killing. He fought with the evil sheriff and he stole from the rich to give to the poor and he got the beautiful Lady Marion and all that business; but he did it all with a swashbuckling smirk on his face and a fancy little kick to his step. Errol Flynn in green girlie tights.

"But this was real life. It was dirty and bloody and just plain ugly most of the time."

I didn't say anything. Just stared at him.

"Sure, we made a lot of people happy, even saved some lives, but it cost us. I wasn't there the night my Annie passed on. Elizabeth held her hand as she drew her final breath, but her other hand was empty. Instead, I was running around in the valley helping strangers I would never see again. I still have nightmares about some of the things we saw and did. And we lost a lot of good men ourselves. Some of them died in my arms."

I looked down at my feet. "I'm sorry."

He waved a hand at me. "What do you have to be sorry for? You weren't there."

"I just meant that—"

"I know what you meant. What say you hush and let me finish now?"

AFTER THE FIRST half-dozen or so raids, it became too difficult to keep what we were doing a secret.

First of all, we had to keep coming up with stories to explain why we were leaving town and then even more stories to explain where in the heck we were finding all the supplies we were lugging back with us.

Secondly, there were too many people running their mouths by then. After awhile, any stranger that crossed our path was more likely than not to be blabbing about this mysterious Robin Hood fellow and his giant of a companion.

When we finally explained the truth, my wife didn't speak to me for three straight days. Annie was a sweet old girl, but nastier than a pack of yellow jackets when she was angry. And, boy, could she hold a grudge.

It was Joseph who finally convinced her to forgive me. To this day, I don't know what he told her, but whatever it was, it worked, and I was forever grateful. Six months later, I would lose her to the sickness. One week Annie was fine; the next, she was gone.

That was just like Joseph, too. He was always keeping the peace in town. He went out of his way to be kind and helpful to folks, and they loved him for it. Especially the children. We called him the Pied Piper, because he always had a line of happy kids trailing behind him wherever he went. He was also the first to step up and volunteer for any job, and he worked twice as hard as any man in town. People respected him. And not just because of his size and strength and willingness to work. He was a good man, with a good heart, and we learned a lot from each other.

As the next few years passed, Joseph and I, along with other men from town, continued the missions—always giving some of what we captured to those less fortunate than us—but over time, we saw less and less of Camelot's guns-for-hire. We ran across other bad guys now and then, including the group who had ambushed us at Tanner's cabin all those years earlier, and we took care of them with the same swift and merciless efficiency.

But Camelot remained a quiet mystery.

"WHY DIDN'T YOU just go to Camelot and see for yourself? Joseph knew the way..."

"We were days away from doing exactly that, Mr. Smartie Pants," the old man said, adjusting himself in his chair. "When the answer came to us instead."

ON THE LAST day of Spring, a group of nineteen survivors approached town from the Northwest. They carried with them enough supplies for a small army. They said they had been held captive inside a walled city for a number of years and made to work as slaves; but that an uprising had taken place and the soldiers had been overthrown. Much of the city had been burned to the ground, but the warehouses storing food and water and medical supplies had survived. Some folks had decided to stay and rebuild. Others left to find a new place to start over.

We welcomed these newcomers into town, and within a week they had decided to stay. Joseph, as usual, was one of the first to make them feel comfortable in their new home.

Now I reckon I've rambled long enough about my life after the bombs, and I doubt you've heard what you came for. So, now, I will try to help you, my friend.

The years from then until now have mercilessly been quiet ones. Very few moments of bloodshed or violence. It seems that people are finally getting tired of fighting each other. Now, we fight only to live. Death and sickness still blanket us like a dark cloak, but there is nothing we can do about that. Each sunrise is a gift. We live or we die. The dirt no longer yields fresh crops the way it once did. No one understands why it suddenly stopped last spring. But the world is like that now. Full of dark mystery and more questions than answers. Some give birth to healthy babies now. Others to monstrosities. Some animals have returned in great numbers. Others have disappeared. One evening, I sit by the fire and my eyes are tired but fine. The next morning, I awake with the sun and I am blind. Again, there seems no reason for any of it.

Your father Joseph died three years ago. He went peacefully on a Thursday evening not far from here. I held his hand and together we stared at the setting sun; Elizabeth held his other hand. The sunlight touched his face one final time, and he smiled that wondrous smile of his and closed his eyes.

I STARED AT the old man in shock. Tears in my eyes.

"How did you—?"

"I knew from the moment you walked in and sat down and started talking."

"But *how?*"

"I lived and breathed with your Daddy for a lot of years. I knew the sound of his voice as well as I knew my own. You sound just like him, son."

I wiped the tears from my eyes.

"He talked about you, you know. It took him awhile to trust us with your name and your memory, but once he started, he never shut up. He had a favorite story that he told over and over again. I used to love to listen to him talk about you..."

HE TOLD ME your name was Noah and that your Momma had died when you were just a baby. So, it had always been just the two of you. He said you took care of each other; you and him against the world.

You lived in Baltimore. He was a police officer during the day, a security guard at a factory after you went to sleep each night. He worked hard to earn enough money to send you to a good school outside of the city.

He told me you were away on a field trip with your school the day the bombs fell. A field trip to Washington, D.C. The city had been leveled. He thought you were dead. He'd searched for you for years, just in case, but he'd never found you.

He said you came to him in his dreams, and I believed him. I used to hear him cry out for you in his sleep sometimes when we were on the trail together. It was one of those dark nights, sitting by the fire, that he told me this story...

He said one of your favorite things to do together was watch baseball games before bedtime. Sometimes you would fall asleep, your head on his chest, and he would carry you to bed and kiss you goodnight before heading off to work at the factory.

He told me that for your ninth birthday he surprised you with box seats for the Orioles game. Right behind home plate. He described to me what your face looked like when you walked up the ramp and saw the field in person for the first time.

"It's so green!" you said. He would always laugh and laugh at that part.

And then he would tell me every single thing you ate during the game. Peanuts and hot dogs and pretzels and ice cream. He remembered everything you said that night. Everything you did.

He said the game went into extra innings and that one of the players fouled off a fastball into the stands and he stood up on his seat and caught it and gave it to you. And you smiled so big and hugged him so tight.

The Orioles beat the Yankees that night, 4-3—and the two of you walked home holding hands and singing silly songs. He said it was the happiest day of his life.

TEARS WERE STREAMING down my face now, and I made no effort to stop them.

"He remembered..." I said.

The old man leaned forward in his seat, his face drawing close enough to mine that I could smell his breath. "He remembered *everything* about you, son. He said you were his compass in the night sky."

I reached down to my side and took something out of my satchel. Placed it in the old man's hand, so he could feel it. He closed both his hands over it.

"The baseball," he said with a beautiful smile. Tears slid from his eyes.

He reached over and placed a rough hand behind my neck and pulled me closer until our heads were touching. I felt his tears on my face. I closed my eyes and remembered my father.

We were still sitting like that, the old man and the black giant, when Elizabeth came out onto the porch.

I looked up at the sound of her footsteps and had to smile at the surprised expression on her face.

"Are you two okay?" she asked.

The old man laughed through his tears. "We're better than okay. Set another plate for supper tonight."

He took my hand in his and placed the baseball back into my palm. "Joseph's long lost son has finally come home."

LAST WORDS

I WAS ALONE WITH HIM when it happened. Sitting by the window in a shaft of lazy September sunlight reading a paperback. It was after lunch, and the day nurse had just gone downstairs with a plate of fruit and a cup of pudding, both of which were barely touched. He had been dozing most of the morning thanks to his pain meds and hadn't bothered to wake up enough to eat much. He wasn't eating much these days even when he was awake.

I marked my page and watched two boys walking on the sidewalk outside, fishing poles perched on their shoulders like rifles, when I heard him whisper something.

I turned to him. "What did you say, Pops?"

His eyes were slits. He could have still been sleeping, but his lips were moving. I got up and walked closer. "You need something?"

A barely perceptible shake of his bald head and then his eyes opened. Cloudy and dull. A snapshot of memory flashed in my mind: this same man leading a conga line at my wedding reception, shirt untucked, tie loosened, those same blue eyes twinkling with mischief and scotch.

"Treasure...hunt," he whispered.

I smiled through sudden tears. "I remember, Pops. Of course, I do."

Another shake of his head. A little harder this time.

"Find the map." He started coughing, his entire body shaking with the effort.

"Here…drink this." I lifted the cup to his lips.

He took a noisy sip of water and closed his eyes. After a long moment, I thought he was asleep again and started to move away when he whispered, "Find the map. Before they do."

I stood there and watched his chest rise and fall, rise and fall.

Fifteen minutes later, he was gone.

MY MOTHER AND father died in a car accident on I-95 the weekend before my seventh birthday. They were on their way home from buying my presents at the mall, and the guilt I felt because of that at age seven is something I have never entirely outgrown.

My grandfather, widowed himself only two years earlier, raised me and my brother. Like many veterans, he was a complicated and proud man. Prone to long stretches of silent thoughtfulness and restlessness, he was also a wonderful storyteller and a man with an amazing and generous heart.

It was my grandfather who gifted me my love of books and the out-doors and classic movies. He was the one who taught me how to fish and swim and throw a curveball. Everything was a lesson to be learned to Pop, but he made it interesting and fun. He was the best teacher I ever had.

I remember one night after a drenching rainstorm, he handed me a flashlight and led me outside to catch nightcrawlers in the back yard. We filled a coffee can and you would have thought he had revealed the secrets of real magic to me that night.

In a way, he did.

AND THEN THERE were the treasure hunts…

They were my absolute favorite when I was a boy.

My brother, Lee, and I would wake up to find a hand-drawn map on the nightstand between our beds. We would hurry up and get dressed, rush through breakfast and our morning chores, and slam out the screen door into a brilliantly blue summer day to follow the map's instructions.

The first time we found the map Pops denied involvement and swore that someone else must have snuck into our bedroom under the cover of darkness and left it. Pirates, maybe.

By the time I was ten and Lee was nine, we knew better. But it didn't matter. All that mattered was the hunt.

The treasure maps would lead us across golden fields and grassy hills, into deep dark woods and along shade-cooled creeks where trout and frogs would chase bugs. We would cross those creeks on moss-covered rocks and follow crumbling stone fences until we eventually spotted the towering oaks or weeping willows or fern-choked gullies that marked our destination.

Soaked with sweat and bursting with excitement, we would set to digging and when our shovels clanged on metal, we would drop to our knees and finish with our hands, racing to unearth our treasure.

Our "treasure" usually ranged from new John D. MacDonald paperbacks to carefully wrapped bags of candy to piles of nickels and dimes and pennies. But sometimes more exotic treasures awaited us: a pair of pocketknives, foreign coins from Pops' Army days, one time even a genuine Japanese bayonet from the war.

Eventually, as we got older, Lee grew bored with the treasure hunts and disappointed with our findings, and he stopped going. Not me. I never cared what I found buried in the ground. For me, it was the thrill of the hunt.

It wasn't until I was almost a man that I understood what Pops was doing with these hunts of his. What a gift they were to us. What he was teaching us...

WHEN I CALLED Lee and a handful of other living relatives—a couple of cousins and one sister too far gone senile to remember she actually had a brother—to tell them that Pops had passed away, the conversations were short and devoid of many details. Pops had been sick for awhile, so it wasn't unexpected news.

Only Lee asked if Pops had said anything on the day he died.

The question surprised me, and for some reason, I changed the subject when he asked.

I didn't want to lie to him...but I also didn't want to tell him.

Pops' last words belonged to me.

WE BURIED POPS on a cloudy autumn Thursday.

Lee and his wife, Annie, and their two girls flew down from New York for the service. I offered they could stay at the house with me, but they opted for the local Holiday Inn, as they had the handful of other times they had visited.

With the exception of old Mrs. Potts, Pops' next door neighbor, the rest of the funeral attendees were made up of mostly strangers. What remained of Pops' friends from church and the VA hospital and the VFW. They all shook my hand and clapped me on the back and said nice things in tired, whispery voices.

I held it together until the honor guard fired their rifles and folded the American flag that draped Pops' casket and the bugler played Taps. I accepted the flag from a soldier not much younger than myself with tears streaming down my cheeks.

It was a nice service, and I was grateful to everyone who attended.

On the drive back to the house from the cemetery, I could almost hear Pops' voice from the seat beside me: beautiful day like this is meant for fishing and not much else.

Lee and I said our goodbyes later that night in the Holiday Inn bar, neither of us talking very much about Pops or the past, choosing instead to discuss the upcoming baseball playoffs and his little girls and how his photography business was really taking off. He asked me what the book I was writing was about, but as usual I didn't sense real interest, merely a polite gesture meant to extend the conversation.

We had been best friends growing up, all thru our school years and into college, even though we attended universities more than five hundred miles away. But sometime after Lee got married and moved to New York, we started to drift apart the way best friends and even brothers sometimes do.

I had married—and then divorced—my college sweetheart. Wrote and sold my first novel. Quit my job at the newspaper and became a full-time writer. Shortly after, I moved back to the old neighborhood, just a couple of blocks away from Pops and the house we grew up in.

The move made sense to me. I could write from anywhere. And I missed Pops. He was my family and this was my home.

I COULDN'T SLEEP. That's why I ended up at Pops' house at midnight, banging around in the dark, looking for the damn map.

I'd laid in bed, running Lee's visit through my head, searching for meaning in the things he had said and the things he hadn't said. Was he still disappointed in me for returning to our little town and writing the kind of books I wrote? Did he think I had settled for this life?

And the loudest voice inside my head: when did I start caring so much about *what* my little brother thought?

Somewhere between thinking about what Lee had said at the funeral about Pops' will and what he'd said at the hotel bar about buying a new Cadillac, I remembered Pops' last words: *"Find the map. Before they do."*

Fifteen minutes later, I was slipping my key into Pops' front door and slipping inside like a thief in the night.

I LEFT THE lights off. I told myself I didn't want old Mrs. Potts to see a light on in the house and come over to investigate. But I think it was more than that. I don't think I was ready to see the silent remnants of Pops' life. His battered old reading chair. His collection of autographed baseballs on the bookshelf. The family photos on the wall. His faded war memorabilia.

Besides, if there was a map to be found, I knew where I would find it.

I crept up the stairs and down the hallway to my old bedroom and pushed open the door. A sliver of moonlight peeked in through the window. The pair of single beds remained, as did the faded and chipped nightstand that sat between them. A lamp sat on the nightstand. And nothing else: no map.

I opened the single drawer. Empty.

Disappointed, I started to turn and leave when one final thought occurred to me. I picked up the lamp and looked underneath...

...and there it was.

I picked up the piece of paper and unfolded it—and discovered that it was actually two sheets of paper.

I walked over to the window and took a closer look.

The first sheet was a map. Even in faint moonbeam, I could see that it was drawn in the same detailed fashion as the maps of my childhood. A wave of bittersweet nostalgia racked my heart.

I unfolded the second sheet of paper and found a list of names.

Nine names.

I SAT IN my truck in the driveway and Googled the names on my phone.

They were all young women between the ages of 22 and 30.

And they had one other thing in common: they were all missing.

I PARKED MY truck in Pops' driveway at daybreak and climbed out with the map and a shovel. Pops had taught me how to dress for the land back when I was a kid, so despite an unseasonably warm September morning, I was wearing jeans and hiking boots, a flannel shirt and a baseball hat. I locked the truck and set off.

For the next ninety minutes it was like walking through a time machine and traveling two decades back in time to my childhood. I walked the same fields and paths and creek beds as I had as a fifteen-year-old dreamer.

Of course, nature had had its way with the land, yet somehow it was just how I remembered it. A sense of peace and calm settled over me as I walked deeper and deeper into the wilderness. All the years I had lived here after moving back and it had taken one of Pops' treasure maps to get me out here again. Maybe that was the point of all this…Pops still teaching me, even after he was gone. The thought made me smile and my pace quickened.

I thought about the list of names as I walked, but those thoughts got me nowhere. Had Pops even meant to include the names with the map? Had he been somehow investigating the disappearances? Maybe playing amateur detective like a character from one of his old pulp novels? It was something I could definitely imagine him doing—scanning the daily newspaper for details, listening to the nightly news reports—especially in his later years after he'd retired from the mill.

After just a single misstep when I miscalculated the distance between two towering pines, I easily found where "X" marked the spot on Pops' map. He had hidden his treasure at the base of an old weeping willow overlooking a lily pad-choked pond. It had taken me exactly ninety-seven minutes to find it. More than 20 years after my last treasure hunt, I still had it. I would have to remember to call Lee later in the morning and do a little bragging.

I pushed the log off to the side and stabbed at the dark earth with my shovel. Just as I expected, it was firm and unyielding. Pops hadn't left the house in four months before his death, so unless he'd had help, he had planned this little adventure many months in advance.

The thought only added to my excitement and curiosity.

I started digging, stopping after just a few minutes to remove my shirt. A fish jumped in the pond. A fat squirrel showed up to watch my progress. A crow cursed at me from the treetops.

I was just about convinced that I was in the wrong spot after all when the shovel hit something that wasn't dirt.

I dropped to my knees and used my hands to uncover what I had found. Once again, feeling time slip away, my dirt-crusted fingers racing faster and faster…

…until they pulled an old cigar box out of the deep hole.

The box was secured with a twist of rotting, black string. I scrambled to untie the knot, my fingers muddy now with perspiration. I could hear a strengthening breeze stirring the trees, and I realized I was holding my breath.

I tossed the string aside and opened the box.

Inside, I found a tangled mound of gold and silver jewelry. Bracelets. Earrings. Necklaces.

And a small stack of driver's licenses rubber-banded together.

I undid the rubber band and flipped through the licenses.

And then I counted them.

There were nine.

IT TOOK A lot longer to make it back to Pops' house. Almost three hours. Nothing looked familiar anymore. I made a lot of wrong turns.

My head hurt.

My heart hurt.

I couldn't stop thinking about the nine women.

I couldn't stop seeing their faces on those driver's licenses.

And I couldn't stop thinking about the second map I had found tucked inside that rubberband with their licenses.

NIGHT
CALL

December 31
6:03 pm

THE FIRST THING I noticed when I pulled over to the curb was Frank Logan's bald head shining in the outdoor Christmas lights. Even with all the commotion and camera flashes and all the people moving around, his head stuck out like the beacon from a lighthouse. He spotted me right away and made a big show of looking at his wristwatch. I grinned and showed him both my middle fingers.

Frank Logan was my partner. Had been for the past eight years; ever since I made detective. He was a good man. A first-rate cop.

He stood there in the doorway and watched me get out of my car and walk up the front sidewalk. I got close enough and he said, "Nice of you to show up."

I shrugged my shoulders. "Traffic was bad."

"Yeah, I know. Only been here a couple minutes myself."

"So what's with the suit?" I asked. He was all decked out—a black, three-piece. It wasn't very wrinkled, and he actually looked pretty good. His tie was bright red and covered with tiny white reindeer, and it wasn't stained. Even his shoes looked shined. All this was new territory for Frank.

"Tonight was Susan's dinner party. Over at the Hilton."

"Oh, shit. She pissed you had to leave?"

"You know it."

Right then I glanced over his shoulder at the front door. "Hey, is that what I think it is?"

"Uh-huh."

"Jesus."

"This guy's one sick son-of-a-bitch."

"You're not kidding."

"Sliced her goddamn ears off—"

"And pinned 'em to the front door," I said, shaking my head.

"Wait 'til you see the upstairs bedroom."

"How come?"

"Because that's where her hands are."

"Her hands?"

"That's right," he said, nodding. "Rest of her's in the kitchen."

"Jesus."

"Third one in three weeks, Ben...I think we might have some real trouble here."

"You're not kidding."

"You eat dinner yet?"

"What?"

"I didn't have time to eat at the party. You hungry?"

"A little," I lied.

"How 'bout we finish up here and go grab a pizza?"

"Sounds good to me."

"Pepperoni and mushroom?"

"Sounds good to me."

We went inside.

9:47 pm

THE RAIN HAD changed over to snow about an hour ago. Almost an inch on the ground already. The guy on the radio was promising six-to-eight by morning with plenty of ice on the roadways. The morgue would be a popular place tomorrow.

The Christmas lights had been turned off. Yellow police tape lined the front yard and driveway, fluttered in the night breeze. It was a lonely sound, a lonely place now. The squad cars and news vans had left some time ago. Even the neighbors had disappeared—gone back inside to their parties, their television sets, their nice warm beds.

Inside the two-story brick colonial, every light in the house was burning bright. The cleanup crew was on the clock and earning overtime. Three single mothers from up north in the suburbs. Over the past year, I'd gotten to know them pretty well. Frieda, Sandra and Lorraine—all in their early forties. Hard-working and friendly women. I liked them very much. Friends since high school, they'd quit their jobs and formed their own company early last year after watching a television program about a similar business venture in Chicago. Ask any of the three and they'll tell you: it's ugly work, real ugly—some days nothing but blood, urine and human waste, and the smell's enough to kill you—but it sure beats making minimum wage and having your ass grabbed every day by a bunch of smug lawyers. Sure, the hours may stink, but the pay more than makes up for the inconvenience. And it's simple work, really. First thing: turn on all the lights. Especially at night. Then, if necessary, start upstairs and work your way down. Keep your mind focused on something else—*anything else*—and scrub everything as clean as possible. Spray it all down with disinfectant. And, last thing before you lock the front door, set up the air-fresheners. Typical job takes between two and six hours, depending on the mess and the number of victims. Longer if they have to call someone in to move furniture or pull up the carpet.

Tonight's victim—Mandy Frymann, a thirty-seven year old middle school teacher, 5'2", 125 pounds, brown hair, brown eyes—was already making her way downtown. Zippered tight inside a shiny black body bag. The thing was: this particular bag was designed for a male victim and it was too long to properly secure a 5'2" female, so the coroner's assistant was forced to improvise. He folded the bottom of the bag up over her feet until it practically reached above her knees and then he weighted the extra flap in place with both of her severed hands, both of her ears, and her right foot—each sealed tight inside heavy duty plastic evidence bags. This was not proper transfer procedure, but the assistant didn't much give a damn. He was supposed to be home by seven, and he was late for a party.

9:54 pm

"YOU GOT CHEESE in your mustache," I said.

"Huh?"

I pointed to my own mouth. "In your mustache. Cheese."

"Oh, thanks."

He located the string of mozzarella and popped it into his mouth. Raised his eyebrows at me. I pretended to be disgusted.

We were sitting across from each other in a booth near the front window of Bountempo Brothers, Frank's favorite pizzeria. He loved this place—with its clean red tablecloths and authentic Italian music on the sound system—always talked about buying a joint just like it when he retired. He wanted me to invest when the time came; that way we could stay partners, he said. Frank was full of crazy ideas.

"Something wrong with you tonight?" I asked, after a few minutes of silence. "You been kinda quiet."

He shook his head. "Just tired I guess."

"You know we'll find this guy, Frank. You know how it is with the violent ones. He'll get messy, make a mistake and we'll—"

"I'm fine, I tell you."

We stared at each other for a moment, both of us trying to look convincing.

I looked away first, watched a young couple cross the snow-covered street, holding hands. They turned the corner, and I looked back at Frank; he'd been watching them, too. There was something in his eyes I didn't recognize.

"Come on, Frank. You don't think I'd know if something was bothering you."

"Jesus Christ, you're a pest. You know that. A goddamn pest."

"That's right," I said, reaching across the table and poking him in the forearm. "I'm a pest and sometimes you're worse than a goddamn woman. Now tell me the truth."

He took a sip of his soda and shrugged. "There's nothing to tell."

I pointed at him. "You…are…a…liar."

He pointed back. "And…you…are…a…asshole."

I shoved the tip of a slice of pizza in my mouth and flicked him the bird.

We sat there in silence, watching the rest of the pizza get cold.

About a minute later, he spilled it, just like I knew he would.

He said it very quietly. "Susan wants a divorce. She told me tonight."

"Jesus, Frank."

"She's serious, too. You shoulda heard her. She swears she's not seeing anyone else. She's not even thinking of anyone else. She just doesn't love me anymore. Said she doesn't even know me anymore."

"Ah, hell, I'm sorry."

He nodded his head sadly. "Me too."

"Maybe she'll change her mind. Maybe she's just pissed off, because of you missing the party and all."

"I don't think so, Ben. I really don't think so."

He locked his hands together, rested his chin on them, and stared out the window. He looked like he was praying, and maybe he was.

"So what'd you say to her?" I asked.

He kept looking out the window at the falling snow. "What could I say? I told her we would have to talk about it in the morning. That there was a lot we needed to talk about."

"And?"

"She said the time for talking had come and gone. That it was time to move on. She said her mind was made up."

"Jesus, Frank. She really said that?"

He looked at me and nodded. He was close to tears. "She really said that."

"Damn, I'm sorry, Frank."

"You already said that."

I opened my mouth to say something else, and that's when our pagers went off.

10:19 pm

"YOU BELIEVE IN any of this millennium bullshit?"

"You obviously don't," I said.

We were heading north on 95 but moving slow because of the storm. The snow was coming down thicker now. Bigger flakes and wet. It was sticking to everything.

"How do you know I don't believe?"

"You said millennium *bullshit*. If you think it's bullshit, then you obviously don't believe in it."

"I didn't mean it that way. Jesus, Ben, sometimes you're a pain in the ass."

"What did you mean then?"

"Okay, we're about to hit a new century. Not a new decade, a *century*. I realize that's pretty damn significant. A big deal even. But now we've got nutcases running loose all over the damn place. Even more so than usual. And why? Just because of the damn calendar. Turn on the television and what do you see? Stories about psycho cult members offing themselves so that they can be transported to another planet. Little kids walking into schools with machine guns in their book bags and blowing their friends away. Murderers and rapists all over the fucking place. Serial killings on the rise. And why? Because a voice told them to do it, because the end of the world is coming, because Judgment Day is upon us all. Jesus Christ, what a bunch of shit."

Frank got like this once in awhile—all red-faced and stuttering and pissed off at the world. A heart attack just waiting to happen. And when he did, it was best to just sit there and listen and not open your mouth. Maybe nod your head once every couple minutes to show that you understood.

"And then when the news is over, you get the goddamn commercials. Fortune tellers, mind readers, psychic healers, mystic forgivers. You tell me, Ben, what the fuck's a mystic forgiver?"

I shook my head and tried not to laugh.

"And people trying to sell you goddamn everything. What does some crystal you wear around your neck have to do with the year 2000? What the hell can you do with 60 different types of organic herbs? I'd like to shove those herbs up their asses is what I'd like to do…"

I steered onto Exit 23, our tires cutting fresh tracks in the deep snow, and turned right at the first stoplight. A bunch of kids were having a snow-ball fight on the front lawn of an old elementary school. There had to be at least twenty of them out there.

About a mile up the road, I turned left and we were there. Squad cars and flashing red lights everywhere. Couple of ambulances. One drove right past us when we pulled to the curb.

"Looks like a goddamn traffic accident," Frank said. "What'd they call us out here for?"

"Let's check it out." I turned off the car and got out. Took a half-dozen steps and wished for a warmer jacket. Maybe a scarf. In the police lights, the falling snow was the color of blood.

It was a working class neighborhood. Small houses built forty, fifty years ago, narrow front yards—run down and neglected now, peeling paint and cracked driveways. Even the snow couldn't make it look pretty.

There were two cars sitting in the middle of the street. Connected nose to nose by twisted metal. The smaller car was missing a windshield. Frank was right; it looked like a head-on collision.

I looked around. None of the folks involved in the accident appeared to still be at the scene.

I spotted Harvey Weidemann standing next to the ambulance and walked over. Frank stayed behind, talking to one of the uniforms.

Harvey used to work city five, six years ago, but then he got married and moved out to the county. Wife's orders. They were going to have kids and she didn't want to raise a family on her own. Smart lady. Harvey's a big man. Real big—six-six and more than two-fifty. These days, most of it's fat, but not all of it. He's still pretty impressive to look at.

"Hey, Harv. What's going on?"

He looked up from his notebook and smiled warmly.

"Christ, look what the cat dragged in."

We shook hands. The bastard was wearing leather gloves. And a scarf.

He glanced over my shoulder, squinted in the falling snow and flashing lights. "And, hey, there's your better half. And wearing a goddamn suit.

Never thought I'd see the day." He shook his head, pointed at the cars in the middle of the street. They were quickly disappearing beneath the snow. "You believe this shit?"

"What's the story?" I asked.

He smiled again. A big fat grinning pumpkin. "You're not gonna believe it."

"Try me."

"Red Cavalier is Marcus and Joanna Firestone. Husband and wife. Live up the street on Hanson. According to their statement they been drinking all day, since before noon."

He walked over and patted the hood of the other automobile—the one missing a windshield—a dark-colored Toyota. "This one is Freddie Jenkins. Next door neighbor to Marcus and Joanna Firestone. The three of them started partying together before lunch. Nothing too serious—beers and a couple of joints. Then a few friends come over and things really start cooking. New Year's Eve comes a little early, if you know what I mean. Seems that sometime around three or four, Marcus catches Freddie making time with his old lady in the upstairs bathroom. Right on the fucking sink. Only he doesn't say anything at the time. Doesn't let on that he knows.

"Around seven, the party gets even bigger and moves across the street to another neighbor's house. But before heading over, Marcus and Joanna drive over to Luskin's Liquor Mart for a beer run. They get their beer and on the way home, they start arguing. Marcus comes clean with her about what he'd seen, even starts crying while he's driving. Now get this: the old lady gets pissed off. You believe that shit? She gets royally pissed off. Starts screaming at him about not trusting her and spying on her and bullshit like that. Starts beating on him while he's driving.

"Anyway, while they're weaving up the street, already drunk and stoned off their minds, here comes their neighbor Freddie Jenkins cruising in the opposite direction."

I rolled my eyes and whispered, "Oh, shit."

Harvey's smile got wider and he held up a finger and said. "It gets better. So Marcus sees Freddie coming his way and with his wife's fingernails digging into his neck and her screaming in his ear *YOU DON'T TRUST ME!*, the poor guy does what comes natural. He fucking loses it.

He backhands his wife until she shuts up, crashes head-first into Freddie's Toyota, grabs a gun from under his front seat, jumps out of the car and onto the hood of Freddie's car, kicks in the windshield, pulls Freddie out and gut-shots him right then and there. Then he does the wife."

I shook my head. "Jesus."

"When the first car got to the scene, the officers found Marcus sitting on the trunk of his car, drinking a Budweiser. They said he was just sitting there, waiting, and he wasn't wearing a shirt; they found it in the front seat of his car, draped over the steering wheel, soaked in blood. Freddie Jenkins was laying on the road, already dead, and Joanna was still in the front seat. She got it in the head…twice. She was a mess. Paramedics said she's eighty-twenty."

Harvey wasn't smiling anymore.

"Marcus wanted to give a statement right then and there, so they let him do it. He was crying the whole damn time. They finally took him downtown 'bout a half-hour ago. The poor son-of-a-bitch. I felt sorry for him. I really did."

"You're not kidding."

I thanked Harvey and told him it was good to see him. I took a few steps and turned and asked about his wife.

"We're divorced," he said. "Two years ago. She got the kids."

I told him I was sorry and found Frank waiting by the car.

We got out of there.

11:57 pm

"WEIRD COUPLE OF calls, huh?"

Frank looked at me and raised his eyebrows "Hey, it's the millennium, remember?"

I couldn't help but smile.

"Not really so weird anyway," he said. "Not so much out of the ordinary."

I nodded. "You're right. Just kinda felt that way tonight is all."

We were sitting at the end of the bar in the Brass Horse Saloon. Best cream of crab soup in the city. And the prettiest waitresses too. None of that mattered tonight, though. It was a mad house—New Year's Eve and all.

Frank had wanted to go someplace quieter. But I thought it might do us some good to be around people for awhile. Normal, everyday, regular-joe, happy, non-homicidal people.

Of course, when we pulled up, there was a fistfight out in the parking lot. Two big guys fighting over a woman.

I finished my drink and looked over at my partner. "You gonna be alright?"

"Susan, you mean?"

I nodded my head.

"I don't know." He shrugged his shoulders. "I really don't know."

People around us starting counting.

"You know, you need a place to stay for awhile, you always got me."

He looked up from his drink, and I saw the fear in his eyes. It was the wrong thing for me to say and the look on his face made my fucking heart ache. I turned away and ordered another round, but the waitress didn't hear me.

"Frank, I didn't mean—"

The place erupted then. Streamers and confetti and annoying little party horns. Hugging and kissing and yelling.

A man I had never seen before in my life slapped me on the shoulder and gave me a thumbs-up. A very fat redhead kissed Frank on the cheek, then moved over and did the same to the man sitting behind him. A couple of college kids jumped up on the bar and started dancing.

Frank and I just sat there and looked at each other, both of us thinking the same thing.

After a few minutes of this, Frank leaned over and raised his voice above the crowd. "Hey, great idea, coming here. Thanks for cheering me up, partner."

I showed him my middle finger and said, "Happy New Year, Frank. Happy fucking New Year."

He smiled and raised his glass.

My glass was empty but I raised it anyway.

THE LAKE IS LIFE

POLICE OFFICER: WHEN DID you realize something was wrong?

Witness: When I saw the blood.

Police officer: Where was the blood?

Witness: Everywhere.

MY PARENTS DECIDED to separate the summer I turned fourteen.

It was a bad time. Not a lot of screaming or yelling or fighting. Just long, awkward silences and the occasional sniffle or dirty look exchanged between Mom and Dad.

June passed in a blur of family counseling sessions and solo shopping dates with Mom and dinner dates with Dad. When I wasn't being dragged to one place or the other, I was hidden away in my old treehouse. Rereading Harry Potter or listening to my iPod.

By the time July rolled around, Dad was drinking again and I was living with Mom in a second floor condo near my school and going alone to counseling twice a week. I had finished all the Harry Potters and had moved on to my mom's old Sidney Sheldon paperbacks. A little racy, but I was growing up fast by then.

On the fourth of July, Mom and I went to dinner at Harrisons and watched the fireworks from the pier with about a billion other people. On the way home, she broke the news to me:

In a week, I was heading to Grandma's house at the lake. I was going to spend the rest of my summer there, while she "sorted out some things."

I COULD TELL Mom thought I might be disappointed with the news. Maybe even angry. But I wasn't.

I loved the lake with its quiet coves and peaceful woods. And I adored my grandma. She was the one who had taught me how to fish and pick berries and mark a trail. She was the one who had taught me my love of books and astrology.

I felt bad thinking it, but when Mom told me, I was actually relieved.

I was tired of my counselor's voice and the way my friends all looked at me. I hated the condo, it smelled funny, and I was starting to be scared of my dad.

The lake sounded wonderful.

It felt a little like running away from home.

"MY GOSH, BECCA, look at you! So tall!"

I rolled my eyes, but I was smiling as I lifted my suitcase out of the trunk of Mom's car. "Grandma Maggie, you just saw me a month ago."

"I know I did, and if you haven't grown another inch, I'm Raquel Welch."

I hugged her in the driveway, and she hugged me back twice as hard. It felt good. It felt like what I remembered happy to feel like.

"Don't break her, Ma."

Grandma laughed at that and hugged my mom next. "Don't break me either!"

Then we were all laughing and staring out at the lake. A boat buzzed by and we could hear muffled laughter on the evening breeze.

"It's so beautiful," I said, mostly to myself.

In my peripheral, I saw the two of them exchange a look that said: *we did good bringing her here.*

"You know what your grandfather always said…"

Grandpa had died of a heart attack when I was seven, but I remembered him well. I smiled. "The lake is life."

"Yes, indeed." She laid a wrinkled hand on my shoulder, and I touched it with my own. "The lake is life. So let's get on living it."

We walked inside the house together.

I SAW THE boat again three days later.

I was sitting on the pier with my toes in the water, writing in my journal and soaking up the sun, when I heard the whir of a small outboard. I looked up just in time to see a dingy round the point and come into view. There was only one person in the boat and as they drew closer, I could see that it was a boy. Probably not much older than I was.

I felt exposed sitting there, so I pulled my feet up out of the water and propped my legs up under my chin.

The boy was shirtless and wearing a red baseball hat. Even from fifty yards away I could see that he was tan from the sun and had muscles. I guessed then that he was older. Maybe even old enough to drive.

He waved as he passed me, and after a moment's hesitation—born of equal parts sheer panic and excitement—I casually waved back, and then looked down at my journal again.

I counted to ten. Slowly. And then I looked up again.

The boat and the boy were gone.

WITH ONE EXCEPTION, my first week at the lake passed in a kind of drowsy haze, as time there usually does, and I was happy to settle into a daily routine.

Each morning I would wake early and eat breakfast with Grandma Maggie out on the deck overlooking the lake. After we did the dishes together, we would walk the winding dirt path to the point and back. Grandma was in pretty good shape for a woman her age, but she was finally slowing down, so I never pushed to go further. I saved those longer hikes for the afternoon and did them solo.

In the evenings, we cooked dinner together and often left our dirty dishes on the table to sneak away and fish for crappie or sunnies or bass before the sun went down. Other times, we cleaned up our mess and sat in rockers on the porch and read or talked. She had a television in the den, but we rarely watched it until bedtime.

We barely talked about Mom and Dad and what was going on at home. Sometimes, she would tell me stories about Mom when she was my age or when she was in high school. I had mostly heard them all before, but I still liked listening to them. And I know it made Grandma happy to tell them.

Grandma never mentioned it, but I'm sure Mom had told her all about my mini-breakdown and the resulting appointments with my counselor. I was pretty certain it would come up in time, but for now I was grateful it hadn't.

Mom called to say goodnight every evening around nine, but I didn't ask many questions and she didn't offer much in the way of news. It was still good to hear her voice. My dad hadn't called yet. I had tried to call him a couple times, but it always went straight to voice mail. I didn't mention this to Mom, and she didn't ask.

It was a good first week.

THE EXCEPTION HAPPENED as I was getting ready for bed one night.

Grandma was already asleep in her room, and I had just come upstairs after watching a late movie by myself. I was certain that my bedroom window was closed because I remembered pausing to close the curtains right before I took my shower.

But when I came out of the bathroom fifteen minutes later, freshly clean and wrapped in a towel, I saw the thin curtains fluttering in the night breeze.

I stood there in the bathroom doorway, staring at the window. Momentarily frozen with fear. Holding my breath.

Then, as if waking from a dream, I quickly glanced around the room, searching for an intruder. I found nothing out of place and realized there were only two places someone could hide: under the bed and inside the closet.

I considered yelling for Grandma Maggie or making a mad dash for her room, but the longer I stood there, the more foolish I felt. I had just watched a stupid horror film. My imagination was probably running wild. *What did I expect?*

I took a deep breath and, before I could change my mind, dropped to a knee on the floor and checked under the bed. Nothing but dust bunnies.

Emboldened, I walked over to the closet and flung open the door. Nothing inside except my summer clothes.

I walked over to the window and pushed it closed.

Just as I was turning around, I saw a flash of movement in the yard. A shadow shifting within a larger, darker shadow.

I stared outside for a long time, and then I locked the window and went to bed.

POLICE OFFICER: WHAT were you doing in the woods again?

Witness: I told you, we were playing a stupid game.

Police officer: (checks notebook) Hide and seek?

Witness: (nods) Yes.

Police officer: Aren't you all a little old to be playing a kid's game?

Witness: I said the same thing to Benjamin.

Police officer: And what did Benjamin say?

Witness: He said they played it all the time. They liked to scare each other.

TWO THINGS HAPPENED on the Monday of my second week at the lake:

Grandma Maggie brought up the "D" word for the first time and I met the boy from the boat.

We were on the way home from our morning walk and Grandma had been extra quiet, so I wasn't at all surprised when she finally asked, "What would you think, Becca, if your parents got a divorce?"

I think she expected me to stop walking or start crying or something equally dramatic, but I didn't have it in me. "Why? Did Mom say something to you?"

Her eyes widened and she shook her head. "No, no. Nothing like that. I was just wondering if now that you're feeling better...if you had thought about the future."

I shrugged my shoulders. "I don't think it really matters what I think, do you?"

"Of course, it matters, honey."

"Not really." I helped her over a fallen log. "I'll be okay with whatever happens. I have to be."

She took my hand in hers, and that's how we walked the rest of the way home.

"HEY, YOU'RE REBECCA, right?"

Startled, I looked up from the shallow stream bed, and there he was: the boy from the boat.

And standing next to him, a very tall and very pretty blonde girl. Wearing very short cut-off jeans.

"Sorry, didn't mean to scare you."

He was shirtless again, and barefoot, and wearing the same red base-ball hat.

"I'm Benjamin."

I stood up. "You didn't scare me. I was...I was just looking for crayfish."

He stepped forward and smiled, and it lit up the entire forest. "Not many crayfish round here, but if you follow it back a ways, you'll find a deep pool crawling with 'em. Just watch out for snakes."

And then that smile again.

"How did you know my name?"

"My Ma knows your grandmother. Told me you were staying the summer here."

I waited for the inevitable "sorry about your folks," but it didn't come.

The blonde girl shuffled her feet and made a noise in her throat.

"Oh, yeah, this is Kelsey."

I started to step forward to shake her hand, but stopped. *Don't be stupid,* I thought. "Hi. I'm Becca."

The girl looked away, disinterested. "I know."

I looked down at my feet, embarrassed.

Benjamin flashed the girl a dirty look I wasn't supposed to see and said, "We're running over to the north side to see some friends. You wanna come?"

I hoped my face didn't show how surprised I was by the invitation. "Thanks, but I can't. I have to help my grandma with dinner."

Kelsey grabbed his arm, held it possessively in both of her hands. "Can we *please* go now?"

I started walking away. "I have to get back anyway."

"Hey, we're thinking about having a bonfire tomorrow night," Benjamin said from behind me. "You should come."

I stopped walking. I could feel my face flush. "Maybe."

"I'll clear it with your grandma and pick you up."

I heard Kelsey hiss something under her breath.

And then they were gone.

BY THE TIME I got back to Grandma Maggie's house, it was dusk and a light rain was falling. I was twenty minutes late for dinner and in a daze, wondering if I had imagined the whole thing.

POLICE OFFICER: HOW long were you up in the tree?

Witness: A long time. My legs started to hurt.

Police officer: Give me an estimate…ten minutes?

Witness: Longer. Maybe a half-hour.

Police officer: You say you didn't see anyone?

Witness: (shakes head) No.

Police officer: Did you hear anything?

Witness: Just what I told you before. Footsteps in the leaves. Some branches breaking. And then a scream.

BUT I HADN'T imagined it.

At breakfast the next morning, I told Grandma about meeting Benjamin and the girl in the woods, and she told me all about Benny—she had known him since he was a baby and that's what she had always called him—and his mother, too. Benjamin's father had died in a logging accident when Benjamin was only five, and Grandma and his mom had grown close over the years. Just a couple of lonely widows, she joked, without a smile.

"I'm glad you ran into Benny," she told me, munching on a piece of dry toast. "They're good people."

"So, it would be okay…if I went with him to the bonfire?"

"Do you want to go?"

I tried to play it cool. "I'm thinking about it."

Grandma saw right through me, as she often did. "Uh, huh, I can see that," she smirked. "You just keep on thinking about it and let me know when you come to a decision, okay?"

I flipped a hand at her and didn't even try to hide my smile. "You hush, Grandma."

"YOUR CHARIOT AWAITS," he said with a dramatic bow, as the boat settled alongside the pier.

He was wearing a t-shirt this time. Faded jeans and tennis shoes. And no hat. He looked beautiful.

He reached out a hand and helped me onto the boat.

I was wearing a sleeveless sundress, the only one I had brought with me, and although I felt overdressed, I didn't care. I never wanted to let go of his hand.

I sat down at the front of the boat, facing him.

He pushed off from the pier and cranked the throttle on the outboard and we were off, Grandma's house growing smaller and smaller behind us.

I waved goodbye because I knew she was watching from somewhere inside the house, and then my eyes went right back to Benjamin.

His curly brown hair danced in the breeze and the muscles of his arm flexed as he maneuvered the outboard. He smiled at me and raised his voice above the motor. "You look nice."

I felt my face get hot. "Thank you."

"You ever been out to Soloman's Island?"

I shook my head. "The old prison?"

He put a hand up next to his ear: *can't hear you.*

Louder this time: "Is that where the old prison was?"

"Yeah," he nodded. "From the Civil War. Nothing left of it now except some crumbling sections of wall and part of the old watchtower."

"That's where you have your bonfires?"

"Usually, yeah. Sometimes, we even camp overnight."

"My grandma said I had to be back by ten o'clock."

He laughed. "I'll have you back in time."

I silently scolded myself for sounding like a dumb kid.

"So, do you have a boyfriend back home?"

I shook my head and wanted to ask if Kelsey was his girlfriend, but I didn't dare.

"Why the heck not? You're gorgeous."

I blushed again and then I was smiling, and I didn't remember a single thing either of us said after that until we reached the island.

THE ISLAND WAS gross.

That was my first and lasting impression. I think I expected a secluded and tranquil paradise, and instead what I found was a rock strewn chunk of land littered with beer cans and cigarette butts and used condoms. There weren't even that many trees.

It was an ugly place, but I understood why they all liked it there. The island belonged to them.

When we beached the dingy and jumped ashore, the bonfire was already raging, and I could see maybe a dozen or so kids clustered around it. Drinking and smoking and dancing to a boom box.

I recognized one of the dancing girls as Kelsey, and when she saw us, she made a beeline to a couple of other girls, and then they had their heads together, whispering and scowling.

I started to think I should've stayed home, and it was as if Benjamin read my mind.

"C'mon, it'll be okay," he said. "You'll have fun."

I looked at him doubtfully and he just had time to take one more step before he was tackled off his feet by one of the largest kids I've ever seen.

"Benny boyyy!"

Benjamin and the human boulder crashed to the ground and rolled to a stop a full five yards away from where they had started. Somehow, Benjamin ended up on top and was holding the much larger boy down by the arms.

"Jesus, Mark. You *gotta* stop doing that."

Benjamin released his grip and got to his feet, brushing dirt from his jeans and t-shirt. He reached down and helped Mark to his feet. I stood there staring at them both, unsure of what I had just seen.

"Mark, this is Rebecca. Rebecca, Mark Andrews. All-Conference linebacker on the football team. All-Conference *retard* everywhere else."

I couldn't help it. I started to laugh.

"Rebecca, my dear, I am charmed." Then he actually took my hand and leaned down and kissed it.

I looked at Benjamin, speechless, and then we all cracked up laughing, and I thought: *maybe he's right; maybe this will be fun.*

IT WAS LIKE a scene from one of my books.

A bunch of teenagers huddled together in the dark around a campfire. Telling scary stories. Except it was real, and I was actually living it.

I sat on a blanket on the ground between Benjamin and Mark. Kelsey was with her friends right next to us, and every once in awhile, I caught her whispering about me or staring at me. I always looked away first.

When it was Benjamin's turn, he surprised me by telling the story of the Soloman's Island slasher. According to legend, there was once a drifter who had gone crazy and started kidnapping local girls and bringing them here to the island. Once he had them trapped here, he would let them go and then hunt them down in a sadistic game of cat and mouse, ultimately capturing them and slicing them to pieces with a hunting knife. Eventually, the townspeople discovered what was happening and they tracked the drifter to the island, where they caught and executed him with the same hunting knife he used to kill his victims.

But the story didn't end there.

For the grand finale, Benjamin got to his feet and walked closer to the bonfire. Turned around and faced us. "According to the legend, the drifter's evil spirit still inhabits this island. And on very special nights, when the wind and moon are just right, you can actually still hear him taunting his victims, calling out to them as they cower in terror."

He lowered his voice for this last part: "But, most frightening of all… it is also said that the drifter's *spirit* remains here…waiting…waiting for someone else to come to this island so he can possess them. Someone with dark thoughts and even darker potential. Someone to carry on his evil legacy and—"

"DIEEEE!!!"

The bushes suddenly exploded and there was the flash of a knife blade in the firelight, followed by a fleeting dark shadow—and I screamed and scuttled backward on my feet and elbows like a sand crab.

I screamed until my throat was sore, and I realized everyone else was rolling on the ground—laughing.

I looked up at the shadow standing above me and watched as Kelsey pulled the hood of her black sweatshirt down and dropped the knife to the ground.

Benjamin brushed past her and snatched up the knife. "That was a shitty thing to do and you know it."

"God, I was only joking," she said with a victorious smile.

And then Benjamin was helping me to my feet. "Are you okay, Rebecca?"

"I...I just want to go home. Now."

He took my arm and guided me away from Kelsey and the others. "She didn't hurt you, did she?"

But I couldn't answer. Tears were spilling down my cheeks and it was all I could do not to burst out in sobs.

"Hey, it's okay," he said, wiping my cheek with his hand. "It was just a stupid prank. I never would have let her do it if I had known."

He helped me into the boat and dropped the knife at his feet before cranking the motor. He held my hand the entire way back to Grandma Maggie's, and by the time he walked me to the front door and said good-night, I had almost forgotten about Kelsey and her dirty trick.

Almost.

I WAS EATING cereal on the deck the next morning when I heard the sound of tires on gravel in the driveway. I looked up and saw Mom parking next to Grandma's truck.

"Mom?" I left my bowl on the table and jogged down to the driveway.

She got out of the car and smiled at me, looking better than she had in months. She pulled me into a long, tight hug. "God, I missed you, baby."

"What are you doing here? Why didn't you tell me you were coming?"

She laughed. "Whatever happened to 'I missed you, too, Mom?!'"

"I did miss you! I *do* miss you! So much. I'm just surprised."

From behind me: "That was the point, kiddo."

I turned around to find a beaming Grandma Maggie standing there with her hands on her hips. "We wanted to surprise you."

"Well, it worked." I hugged my mom again. "I'm so happy you're here."

"I have a present for you, too." She walked back to the car and pulled a plastic bag from the back seat. Handed it to me.

I opened the bag and pulled out a stack of brand new Stephen King paperbacks. I squealed with delight. "Thank you! Thank you! Thank you!"

"There's also a new journal in there, so you can write if you feel like it."

I gave her a look. "Is that my counselor talking? Or you?"

"It's from *me*, you little smart aleck." She looked at Grandma. "Now am I too late for breakfast? I've been driving all morning and I'm starving."

"Let's see what I can whip up," Grandma said, and I watched them walk into the house arm in arm like schoolgirls.

It was the happiest I had felt in weeks.

AFTER BREAKFAST, MOM and I went for a long walk in the woods. Just the two of us.

We hiked past the point and into the valley beyond where the lake had long ago eaten into the land forming what Grandma always called Tranquility Cove. It was my favorite part of the shoreline and we spent a lazy hour there, skipping stones on the glassy surface of the lake and looking for driftwood.

And Mom talked a lot. Of course. I could tell she was worried about me.

"I'm fine, Mom, I promise."

"And you've been taking your pills?"

"Like clockwork."

"No more episodes?"

"I told you, I'm fine."

She sighed. "You always say that."

I tossed another stone and counted. Four skips. Not bad.

"I heard you met a boy."

I nodded. "He's just a friend."

Another stretch of silence, then:

"You know what the counselor said. You can't keep it all inside you. You'll explode again. It has to have a release."

I looked up at her. "*This* is my release," I said, gesturing to the lake and the trees and the sky around us. "This is where I come to feel better."

She looked around, *really* looked, and I could tell I had said the right thing.

"You promise you're still taking your meds?"

I crossed my toes inside my right boot.

"I promise."

POLICE OFFICER: DID you recognize the voice of the person screaming?

Witness: (shakes head) No. Just that it was a girl.

Police officer: Then what happened?

Witness: The screaming stopped.

Police officer: And then?

Witness: I heard more footsteps. Running away.

Police officer: What did you do next?

Witness: I waited. For what felt like a long time. Then I climbed down out of my hiding place.

I SAID GOODBYE to Mom the next morning after breakfast. She had to work that evening and wanted to get back in time to shower and change clothes. I thanked her again for coming and for the books and watched her drive away until her car disappeared around the bend.

Grandma was feeling tired—probably because her and Mom had stayed up late talking in the den—so we skipped our morning hike, and instead I walked down to the pier to read.

The sun was already hot, so I rolled up the sleeves of my t-shirt and dropped my feet into the water. I turned the page and for the next couple hours, I found myself lost in a small Maine town infested with vampires.

I was just getting ready to take a break and check on Grandma Maggie when I heard the buzz of Benjamin's outboard. I looked up and there he was: typical Benjamin. No shirt. No shoes. Dirty red hat. Big beautiful smile.

He cut the motor, drifted the final twenty feet to the pier, tied off the bowline, and plopped down right next to me. I could smell his sweat.

"What ya readin?"

I showed him the cover.

"'Salem's Lot. Any good?"

"Better than good. It's amazing."

Neither of us said anything for a time. Both of us just staring out at the lake. Then, he moved a little closer, and I could feel the warmth of his leg against mine.

"Sorry again about Kelsey. She can be a bitch sometimes."

"I won't argue with that."

He laughed. "She's not always like that. She can be sweet, too. I guess she's just jealous."

"Jealous? Of what?"

He leaned forward so he could get a better look at me. "Of *you*, silly."

"Well, she obviously has nothing to be jealous about. I'm…me. And she's…*Kelsey*. All legs and boobs and blondeness."

He laughed again. "She *is* a big deal around here. But you're…*different*. And she knows it."

"Different," I repeated.

He splashed the water with his foot. "And she knows I like you."

I didn't say anything. I couldn't.

I felt the pressure on my leg increase, and before I realized what was happening, he was leaning in again, this time so close I could feel his breath on my cheek and then *oh, my God*, we were about to kiss…

"Howdy, kids." Right behind us. "Beautiful morning, isn't it?"

I jumped and he pulled back, and it was over. Just like that.

Benjamin stood up first. "Morning, Mrs. Maggie. How are you?"

"I'm right as rain. And you?"

"I'm good. Was heading home and saw Rebecca on the pier. Thought I'd say hello." He glanced at his boat. "I should probably be going now."

"No need to rush off on my account."

"Thanks, but I'm already late and you know how my ma gets."

Grandma Maggie smiled, and I saw the beautiful young woman she once was. "Your ma is a saint, boy, and don't you forget it. You say hi to her for me."

"Yes, ma'am. I sure will."

He hopped down into the boat with practiced ease. "I'll see you later, Rebecca. Thanks for telling me about your book."

"Bye, Benjamin."

He cranked the engine and pushed off.

Grandma Maggie walked up next to me, watching him motor across the lake.

"Thanks for telling me about your book? Uh huh."

"Hush, Grandma."

She giggled like a little girl and headed back to the house.

I turned to follow her and my good mood vanished when I saw a flicker of color in the woods along the far shoreline.

I stopped and stared and saw it again, just a flash of yellow shirt, and then it was gone.

Someone had been watching us.

I WAS WATCHING a *Big Bang Theory* rerun in the den when the phone starting ringing.

"Got it," Grandma called from the kitchen.

I glanced at the clock: *early for Mom.*

Grandma Maggie came in holding the phone against her chest, a strange look on her face. "It's your father," she whispered.

I took the phone and stared at it for a moment before lifting it to my ear. "Hello."

"Hi, baby, it's Dad."

I didn't say anything.

"I'm so sorry, Becca. Let me explain."

"Let you explain why you haven't called me or returned my calls for three weeks?"

"I understand you're angry. I really do. But if you hear me out, you'll—"

"I'm not angry, Dad. I'm confused. I was worried."

"I'm at a place getting help, Becca."

"What kind of place?"

"A *good* place. The kind that helps people with their addictions."

"You're in rehab?"

He laughed. "Well, yes, honey, I'm in rehab."

"How is it?"

"It's going really, really well, baby. I wish I had done this sooner."

"How come you didn't tell me?"

"Today's the first day I was allowed to call anyone. I only have another minute and then I get to call your mother."

"You're gonna call Mom?"

"I am. Hopefully, she'll listen and maybe even come to visit me."

A flood of emotions washed over me. I didn't know what to think or say.

"Honey, I have to go now, but I'll call again next week. I promise."

"Okay."

"I love you, Becca. It's gonna be okay."

"I love you, too, Dad."

We said goodbye and hung up.

And then I started crying.

POLICE OFFICER: WHEN did you realize something was wrong?

    Witness: When I saw the blood.

    Police officer: Where was the blood?

    Witness: Everywhere.

I SAT ON the sofa and rested my head on Grandma Maggie's shoulder until the tears stopped coming. She stroked my hair with her fingers, comforting me like a little girl.

"Just when I had convinced myself everything would be okay one way, it changes and now the other way is a possibility again."

She nodded. "I understand how confusing it all must feel."

"Confusing and scary and—"

Before I could finish, the doorbell rang.

"Now who could that be," Grandma said, getting up to answer it.

I heard voices in the foyer, and then she walked back in the den with Benjamin trailing behind her.

"You have company, Becca."

I sat up straight. "Hey, what are you—"

"You ever play flashlight tag before?"

"What in the world are you talking about?"

He smiled and came closer. "Flashlight tag? Hide and seek?"

"Umm, yeah, when I was like ten."

He pretended to be insulted. "Well, unlike you fancy city folks, us dumb country bumpkins have to make our own fun around here." He reached out a hand. "C'mon, let's go."

I took his hand and let him help me up. "Go where?"

"I told you. To go play games in the dark. Your grandma said it's okay."

I looked at Grandma Maggie. "You sure?"

She smiled and nodded. "Might be good for you, honey."

TWENTY MINUTES LATER, I was standing in the dark woods just past the point with Benjamin and Mark and Kelsey and a half dozen other kids I had met earlier on the island. Several of them were passing around a bottle of wine and a joint. I turned both down when they were offered and did my best to stay clear of the smoke.

"Jimmy, you're it first," Benjamin said, gesturing to a tall kid dressed all in black.

Then he looked at me. "We get to the count of a hundred to hide and then he comes looking for us. He can use the flashlight to find us, but he has to tag us with his hand to win."

He pointed at a cluster of large rocks. "Get back to base without him touching you, and you're safe."

"We don't get flashlights?" I asked, feeling a little foolish.

"Only the hunter gets the flashlight."

"Why? You scared of the dark?" Kelsey asked, smirking.

"Just making sure I know the rules," I snapped. I was actually proud of myself for standing up to her.

Jimmy turned on the flashlight and shined it on his face. "I'm coming to get youuu, Barbaraaa!"

Everyone laughed and starting spreading out in anticipation of the game starting.

Benjamin came up close to me, lowered his voice. "You gonna be okay?"

"I'll be fine. It's just a game."

"If you need me, call out and I'll come find you."

Jimmy started counting in a booming voice. "One, two, three..."

"Thanks, I'll be fine."

He looked at me, making sure.

"Go!" I said and pushed him playfully away. He flashed me a grin and took off into the woods.

"...nine, ten, eleven..."

I looked around. Only Kelsey and I remained in the clearing. She had been watching us the whole time. She glared at me, and then without a word, spun on her heels and disappeared into the shadows.

"...fifteen, sixteen, seventeen..."

I took off running.

THE TRUTH WAS I *was* scared.

I had been hiking in these woods dozens of times but never at night. Never alone in the dark.

There was a sliver of moon high in the August sky but not enough to do anything except cast more shadows. I felt like I was lost in a haunted house.

I stopped running after a few minutes and caught my breath. I looked around for a place to hide, deciding it would probably be better if I stayed close to base.

I worked my way toward the shoreline, looking for a stand of thick enough bushes to hide under. The night was sticky and hot and I could feel mosquitos buzzing my arms and neck. Suddenly, the idea of crawling under a bush or a fallen log didn't seem so appealing.

Instead, I looked for a tree to climb and found the perfect specimen only a few yards away from the lake. It was an ancient weeping willow, gnarled and bent over, like a tired old man waiting at a bus stop.

I scuttled up a thick branch and found a natural nesting ledge where two other limbs branched off. It was perfect.

I sat there in silence and waited for something to happen.

I didn't have to wait long.

Maybe five minutes passed before I heard the crash of heavy footsteps in the woods below. Leaves crunching. Branches breaking. Whoever it was wasn't being very cautious or quiet.

And then I saw the stab of a flashlight beam on the ground below and understood why. It was Jimmy. No need for him to be as stealth as the rest of us.

I held my breath, a chill of nervous delight spreading through me, and remained perfectly still.

He paused for a second, fanned the light out over the water, and then continued on his way.

I let out my breath and relaxed.

If Jimmy was heading down the shoreline, away from base, shouldn't I make a break for it? Or was it a trick and he was down there hiding? Waiting for someone to make a move?

I thought about it some more and had just made up my mind to climb down and sprint for base…

…when I heard more footsteps, and then whispering:

"You're being silly, babe."

"Don't you dare tell me that. I heard what you said to her."

I chanced a peek—it was Benjamin and Kelsey.

"*If you neeeddd me, call out and I'll come find youuuu,*" she mocked.

"I was just being nice, babe."

"You were flirting."

"She's a kid, Kels. I told you what my ma said about her folks, and her having a nervous breakdown."

"I don't care if she's some kind of mental case."

"She's not a mental case. She's just a dumb kid. My ma's making me be nice to her."

"I don't care what your mom says. I don't like it."

"Babe—"

"Let someone else be nice to her. You've done your charity work for the summer."

I didn't remember anything else after that.

Like before, my brain shut off then…and everything went black. And then it went red.

POLICE OFFICER: IT'S okay to tell the truth now, Rebecca. We found the knife.

Witness: (starting to cry) I *am* telling the truth.

Police officer: We found Benjamin, too.

Witness: Benjamin?

Police officer: His body. Floating in the lake, Rebecca. Covered with the same knife wounds we found all over Kelsey.

Witness: (crying; unintelligible)

Police officer: We know, Rebecca. We know what you did.

Witness: (crying) No. I was hiding in my treehouse.

Police officer: We know you killed Benjamin and put him in the lake, and then you ambushed Kelsey in the woods.

Witness: (crying) No. The lake…is life.

Police officer: Just help us understand why.

Witness: I was in my treehouse.

Police officer: Your grandmother is downstairs and your mother is on the way.

Witness: The lake is life. The lake is life. The lake is…

Police officer: (to Officer 2) I think we're done for now. She's already been photographed, but we need to get her clothes logged in evidence.

Police officer 2: Yes, sir.

Police officer: Be careful. She's covered in their blood.

Witness: The lake is life…

THE GOOD OLD DAYS

THE LETTER ARRIVED EARLY this morning.

A plain white envelope.

No return address.

I found it mixed in with a holiday catalog from Sears, a couple of sale flyers from the local shopping mall, and a bill from the telephone company.

I am nothing if not an old fool; each month I send off my twenty-three dollars and fifty cents for my telephone service, yet there is no one for me to call. And certainly no one to call me. I have an unlisted number, so I don't even hear from complete strangers trying to sell me something.

I am alone, and that is how it should be.

Still, sometimes I can't help myself; I find myself dialing one of the department stores and inquiring as to whether or not certain merchandise is in stock—even though I have no interest whatsoever in the product. Or I find myself calling and ordering a pizza pie from the corner shop, even though I am not the least bit hungry. Hell, I don't even like American pizza. And still other times, I call long-distance to the airport to request specific flight information—checking on arrival times for out-of-town guests who exist only in my mind.

All this—all this foolishness—just to have some measure of human contact in my life.

I know how awful this all sounds, how pathetic…but some days I just can't stop myself. And when the night comes and I'm lying there in bed with nothing else to think about, I feel so ashamed and embarrassed and so very, very old. It's a horrible, lonely feeling, and on nights like this, I rarely fall asleep before dawn.

One of these days, I'll have to get rid of the damn telephone. Throw it out by the curb with the weekend trash. Rid myself of all temptation.

The little boy across the street saw me standing there by the mailbox, and he smiled and waved at me. His name is Brian. He is six years old and seems a happy child.

I returned the wave—but not the smile—and carried my mail inside the house. I flavored my morning coffee with a shot of brandy and sipped it while standing at the kitchen counter, staring out the window. When the cup was empty and my courage was there, I sat down at the table and opened the letter…

THERE ARE MANY ways to kill a man.

We were trained in dozens of methods.

Some quick and clean.

Some not so quick.

And some not so clean.

I've used them all…

My first kill: a young man, barely out of his teens. A scientist. A *genius*, I was told. He was German and very ugly. A pale, pasty face covered with pimples and ratty little sprouts of black hair. Ugliest man I've ever seen. He was on a train traveling west across the heartland of Europe. A stoop-shouldered troll in a too-tight dark suit and a sweat-stained hat. Guarded by three men so alike they could have been brothers. Three very stupid men. But this was before the war, and people were not as careful then.

Sitting across the aisle, I watched him eat his dinner—roast beef with gravy, mashed potatoes and steaming sweet carrots—then I followed him inside the lavatory and choked him to death while he was washing his hands. He was weak and soft and went very easily.

As planned, I slipped off at the next stop and found a car waiting for me two blocks north of the station, parked in a narrow alleyway behind a noisy tavern. The trunk was unlocked. I found keys and instructions beneath the spare tire, and two days later, I was drinking tea and window-shopping in New York City. I never read about his death in any newspaper.

Several months later, I was just beginning a new assignment in London when Pearl Harbor was attacked. Suddenly, I was a very busy man. A very *important* man. By the end of the war, I had killed nearly a dozen men on each continent. Some of these men were great warriors, and not all gave their lives as easily as my ugly, young scientist friend. Those four years marched hard across my back. Still harder inside my heart.

Twenty-three kills. Twenty-three lives taken by my own hands. Many times I remember staring at those hands in the darkness and thinking: *Twenty-three is not so many. There were thousands of lives lost. No, twenty-three is not so many...*

At the time, I had thought that with the war winding down and the world undergoing such dramatic change, my life would soon be different. That the killing would eventually stop, and they would find other—more significant—tasks for me to consider.

I was wrong.

IT WASN'T MUCH of a letter.

Four words—that's all there was to it.

Four simple words.

Red ink on a folded sheet of white tablet paper.

I recognized the handwriting immediately.

THE LAST LETTER had arrived eight months ago. Back in springtime, when I was busy planting my vegetable garden in the side yard and my arthritis was doing so much better.

He'd been living in south Florida then. Somewhere on the Gulf Coast with a lovely gray-haired lady by the name of Eve. There'd been a color photograph of the two of them enclosed—tanned and smiling and holding hands—and the P.S. joked that he was thinking of changing his name to Adam after the wedding service.

Jesus, I did some belly-laughing *that* afternoon. It was just like Peter— eighty-three years old and getting married again (What was it? His fourth, fifth time?). He was still a pistol, that's for sure: having his picture taken with senior citizen beauties, casting a line out into the clear blue surf every damn morning, and probably taking side bets at the shuffleboard court. And still smiling…God bless him, always smiling.

I didn't see how he could do it—even after all these years—but that was just me being me.

At least that's what Peter would have said. I could just see him now: he'd flash me one of his thousand-watt grins and rabbit punch me in the shoulder a couple times and say: "Ya gotta stop carryin' the world on your shoulders, Frankie-boy. Ain't enough room up there for the whole damn world. Start enjoyin' life a little more. C'mon, now, lad, live a little." And then he'd wink at me. Some nights, I can still hear his voice in my dreams…

We had *always* been like that, though—like night and day. He was so loud and boisterous. God, you couldn't shut him up once he got going. And, Christ Almighty, he was a handsome bastard. A real charmer with the ladies. We used to call him "Movie Star," and the name fit him like a glove.

And then there was me: the quiet one, the careful one. Like a machine, he always used to tease me. "That's why you're so damn good at your job," he would say. "Like a goddamn machine…"

But as Joseph often used to point out: we were *all* different but the same. Different on the outside, but the same on the inside…and that's where it counted.

That's right—there were three of us back then.

Me and Peter, and that crazy son-of-a-bitch Joseph…God, I still missed him something awful.

Joseph passed away a while back. At the time, he was living in a townhouse in downtown Baltimore, with his eldest son, an unemployed computer salesman. After we'd "disappeared," he'd changed his name to Thomas Holt and married some Mexican woman he'd met in a west Texas Bingo hall. I never saw her picture, but he wrote about her in a couple of letters. Supposed to be a real looker and a helluva cook. Several divorces and almost thirty years later, Joseph went out and caught himself a killer case of pneumonia while shoveling snow off his front porch dressed only in a bathrobe.

That was Joseph, all right—always the reckless one. Always taking unnecessary risks. Even in his old age. Trust me, back in the good old days, Peter and I covered his skinny ass on more than one occasion. And, of course, he covered ours, too.

The same day that the letter arrived—bringing news of Joseph's illness—Peter flew up to the hospital where our friend was being treated.

Of course, Joseph had written to both of us.

Peter arrived late that night and found him in a private room on the third floor. They sat together on the bed and talked for more than an hour—mostly about the good old days. About the three of us—the places we'd gone, the things we'd seen, all the good times and the not-so-good times. Peter said they laughed so loud a fat, old nurse had to poke her head inside the room and warn them: *This is a hospital, gentlemen, and there are sick people to consider. Please turn down the volume.* Unfortunately, this scolding only made Joseph laugh that much harder, and as a result, he accidentally popped his IV tube out of his arm. Needless to say, the nurse was not amused.

But Joseph eventually grew weak and tired, so Peter hugged him good-bye, kissed him on the forehead, and called himself a cab from the phone outside in the hallway—

—and then he snuck back inside the room and smothered Joseph with his pillow.

Peter told me all of this in a two-page letter. He wrote it during the flight home and dropped it in a mailbox outside the airport.

That was three years ago.

THERE WERE THREE of us back then.

The three horsemen. That was our code name, and maybe a dozen people in the entire world knew this information. Half that number knew our true identities.

Let me tell you, back in those days, there was no one better. No one even close.

We did the impossible. And we did it time and time again. Like goddamn phantoms in the night.

Even some of our own people were scared of us. And we liked it that way. It made things easier for a while.

But then things changed.

And we got older...

WE DISAPPEARED IN 1968.

After twenty-nine years of loyal service.

The world was changing...and not for the better.

I guess you could say that we saw the handwriting on the wall.

So, we formulated a plan.

You have to remember now, men in our profession did not exactly retire with a gold wristwatch, a handshake, and a big fat pension. It was an unspoken truth, but it existed nonetheless.

In theory, our plan was simple: stage an accident and provide a trio of burned and disfigured bodies as proof of our demise. Then split up and go our separate ways, alter our appearances, change our names, and start new lives. And no matter what—never, ever directly contact each other. Not by telephone and certainly not in person.

Only unsigned letters and only occasionally—once or twice a year.

Keep the trail to a minimum.

And when the time came, we would be there for each other. In the end, we would be there...

That was the promise we made to each other so many years ago.

That was part of it anyway.

IN THEORY, THE plan sounded so simple.

In reality, it was something else entirely. Even if they believed our little "accident," they would be sure to take the necessary precautions. They had no choice in the matter. The simple truth was: we would always be three of the most hunted men on the planet. No matter what, we knew they would never stop searching for us. They couldn't afford to—we knew too much. We'd seen things no one ever dreamed of. *Done* things no one could even imagine. And this knowledge was very, very dangerous. With this information, we could change the course of world history at any moment in time...

During the war, it had all been relatively clear: scientists, soldiers, spies, a couple of politicians. There was blood everywhere in those days. No one was clean; everyone had it on their hands. We were simply a working cog in a much larger war-machine. An honorable and noble machine—we truly believed that.

It was years later that it all became so *strange*. That's the only way I can describe it for you. It just got so damn *strange*. Hell, for a time there, it was hard to figure out who was our enemy and who was our ally. It all got so mixed up and messed up, and we didn't know who we could turn to, who we could trust.

Only that we had each other—we *always* had each other.

And some of the assignments...Jesus. Mostly they broke down into two categories: those who *knew* the wrong things. Politicians and military folks mostly—all over the world. And plenty here in the States. Generals, congressmen, even a President. But there were others, too. And *they* were the tough ones. People in the wrong place at the wrong time. Folks who had snooped a little too deep under the covers. Journalists and reporters. Doctors and professors. Businessmen, big and small. Even a few housewives who happened to be victims of bad timing and even worse luck...and there were children, too.

It all got so confusing. For a while there, it seemed like we were being ordered to terminate just about everyone.

During the war and the years that followed, we looked at the assignments as our job—as our duty to our country—but then it all got to be such madness. Such goddamn madness.

And still we did the job we were trained to do.

And we did it well.

IT'S TIME. HOSPITAL. Come.

I sat there at the kitchen table, my hands trembling, and read the letter a dozen times.

The words didn't change.

It's time. Hospital. Come.

I always knew this day would arrive.

I crumpled the letter into a ball and took it out to the garage. Placed it in an ashtray on my workbench and burned it. Scattered the ashes in the back yard.

I went inside and took a shower.

Then I packed a suitcase and called the airport.

I knew the phone number by heart.

IT'S A SHORT flight to Wichita. A little under four hours, with a thirty-minute layover. If there are no delays, I should be there in time for dinner.

Plenty of time to think about things...

My name is Aaron Thomas Schumacher. Aaron is my birth name, the name given to me by my father and mother eighty-four years ago.

But if you know me today, you know me as John Cremins. Retired postal worker from Arizona. Relocated to North Carolina a decade ago, just after the death of my wife, Anne. We were high school sweethearts, married fifty years, until she died of bone cancer. Yes, sir, John Cremins has himself quite an interesting history. He was even a combat veteran.

Over the past thirty years, I've lived under four other aliases. Made my home on three different continents—been a citizen of several foreign countries and a resident of a half-dozen states here on America soil.

I've altered my appearance five times. Nothing permanent—other than a nose job—and nothing too drastic; just enough to get the job done.

The only thing that has remained constant over these many years is the company I have chosen to keep: I have *always* lived alone.

And that is the way it should be—at least for me.

I am an old man now. Horrible arthritis. Deaf in one ear. I walk with a limp even when it's warm outside, and some days I have trouble going to the bathroom. I also do not sleep well.

I am an old man—and often afraid.

Perhaps this is my penance, although I do not believe so.

Look at Peter. Eight months ago, he was still smiling. Still living the good life in the warm sunshine of Florida. How he got to a Kansas hospital? How he is dying? Where his golden-haired bride by the name of Eve is? These are all questions I cannot answer.

But I *can* tell you this:

In a little more than five or six hours, I will take my best friend's life. I will study his face as his eyes close for the final time and watch as his spirit leaves his body. I will hold his hand in mine, and when I am finished, I will wait and make sure he is truly gone.

Then I will ride back to the airport and board my flight. If there are no delays, I will arrive home sometime after midnight.

And my final assignment will be completed.

I ALWAYS KNEW this day would come.

We all did.

Maybe this is all just foolishness; an exercise in madness. Maybe enough years have finally passed, and it is no longer necessary. But a promise is a promise. Especially one made to a friend such as Peter.

I have to admit, though—it makes me wonder about my own death and that frightens me.

When the time comes, who will be there to take care of me? To send me on my way? Who will be there to make sure that I do not panic in my moment of truth and release my treasure chest of secrets? Who will be there to stop pen from touching paper…?

First Joseph, and now Peter.

Soon, it will be all three of us...

My God, we were something back in the old days—three young men, different but the same, the best of friends, trained in the fine art of killing.

Like phantoms in the night.

Death could not take us, then.

And we would not allow it to take us now.

Only *we* would take each other.

And the last one standing...

Well, he would have to find his own way.

That was the promise we'd made to each other.

All those years ago.

Me and Peter and Joseph—the three horsemen.

My name is Aaron Thomas Schumacher.

I am an old man.

And I am afraid of the dark.

GRAND FINALE

1

"**D**OES THAT FEEL GOOD, baby?"

A twitch of candy red lips. A crooked smile. "Ummm, incredible."

He flicked his tongue across the silky smooth skin of her thigh, snaked it closer to the center of her body. She moaned with pleasure and squirmed on the tangle of white sheets, then reached down and forced his face between her legs. This time, he stayed there. She was past the point of no return now; completely his for the taking. As if to confirm his thoughts, she leaned back and gripped the bed's brass headrest with both hands and closed her eyes.

Her name was Jill; he didn't know the last name, and didn't plan to ask. It wasn't important. She was the front-row beauty from his Senior Finance class. Tall. Golden tan. Brunette. A real knockout; and that's what *was* important. Earlier, he'd taken her to a new dinner club downtown, but they'd quickly grown bored with the older crowd and returned to his place.

"His place" was actually a luxury condominium suite. Two levels, complete with spacious dining and living rooms, sunken den, two bathrooms, and a bedroom loft, which was now occupied by the sweat-slicked couple.

Top to bottom, the place reeked of wealth. The floor covers and furniture were imported, the art on the walls, originals. The downstairs bar and wine rack were always overstocked. The sound system—also located downstairs, along the far wall of the den—cost more than a full year's tuition at the university. The second-floor balcony overlooked the bay out back, and on clear nights like tonight, one could see the resort lights aglow on the far shore.

It was extravagant by any means, but especially so for a 22-year-old college senior.

But then again Brian Lewis was anything *but* a typical college student. The only son of Manhattan publishing tycoon, Bernard Lewis, Brian lived a privileged life. He enjoyed an unlimited expense account and the freedom to do as he pleased, with only one strict requirement: that he continue to receive his "B" average at the university and graduate along with his class. After completing that task—his "growth and responsibility period," his father called it—the rest of his life was his to do with as he pleased.

Upstairs in the loft, Brian slid on top and inside of his date, his shoulder-length brown hair tickling his back. The Justin Timberlake disc he'd put on earlier was between songs, the couple's hungry breathing momentarily the only sound in the condo. He shifted, tried to catch his breath, but she wrapped her legs around his back and pulled him inside further, tightening and loosening her grip until she found a satisfying rhythm. *Christ*, he decided, *she's even better than I thought.*

He kicked away the blanket, braced his feet on the bed's footrest and pushed hard, gaining strength with each thrust. Two songs later, after her second orgasm, they switched positions, fumbling over each other in the dark. She immediately responded, rotating her hips in a lazy but forceful circular motion. This time, it was Brian who reached back for the bed rails, enjoying the ride and the *view.*

When she finally came, only moments later, she collapsed atop Brian's chest, allowing him to glance over her right shoulder, up at the thick wooden rafters above the loft. And to smile at the hidden video camera, which had recorded the entire night's action.

<u>2</u>

THE NEXT EVENING...

Brian Lewis was thinking three things as he slid the key into his front door at twenty minutes past midnight: Chet Avery's party had been a real bomb; so much so, in fact, that he hadn't even gotten laid; and, foremost on his mind, he was hungry as hell.

He stepped into the den, flipped on the television—a 52-inch Sony—and sat back on the sofa, a grease-stained pizza box resting in his lap. With one hand, he stuffed the tip of a pepperoni and sausage slice into his mouth, and, with the other, he lifted a heavy leather case from atop the end table and rested it beside him. He popped the clasp and opened the lid. Inside were several dozen videocassette tapes, protected in clear plastic cases. Each tape was labeled on the spine in neat blue magic-marker print. A few of them read: BARBARA, Sept. 12. JANICE, Dec. 24. TERESA, Feb. 13.

Brian selected a tape from the top row, one marked "JILL, July 23." He struggled up from the sofa and popped it into the cassette recorder. He sat back and pointed a palm-sized remote control at the television. The VCR whirred quietly and the screen immediately filled with a blurry, shadow-scarred image. After a few seconds, the shadows lifted, the picture sharpened, and Brian recognized the loft, his bed, last night's date, and his own naked white ass. Grinning at the picture, he traded the remote for a tightly-rolled joint from his shirt pocket and another slice of pizza.

He'd started videotaping his dates several years ago, while only a freshman. He had always been a whiz with various types of mechanical devices, and cameras were his specialty. Shortly after coming to the university, it occurred to him that it was only natural that he combine his technical talents with his other favorite pastime: women. And with his casual good looks and well-publicized bank account, the women were his for the picking. He even had two female instructors from the university—a 32-year-old, married English professor included—among his tape collection. Over the years, he'd perfected his spy system to the point where he could now activate the camera with a special vocal command, and even control the zoom lens with a hidden switch located in the upstairs bathroom.

Only one time had he almost been caught. During the spring semester of his freshman year, the first camera he'd used—a store-bought model—had malfunctioned and a warning alarm had sounded from the camera, scaring his date half to death. He'd simply claimed it was the smoke alarm and scooted the girl downstairs to wait while he "fixed" it. He'd learned a valuable lesson that night, and as a result, he now used only the most expensive surveillance equipment available.

Six slices of pizza and two joints later, Brian stretched out on the sofa and reached for the remote, ready to turn the tape off for the night. About to hit STOP, he realized from the position he and Jill were in that the tape was almost finished, so he let it run. He'd been especially strong last night. And, as he always said, there was nothing quite like the grand finale.

A close-up view. High and tight. Her on top, riding him hard, muscles flexing, hair flying everywhere like she's on the dance floor: she was dancing all right. Mouth open, tongue darting in and out, not seductively; animal-like, gasping for air. Camera angle pulls back, swings a degree left, and you see Brian on his back, you see his face, his sweating, smiling face. And as Jill comes, she falls onto him, and he smiles a big grin for the camera and winks a secret salute of success. Then she plants a tender kiss on his lips and crawls out of the bed, heads for the shower.

That *was* exactly what had happened last night...

But that was *not* what was now playing on the videotape...

That was *not* what Brian was seeing...

The screen *did* show Jill pecking Brian softly on the lips, but instead of getting up to take a shower, as she most definitely had the night before, *she reaches behind her back and her right hand swims into the camera's view holding a gleaming butcher knife, and then the lens isn't fast enough to capture any more detail because then she's slashing at Brian's face and chest and all you can see is a bloody pulp...and the crooked smile on the brunette's blood-spattered face, as she stares directly into the camera.*

"Jesus," Brian whispered, shaking his head and pushing the pizza box to the floor. He looked at the residue of ash scattered on the sofa cushion, blinked at the marijuana smoke, which hung thick in the room. "Powerful shit," he mumbled, and leaned back on the sofa, instantly asleep.

3

MORNING GREETED BRIAN Lewis just before nine, and a killer headache came along for the ride. Within half an hour, he'd already swallowed a couple glasses of juice and a half-dozen Tylenols, but relief wasn't on the way yet. And so he suffered at its mercy, sitting perfectly still in the dark bedroom. Finally, when he could wait no longer, he pulled on a white polo, tucked it into his khakis, and went downstairs.

The den was a mess. Stale smoke hung heavy in the air like early-morning smog. Sofa cushions and pizza crusts were scattered across the carpet. All of the lights were still on. And the entire room smelled of pizza grease. He had slept soundly on the sofa until just before six, when he'd rolled off and almost lost some teeth on the corner of the coffee table. Only then had he retreated to the loft.

He poured himself yet another glass of orange juice and sat on the only remaining sofa cushion, flipping absently through his tattered notebook. The words were too blurry to read, so he merely glanced at the charts and diagrams. His head was feeling worse by the minute, but he had already missed two labs this summer semester and couldn't afford to skip another.

He was about to slam the notebook shut when he suddenly remembered the dream from the night before. White-hot flashes of a remarkably vivid dope dream. A horrifyingly real nightmare in which he'd watched himself being stabbed to death.

He dropped the notebook on the sofa. Flicked on the television and the VCR using the remote. *Just to make sure I'm not whacked*, he thought, shaking his head.

He pressed PLAY.

The screen flickered once, changed a darker shade, but remained blank. The dark gray picture and accompanying static hum of a blank videotape.

Wait a minute, this tape wasn't blank, Brian thought. He punched REWIND, waited a moment, and then hit PLAY again.

The same picture.

Puzzled, he stood up and ejected the tape manually. It *was* the right tape. The label on the tape's spine read "JILL, July 23."

Something's wrong here, he thought. He pushed the tape back in, tried it a third time. Nothing.

Jesus, could I have erased it last night?

Brian glanced at his Rolex—eight minutes to ten—and clicked the power off on both machines. He locked the door behind him, still shaking his head.

4

BRIAN PUSHED THE tape marked "PENNY, March 9" into the recorder and returned to the sofa. The tape's selection had been random, and he realized he couldn't even remember what Penny looked like, much less anything else about her. He thought she might be the cute little blonde he'd met at a football game sophomore year, but wasn't sure.

The mystery tape from this morning rested on the end table. He'd already played it a fourth and fifth time, checking it from start to finish. He'd even tested it on the upstairs camera for possible damage. The result: the tape itself was technically fine, but it was undeniably blank.

Earlier in the afternoon, after lab, he'd tried to work on a research paper in the campus library, but he'd found any form of concentration impossible. All he could think about was the disturbing dream from the previous night, and the blank tape from this morning.

He didn't know why he was so preoccupied with what was obviously just one of life's weird little coincidences. Okay, so what? First, he dreams—or Christ, maybe he'd hallucinated the whole thing—about watching himself getting sliced up by Jill. Everything perfectly filmed on video. And then the tape of his "real" date with Jill shows up blank the next morning.

Coincidence, right?

For whatever reasons, he didn't think so.

Despite the manner in which he lived his life. Brian Lewis was no dummy. He was at least bright enough to consider rational explanations. Maybe the whole thing was just some sort of warped revenge fantasy his mind was laying on him. Maybe it was a bad combination of drugs. Or the lack of sleep. Reasonable explanations, one and all.

But none of them explained the blank tape. And if there was one thing he *was* positive of, it was that he hadn't accidentally erased the tape. No, sir. Something weird was going on here, and he was going to get to the bottom of it.

Now, at forty-five minutes before midnight, he was prepared to sit through his entire collection of videos if he had to. He didn't know what to expect, or even what he was looking for. One voice inside his head kept telling him that all he was going to see were a bunch of old homemade porno flicks and that he'd feel stupid as hell by the end of the night. But the other voice...

Brian noticed the time on the VCR and stifled a yawn. He had wanted to start earlier, but had allowed himself to be talked into smoking a few hits of hash with some frat boys on campus. Their treat, of course. People were always eager to share a drink or a smoke with someone of Brian Lewis's stature, and he'd not yet learned to say "no."

He finally pressed PLAY, and the screen came to life. Same setting—upstairs in the loft. Different angle, though. Lower and a bit fuzzier. This was an older tape, an earlier conquest.

He was on top in the video, driving himself into his almost-hidden date. Long, shapely legs wrapped his back, taut arm muscles flexed as she clutched at him.

As Brian watched, memories of Penny and their "date" came back to him. Blonde. Tall, almost six feet. A freshman from somewhere out west; Oregon, maybe. An art major, head full of foolish dreams and ideals. Too much of a talker. But she'd been incredible in the sack. A genuine virgin when she first arrived here, now one of the easiest and best lays on campus. They'd gone to a lawn party that night. Left early.

The tape continued for twenty minutes, the two of them changing positions several times. Nothing out of the ordinary.

Then...it happened.

The tape quality seemed to improve, grow noticeably clearer, as Penny climaxed for the final time, crouched on her hands and knees, head and back arched. Brian was just slowing down behind her when she pulled her hand out from underneath a blanket and the camera closed in tight on a shiny black revolver.

Brian's mouth dropped open, eyes widening. He leaned forward on the sofa, feeling the skin on his hands grow slick and clammy. Then, as the blonde twisted around and pointed the pistol, his image on the tape mimicked his real-life facial expression. The younger version of Brian opened his mouth wide in surprise, just in time to catch the full force of the gunshot. His head exploded like a watermelon dropped from a speeding car. A red and black fountain.

Brian quickly punched STOP on the remote, hands shaking violently. Stood up. Began pacing the carpet. Despite the air conditioning, he was drenched. *It's the hash*, he thought. *It's bad. Probably laced with something nasty. Making me see things that aren't there. Same with the joints last night. Too many drugs, that's all. Been doing too much lately. Especially the hard stuff. You're letting this get to you, man. Means nothing.*

He walked across the den and took an unopened bottle of Scotch from the bar. *This'll help you relax*, he thought, returning to the sofa.

Two hours later, the bottle of scotch was empty.

As was the pill bottle sitting right next to it on the coffee table.

And Brian was bouncing off the walls. He had watched a dozen more tapes from start to finish, and in each instance, the story was the same. Each and every video showed Brian with a different date, and the action was always exactly as Brian recalled until the very end—until the grand finale.

Then everything changed. Then everything went absolutely bugshit crazy.

It was horrifying to watch. Murder. Mutilation. Torture. The end result was always the same, only the method differed each time. *Knives. Guns. Razors. A power drill. Strangulation with nylon pantyhose. Poison in his drink.* The last girl—one he'd truly thought he was falling in love with at the time—had actually bitten off his penis. He'd watched himself bleed to death, as the girl smiled and giggled for the camera, her pretty face dripping with gore.

Strangely enough, despite watching himself being brutally murdered over and over again, the girls' reactions were what bothered Brian the most. Somehow, they *knew* about the camera, were aware of its presence, and it was almost as if they were performing solely for the camera's benefit.

Smiling and waving and carrying on. Acting as if the whole thing was just a sick, sick joke.

Sometime later, dawn still several hours away, something inside Brian Lewis's mind snapped, and he fled into the dark embrace of night.

5

TWO WEEKS LATER...

Before Brian could close and lock the front door, his date ran into the den with a squeal and did a belly-flop onto the couch, her black mini-skirt bunched around her waist. He watched from the hallway and laughed.

Her name was Bette, like the fat, redheaded actress whose movies his father liked so much, and she'd had too much to drink at the restaurant. She'd been drinking vodka tonics with her salad and stuffed shells, and Brian had lost count after four glasses.

Unlike the famous actress, this Bette possessed wavy brown hair, a voluptuous, if not model-thin body, and the deepest, bluest eyes Brian had ever seen. He'd met her just yesterday at the Student Union Bookstore. She'd been in front of Brian in the cashier's line and when her credit card was refused at the counter, he'd valiantly stepped in and, despite her objections, added her charges to his Platinum Card.

An hour later, after sharing a shrimp salad sandwich and a paper plate of potato chips in the cafeteria, they had agreed on a date for tonight.

He'd picked her up at her apartment at exactly six o'clock. From there they'd gone to Giovanni's, one of Brian's favorite Italian restaurants, for dinner, and finished the night off with a moonlit stroll along the shore.

Now, they were both ready for the nightcap.

Brian tossed the keys on an end table and walked across the room and turned on the stereo. He felt good tonight...*damn good*. His head was clear, just a beer or two and a few lines of toot. He'd been strung out big-time for over a week following the video incident. A week of living hell, in which he'd missed classes, hadn't slept, barely eaten, and spent over five thousand dollars on assorted dope. Each night had been a drug-clouded series of horror movie screenings...

No matter how much he'd wanted to, he couldn't stop watching the videos.

Then, late Tuesday night, dangerously close to slipping over the edge forever, while waiting in a Burger King parking lot to meet his supplier, the solution to his problem wormed quietly into his fried brain like a heaven-sent prayer. And in a flash, he knew all the answers. Was no longer scared or confused. In fact, he'd thought at the time, *I'm a friggin' moron. I should have figured it out right away. It all made such perfect, logical sense.*

Yes, sirree, Brian thought, pulling a CD from its case, *feeling just fine and dandy tonight.* He slid it into the stereo and turned the volume up very loud.

Bette rolled gracefully to a sitting position on the sofa and motioned with a curl of a finger and a lick of the lips for Brian to join her. She smiled, then crossed her legs, and flipped off her pumps to add incentive.

Brian didn't need any.

He moved smoothly to the sofa, uncrossed her legs, and knelt down in front of her. Starting at her ankles, he nibbled and licked each of her legs, working slowly, methodically. When he finally reached the center of her trembling legs, he ran his tongue across the soft wet cotton of her black panties, and then stopped. She shuddered and groaned her disapproval, but before she could protest, he stood and lifted her from the couch. She melted into his arms, hands knifing through his hair, lips caressing his neck.

As they worked their way up the stairs, Brian suddenly thought of the camera—waiting silently in the dark—and the little voice inside his head betrayed him, screamed out in terror: *Don't go! Stay away from the camera! Whatever you do, stay away from the camera!*

But then the other voice spoke to him, and it was so much stronger, and it was this voice that he listened to.

6

DAGGERS OF BRIGHT sunlight slanted through the open windows. A strong breeze off the bay danced with the curtains, breathing clean, cool air into the condominium. The den vibrated with the frantic chatter of early morning cartoons from the television set.

Brian Lewis, dressed only in a pair of red silk boxers, walked into the room and sat down on the carpet in front of the television. In his right hand, he carried a steaming cup of coffee; in his left, he held the remote control. He crossed his legs Indian-style, placed the coffee down at his side, and punched PLAY on the remote.

Twenty seconds of blank screen. Then two figures clutching at each other in the shadows, pulling, ripping at each other's clothing. A gradual close-up... Brian already naked in the bed; Bette dancing seductively, swaying, giggling, stripping off her bra and panties, tossing them aside, touching herself before climbing in beside him. A furious meeting of flesh; legs and arms intertwining, uninhibited screams of pleasure...

His fingers itched to press FAST FORWARD, but he forced himself to be patient. Take it slow. Watch every second. Make sure there were no surprises.

They were laying on their sides now, Brian behind and inside her. She was grasping his ass with an open palm, guiding his thrusts. Her eyes were closed in ecstasy as he worked at her shoulder and neck with his tongue and teeth...

He watched silently, face expressionless. The mug of coffee sat untouched at his side, no longer steaming. The sunlight slowly crept to the far side of the den, leaving him in shadow, except for the soft, flickering light from the television. The digital clock on the VCR blinked the passing time in red neon. Brian noticed none of this.

Then, after a short time, he shifted ever so slightly. Stretched his right leg. Cleared his throat. His eyes widened just a hint.

The end was approaching.

He playfully slapped her on the ass, tight flesh barely moving. She rolled over and pulled him on top of her, legs spreading to accommodate him fully...

His hands came together, fingers interlocking. His heart raced. In several minutes, Brian knew, both would reach orgasm together, for the final time of the night. *So far, so good,* he thought. Every single movement, every word spoken—the same as the night before.

Only the grand finale awaited.

Brian was still on top. Backside glistening with sweat. Fingers gripping at the headrest behind her. Bette's breathy groans the only sound on the tape. The rhythm quickening. Her voice growing louder. A quick close-up of their faces. *Pressed together, pulled apart, pressed together, pulled apart...each time in rhythm with their movements. Tongues clashing together, then tasting only air. Suddenly, she convulses, her hands tearing at his slippery back. He releases the headrest and hugs her closer, tighter, climaxing in unison...*

This is it. Please God, let me be right, he prayed, his fingers squeezing still tighter.

He watched...

As the passion slowly subsided. As the movement finally ceased. As his hands moved slowly, tenderly, from her shoulders to the sides of her neck...and closed there. Cutting off the passage of air, the breath of life. Closing tighter. Crushing the windpipe. Still tighter. Until her arms fell limp to her sides, an expression of surprise and betrayal haunting her face.

And he watched:

As his video image looked up at the camera and smiled a tired but triumphant grin of relief.

And, this time, Brian Lewis returned the smile.

THE
ARTIST

THE ARTIST WAS DYING.

His cries had stopped almost an hour ago, and now the only sound we heard in the freezing darkness was the rhythmic pelting of falling sleet on our helmets.

Word had spread down the line that Doc had managed to slow the bleeding, but he was out of bandages, out of morphine, out of everything.

It was just a matter of time now—for the artist, and the rest of us, if help didn't arrive soon.

There were nineteen of us left. Scattered amongst a dozen foxholes. In the forest around us, a full company of Germans waited for daybreak to finish what they had started.

The artist's name was Henry Reed. He had red hair and wore wire glasses. He was from Boston. A thin, well-spoken boy of eighteen, he had three older sisters at home.

Most of us replacements were eighteen, much to the disgust of our Sergeant. It had gotten to the point where I had started telling the new guys to lie and say they were nineteen, if only to save us all from the inevitable lecture. The Sergeant was a hard man. He didn't speak so much as bark. And his eyes weren't right; like he had seen and done too many bad things to ever find his way back.

We called Henry the artist on account of the sketchbook he carried in his pack. Drawing was relaxing, he explained one day after Corporal Fleming questioned him about it. It calmed his soul and reminded him of home; it was a safe place to visit in a very unsafe world. Henry talked differently than the rest of us. He was educated, but it was more than that. He had a kind of peace inside of him the rest of us didn't. Even here in the frozen forests of Europe. I asked him about it once when we were alone on guard duty. He got quiet and stared off at the distant treeline and didn't answer me for such a long time that I started to think he'd forgotten what I'd asked him. But then he'd blinked his eyes a couple of times, like he was waking from a dream, and looked back at me and said, "From the time we were very young, my father taught us that inner peace comes from understanding. Understanding one's true self, and the world around us. I don't pretend to understand this war, I don't think any of us can, but I *do* accept my role in it. I have a duty to serve. A duty to my country, my family, myself, and to all you boys here with me. All I can control are my own thoughts and actions; the rest is up to something else entirely."

"You talking about God?" I asked, in awe of the words he had just spoken to me, with apparently no more effort than if he had just ordered lunch at a cafe.

"I am," he said and smiled. "Your God, my God, Bernstein's God… it doesn't really matter which. My path is set. All that remains now is to follow it."

I remember nodding my head, pretending to understand better than I actually did, and then we both went back to watching the distant treeline in silence.

PARKER LOOKED UP from cleaning his rifle and said without looking at me, "You think anyone will come?"

I placed my pencil atop the journal resting on my lap. Nodded and tried to sound reassuring. "They will if they can."

"But I mean…do you think they will come in time?" he said, and now I realized he was scared to look at me. Scared to see the truth in my eyes.

Parker was a good soldier, brave and decisive on the battlefield. We were all scared.

I thought of Henry's words before I answered. "They will either come or they won't. We can't control that, Parker. We can only control what we do in the meantime. But my money's on them showing up before the sun comes up."

It was what he wanted to hear. He risked a quick glance at me, nodded, and returned to cleaning his M1.

I picked up my pencil and started writing again.

IT WAS HENRY'S idea that I keep a journal.

I argued that I had nothing to write about, and he laughed at me.

I got angry, and he laughed harder.

He waved his arms. "Look around, Cavanaugh. We're in Belgium, for Godsake. Surrounded by bad guys and endless haunted forest. Last month we were in France, marching through bombed-out towns with names we couldn't even pronounce. Every day, side by side with men from cities and states we've never set foot in. Write a story about what you see, what you hear, what you *feel*. Write about the Sergeant. Or, hell, I don't know, write about home if you want."

"Home?"

"Sure, why not? All I know is that you're never happier than when you talk about those stories you used to write when you were a kid."

"Exactly. Kid stuff. Monsters and aliens from outer space. It was dumb."

"Not dumb, and if you think that, then write about something else. Keep a journal."

I thought about it for a quiet moment.

Henry pushed himself up from the tree he was sitting back on and thumped me on the shoulder. "Just make sure you write something good about me, Cavanaugh. C'mon, let's go grab some grub."

A QUICK THUD of footsteps sounded from behind us. Before I could even reach for my rifle, Sergeant Thompson was kneeling beside our fox-hole, reaching down to Parker with a box of ammunition.

"All you get until reinforcements show up."

Parker opened his mouth to say something, then decided against it. He took the box and found a dry spot for it inside our hole.

"Henry?" I asked, scared to hear the Sergeant's answer.

"Hanging on. Not hurting anymore."

I nodded and adjusted my helmet. When I looked up again, the Sergeant was gone.

MOSTLY, I WROTE about the guys or things I missed back home.

Fishing for perch in Hanson Creek with my little brother. Playing with the dogs. Catching fireflies and watching the girls in their Sunday dresses. Listening to my Mom and Pop teasing each other.

Henry was right; it came pretty easy to me. The feelings and the words. Words I never would have even dreamt of saying out loud flowed onto paper as quickly as I could scribble them.

Last week, I wrote about a skirmish we had gotten into with a handful of Germans holed up in a machine gun bunker. Everything I remembered seeing and feeling and hearing and smelling...I wrote it down. Henry asked if he could read it and liked it so much, he read it aloud to some of the other boys. It was embarrassing to listen to their compliments, but I also kind of liked it. Even the Sergeant said it read like something from a newspaper or *Life* magazine.

After that day, I thought about turning it all into a book if I ever got home again, but I didn't share that with anyone. Not even Henry.

At least once a week, he would remind me: "Don't forget to write something good about me."

I would smile and shake my head and joke back at him: "Do something good for a change, Henry, and maybe I will one day."

MY "JOURNAL" HAS now grown to fill most of three notebooks. The kind you see school kids tucking under their desks before the first bell rings every morning. I traded two bars of chocolate to a guy in supply for the first notebook. A German helmet for the last two and a new box of pencils. Each notebook contains about a hundred pages and every page is filled except for the last twenty or so of the last notebook.

I never would've dreamed I could write so much, but it just keeps coming out of me.

I miss my mother more than anyone else back home, but I think the best thing I've ever written is about my father. More words I could never say out loud—especially not to him. Henry said it almost reads like a poem, and I agree with that. After some thought, I even gave it a title. "Heroes":

I've always watched him. Secretly. From the time I was a child. Watched the way his eyebrows danced when he laughed. The way he lit his pipe or handled a tool, like a magician wielding a magic wand. The way he walked the family dog; bending to talk with it or ruffle its fur, but only when he was sure no one was watching. The way he read the newspaper or one of his tattered old pulps, peering over the worn pages every few minutes to keep me in check. The way his eyes twinkled when he called me "son." I've always watched him.

That's just the start of it, but for me, writing those words was like traveling back in a time machine. It was like…magic.

THE MORTARS STARTED again just minutes ago. Screaming overhead. Getting closer. Great chunks of shattered trees and frozen earth showering us in our holes. When the mortars go silent, they will come, with guns and bayonets. There are only eighteen of us left now. Word came an hour ago that the artist had died. No more fancy Yankee talk. No more drawings. No more goofy smiles.

He'd sketched most of the men at one time or another. I take out a folded piece of heavy paper from my journal and unfold it. It's my face, but older and thinner than I remember it. It's good. It's better than good; it's *magic.*

I fold it back up and tuck it in my journal.

Help isn't coming. At least not in time for us.

I know that now; maybe I always knew.

Parker is huddled at the bottom of our foxhole like a frightened rabbit. Eyes like quarters. Stuffing cotton in his ears.

I grab my rifle and secure my helmet and think one last time of Henry. Henry the artist. So much talent. So much joy. Gone.

If I make it home, I will visit his folks, his sisters. Sit with them and drink lemonade and tell them what a fine young man they had gifted to the world. If I don't make it, I hope what I have written is enough.

It will have to be.

(Item 174765C—Bound Notebook—Found in Ardennes, Belgium; property of Private James F. Cavanaugh; Worthington, South Carolina; 99th Infantry Division; killed in action January 14, 1945)

(for William V. Chizmar and Richard Matheson)

FAMILY TIES

1

A COUPLE YEARS AGO, MY momma told me about the one and only time she saw her daddy cry. It was a very long time ago at his youngest brother's funeral. Uncle Bobby was her favorite uncle in the whole world, Momma said, and he'd got himself killed at the factory. Momma told me it broke her heart to see her daddy that way. Felt like something inside of her was dying, like her heart was just ripping apart.

That's how I felt when they brought Jason into the courtroom.

Like something inside of me was dying.

He seemed so small. So scared. His arms looked so skinny in the handcuffs. And he wouldn't even look at me.

He hadn't been the same big brother for a long time now, that's for sure, but the old Jason still lived inside my head. The way he used to wink at me and laugh when he was up to no good or fooling around teasing Momma. The way he used to take charge of a bad situation out on the street and turn it around. Or the way he could look at you with those big brown eyes of his and make you believe you could do almost anything, even fly if you wanted to. I was his Little One, and he was my big brother. Always so strong and sure of himself.

Now, sitting up there on the witness stand, as the lawyers and the judge asked him questions, he mostly just stared at the floor in front of him. Nodded his head every now and then. And when he did look up, it was like staring at a stranger. Like someone you passed on the street corner and never thought twice about.

A tear rolled down my cheek, and before I could wipe it away with my shirt sleeve, Momma did it herself with a balled-up Kleenex. "You okay, honey?" she whispered.

I nodded and tried to smile.

Momma knew I wasn't okay. She'd been through this before a couple of times with one of her nephews, but this was my first time inside a courtroom. It sure looked different than on television. Everything was so big and the ceilings were so high and the furniture didn't look all shiny and pretty. And there weren't a lot of fancy-dressed people running around yelling and giving speeches like on television either. Just me and Momma and Jason, the judge, and a bunch of fat lawyers and policemen. And some lady with curly red hair who was typing everything that was being said.

It was cold, too. Real cold. Didn't they have heat in a place like this?

I hugged myself and shivered. It all made me feel so small. Like a little girl. Much younger than fourteen years old. It all made me want my big brother even more.

"I'll always be there to watch your back, Little One," he used to tell me. "Try not to worry so much. I'll take good care of you."

And he had. Up until six or seven months ago. Until everything changed...

2

JASON HAD BEEN more than just a big brother to me. He'd been my father, protector, teacher, playmate, my best friend in the whole world. He and Momma were everything to me. Our daddy had taken off soon after I was born. Left one morning for work and never came back, Momma told me. Rumor was he moved down to Baltimore with some other woman. Jason was three at the time. I saw a picture of my daddy once. It was old and wrinkled and faded, but he didn't look a thing like Jason or me. Just some stranger is all.

From the time he was old enough, Jason took care of me. Took good care of me, too. Making sure I was dressed for school on time and had some breakfast. Making sure I did my homework before watching television. Teaching me to read better than anyone in my class and how to write cursive. How to wash my clothes and help keep the apartment clean. Always checking on me after school and making sure I wasn't smoking cigarettes or hanging around with what he called "the bad kids."

Momma did the best she could with both us kids. And her best was pretty darn good. We started out in the projects. Rats, roaches, brown water, and a whole lot worse. But Momma worked two jobs all day long and took in some baby-sitting whenever she had a couple of free hours. When I was six, we moved three blocks north to a two-bedroom apartment. It was still pretty cold in the winter; heck, I've never lived anywhere where the heat works the way it's supposed to; but we had hot food on the table and store-bought clothes on our backs. No more food stamps or charity for us. Momma was a proud woman, and she taught us kids to be the same way. Most nights, she'd come home from her first job, shower, grab a bite to eat or squeeze in a nap, and then she was gone to the bus stop and her night job. Seven days a week it was like that. Sometimes we teased her and called her the Phantom.

"It won't always be like this, kids," she'd promise us. "It'll keep getting better and better. Just you wait and see."

And we believed her, too.

In the meantime, it was up to us to take care of ourselves. But it wasn't all work either. We had fun together. Lots of it. We'd play board games when it was raining outside and watch movies on television. Jason even pretended to like to watch cartoons with me. Sometimes we'd play Stratego or Monopoly or cards at the kitchen table and bake chocolate-chip cookies or cupcakes. I can still see Jason now, walking over to check on the cookies and me pretending to sneak a peek at one of his game pieces. He'd give me one of those I-know-exactly-what-you're-doing looks and wink at me. He never once yelled or got mad because he knew I wasn't really cheating; just teasing him and trying to get a rise outta him.

The summer I turned ten years old, Jason taught me how to play basketball. How to dribble and pass the ball. How to shoot and play good defense. He was a great teacher; he was real patient and hardly ever got mad or frustrated, even when I didn't listen to him. And he was tough with me, too. Didn't treat me like a sissy or anything. Later, when I started playing rec ball at the YMCA on Saturday mornings, he came to every game and sat in the stands with his friends from school. I could tell he was proud of me.

And, of course, it was Jason who brought Simon home three days before my twelfth birthday.

Simon was a skinny little runt of a gray kitten. The first time I laid eyes on him he looked more like a baby beaver than a cat. Jason had found him inside a Dumpster behind the Laundromat meowing away in a rainstorm. Said he was afraid the poor thing might've drowned if he hadn't come along. Figured the kitty could keep me company when he was at basketball practice after school or working down at the video store. That evening, we went down to Fisher's Pet Store, and he bought me a collar, a food and water dish, some cat food, and a place for Simon to use the bathroom. He gave me a big hug out on the sidewalk in front of Fisher's and wished me an early Happy Birthday. That's how I like to remember my big brother.

A few months later, when I started whining that Simon liked Jason more than me, he really surprised me and brought home another kitty. A girl kitty this time. He named her Samantha—after the mom on *Bewitched*—and we made a return trip to Fisher's Pet Store. Simon and Samantha took to each other like brother and sister, and Samantha grew to be as fond of me as Simon was of Jason. Some nights she would sit on my lap for hours and watch television, and she slept at the foot of my bed every night, curled inside the covers.

It was around that time that Momma got her promotion at the store, and she was finally able to quit her night job. Good thing, too, because before long she was busy at the store every night until eight or nine o'clock. She usually came home about an hour before my bedtime. *But just wait and see, kids,* she told us a few weeks into her new schedule. *It'll be worth it. It comes with a good pay increase and a lot of responsibility.* My gosh, we were so proud of her. I remember we celebrated with dinner at Pizza Hut and a movie afterward. Jason gave a toast at the restaurant, and Momma started crying and laughing at the same time, and then I did, too. Jason said we were both crazy ladies and acted all embarrassed and ran off to the restroom, shaking his head at us.

So, things were good for us then, and for about a year after that. We both kept on missing Momma, but Jason and I understood why she had to be gone so much. And we still had each other. It was probably the happiest time of my life.

Then, just like that, things started to change.

Jason started to change.

It was little things at first. I noticed he didn't smile as often as he used to. He wasn't as funny as he once was—not as many wisecracks or practical jokes or silly faces. And he didn't spend as much time hanging around with me either—watching television, playing games, or playing with Simon and Samantha. Some days after practice he went right to his bedroom and stayed there until dinnertime. Some mornings I had to wake him up for school, when it had usually been the other way around.

And then it got worse. He went from being a little moody to down-right grumpy. Some days he was mean to me; other days he just ignored me. I couldn't believe it. I hadn't done anything at all to make him act this way. Some nights we'd sit at the kitchen table eating dinner and not say a word to each other. It was like living with a different person.

I talked to Momma about it, and she told me it was probably just "girl trouble." That's exactly what she called it—*girl trouble*. Promised me that she would talk to him. Said all teenagers went through it, and you just watch and see, he'll be back to his old self before we know it.

But she was wrong. It just kept getting worse.

Soon, I started noticing other things. Jason didn't shower as often as before. Sometimes I could smell the sweat and the stink on him all the way across the room. And his clothes were always wrinkled and dirty. For someone like Jason, this was a big deal. In the old days, he used to be such a sharp dresser, so handsome and cool; all my girlfriends used to say so.

And then there was school. Once basketball season was over, he started missing classes. Some of my friends would tell me they saw him leaving school early, or once in a while, he would tell me he was sick and for me to leave without him in the morning. He would promise that he was coming in late, and then he'd never show up at all.

I tried to tell Momma what was going on, but she was real busy at work, and Jason always had an answer for her anyway. He was good like that; he always had it covered.

One of the worst things of all was how Jason started treating Simon and Samantha. First he just ignored them. He didn't feed them anymore or clean their litter boxes when it was his turn. He didn't play with them. He pretty much pretended they didn't exist. That was bad enough, but then he got mean. He started pushing them away when they slinked over to him for attention. He tried to kick them when they got in his way. That kind of thing. I couldn't understand how he could do those things, but soon he was like that pretty much every day.

Then, one day, I found out his secret. His dirty little secret.

I came home early from practice one Saturday afternoon and walked in on him in the bathroom by accident. The door wasn't locked, and I didn't even know anyone was home. Jason was bent over the sink, smoking a little glass pipe. His face was all red and sweaty and his eyes were wild and glassy. I knew what he was doing right away—smoking crack cocaine. I ran into the kitchen crying, and he followed me, the pipe still in his hand. I was hysterical, screaming and crying. Jason sat me down at the table and calmed me down, but first I made him put the pipe away; I couldn't even stand to look at it. We talked for almost two hours that night, and this is what he promised me:

He said it was only a phase he was going through. Kind of an experiment. Everyone was doing it at school, and he wanted to try it. But he knew it was stupid, and he'd already decided that it wasn't for him. Today was only the third or fourth time he'd tried it, he swore to me. So, no problem, he would stop. He didn't like the cocaine, and he certainly didn't need it. He would stop. It was as simple as that.

I wasn't sure if I should believe him or not, but he was so convincing. So much like the old Jason. God, it felt good to see and hear him like that and to be able to talk to him again. He wasn't at all like the stranger I'd grown to know.

So, by bedtime that night, Jason agreed to never take drugs ever again. And I agreed not to tell Momma anything and to trust him. We were sister and brother again, and we watched television—Simon and Samantha on our laps—until Momma came home from work. I honestly thought things were going to be better from that night on.

This time it was my turn to be wrong.

Things were better for about a week.

But then came the next couple of months…Jason losing so much weight and quitting his summer-league basketball team; Momma complaining that money was missing from her purse and a necklace was gone from her top dresser drawer; Jason quitting his job at the video store…

Call me stupid, but I never thought it was the drugs. People got hooked on dope all the time—especially in my neighborhood—but not my brother. He was too smart for that, for goodness sake. I just thought Jason had changed. That happens a lot of times, you know. Plenty of my friends were close to their sisters or brothers when they were younger and then as soon as they reached a certain age, they drifted apart. I just thought that's what was happening with Jason and me.

It all came to a head a few days after Jason's seventeenth birthday. I came home from school and found him sprawled on the kitchen floor. His face was a bloody, swollen mess, and his arm was bleeding. The kitchen table was overturned, and a chair was broken. Samantha was going crazy in the corner behind the trash can, meowing and whimpering louder than I had ever heard her.

Jason refused to go to the hospital, so I wet a washcloth and started cleaning his face. I kept asking him over and over again what had happened, but all he would say was: "I'm sorry. I'm sorry. I'm so sorry…"

I was just finishing with his arm when suddenly a sick feeling came over me, and I asked him: "Where's Simon?"

He shook his head and started crying.

I felt the panic in my stomach. "Jason, what happened to Simon?"

"I'm sorry…"

Louder this time. "Jason, where's Simon?"

And that's when he broke down and told me everything: about the drugs and the money he owed. About how they warned him this would happen. How they were waiting for him inside the apartment…and finally, about what they'd done to poor Simon, as his final warning to come up with the money or else.

My hands were shaking. I couldn't believe this was happening. Happening to us. Inside our own apartment. I picked up Samantha and walked into the living room. Sat on the sofa and cried for a long, long time. Poor Simon. God, I was going to miss him.

Before Momma came home, we cleaned up the mess and made up another story. I never asked exactly what happened to Simon; I was afraid to.

And, of course, Jason promised to stop again. He owed the men two hundred dollars. I loaned him all the money I had—just over sixty—and he swore he would borrow the rest of the money from his friends and get his job back at the video store and repay me. He promised me, and I believed him. He was my best friend in the whole world.

Two weeks later, money wasn't a problem any more. But he wasn't working at the video store. Instead, he came home one evening, and I noticed the changes right away: a fancy gold watch on his right wrist, a thick bracelet on his left. A beeper clipped to his belt. A new leather jacket and kicks. And a swagger to his walk that hadn't been there before. He walked up to me, pulled a wad of bills from his front pants pocket, and peeled off three twenty dollar bills and handed them to me. Walked into his bedroom without saying a word and closed the door.

I knew the truth then. He was never going to stop. Never. He was dealing now. Using was bad enough, but dealing…

For the next few days, I tried to think of how to tell Momma without breaking her heart. She was working so hard and was so proud of us, I couldn't bear the thought of telling her, or disappointing her. But she had to know.

That weekend, Jason brought home another cat for me. He had a gold-studded collar and a fancy gold tag that read *SIMON 2*. I kept the cat, but threw away the collar and tag. I named him Jordan, and by Monday he and Samantha were old friends.

Jason had no problem flaunting his newfound wealth in front of me, but Momma was another story. If he knew she was going to be home, there was no jewelry, no flashy new clothes or pager on his belt. To Momma, he was still the old Jason, a little more distant maybe, a little more grown-up, but still her baby boy. He still came home every night, but he'd started sneaking out after Momma fell asleep.

One night, when I knew he was gone, I heard a story on the news about a drive-by shooting over on Madison, two blocks north from where we live. The man on the news said it was drug-related and three young men were killed. I cried myself to sleep that night with worry, and when I saw Jason the next morning in the parking lot in front of our apartment building, getting out of the passenger side of a shiny new Jeep Cherokee, I was relieved and furious at the same time.

I ran up to him and hugged him as the truck drove away.

"Oh my God, Jason," I cried. "I thought you were one of those men on the television, the ones that got killed"

"Hey, hey, Little One. It's okay," he said, wrapping his arms around me. "It's okay. I ain't never gonna be the one, so you just stop your worrying."

I looked at him, at his glazed eyes, his crooked smile. He was high as a kite.

I hugged him as tight as I could, and he hugged me back. I kissed him on the cheek and said, "I love you, big brother," and I walked to school.

A couple days later, on a rainy Sunday afternoon, it finally happened. Three policemen knocked on our door. They had their hands on their guns and a search warrant. There had been a middle-of-the-night robbery at Hardesty's Pharmacy, where Momma worked, and evidence at the scene pointed to Jason: a spare key, which was evidently used for entry, was found there, and the serial number was registered to Momma. And a wallet with Jason's identification was also found on the floor of the pharmacy.

Although it was almost noon, Jason was still asleep when a stunned Momma let the officers into his bedroom. He was in handcuffs before he was fully awake. The policemen discovered five stolen watches and several baggies of cocaine underneath the mattress of his bed.

Jason never said a word when the officers walked him out of the apartment. Not to Momma, not to me, and not to the policemen.

3

EVEN JASON'S VOICE sounded strange to me. The courtroom was so big and empty that it echoed off the walls. Or maybe it was the microphone, but he sounded like an old man, not my seventeen-year-old brother.

I listened to him talk:

"I didn't steal no watches."

"I wasn't in no fool store."

"No, sir, I don't know where they came from."

"No, Your Honor, I don't take drugs. Never have, never will."

I could tell he was trying to sound strong and smooth and in control—like the old Jason—but his voice reminded me of that afternoon when I found him beat-up and laying on the kitchen floor. Right before he'd started to cry and tell me how sorry he was.

I reached over and took Momma's hand. I gave it a little squeeze, and she did the same.

Twenty minutes later, with Jason sitting next to his lawyer, the judge pronounced Jason guilty and shook his head sadly as he handed down his sentence. "You leave me with no choice, young man. The evidence was found at the crime scene. You were caught with stolen property and crack cocaine in your bedroom. Yet you refuse to take any responsibility for the crime. I've listened to all the testimony and taken into account the fact that you are a first-time offender, but…"

And then the judge sentenced Jason to a juvenile boot camp upstate until his twenty-first birthday.

I heard Momma start to cry. I squeezed her hand again. I knew how hard this was for her.

"Removing you from this environment may be the best thing for you," the judge continued, and for the first time Jason met his eyes. "It's still not too late to turn your life around. There are people in this courtroom," he said, pointing to Momma and me, "who are counting on you. You've let them down. And now you will have three and a half years to straighten yourself out and become the man you think you are."

And just like that, the judge banged his gavel and walked out of the room.

Suddenly, the room was full of conversation and activity. The sound of shoes on the hardwood floor. Lawyers chattering away and shuffling papers. Briefcases being closed. Police officers huddled together talking. In a matter of minutes, Jason was headed for a side door, on his way out of the courtroom. He looked over his shoulder at us. There were tears on his face.

Momma stood on her tiptoes and waved and cried, "I love you, baby! I love you!"

And then he was gone.

We hugged right there in the courtroom. We hugged tight and for a long time, searching for hope in each other's arms. And then we headed home on the subway.

Three and a half years wasn't forever. And then we would be a family again. In the meantime, it was just Momma and me, and Samantha and Jordan. Just the four of us, waiting for Jason to come home again. Waiting for things to be the way they used to be.

All the way home, I thought about Jason. I thought about only the good times. Back when we were kids, playing those silly games and watching television for hours. Running around the apartment chasing Simon and Samantha.

I thought about that smile of his and how he used to wink at me. How much he used to love me and Momma.

And I knew I had done the right thing. Stealing Momma's key from her purse and sneaking into the store that night. Taking those watches and hiding them under Jason's mattress. Leaving his wallet behind.

That night I fell asleep on the sofa with my head in Momma's lap, and I dreamed about my big brother coming home again.

(written with Barry Hoffman)

MISTER PARKER

BENJAMIN PARKER—MR. PARKER or Bulldog Parker, behind his back, to his eighth grade English students—lived a simple life.

By choice, he had no wife, no children, and no pets. He lived in a practical two-story house in the suburb of Forest Hill. The house was practical because it was located three miles from the middle school at which he taught—close enough to save on fuel costs, but far enough so that he didn't have to live amidst his pupils—and because it was a perfect fit for his daily needs and extensive library.

Parker mostly kept to himself, although he attended a weekly book club every Thursday night and a monthly Friday night poker game with five other teachers from nearby schools. He spent most afternoons reading student papers and grading tests; most evenings in the library or in the back yard with his telescope.

Parker had two great loves in his life: books and astronomy. Naturally, his library featured many volumes that focused on his lifelong obsession with the night sky, but it was hardly limited to that subject.

Classic literature. Poetry. History. Biographies. Folklore. True crime. Photography. Cooking. Pop culture. Even modern fiction.

It was all there. Each volume categorized by genre; each author alphabetized; each book protected within carefully applied Mylar sleeves.

When Parker was a younger man, he often spent his weekends driving to various rare or used bookshops, searching for hard-to-find titles to fill out his collection. Of course, he could have done much of this buying via the telephone or mail order catalog, but he enjoyed his treasure hunts, as he referred to them. He never felt lonely on these road trips; quite the contrary. He enjoyed driving the winding back roads and listening to music while the wind whipped through his hair and cooled his cheeks.

But, as the years passed and the internet forced many booksellers out of business, these trips dwindled from weekly to monthly to every other month until finally, Parker barely managed two or three road trips a year.

Now most of his book purchases were completed through numerous online websites and occasional slumming on ebay—which is precisely what Parker was doing when Kelly Rutherford walked into his classroom after the final bell on Friday and interrupted him.

"I'M SORRY TO bother you, Mr. Parker."

Parker started and looked up from his computer screen in surprise; he hadn't heard anyone come in. He closed the laptop and put on his best English teacher smile.

"No bother at all, Miss Rutherford. How can I help you?"

"I was wondering..." The girl started shuffling papers out of a bright pink notebook. "...if you wouldn't mind reading my paper this weekend if you're not too busy." She dropped one of the pages onto the desk, quickly grabbed it and almost knocked over Parker's coffee mug. "I know it's not due until next Friday, but I finished early and I'm a little worried if I'm on the right track or not."

Kelly Rutherford was a straight "A" student, class president, and *always* worried if she was on the right track or not.

Parker stood up and walked around his desk. Took the outstretched pages.

The girl shrugged apologetically. "I understand if you're too busy, I just thought—"

"It's fine, Miss Rutherford. I'd be happy to give it an early read." He opened the briefcase on his desk, placed the paper inside, and clicked it shut again.

The girl beamed in relief and squeezed her hands together in a gesture Parker found both odd and charming. "Thank you *so* much, Mr. Parker. I really appreciate it."

Parker, for reasons he couldn't have explained if he tried, steepled his own hands together and gave a polite, little bow.

The girl looked momentarily confused, then broke out in a giggle. "Well, thanks again, Mr. Parker."

She practically skipped out of the classroom before pausing by the door and looking back over her shoulder. "Oh, yeah, and Happy Halloween." She flipped him a wave and was gone.

The smile faded from Parker's face, his eyes troubled. He picked up the mug from his desk and took a long swallow of lukewarm coffee. "Happy Halloween, indeed."

BENJAMIN PARKER LIVED a simple life. He was a strict and respected teacher. A quiet and courteous, if not overly friendly, neighbor. And a kind and trustworthy friend within his small circle; even if they all tended to tease him about his eccentricities and overly private nature.

Parker was a man of moderate taste, temperament, and behavior. He was, as the self-help gurus liked to say, very comfortable in his own skin. In fact, he often thought to himself: *I have my stars and my books and my peace of mind; that is more than enough for any man.*

Most people would have been shocked to learn that there were indeed two matters Parker despised with enough passion to upset his calm exterior: drunks and Halloween.

His father had been a drunk—a violent one—and Parker had suffered at his hands. A broken arm one night after the old man had lost yet another job. Three broken fingers when Parker had made the mistake of sticking up for his mother after she burned a pot roast dinner. Permanent scars on his back and buttocks after Parker had accidentally knocked his father's beer off a tv tray or left his bicycle in the front yard overnight. More black eyes and bruises than he could count or remember. Parker eventually learned to antagonize his father when he had been drinking, to invite his aggressions, in an effort to spare his mother. All this by the time Parker was eleven years old.

The nightmare lasted until his father's death in a hit-and-run accident shortly after Parker's fifteenth birthday. The old man had been drunk, of course, staggering home from a bar in the middle of the night—*and* the middle of the road. Someone simply came tearing around the bend on old Route 22, drove him down like a stray cat, and kept right on going.

Two days later, they buried him on a rainy Sunday morning. Only three people stood at the gravesite: Parker, his mother, and the preacher. His mother had a black eye. There were no tears that day.

PARKER TOOK A left on Hanson Road and drove slowly down his street. It was too early for trick-or-treaters, but he was by nature a careful man. The speed limit was 25 miles per hour, so he drove 25 miles per hour.

He focused on the road ahead of him, doing his best to avoid looking at the garish Halloween decorations adorning his neighbors' houses. He was particularly grateful that it was still light out and none of the fat orange pumpkins sitting on front porches were smiling their jagged, glowing grins.

Parker signaled a right hand turn, slowed, and pulled into his driveway. He turned off the ignition and sat behind the wheel for a moment. He didn't feel quite right. At first, he had thought it was the usual trepidation he felt toward the final night of October, but now he was starting to believe he was coming down with something. His heart was beating too hard and his head felt swimmy and unfocused.

He grabbed his briefcase from the seat next to him and got out of the car. As he was walking up the front walk, a voice called out to him from across the street.

"Happy Halloween, Benjamin!"

He turned and saw his neighbor, Carol Perkins, raking leaves into narrow, makeshift burial mounds, each one centered in front of a fake, Styrofoam tombstone.

Parker gave her a half-hearted wave and continued onto his front porch and into the house. His briefcase felt heavier than usual. He needed to rest.

IF PARKER WERE ever forced to acknowledge and then explain his loathing of Halloween, he probably would have opted for the simplest explanation: it was a frivolous tradition that bordered on the sacrilegious; a greedy retailer-manipulated holiday based on cheesy decorations and cavity-inducing sweets.

But Parker knew that day would never come. Only two people in the world knew about his true feelings toward Halloween. He was the first (and he wasn't talking), and his mother was the second (and she wasn't either; Parker had buried her two decades earlier in a cemetery far away from where his father's corpse lay rotting).

The truth of the matter was Parker hated Halloween because of his father. No surprise there.

Parker's father wasn't big on holidays. Most Christmases he was solidly in the bag by the time presents had been opened and the smell of ham was just beginning to waft out of the kitchen. Thanksgiving was a blurred nightmare of football blaring on the television and loud, drunken complaints about food preparation. The fourth of July was more than likely a fistfight at the neighborhood picnic and an early exit, thus guaranteeing that Parker would once again miss the fireworks display after dark.

But Halloween was the worst of all…because Parker's father actually *liked* it. He would start decorating the house and planning his costume by mid-October—paying little attention to Parker's own costume or excitement—and by the time the thirty-first rolled around, their house was a gaudy mess of fake spider webs and ghosts hanging from trees; plastic tombstones scattered across the front yard; and nearly a dozen glowing jack o'lanterns lining the porch and front walk.

As dusk darkened the October sky on Halloween night, Parker's father would appear in full costume—the most memorable being an incredibly life-like Frankenstein, complete with stitched, green skin and nuts and bolts in his skull—and inevitably he would be reeking of liquor.

When Parker would come downstairs dressed in his own costume—a hobo or a clown or a fighter pilot; usually something his mother helped him make—his father would make merciless fun of him, calling him "fag" or "sissy" or "homo."

Then he would spend the rest of Halloween night sneaking sips of whiskey and jumping out from behind the tall shrubs that bordered the front porch and terrifying unsuspecting trick-or-treaters. Many of the children would scream in terror and run crying back to their parents waiting on the sidewalk—but very few of those parents would complain; Parker's father was a very large man.

Eventually, as the years passed, fewer and fewer children came trick-or-treating to Parker's house, and he knew his sadistic father was to blame.

Parker learned to hate his father even more for ruining Halloween.

PARKER DOUBLE-CHECKED THAT the front porch light was turned off and retreated to his library. Dropping his briefcase to the hardwood floor, he practically collapsed into his favorite reading chair, immediately feeling at home in its soft leather embrace. He closed his eyes for a moment and tried to settle his breathing.

He was feeling worse. He'd decided to skip dinner—he wasn't very hungry at all, which was unusual—and spend his evening reading and listening to music.

Parker pushed on the armrests and the chair readjusted itself into a lounger. He reached over and took his book-in-progress from the end table and rested it on his lap. He closed his eyes again (*just for a second*, he thought), and just as he heard the first distant chatter of trick-or-treaters out on the street, he drifted off to sleep—and dreamed of his father dressed as Frankenstein chasing him down a dark sidewalk.

IT WAS LITTLE surprise that a beloved book resting in his lap had helped to lull Parker to sleep. In many ways, books were his security blanket and salvation.

Not surprisingly, he had learned his love of literature from his mother. As far back as his memory stretched, he could remember his mother borrowing stacks of books from the local library and reading to him in his tiny bedroom. Reading wasn't limited to bedtime in their house; it was an any-time-of-the-day activity. It wasn't until Parker was a little older—and reading himself—that he understood what his mother was doing, what she was *providing* for them both.

An escape.

An escape from the nightmare world they lived in.

An escape to faraway worlds and experiences that were often magical and mysterious and, most importantly, *happy*.

This certainly explained why his mother read two or three books herself each week. She couldn't defend her son from the almost daily physical blows and psychological torment, but she *could* teach him that other worlds—better worlds—existed within his reach.

After she was gone, Parker realized that his mother had blessed him with the most precious gift of his lifetime—hope.

PARKER AWOKE WITH a start, heart thudding in his chest, face bathed in a sheen of sweat. He jerked to a sitting position, and the book tumbled from his lap onto the floor. He couldn't remember his nightmare, but he knew it had been a bad one.

He looked around the dark room, confused, the flickering orange flames from the gas fireplace the only available light.

Something was wrong—with him *and* the room.

I could've sworn I switched on the lights in here...and I know I didn't turn on the fireplace...and why was everything so damn blurry and out of focus?

Parker bent over and picked up the book and placed it back on the end table. His hand was shaking. He carefully got to his feet, steadying himself against the chair. He was dizzy and could feel a blue-ribbon headache blooming in the back of his head.

I'm dehydrated, he thought. *Need water.*

He started to shuffle his way out of the library—but stopped abruptly, legs frozen, eyes wide, when one of the shadows in the corner of the room detached itself from the wall and slithered behind a tall potted plant.

"Who's there?" Parker asked in a trembling voice. "I saw you. You can't hide in here."

There came no response.

Parker held his breath, listening for a sound of any kind.

Nothing.

Summoning courage, he took a slow, silent step forward—just as someone banged three times on the library window.

Parker let out a little scream and almost knocked over the big, museum quality globe that was the centerpiece of his library. He steadied himself again and focused on the lone window in the room, a dark square floating against an even darker backdrop. *Had someone knocked on the outside of the window—or the inside?*

The thought made Parker's head spin, and he brushed it aside.

Enough of this, he thought, and deliberately made his way out of the library and into the hallway. The foyer ceiling light was on, and he shielded his eyes from the sudden brightness. He started for the kitchen—

—and the front doorbell rang.

Parker froze and looked at the door. *Stupid kids.*

The doorbell rang again.

"Go away!" he bellowed. "No trick-or-treaters allowed!"

He was answered by a violent pounding on the door—BOOM! BOOM! BOOM!

Using the wall to support himself, Parker shuffled into the foyer and took out an umbrella from the base of the coat rack. He held it high over his shoulder, poised to strike, and reached for the doorknob.

PARKER YANKED OPEN the front door—"I told you kids to get out of here!"—and found the porch empty.

He squinted into the darkness, peering up and down the silent street. It was later than he thought—*how long had he slept?*—and the sidewalks were devoid of trick-or-treaters.

A sudden rustling noise came from the bushes that bordered the right side of the porch. Parker lifted the umbrella high above his head. "Who's there? Come out and show yourself!"

When no one answered, Parker leaned back inside the doorway and flipped on the front porch light.

He turned back to the bushes on the side of the porch—and froze in terror.

His eyes locked on a large, green puddle of rubber—*a Frankenstein mask*—lying on the edge of the concrete porch, and right next to it, scrawled in big, dripping red letters, a single hateful word: **FAG**

"Nooo!" Parker wailed.

He stumbled toward the mask, his face twisted in disbelief, and then he sniffed the faint scent of liquor in the night air. The smell struck him like a physical blow and he slammed back against the house, hitting his head against the brick and dropping the umbrella. *Dad?*

Rustling came from the bushes again, and this time, Parker could see the shrubs moving.

"Dad?" he whispered, not recognizing the sound of his own voice. "Is that you?"

The shrubs abruptly stopped moving. A gentle breeze stirred the bare trees. A dog barked. Somewhere down the street, a car started and drove away.

"It can't be you." Parker took a step forward, his voice louder now, already edging into panic. "You're dead. It can't be you."

Another step—and the smell of liquor touched his nose again. "Nooo! It can't be! I killed you, you son-of-a-bitch!" He surged forward. "I ran you down like the junkyard dog you are!"

He dropped to his knees and picked up the mask in both hands—and that's when his tired heart finally burst inside his chest.

Parker, a simple man with simple hopes, had just enough time to look at the mask and think *Wait, this isn't Frankenstein; it's Shrek, isn't it?* before everything went black and he collapsed dead to the porch floor, still grasping the rubber mask in both of his hands.

November 6, 2016 edition of the Baltimore Sun newspaper:

JUVENILES ARRESTED FOR
HALLOWEEN PRANK GONE AWRY

Baltimore County Police Detectives made several arrests yesterday in the tragic, accidental death of Forest Hill resident and longtime Fallston Middle School teacher, Benjamin Parker.

Names are being withheld because the suspects are juveniles, but numerous sources report that three arrests were made yesterday afternoon at Fallston Middle School, including one female and two male students.

Parker, 51, a resident of the 1900 block of Hanson Road, was found dead on his front porch the morning of November 1, 2016 by concerned neighbors.

An investigation was launched after police found a hate message sprayed on Parker's front porch and a mysterious rubber mask still grasped in the deceased's hands.

While the coroner's report listed cardiac arrest as the official cause of death, subsequent toxicology reports indicated the presence of an unusually high dosage of a yet-to-be-named drug, which most likely caused blurred vision, severe confusion, heightened anxiety, and hallucinations.

An unnamed police source revealed that one of the students allegedly spiked Parker's coffee during school hours, then all three students allegedly appeared at Parker's Hanson Road home later that October night to play a Halloween prank on him.

All three suspects are being held in the Baltimore County Eastern Precinct until a bail hearing can be arranged…

MONSTERS

"DID YOU HEAR IT *this* time?"

Manning leaned forward in the driver's seat and cocked his head to the side, a movement designed to show that he was *really* listening this time. He shrugged his shoulders. "Just the crickets, baby. And the wind."

Baby shook her head and shivered and felt an army of goosebumps march across her forearms. The night air *was* unseasonably cool, but not *that* cool. Her eyes searched the darkness, found only tall trees dancing in the summer breeze beneath a fingernail moon, shadow partners following their rhythmic lead.

Her name was Mary Beth and she hated being called "baby" almost as much as "darling" or "gorgeous," but now was *not* the time and this was *not* the place to start an argument. It was downright spooky out here in the middle of nowhere and she just wanted to get it over with and get back to the motel to a big glass of iced-tea and the clean, cool sheets of her bed.

"Don't worry, little darling, I'm right here to take care of you." Manning put his arm around her and pulled her closer. He smelled of sour whiskey and cheap aftershave. His Trans-Am had designer bucket seats—leather, of course—and with a blanket stuffed down into the space between the seats it allowed for comfortable cuddling. He'd learned that trick many years ago.

"What would you do if something came out of the woods?" she asked, looking nervously out his side window. Her window was barely cracked, but his was more than halfway down. "A monster or something?"

He laughed loud and harsh and mean. "A monster? You mean like the Mummy or Frankenstein?" He shook his head, arched his eyebrows. "Shee-it! I ain't never seen no monster before, but you can bet I'd jump on out and go right to ass-kicking if I did."

Mary Beth almost laughed and was glad she didn't. Manning was a lot of things, she knew, but an ass-kicker wasn't one of them. She had played the dumb redhead role perfectly when they'd met earlier at the bar, but the facts were all committed to memory. Parker Manning. Twenty-nine years old. Ran his father's furniture factory over on Elf and 14th. Spent money like it was paper. Local playboy, especially with the teeny-boppers. And worst of all—and this was her favorite—he still lived at home, with his folks, in an attic-converted apartment.

"You mean you wouldn't be scared?" she said.

"Hell no."

"Why not?" She made her eyes wide and fascinated.

"First of all, because there ain't no such thing as monsters." His chest was swelled out now and his heavy breathing filled the car with the flavor of cinnamon chewing gum. Again she swallowed a giggle. "Second of all, because I'm Parker Manning and I'm not afraid of anything."

"So you'd protect me?" she purred, leaning in a little closer and kissing his earlobe, flicking it with her tongue.

"You're damn right I would . What kind of a man do you think I am?"

And then, with the frantic grace of a fourteen-year-old in a dark movie theater balcony, Manning made his move. He rolled his bulk onto her, his chest pinning her tight against the seat, and then his tongue was inside her mouth like a fat, sloppy slug. His fingers found the three buttons at the top of her blouse and roughly pulled them open.

Christ, she thought, this was Mr. Playboy's idea of romance and seduction in the moonlight. Ten minutes on a deserted dirt road, a little sweet-talking, and then get right to the good stuff. Jesus, she sure could pick 'em.

He paused to catch his breath and she took advantage of the break. "How 'bout we go outside, big boy? Take a blanket and have some fun underneath the stars." It was still creepy as hell out there, but she no longer felt she had the advantage inside the cramped front seat. She wanted out.

"Nuh, uh," he said. "Ain't no stars out tonight. How 'bout we get that shirt off instead." He yanked the bottom of her blouse out from her jeans and began to pull it up over her head. He let out a whistle when he caught a glimpse of her pale breasts.

Instinctively, her arms came up to stop him...and she panicked. With one swift movement, she pushed him off her and raked at his face with her left hand.

He shrieked and reacted with a backhand slap to her face. "You bitch. You stupid, stupid bitch." He started the car and the engine was painfully loud, the stereo still louder.

"Get out," he screamed above the music.

Mary Beth slowly reached over and unlocked the door, ignoring her stinging cheek. She knew exactly what would happen next: she would swing a leg out the car door and just before she got out, she'd turn back to him, lips pouting, big eyes blinking, and apologize and promise to make it up to him...

She pushed open the door, held it slightly ajar, so that the inside light flashed on. Manning's face was flushed red and thin railroad tracks of blood crossed his forehead. Mary Beth opened her mouth—

—and he surprised her.

He gave her a hard two-hand shove and slammed his foot on the gas pedal. The Trans-Am swerved wide, tires spinning, sending her tumbling out into the night, screaming like he had never, ever heard a person scream before...

MANNING SPED HOME in silence, windows rolled down, the air cool and soothing on his ravaged face. You sure can pick 'em, he thought. Crazy, crazy bitch. That's the last time I pick up a stranger. Acting all hot and bothered at first, then all scared, then friggin' crazy as a mountain man. And all that screamin' and hollerin', like she was back there dying or something. Christ, all she had to do was pick her skinny ass up off that dirt road and hike a few miles into town. Not like I abandoned her in the middle of nowhere.

He pulled to the curb in front of his parents' split-level house and switched off the ignition. It felt damn good to be home again. He was halfway up the driveway—no one *ever* walked on the grass, not even the mailman—when he smelled rain in the night air and turned back. Both car windows were still open.

He yanked open the passenger door and screamed.

An upstairs light clicked on inside the house.

He screamed louder.

The front door opened and he heard his Daddy's voice behind him, tired and clearly agitated. "What the hell's going on, boy?"

Manning dropped to his knees and lost his club sandwich and bourbon dinner on the neatly-clipped grass.

When Daddy reached his side, Manning motioned inside the car—

—to the gleaming metal hook which was swaying gently on the *inside* door handle, a bloody stump of flesh dripping red and black onto the leather seat.

Manning's final thought before he fainted at his Daddy's feet was of the woman's tortured screams echoing in the wind-blown summer night.

LIKE FATHER, LIKE SON

FATHER'S DAY WAS ALWAYS a big deal when I was growing up. The old man loved it. Breakfast in bed. (And let me tell you, back in those days, Mom made a ham and egg omelet so big the plate could barely hold it). Afternoon barbecue in the back yard. Horseshoes. Ball-tossing. Lots of laughter and silly stuff. And then an evening drive downtown for ice cream cones and milkshakes; all four windows rolled down, cool spring air blushing our cheeks; Dad at the wheel, singing along with the radio in that crazy voice of his, big hands swallowing up the steering wheel; Mom, sitting sideways in the passenger seat, rolling her eyes at us, feigning embarrassment.

There were three of us boys—the three stooges, Dad always called us. I was the oldest and most of the responsibilities fell on my shoulders. Come the big weekend, I was in charge of making sure the lawn was mowed, the hedges clipped, and the sidewalk swept. I was the one every year who bought the card down at Finch's Grocery Mart and made sure that Marty and Lawrence signed it. And, most importantly, I was in charge of organizing the gifts. Of course, back when we were kids, our presents were never very expensive or fancy. Usually just something simple we'd each made in school.

Individually wrapped and sealed tight with a few yards of shiny scotch tape so as to prolong the official gift opening ceremony after breakfast.

The first gift I can remember making was an ashtray in the shape of a bullfrog. Painted green, of course. Very bright green. The only frog in class with big yellow teeth, too. Dad loved it. Let out a bellow that rattled the bed frame when he pulled it from the box. Shook my tiny hand and told me how proud he was of me. And he was too; you could just tell.

Then there was the year that Marty gave the old man a wooden pipe-holder for his desktop. Sanded and polished and varnished to a fine finish; it was a thing of beauty; it really was. To this day, I think Marty could've had a successful career as a craftsman; it was that nice a job.

Lawrence, who was the youngest and the brightest, was the writer of the family and for a three year period in his early teens, he gave the old man an "original Lawrence Finley book" each Father's Day. Each "book" was composed of five short chapters and each chapter ended with a suspenseful cliff-hanger. They were typed out in dark, clear script on folded construction paper and carefully stapled down the middle. A remarkably-detailed pencil sketch decorated the title page of each new volume. The story itself was equally impressive: it featured the old man as an outlaw gunfighter in the Old West. Strong and brave and with a heart of gold. A mid-west Robin Hood with a six-shooter on his hip and a fast, white horse named Gypsy. Of all the gifts the three of us gave him back when we were kids, I think these stories were the old man's favorite. Not that he ever would've admitted it, of course.

Years later, when all three of us were over at the University and working good part-time jobs, we each saved up and chipped in for something special: a John Deere riding mower. A brand spanking new one with a big red ribbon laced through the steering wheel. We surprised him with it right after breakfast that year, and he flat out couldn't believe his eyes. Neither could we; it was the first time any of us—Mom included—had ever seen the old guy speechless. Makes me smile even now just to think about it. Makes me smile even more when I remember all the times I called home from college and Mom would tell me he couldn't come to the phone right now because he was out cutting the lawn…again…for the second time that week.

Yes, sir, Father's Day was always a big deal back when I was growing up.

THE DRIVE OUT to Hagerstown Prison takes just under three hours on a good day. I figure the traffic to be a bit heavier than usual this morning, so I leave when it's still dark outside. I ride with the radio off and the heat on; it rained last night and the June air has a nasty little bite to it.

I drive the winding country roads faster than I should, but visiting hours have been extended because of the holiday, and I want to show up a few minutes early to get a head start on the registration forms and to check in the gifts I've brought along with me. In the back seat, I have a big bag of freshly-baked chocolate chip cookies, a stack of brand new paperbacks—westerns, mostly—and a half-dozen pouches of his favorite pipe tobacco.

The road is fairly clear and the trip takes two hours and thirty-five minutes. Plenty of time for a man to think…even if he doesn't want to.

When I step out onto the gravel parking lot, the morning sun is shining and the chill has vanished from the air. I can hear birds singing in the trees across the way, and I can't help but wonder what they must sound like to the men locked inside these walls.

There are already a scattered handful of visitors waiting inside the lobby. Mostly young women with pale, dirty, restless children. But a few older couples, too. None of them look up at me when I take off my coat and sit down, but the hush of whispering momentarily fades to silence then picks up again. In all my visits here, I've never once heard anyone speak in a normal tone of voice in this room; only whispers. It's always like this in the waiting room. There's an awkward kind of acceptance here. No one gawks or stares. It's like we're all charter members of the same club—each and every one of us joined together by our love for someone behind these bars and each of us sharing the same white-hot emotions of embarrassment and fear and despair that coming here brings to the surface.

My father has been here for almost three years now. And unless his case is reopened—which is very unlikely—he will remain here until the day he dies. I don't like to think about that, though. I'd rather dream about the day when he might be free again to spend his retirement years back where he belongs—back at the house with me.

But we both know that day will never come. He will never come home again…and still the old man claims he has no regrets. Swears he'd do it all over again in a heartbeat. After all, he tells me, I was just protecting my family.

SOMETIMES FAMILIES JUST drift apart and it's almost impossible to put a finger on the reason. Age old secrets remain secret. Hidden feelings remain hidden. Sometimes the family was never really that close in the first place, and it simply took the passage of time to bring this sad fact to light.

But you know that's the funny thing. We never drifted apart. We remained close right up to a point and then *boom*—it was over. One day we're a family; the next day we're not. It was almost as if Marty and Lawrence had gotten together behind our backs and planned the whole terrible thing.

After college, Marty went into real estate. He married a fairly snobby woman named Jennifer (not Jenny or Jenn, but Jennifer) and moved east to Annapolis and earned a six-figure income selling waterfront property to yuppies. By the time he was thirty-five, he'd had two boys of his own, divorced Jennifer after discovering that she'd been unfaithful with a co-worker, and entered into a second marriage, this time with an older woman who also worked in real estate. I've never met her, but her name is Vicki and she has a very pleasant voice and is downright friendly on the telephone (although I've only spoken with her twice.)

Lawrence, who turned out to be not only the brightest, but also the hardest working Finley boy, put his creative skills to profitable use—he went into advertising. He worked a back-breaking schedule and squirreled away his pennies for damn near a decade then opened his own small agency in downtown Baltimore when he was still in his early thirties. Just a handful of years later, he was one of the field's fastest risers, appeared regularly in all the trade magazines, and oversaw an operation of some two dozen employees. Last year (and I read this in the newspaper, we haven't spoken in over five years), he opened a second office—in New York City.

But for all of their successes, it quickly became apparent that Marty and Lawrence had changed—and not for the better. Sure, there were gifts and cards at Christmas and on birthdays, but that was pretty much it. Mom and Dad and I rarely spoke with the two of them—much less saw them—and whenever friends and neighbors asked, our responses were quick, our smiles forced. For a couple of years we kept trying, we honestly did, but our letters went mostly unanswered, our phone calls ignored. The whole situation made Mom and Dad furious. They'd sit around the dining room table, nibbling at their desserts and say, "If they're so ashamed of their small town roots and their small town family, then so be it. Couple of big shots is what they think they are. Good riddance to them." But I could see past their bitterness and resentment. At the end of the day, they were just like me—they were left feeling hurt and confused and abandoned. And it was a miserable feeling, let me tell you. Things like this might happen to other families, but for God's sake not the Finleys.

And so, just like that, we became a family of three.

And, soon after, a family of two.

Mom died in her sleep on Easter weekend 1989, and everyone—including Dad—thought it was a good thing. She'd been suffering something terrible. Lung cancer, if you can believe that. Only fifty-three years old and never smoked a day in her life.

Of course, neither Marty nor Lawrence made it home for the funeral. And if you ask me (and the state police boys *did* ask me in a roundabout way later on), Mom's death coupled with their failure to show up at the service was the final straw. Something inside the old man's mind snapped like a soggy twig and he was never the same again.

Shortly after, he began bringing home the cats. Strays, store-bought; it didn't matter a lick. Sometimes as many as two or three a month. His new family, he called them. The two of us need a family to take care of, he'd say. A family that will stay together and live under the same roof. Just wait and see.

By Christmas later that year, we were living with over twenty cats of various sizes, shapes, and colors. The old man had a name for each and every one of them. And I have to admit, he was right; we were like a family again. He must have felt it, too; he was the happiest I'd seen him in a long time.

Then, just after Easter, right after the first anniversary of Mom's passing, the old man lost it and killed the Benson kid and all hell broke loose.

THE DRIVE HOME takes forever. It's raining again—really coming down now in thick, flapping sheets—and it's all I can do to keep the tires on the road. I change the radio station, try to think of something cheerful, but I can't stop myself from thinking of his eyes. Sparkling with such happiness and love, pleased with my gifts, overjoyed with my presence on his special day. But then, as always, the conversation soon turns and he is asking about his family, and his eyes are transforming into something alien and frightening. Eyes so focused and intense and determined, they belong to someone decades younger; they are the eyes of the stranger who stormed out of the house and chased down the Benson kid that long ago night.

So, that's when I take his trembling hand and gently squeeze and tell him what I always tell him: that they are fine. That I am taking good care of them. That his family is safe and sound, and they are all very happy and healthy.

Before I leave he almost breaks my heart when he thanks me with fat tears streaming down his cheeks, and in a quaking voice tells me that I am the man of the family now, that I am the one responsible for their care.

It is after midnight when I pull into the mud-streaked driveway. In the shine of the headlights, I glimpse a blur of black and white fur flash past me and disappear beneath the front porch. For just one moment, I can't decide if I should laugh or cry.

AS FOR ME...WELL, I'm still here. I never did leave this town (except for college and, hell, even then, I was back living in my old room ten days after graduation). I never did marry. Never had children. Never made my first million. In fact, you can still find me six days a week working the desk over at Bradshaw County Library and every other Saturday night taking tickets at the movie theater downtown. Not very exciting, I'm afraid.

But you know, that's okay with me. I turned forty-six a month ago today. I'm finally starting to lose a little ground—going bald on top and a little pudgy on the bottom. Started wearing glasses awhile back too. The kids at the library snicker behind my back once in a while, but they're just being kids; they don't mean anything by it. And, sure, I hear the whispers sometimes, I know the stories they tell—about how old man Finley went off his rocker and strangled little Billy Benson with his bare hands. And all because he'd set one of the old man's cats on fire.

I know they're starting to talk about me, too: about how I'm just as crazy as my old man was. Spending all that time with a house full of stinky old cats. Just like an old blue-haired spinster.

But you know what? I don't mind. Despite everything, I still like this town. I still like my life. There's just something that feels right about it. That's the best way I can explain it. It just feels *right*.

Sure there are nights—usually after drinking too many beers out on the front porch—when I lay awake in bed and stare off into the darkness and wonder what else my life might amount to. I wonder about Marty and Lawrence and why they did what they did. I wonder about Mom and what she would think about all this if she were still alive. And I can't help but wonder about the old man and those haunted eyes of his and that old green bullfrog ashtray and the evening drives for ice cream we used to take back when I was a little kid. But, you know, nothing good ever comes from those thoughts. There are never any easy answers, and those nights are long and lonely and sometimes even a little scary.

But, then, when I awake the next morning and feel the sunlight on my face and smell the coffee in the air and hear the purrs of my family as they gather around my ankles, I have all the answers I'll ever need.

And I'll tell you something else…like father, like son. I have no regrets. Not a one.

THE TOWER

1

T HEY FOUND THE FIRST body on a Thursday.

A couple of kids on their way home from fishing Hanson Creek stopped at the base of the old water tower to take a leak and almost ended up pissing on the missing girl's Nikes.

In the old days, one of the boys would have stood guard over the body while the other ran into town for help. In these sadly modern times, they did what most other kids would've done: they took out their cell phones, snapped a few pictures to show their friends later, and only then did they call 911 to report their finding.

The police showed up remarkably fast, not even ten minutes later. Three patrol cars almost colliding in a nearby gravel parking lot, before making the short hike to the old water tower. They forgot to bring a roll of police tape—seldom used in a town like Edgewood—so one of the officers had to jog back to his car to retrieve it—which is where he met the girl's hysterical parents.

Some things never change, regardless of the times: news travels fast in a small town.

The officer radioed ahead to warn the others that the girl's parents had arrived and were understandably upset. His Sergeant ordered him to hold them there in the parking lot, but that didn't work out so well, as both Mom and Dad bum-rushed the officer and beat him back to the crime scene by a good forty yards.

Once there, the Dad—a bearded construction foreman of nearly 250 pounds—took one look at his daughter's body sprawled there in the bushes and fainted dead to the ground. The kids whipped out their cell phones, of course, and took more pictures, before they were shooed away by the police, with threats to tell their parents. The boys grabbed their fishing rods and stringer full of crappie and yellow perch and beat it. The entire time, the Mom was down on her knees, eyes closed and praying.

An ambulance arrived a short time later, but the Dad was conscious and back on his feet by then, too distraught to be embarrassed by his fainting. A pair of police officers stood with him by a patrol car, trying to counsel him. The Mom was still off praying in the weeds. It took several more hours for the police to finish their initial investigation and remove the body. In that time, a crowd of townspeople had gathered at the scene. There was incessant whispering and pointing and quite a bit more picture taking. There were also two television reporters and a local newspaperman.

But by dusk, the scene was eerily quiet and practically deserted. A lone officer remained, sitting guard on a folding chair—the kind you might see at a backyard barbecue—reading a magazine by the glow of his flashlight and swatting at mosquitos.

Behind him, lost in the shadows, the old water tower watched over the town.

2

THE DEAD GIRL'S name was Bethany Hopkins. She was twelve. Tall for her age, nearsighted, and blonde. A straight "A" student, she was also captain of her swim team and a talented artist. She liked to wear her long hair in braids and was crazy for country music.

Bethany had gone missing the night before. She had eaten pizza for dinner at a friend's house and set out to walk the two blocks home just before eight—but she never made it.

By eight-thirty, her worried parents were combing the neighborhood; her Dad on foot, her Mom behind the wheel of their brand new SUV. By nine-thirty, worry had turned into panic, and they had called in the police. The police did their jobs, and by midnight, every officer in town was on the look-out, a recent school picture of a smiling Bethany Hopkins at their side. Plans were made for a county wide search the next morning, but the two boys discovered Bethany's body before the search could begin. Which explains why the police had been so quick to arrive; they'd all been assembled in the Food Lion parking lot, still going over the details of the upcoming search.

The coroner's report for Bethany Hopkins cited strangulation as the cause of death. There were no signs of sexual abuse or torture. Someone simply choked the life out of the little girl and left here there in the bushes.

The police did their work tirelessly, but there were no leads.

After awhile, people stopped whispering, and life eventually returned to normal.

3

UNTIL THE NEXT body was discovered—and in almost exactly the same spot.

This time by a home-for-the-summer college girl who was jogging along the worn dirt path that snaked through the Hanson Woods and looped past the water tower on its way back toward town.

The old water tower was as much a part of Edgewood as Main Street or the Campus Hills Movie Theater or Tucker's Field, where the annual Summer Carnival and Fall Pumpkin Festival were held. The aging tower stood up there on its hill, overlooking the town, looking all the world like one of H.G. Wells' spindly alien invaders marching over the horizon.

Long ago, when I was a kid, before the trees and thick bramble overtook the slope, we used to sled there on snowy mornings when school was cancelled. I remember playing flashlight tag and kick the can there on countless summer nights, fireflies dancing around our heads, our young, excited voices carrying in the darkness.

Once the woods took over, and the years marched on, the old water tower became known for a different kind of playing.

Instead of sledding, kids snuck up there to party or have bonfires or shoot their fathers' .22s. Too often, the ground was littered with empty beer cans and broken bottles, left behind and forgotten shoes and shirts and even brassieres. There were stories of drunken fights and carnal abandon and even satan worshippers in the Summer and Fall of '76.

There were a number of complaints from the older folks who used that stretch of land for daily strolls or bird watching or getting to and from their favorite fishing spots on Hanson Creek, but none of them really made a difference until the local newspaper ran a front page editorial about the issue. That did the trick, though, and soon after, warning signs were posted and the local police added the area to their daily patrol routes.

The bonfires and drinking went away—simply moved somewhere else, of course; kids will be kids—as did most of the litter and trouble. Most, but not all. Things still happened there from time to time. Bad things. People move away, people forget; but I've done neither. I remember…

A local husband, distraught after he discovered his wife was cheating on him with her best friend's husband, jumped to his death from the water tower in 1986.

A decade later, someone climbed the tower in the middle of the night, and spray-painted satanic graffiti all over the damn thing. Goat's heads. Pentagrams. Inverted crosses. Pretty much everything except a big red 666. It took three weeks and two budget meetings before the town got its act together and painted over the atrocities.

A few years later, a middle-aged, black woman—a stranger—was found hanging from one of the tower's criss-crossing metal support beams. Neither her identity—nor an explanation—were ever uncovered.

Of course, when a series of dark and mostly unexplainable events occur in the same spot over the course of many years, and most especially when these events occur within the confines of a small town, the spot is inevitably said to be cursed or even haunted—and the old water tower was no exception. Stories spread. Legends grew.

The land around the old water tower was unholy ground; it attracted evil. Ghosts and demons roamed there. It was a backwoods meeting spot for drug runners and gang members traveling on I-95 from New York to Florida. An old witch, her face burned and disfigured, lived somewhere back there in the woods; her cabin hidden amongst the bramble.

A local high school boy even wrote a term paper a number of years ago that spotlighted the area's dark history in great detail. He contended that there was once a slave house that stood on that lonely hill. Long before the water tower ever existed. The slave house was burned to the ground one night by a drunken and enraged master, and everyone inside had perished. Then, during the second world war, while the tower was being built in that very spot, it was reported that a half-dozen workers had either died or been seriously injured during its construction. Workers also reported that dozens of dead animal carcasses were found on the property; a reasonable explanation was never found. As a result, the tower was said to be cursed from the very beginning. Then, there was the story of the newlywed bride who, while on an early morning walk the day after her joyous wedding celebration, was bitten by a mysterious two-headed, red snake while resting in the tower's shadow. The woman died of her wound later that evening, and the snake was never found. There was even a lengthy section discussing the long-rumored worship of devils and demons on the grounds and a handful of witness accounts claiming that the area was haunted by the ghosts of murdered slaves.

There was more, much more—29 pages in all.

The fact that there were very few truths to be found in this young man's school report did nothing to diminish its impact. The boy received a "B+" on his report (he was said to be a terrible speller) and became a hero of sorts to his fellow students.

And, with the passage of time, as so often is the case, the many stories became truth, the legends became fact.

I would know. Many of the other old-timers moved away or forgot, but not me. No, sir. I've been here since almost the beginning.

My Lord willing, I'll turn eighty-four years old when this chill October rolls around, and I spent just over forty of those years hauling the mail around this town. I've seen it all, and I've heard it all. Trust me, people like to run their mouths and the only person likely to hear more rambling words than a mailman is the bartender down at Loughlin's Pub. But I've learned that drunk people mostly tell lies and folks standing in their sunny front yards holding onto their mail mostly tell the truth—or at least the truth as they believe it.

Lot of folks around this town think I'm just a friendly, old, senile man. They say their polite hellos and offer up their polite waves and keep right on going when they pass me on the sidewalk.

And they might be right, you know it.

But, don't you forget what I said: I have seen things.

4

THE SECOND BODY was discovered in plain sight. In fact, according to police, the whole thing looked staged.

Our resident home-from-college girl, a bright young lady named Jennifer Ward studying to become a teacher, came jogging around the bend—and stopped dead in her tracks. Her iPod tumbled from her hand down to the ground, yanking her headphones right out of her ears. Justin Timberlake broke the morning silence.

Everyone in town knew Gina Sharretts. She taught math at the local high school and coached the field hockey team.

Gina's limp body lay propped up against one of the water tower's rusting metal legs, her hands folded neatly in her lap. She could have been sleeping if it weren't for her hideously bulging eyes and the dark bruising around her swollen neck.

Jennifer snatched up her iPod and headphones and took off at a sprint. If campus life had taught her one thing, it was that safety was in numbers. Out on the road, she flagged down the first approaching car, and told the driver to call the police.

The patrol cars arrived a short time later, and once again out came the police tape and the picture-takers and the lookie loos, and this time around, it was a distraught brother and sister—Gina was thirty-seven and single on the day of her death—crashing the crime scene.

Once again, in the frantic days that followed, the police did their jobs and did them well—but there were still no leads.

Someone had simply strangled the life out of Gina Sharretts...

...just as someone had strangled the life out of Bethany Hopkins three years earlier.

And left them both there at the base of the water tower.

This clear pattern escaped no one's notice, of course. Most especially that of the police and the press. But even this discovery seemed to lead nowhere. Just one more dead end street in another dead end investigation.

5

THIS TIME IT took longer for the town to return to normal.

People were angry and paranoid. Old grudges and suspicions gained new life. Brand new grudges and suspicions were born. There were more drunken fights down at Loughlin's Pub on Friday and Saturday nights. More arguments and mean-spirited gossip between sunburned moms at the community pool.

Interestingly enough, it was the adults responsible for most of the bad behavior. It was summer break, and most of the teenagers chose to hang out together at the quarry or the Dairy Queen or over in Fallston at the new shopping mall. They seemed to feel safer together, and whether they were a fan of Miss Sharrett's math class or not, there was an unspoken agreement that they had lost one of their own.

It was a strange time to live in Edgewood. The constant police presence made it so, as did the daily newspaper headlines and the local television updates. There was no new information, so the news folk simply chewed up the old information to tiny pieces and spit it back out.

Most days were too hot and humid for an old man like me to spend outside, so I usually sat in my glassed-in back porch and drank iced tea and read my paperbacks. Old oaters, mostly, with the occasional spy novel thrown in for good measure. I used to like mysteries and thrillers, but I was a younger and braver man back then.

On mild evenings, I liked to walk down to the park and sit on one of the benches and watch the town wind down for the day. I'd watch the shop owners flip the OPEN signs to CLOSED (or in most cases now, they simply turned off their glowing red electronic signs). I'd watch the lovers stroll down Main Street hand in hand or arm in arm. The mothers and fathers hurrying after their racing children to stand in line at the Dairy Queen. The tired factory workers shuffling into Loughlin's Pub to drink their paychecks as the streetlights blinked on behind them.

To a stranger, it may have appeared to be a Norman Rockwell-ish scene of small town serenity; the kind of golden-tinted picture that makes city slickers wish they could pull up roots and move to a place like Edgewood. But if you stopped and looked closer, *really* looked, you could see the lovers holding onto each other a little tighter than was necessary; the moms and dads hurrying after their children, not with relaxed smiles on their faces, but expressions of worry and concern; the workers looking more defeated and angry than tired; and what kind of stores closed up for the night at 7 p.m., before it was even dark outside? And then there were the patrol cars making their way up and down Main Street with a much higher regularity than anyone would believe necessary for such a small town.

I saw all this—and more—from my park bench. Most evenings I spent in solitude; a silent observer. But some nights folks would do more than just flip me a wave or mutter a hurried "hello." Sometimes, they'd stop and chat for a moment or two, and once in a great while, someone would even sit down next to me on my bench and chew my ear for a time. Usually it was just Mrs. Brown from the library or Frankie from the barbershop, but it was real nice to have company on those nights.

Company kept me from letting my gaze wander...over to the western outskirts of town...where the water tower stood like some kind of dark sentinel.

Company kept me from thinking too much, and remembering...

I used to sled there as a child. I shot my first squirrel in those woods. I used to play kids' games there at night, the air filled with the laughs and screams of happy children. We used to climb the tower's lower beams and dangle from our legs like toy monkeys on a playground. Kids were kids. Knees got scuffed. Bodies got bruised. The occasional bone got broken. But no one died. Not when we were kids. I never even had an inkling that the place was bad.

Until many years later.

I moved away from Edgewood when I was eighteen years old. Six long, miserable years in the Army, and back home I scurried just as fast as my legs could carry me. My Momma was still alive then, and my baby sister, Amelia, too. I settled back into my old bedroom and took a job at the shoe factory, which was a blessing because that's where I met my Beth Anne, God rest her soul. It would be another four years before I started delivering the mail; that didn't happen until sweet old Ralph Jenkins passed in his sleep, leaving the job opening for me to step in and fill.

Anyway, it was probably a month—a happy month, too, believe me—after I came back home from the Army that I found myself standing at the base of that water tower staring up at its expanse. To be honest, and despite seeing the tower outlined in the sky every damn day on my way to and from work, I had mostly forgotten all about the old thing and the times I had spent there.

But that evening I was on my way to Hanson Creek to try my luck for catfish when I stumbled upon it. I stopped and glanced up, and then I slowly turned and looked around me at the woods and the wild bramble—and the tiny hairs on the back of my neck went all tingly. I've read about that kind of thing happening in countless paperbacks, but I never believed it until that night.

I spun in a slow circle, looking all around, suddenly sure that someone— or something—was hiding there, watching me. I started to hurry away, but then something else stopped me. I stood there, trying to figure it out: was there a smell? was the light somehow different? why was it so quiet all of a sudden? where were the damn birds?

And then it struck me—there was something wrong with the air. I know how that sounds, but I swear to you it's true. There was a thinness to it, almost like being two places at once, like there was another world underneath this one.

I stood there and I swear on my Momma's family bible that I could almost see glimpses of movement in the shadows; that I could hear whispered snatches of words in the empty air right beside me.

I thought of the Ray Bradbury stories I loved so much as a young man, tales of faraway worlds and the mysteries that existed right next door to all of us. It could have been a magical experience…

…but this was different.

I realized that I was frightened.

This was a bad place, and I had just had my first real glimpse of it.

I remembered all this sitting there in the park at dusk, but I didn't want to. Lord, no, I didn't.

I have seen things in my lifetime.

And I have done things.

6

REVEREND PARKER NEVER made it to the church last night to give Evening Mass. There aren't a lot of secrets in a small town, so most people knew that Reverend Parker was a drinker. He would occasionally be a few minutes late to Mass or Wednesday night bingo, and on rarer occasions you might even catch a whiff of whiskey on his breath when he passed you on the street—but he had never missed Mass before.

Still, most of his parishioners weren't overly concerned. Sure, that old bitty Clara Lotz was put off by his absence and told everyone within earshot exactly that; she had better things to do than wait around for someone who didn't even have the decency to show up to do their job. And poor Hannah Pinborough was visibly worried that she might go to hell without her usual Thursday night worship. But most folks just shrugged their shoulders and went on their merry way.

If it weren't for Sophie Connolly, the church secretary, and a renowned worry-wart, the police probably wouldn't have been notified until long into the next day. Instead, after repeated calls with no answer, Sophie drove to the Reverend's house, used her key to open the front door, and upon finding the house empty, called the police to report the Reverend missing.

She happened to glance at the kitchen clock when she hung up the phone and noticed that the time was 7:13 p.m.

According to official reports, the police discovered the Reverend's body at 7:29 p.m.

They had obviously wasted little time before searching the woods surrounding the old water tower—as if they expected to find something there.

And they did.

Reverend Parker was tied spread-eagle to the four foundation posts of the old water tower with four lengths of thick robe. His eyes and mouth were open obscenely wide, a smudge of dried blood crusted his nostrils, and there was severe bruising on his neck. He was still dressed in his preaching clothes, but the gold crucifix he always wore was nowhere to be found. His Bible lay on his chest.

The press had a field day. *Why hadn't the water tower been staked out? Why were there no leads? Was it a serial killer? Why in a place like Edgewood? If the Reverend wasn't safe, who was?*

Stores started closing their doors even earlier. The police and town council were said to be considering a curfew. The Dairy Queen laid off two of the summer help because there weren't enough hours to keep them working. A front page editorial in the newspaper called for the Sheriff's firing.

In the end, the town council called for a Town Meeting on Friday night "to clear the air and inform the townspeople of the appropriate measures which were being taken." Those were the mayor's word, not mine, let me tell you.

Friday night was almost a week away, and most folks weren't buying the "appropriate measures" story. They knew the Sheriff was just trying to buy some time, and who could blame him?

Something very wrong was going on in our town.

Something very bad.

I thought I had a good idea what it was, but there was no one I could tell.

There was no one who would believe me.

7

I TOLD YOU before...I've seen and done things.

Things I'm not proud of, nor fully understand.

I thought I'd forgotten most of it; that the passing years and the burning shame and guilt had erased it from my memory, leaving me a simple old man living out the rest of my days in the town that gave birth to me.

I kept to myself all these years, read my books, minded my business, prayed every night. I tried to be a good person and live a good life. I didn't dare pray for redemption, only peace.

I knew I wasn't that man anymore.

That man who had been infected by whatever evil dwelled in that miserable stretch of land beneath that old damn tower.

That man who had been cursed to hear its calling...and proved too weak to ignore it.

That man who had not only heard its calling, but *listened* to it...

Finally luring a stranger there under the pretense of liquid and carnal sins—only to bludgeon her soft skull until it cracked like an egg from my Momma's coop. I buried her that night in the soft, dark soil behind the tower and went home to my own bed.

Only to awaken and complete this horrible act again...and again... and again.

But not without remorse; not without judgment.

I dreamed many nights of killing myself. Or leaving this town and never coming back. I even considered turning myself in to the police. Once, I went so far as to write my own confession, but I burned it to ashes before I could find the courage or conviction.

I realized that I didn't control my own thoughts anymore than I did my own actions.

These thoughts—and my soul—belonged to someone else. *Something* else.

Until my Beth Anne somehow saved me.

I did not—could not—confess my sins to her, but she knew I was struggling; she somehow knew I was in a battle for my soul.

I don't know why my prayers were suddenly answered or why the voices suddenly vanished. I can only believe it was the immense goodness in my wife's heart and her undying faith in her Lord and in me that was responsible. Beth Anne led me back to God and saved me; she saved my very soul. I have no other explanation.

I only know that the things I saw standing there in the *thin* air surrounding that wretched old tower were not of this world; not of any world that contained even a sliver of goodness.

It was an evil, *hungry* place.

In the years that followed, I prayed more than ever before and did my research. I found no record of a slave house or any other building having existed atop that hill. Two men did die during construction of the water tower, and a third worker was killed during an argument with another worker. There were also many credible reports of animal carcasses being found on the property. Not surprisingly, most of the devil worshipping stories turned out to be nothing but rumors and campfire stories; nothing was substantiated.

I believe now it is the ground itself that is *wrong*. It acts as some sort of mysterious conduit, perhaps even a portal or a doorway to another world or dimension. I believe it allows whatever it is that dwells in that other world to control its chosen one in this world. Why it demands blood? I do not know. The tower itself remains another mystery to me. Does it act as a sort of lure to attract people there, so there are higher numbers to choose from? If so, why was I selected? What did it sense inside me?

I don't know these answers—and that is a blessing.

8

CAN YOU GUESS now how this story will end?

There will be another body soon, of course.

And they will find it sprawled there beneath that stupid old water tower.

I see the tower silhouetted against the western sky most mornings. I watch the setting sun paint it a golden shade of orange most evenings. But I haven't placed a single foot in its shadow for close to four decades.

Someone else has been chosen; I know that now.

Stranger or friend, I do not know, nor do I wish to.

I pray myself to sleep every night.

I pray for the lost soul of the chosen one.

I pray for the lost soul of this town.

And I pray for the deceased.

But most of all, I pray that I don't wake up one morning and feel the urge to slip on my walking boots and pick up my cane and make the long walk up that hill again.

(This campfire story, for Jimmy Cavanaugh)

BROTHERS

1

WHEN I ROLLED INTO the precinct just before eleven that humid August night, I saw my brother Michael walking out the west door.

I'd been able to get him on the force seven years ago, despite a still ongoing hiring freeze, and he was generally doing well. It didn't hurt that at the time I'd just received an award for stopping a man who'd just killed three people in a convenience store. I'd chased him in my car, warning him in the dark alley to stop running. He had turned around and put three bullets in my windshield. I ran him over and killed him.

I'd asked the commander a few times before about hiring Michael. He knew about Michael's past and problems. He'd always said, "Let me think about it."

Since joining the department, Michael had become a dutiful cop. On other matters, which he insisted weren't my business, he wasn't doing well at all.

He worked the same shift I did but he was already in civvies, a crisp white short-sleeved shirt, dark slacks, and a brisk, slightly wood-scented cologne.

He must have been lost in his own thoughts, because he almost walked right into me.

"Hey," he said, looking up. "Didn't see you."

"I wanted to apologize for the other night."

He grinned the grin that had won him a hundred hearts. My little brother got the family's blonde good looks. I got the family's work ethic. Or, as our mother always put it, "Little Mike got the looks, but Chet got the maturity." In her sweet maternal way, she tried to pretend that both attributes were equal. Maturity, in case you hadn't noticed, has yet to get even one female into a bed.

He clapped me on the arm. "Hell, Chet, we're brothers. You were just looking out for me the way you have since Mom died."

When I was sixteen and Chet was twelve, Mom drowned in the YMCA pool after suffering a stroke. Freak accident. The news reports called it that, the Y called it that, the coroner called it that, the priest at the burial site called it that, everybody at the wake called it that. Even fourteen years later I wince when I hear that term.

Dad took over. Or tried. But he'd always been a better cop than a father. It was from his side of the family that the blonde good looks came. For twenty-one years of marriage, Mom had been able to pretend that all the nights Dad spent carousing with other cops were spent bowling and playing nickel-dime poker. The only time I'd ever heard them argue about those nights was when a drunk lady called at two a.m. and demanded to talk to my dad. Bowling alleys don't make those kind of calls.

Other cops, male and female, walked around us now, goodnights and goodbyes on the air thick as fireflies.

"I'm not mad, Chet. I just want to run my own life. You don't need to play dad anymore."

And I had been his dad for five years. Made sure he got a B average, made sure he wasn't into drugs or alcohol, made sure he wasn't hanging around with the wrong boys, made sure he honored the curfew hours I set for him.

Dad spent more and more time away from the house. He got himself what he called a "woman friend" and half-ass moved in with her. One night when he was home and puke-drunk, I heard him sobbing—literally, sobbing—in the bedroom he'd shared with Mom all those years. I went in and dragged him to the bathroom and got him cleaned up and then

ripped the covers with the vomit on it off and got him settled in. He grabbed my hand and gripped it hard, the way he used to. He didn't seem to realize that these days my grip was a lot harder than his. Before he passed out, he said: "You gotta watch Michael. He's gonna turn out just like me. I was such a shitty husband to your poor mother, Chet." He started sobbing again. He wouldn't let go of my hand. "I'm goin' to hell, Chet, the way I treated that woman, always sneakin' off for some strange broad. You got to know that I loved her. She was the only woman I ever truly loved. Those bitches I ran around with didn't mean nothing to me. They really didn't."

MICHAEL LOWERED HIS voice and said, "It's just this little thing I'm having on the side is all. It'll wear itself out."

"That's what you said four months ago."

His face hardened. His tactic was to be amiable, kid you away from serious talk. When that didn't work, he coasted for awhile on irritation that would soon become real anger if he wasn't careful. "Look, I admit I screwed up my life back when I first left home. I gambled, I did some drugs, I married the wrong woman, I couldn't hold a job—and I let you take over my life the same way you did when I was a kid. And that really helped, Chet. And I'm grateful for it. I mean, how could I not be? You found my second wife for me, you got me on the force, and you managed to find a bank that would give me a mortgage even with *my* credit rating."

He put both of his hands on my shoulders. He was three inches taller than I was. "I owe you everything, Chet. Everything. But this time—" He shook his head. Then he shot me the Michael grin again. "This time it isn't any of your business. All right? I know what I'm doing? I'm not going to hurt Laura or the kids. That I promise. But I'm in this thing and I just have to play it out is all." His hands shook my shoulders with mock fondness—mock because he was sick of me trying to drag him away from the affair he was having. The affair that had put him right back into gambling, drinking too much, even getting into a few fights. Fights can get you kicked off the force.

He took his hands down. "So can we leave it like that, Chet? Please? I'll handle it, and we'll get together at Jen's birthday party a couple weeks from now and everything'll be cool. All right?"

He walked away before I could say anything and got in his car. I hadn't known until that moment that he'd bought himself a new Pontiac GTO. I didn't know any other uniformed officer who could afford a new GTO and have any money left over for the wife and kids.

I stood there and watched him lay rubber out of the lot and suddenly remembered what he'd forced me to do the summer he'd turned sixteen…

LOCALLY, THE PLACE was just known as the Pits. It was a sandy area along a stretch of river. Nothing fancy. Generations of high school boys had driven girls out there to get them drunk and hopefully not pregnant. The Pits were eleven miles out of town. A farm house sat on the top of the hill that looked down on the beach area.

I had a pretty bad hangover that Sunday morning when Dad came down to the breakfast table bearing the newspaper and his reading glasses.

Michael and I were finishing our breakfast—cold cereal and orange juice was the usual serving; even idiots could put cold cereal and juice together—when Dad said, "Either of you boys at the Sand Pits last night?"

I shook my aching head. I'd been on a double date in town.

Michael, whose hangover had left him pale and sweaty, cleared his throat and said, "I was for a little while."

"You there when the fire started?"

"What fire?"

I couldn't tell exactly why but the way Michael spoke those two words… I knew something was wrong.

But apparently Dad didn't pick up on it. He went over to the coffee I'd made with the help of an automatic machine. "The people who own the farm up there are accusing your little friend Jeff Cosgrove of setting it."

"Jeff?" I said. "No way. He's one of the nicest kids in town."

"They found him about a hundred yards from the fire and about six or seven feet from a little red gas can that had only a little bit left in it. He was passed out drunk."

Dad looked at Michael. "He's your friend. Did you see him out there last night?"

Michael had been studying the words on the back of the cereal box with a zeal he never visited upon his text books. He looked up as if dazed.

"Uh, yeah. Early, I mean. I mean he rode out there with me, but I didn't see him after awhile. And then Jenny and I left kinda early."

"Well, he's sure as hell in some trouble. The little Stinson girl kept her pony in that barn. Fire killed the pony and destroyed the barn by the time the county boys could get there." He walked over and sat down at the table. "The Stinsons have trouble all summer long with teenagers. I'd just as soon you not go out there."

Yeah," Michael smiled at me. "I'm pretty sure you told us that before, Dad. About six or seven million times."

"This time I mean it, Michael," he said as he fixed up his own cold cereal. "I'm pretty sure the Chief'll ask County to start patrolling out there every night now. And that means a lot of your buddies're gonna get busted for drinking and driving."

This was the point where Michael would usually protest. I didn't always go along with all of Dad's rules and protested at times myself. But given what had happened to the Stinsons last night I knew this was time to keep quiet.

But Michael *never* kept quiet. And cutting off access to the Pit was serious. He should have been erupting from the table and shouting at Dad. He was out there at least two or three times a week with different girls now that he had his driver's license. He'd already come to me twice this summer, terrified that a couple of the girls might be pregnant.

Instead, Michael made a show of looking up at the kitchen clock. He stood up and stretched.

"I've got a date this afternoon. I better start cleaning up my car. Needs a wash for one thing." He was obsessive about his '79 Chevy. It was old to everybody but Michael. I didn't know diddly shit about cars but he sure did. Too bad he didn't take his romantic relationships as seriously.

I sensed he was hurrying out to the garage for another reason this particular morning, so I followed him.

Dad was so engrossed in his newspaper by now, I doubt he even realized I was gone.

The sunlight made a rainbow of the water Michael was splashing over the red Chevy with a hose.

I walked over to him. "We need to talk."

He faced the car. Wouldn't look at me. "I'm kinda busy right now."

"We need to talk about that fire out at the Stinsons."

"Don't know anything about it."

"Yeah. Right." I tried to see his face. "C'mon, talk to me."

Still not looking at me. "We'll talk later if you want to. But there's no point. I don't know jackshit about that fire."

There was only one way to get his attention. The spigot was ten feet away. I walked over and twisted the knob to off.

Now he faced me. Now he was ready for one of our occasional fist fights. Lots of bloody noses and bloody lips but never any serious damage. But this time I wondered. He tossed the hose away and came at me. He threw a right cross before he was close enough for it to land.

Now it was my turn to charge him. While he continued to try to hit me I grabbed him around the waist and hurled him against the side of the Chevy. He landed hard enough to fall to the driveway on his hands and knees.

I stood over him. He wasn't afraid of me, but he stayed down.

"Tell me what happened, Michael. And none of your usual bullshit. You heard Dad. This is serious shit."

"You mind if I fucking get up?"

He had a way of making even the slightest expression, the slightest movement, the slightest phrase insolent. You put enough time in on the streets as a cop and you learned that there are certain people—usually male but not always—that you just can't break psychologically unless you want to beat them near death, which is something I've never done. They are the Fuck You people. Everything they do and say is calculated to let you know that you are an inferior species.

This was Michael and he put on quite the show getting to his feet. Most of us would look awkward struggling to stand up. Not Michael. No professional dancer could have done it more gracefully. The sneer was in place and so was that look of amused contempt.

"What's your problem, *Dad?* I was out at the Sand Pits, so I *must* have been involved, right? You think I'm crazy enough to burn down a fucking barn?"

"You were crazy enough to break into that store and steal baseball equipment. You were crazy enough to steal a car before you were even old enough to drive. And you were crazy enough to accidentally lock that teacher in his closet."

"You promised you'd never tell anybody."

"I haven't, but maybe I made a mistake. Maybe I *should* have told somebody. Because you're still doing this shit. You really going to let Jeff get blamed for this?"

For one of the few times I'd ever known him, he stumbled when he lied. "Well—well, he did it, didn't he?"

"Bullshit. He's afraid of just about everything. That's why he hangs around you and runs all your errands and takes all your jokes about him. So he can feel cool. He's afraid to fight, and I remember he won't go swimming out at the Pits because he's afraid of the water and he hates to go fast in a car because he's scared he will wreck—so this is the kid who set fire to a barn?"

Michael's composure had returned. "The last time I saw him he was really drunk."

"Making it real easy for you to make it look like he did it."

I don't know where Michael bought all his smirks but it was a store with an inexhaustible supply. "You tell Dad all this and he won't believe a word of it. And you know it. Which is why you won't tell him."

"You don't have a record, Michael. If you admit what you did, Dad'll pay for the barn and the horse and you won't have to do any time."

Michael shrugged. "Same for Jeff when he goes to court. And his old man's got a lot more money than Dad, that's for sure."

He walked over and turned on the hose again. "Besides, you can't prove a fucking thing. So like I said, I've got a date and I need to wash my car. But thanks for the lecture. You know how serious I take them."

The whole thing wound up pretty much as Michael predicted. Mister Cosgrove paid for the barn and the horse, and Jeff got probation and no jail time. There was a lot more public outrage over the horse than there was the ancient barn. And Jeff went from the nicest kid in town to an outcast.

He became a target at school and some of my friends with younger brothers and sisters told me Michael cut him loose as well.

Apparently, Jeff had been so drunk he'd just accepted the *fact* that he was guilty as charged. They also said Jeff had started to drink heavily. He was a small kid and got drunk pretty easily. He found himself getting kicked out of the few parties he was invited to, and then he started hanging out with the dopers and the reform school crowd.

As always, Michael and I got past the whole thing in the way we usually did. He apologized finally, although he still insisted on his complete innocence. For Senior year he even got serious about his studies. He ended up with a B+ average. And he even started listening more to me. It was funny but after a few months the only thing I thought about when the barn incident was mentioned was not poor Jeff but that poor pony.

That is until the night that Dad called from the station and told us that a drunken Jeff had wrapped his car around a telephone pole out on the old river road, a deadly stretch that claimed at least one victim a summer. Dead on impact, Dad said.

There was no great mourning in the school community. Jeff had disgraced himself many, many times after his court appearance. There were even a few outraged letters in the papers about how he'd killed that pony.

Dad said he felt bad for Jeff's parents and ordered Michael and I to attend the funeral. I assumed Michael and I would go together but he told me he'd just see me there.

I quickly found out why. He used the occasion to debut his latest and maybe most elegant girlfriend. I saw it as a kind of fuck you. *You want to get all teary and hokey about poor dumb Jeff...well, how about this girl? She's alive and so am I. Jeff was a moron anyway.*

The priest gave a terrible sermon. He'd neither known nor cared about Jeff. He kept sermons like this up his ass. File 239.

Afterward, near the church steps, numerous young men came over to Michael for a closer look at the new one in his life.

Dad went over to talk to a few of the older people, so I was standing there alone when Mister Cosgrove, a handsome, proper businessman and community leader came over to me and blasting me with whiskey breath harsh enough to gag me, hissed, "You're the only decent one in the family and you know it."

Then he was choking on his tears. I touched his arm, but his wife and daughter dragged him bitterly away before I could say anything in return.

The next day Michael smiled and told me that the new one had given him the best blow job he'd ever had.

A WEEK AFTER our confrontation at the station, I saw him downtown, standing by that new GTO. I was on duty. He wasn't. He had called in sick.

He was dressed in jeans and a wrinkled t-shirt, and he looked angry.

I pulled my car over and put down the window. He didn't look happy to see me.

"You okay?"

"Why wouldn't I be okay?" No grin this time. He wasn't in the mood for pretending.

"It was just a question, Michael. You don't need to get upset."

"Yeah, well, maybe sometimes I get tired of your—"

His cell phone rang. He waved me off and answered it. "Where the hell are you?"

Then he walked away, wanting his privacy.

I waited a good five minutes for him to hang up and come back.

When he didn't, I drove away and went back to work.

THERE WERE SIX of us that September night at Jen's birthday party. Me and Jen. Michael and his wife, Laura. And Jen's best friend, Erin, and her doctor husband, Aaron. The kids were at a sitter across the street.

Jen was delighted with the whole affair, and it made me happy to watch her smile and listen to her laughter. She must have thanked me a dozen times before dinner was served.

I grilled steaks outside on the lawn and helped Laura make a great big salad at the island in the kitchen. We ate out back on the deck and drank wine while fireflies danced around us. They would be gone in another week or so, it was already Autumn chilly, but tonight they reminded us of how it felt to be young again.

Laura was pretty quiet while we fixed the salad and again during dinner, but that wasn't unusual for her. Otherwise, she seemed fine.

Michael seemed better than fine. He was relaxed and charming, and he surprised Jen with a signed first edition of her favorite novel. She squealed with joy when she opened it and hugged him.

I was relieved and grateful until I caught him whispering on his cell phone in the bathroom upstairs.

I was standing outside the bathroom door when he came out. I knew who he had been talking to, and he knew I knew.

Before I could say a word: "I don't want to hear it. I'm trying to end it, Chet."

"Try harder," I said, but he was already heading downstairs and back to the party.

THE CALL CAME about a month later. Laura.

"I'm sure you're watching the football game," she said. I'd met her years ago at a grade school. I had been there to tell the kids about being a policeman. Laura was a slender, dark-haired young woman with a very pretty face spoiled only by a quick, nervous smile that revealed the stress she always seemed to feel. This was at the time when Michael had neared the end of his problems—no job, into some gamblers for several thousand dollars, and drinking way more than he should have been. Laura herself was just getting through a divorce, a husband who'd run around on her. Neither of them wanted to meet each other, but I stage-mothered the relationship until it found its own way.

"Actually, no. Joan's volunteering at the hospital tonight, so I'm here with the kids. I just cattle-prodded them into bed, in fact."

A strained laugh. "They're just like ours. They hate going to bed." Then: "Could we talk a little, Chet?"

"Sure. That's what brothers-in-law are for."

So this was to be the night. I knew that it would happen and that when it happened a whole lot of things would change. I thought of what Dad had told me the night he'd drunkenly admitted he'd been such a terrible husband and that I was to keep Michael from repeating Dad's mistakes. I wondered how much Laura knew. I was about to find out.

"I don't think Michael loves me anymore."

"Oh, come on. You know better than that."

"He used to come straight home after work. He'd only hang out at that cop bar once a week. But now—three or four nights a week he doesn't get home until three in the morning. And he hasn't had much to drink. That's what makes me suspicious."

"I guess I'm not following you."

"He always tells me he's just at the bar with the boys. Well, first of all, the bar closes at two, and it's only about a mile away. It sure doesn't take him that long to drive home. But even worse than that—he's never drunk."

"Well, that's a good thing, isn't it, that he's cut back on his drinking?" I tried to put a smile into it.

"But I know him well enough that if he was at that bar, he'd be drunk when he came home." Cop wives always say "that bar" when referring to the Golden Chalice. They hate it because they know all about the cop groupies who hang out there.

She said, "Would you talk to him, Chet?"

"I'd be happy to. But you know how he resents me sometimes."

"You know how I feel about that. And I've told him so. You were in a situation where you were forced to be his father. You had to give up a lot of things other boys your age got to do—and all for his sake. I always tell him that."

"I appreciate it, Laura. But that doesn't mean he'll be any happier if I butt into your marriage."

A long pause: "Then how about a little spying?"

"Spying?"

"Just seeing what he's up to after your shift ends. Where he goes and things like that." This time her laugh was real but sad. "I know this is awful. I'd sure resent it if somebody spied on me. But our marriage—it hasn't been good for quite a while."

For a moment I was back in the parking lot and Michael was explaining to me, as if I was slightly retarded, how everything was under control. He had his mistress and he had his family, and according to him, he was doing well by both of them.

"Maybe I shouldn't have called, Chet. I'm just so—"

She started crying. I let her get through the worst of it. Michael was doing it all over again. He'd lost a first wife who'd been every bit the player he was. But this woman was different. Only through her had he finally put his life on track. And now he was turning away from her.

"I'm sorry, Chet," when the tears became sniffles. "I just feel so isolated, I guess. I'm sorry I called."

"Tell you what. I'm going to do a little poking around. I'll be back to you in a day or so."

"I'm sorry I'm so needy, Chet."

"I'm needy, too. I want to find out what's going on. We've both got a stake in this, Laura, believe me." I made a joke of it before hanging up: "I didn't spend all those years raising him so he'd act this way."

2

THREE O'CLOCK A.M. Sitting in my boxers. Staring at the glow of the guttering fire we'd set to chase the autumn cold away.

I heard Jen coming down the stairs, her slippers flapping with each step. When she reached the living room, I said, "Leave the lights off, please."

She came over, the hem of her long cotton robe whispering across the hardwood floor. She sat on her haunches next to my armchair. Bare branches scraped the windows in the whistling wind. Shadow goblins played on the walls.

"So what seems to be troubling our baby boy tonight?"

"Sometimes I *wish* I was a baby boy." Then: "Michael. Of course."

She touched my wide coarse hand with her long smooth one. "Now I'm going out to the kitchen and get that .45 you taught me how to shoot. And then I'm going to come back and kill one of us. And at this point I really don't care which one of us it is. Because if I ever hear that you're brooding about him again—"

"He's my brother."

"Oh, yes, and you swore to your father you'd raise him right."

"Don't make fun of that. I gave him my word."

"Yes, and that was the right thing to do. When Michael was still a boy. But he's almost thirty now. He has a wife and two children. You got him a job, you found him a wife, and you've been playing daddy to him right straight through. It's not right, honey. Or normal."

For some reason that irritated me. Normal. What was abnormal about taking care of your kid brother?

"If I don't take care of him, who will?"

"Oh, let's see—maybe himself. He's an adult, Chet. At least that's what it says on his driver's license. You have your own family and your own problems you need to take care of. You can't keep spending all your time on him. It's unnatural."

Abnormal. Unnatural.

"You know how selfish that sounds?"

"Selfish? What're you talking about?"

"That I shouldn't worry about my own little brother?"

"Worry, fine. But try to turn his life around—no way." Her hand pulled free from mine. She used it as a lever on the arm of the chair to pull herself up. "You know I don't like him very much. But sometimes I can't help myself—I feel sorry for him, the way you're always putting yourself in his business. I understand why he resents you, Chet. I really do."

And then the line I hated most where my little brother was concerned: "You could always see the police shrink. I really think it's something you should talk through. We've been arguing about this since we first started dating. And it never seems to get any better."

"And you never stop saying that I should see the police shrink."

She was all done with banter. Tears trembled in her voice. "You ever think that's because I love you? You ever think how tired I am of all this? And I meant what I said about Michael. I feel sorry for him sometimes. I really do. But if he's going to screw up his life, that's his business."

"If it's his business, why did Laura call me today and tell me she's worried about their marriage?"

"Laura called you?"

"That's right. So if I'm butting in, it's because she asked me to."

"Oh, great," Jen said. "Now we've got her pulling you into their lives. This whole thing is insane." She started to walk back to the stairs. "I'm going to sleep on the couch in the TV room. You need your sleep, so you take the bed."

I started to object but she stopped me.

"I'm too tired to argue about it, Chet. I'm taking the couch. I'll grab a blanket from the closet upstairs." Six steps up the staircase, she said, in a gentler tone, "I'll see you in the morning."

TWENTY MINUTES LATER, I hugged my pillow in bed and tried not to think about Jen on the couch downstairs.

And I tried not to hear her voice inside my head: *Abnormal. Unnatural.*

I loved her more than anything in this world, but she was wrong. Michael was my brother.

It took a long time, but I finally fell asleep—and dreamed about Michael.

We were younger, in our twenties, and I was picking him up from his first stint at rehab.

I signed him out at a long polished table in a glass enclosed conference room and we walked out together into a bright spring morning.

Michael was grinning that million dollar grin of his and talking my ear off about how much he had learned and how he was going to do this and how he was going to do that and never ever make the same mistakes again, what the hell had he been thinking in the first place doing the things he had done.

I put his suitcase in the trunk of the car and we got in and drove away.

He put his window down and leaned his head out into the wind and closed his eyes. Then he stuck his arm out the window and surfed the wind with his palm, something he had always done as a little boy.

I tightened my grip on the steering wheel and felt sudden tears streaming down my cheeks.

It was a good dream.

3

I DIDN'T EVEN know her name, my brother's mistress.

I had never asked because I didn't want to know, and I'm not sure Michael would have told me anyway.

I had seen her once, just a glimpse, as they drove away from a liquor store I happened to be passing. All blonde and shiny, even at a distance. That was months ago.

Michael didn't know that, and I had never mentioned it.

I asked Kathi Reynolds to do me a favor the next morning and pull Michael's cell phone record. Kathi is a very large and very beautiful black single mom who has become a vital part of our department. If the information you need can be found somewhere online, no matter how difficult the task, she can find it. Kathi thinks she owes me because I once helped her oldest boy out of some trouble at his high school. But it was nothing, really.

She likes to believe otherwise and nothing I say can change her mind. She's stubborn and proud of it. She also likes to call me "boss."

She dropped the file on my desk no more than an hour after I asked for it, and I thanked her for her discretion.

She shooed my thanks away and said, "Anything for you, boss, you know that."

And then she was gone, and I was alone with the file and my thoughts.

I SPENT THE next few days finding out what I could about Jane Cameron and found nothing I liked.

You couldn't call her rich, I suppose, but she did have the remains of a large inheritance to rely on if she needed it for her business, which was public relations. You would have to call her beautiful. College girl beautiful, though she was mid-thirties—fine, clean features; gym-trim body; and a radiant blonde presence in any environment. A ten-year-old daughter conveniently locked away at a boarding school in Vermont. Two husbands, several lovers, at least three of whom had been married at the time. A few very public and very angry scenes with angry wives.

As I sat at my computer looking at her photos, I realized what my little brother was living out here. He'd met her the night a jilted lover of hers had assaulted her in the lobby of her expensive condo. Michael and his partner were the first on the scene. It probably hadn't taken long for Michael to find himself in the sort of bad movie he used to star in frequently. Married cop intrigued by fashionable, vulnerable beauty, cheats on family, honor, good sense.

So, for three nights, I followed him. Twice he left work to meet her at the bar across the street from her condo, the bar where all the successful young lawyers in town like to do their cheating. An hour of drinks there and back across the street to her condo. The third night, still in uniform, he went straight home. In my talk with Laura, she'd said this was his standard pattern. Somehow, she wasn't convinced any of this had to do with a woman. I guess she just couldn't face what was really going on.

One night I took my camera and got some good snaps of them making out in the parking lot of a café.

I put them in a manila envelope and set them in the front seat of his new Pontiac.

The next night, when I got off shift, I found them sitting on the front seat of my own car.

He came over, still in uniform, and slid into the shotgun seat.

"You really think I wouldn't figure out you were behind this bullshit?"

"I wanted you to know, Michael. If you hadn't figured it out, I would've told you."

"You're insane, you know that? Clinically, I mean. Off your damned rocker."

"You know anything about her, Michael?"

"Sure I know about her. She's a very beautiful and successful woman."

"And she has a lot of enemies."

"That's because she's so successful."

"That's because she's slept with so many important men around town."

"People change."

I couldn't help it. I laughed.

"In Japan they get their hymens sewn back in for the wedding. She thinking of doing that, is she?"

"Be careful here, man. You may still be able to take me but I can put a lot of hurt on you."

I stared straight ahead. Sighed.

"So now it's supposed to be serious, Michael?"

"Isn't 'supposed to be.' Is."

"I thought it was going to end."

Now it was Michael who stared straight ahead and sighed.

"I'm not sure what to do, Chet."

"Take out that picture of your kids in your billfold and look at it for awhile. That'll tell you what to do."

Silence for a time.

"You know how good a woman you've got in that wife of yours, Michael."

"Of course I know."

"And you treat her like this, anyway?"

"We're different is all, Chet. You and me, I mean. You're satisfied to sit home and watch TV and I want—"

"Excitement."

"Not exactly. Not the way you mean. Not running around and getting all boozed up and hanging out in clubs. It's just—I'm starting to feel old, Chet. I'm young. But when I met Jane I realized that I'd mentally become an old man. She didn't make me feel young exactly, but I didn't feel old anymore, either. I'm a better cop now because of her. I know that sounds funny but it isn't. She really thinks it's true. I'm even thinking about taking the test for detective."

"Laura wanted you to do that two years ago."

"Yeah, but with Laura it was different. It was just because I'd make more money. But with Jane being a detective isn't just about that, it's because being a detective is—"

"Cool."

"God, Chet, you don't understand any of this."

"I don't think you do, either. You're getting a nice piece of ass on the sly and you think it's worth destroying your family for."

"I'm going to go now. I can't sit here and let you lay all this on me. Remember when I called you the Pope once? Well, you haven't changed.

You think you can run my life from this big ass throne you sit on. But it doesn't work that way anymore, Michael. Maybe I am screwing up my life. I'm not stupid. I know what I'm doing is wrong. But right now I can't pull myself out of it. But you playing Pope isn't helping. You can't order me around anymore, Michael."

He opened the car door.

"One more thing. It's my place to tell Laura. Not yours. So until I tell her about this, don't say anything to her. All right?"

I just stared at my big hands on the steering wheel.

"All right, Chet?" The anger coming back into his voice.

I could barely whisper. "All right, Michael."

THE PHONE RANG that night as I was walking up the stairs to bed.

I hesitated, thinking: *what if it's Laura? What if Michael told her tonight?*

I heard the squeak of bedsprings down the hallway as Jen moved over to my side of the bed to check the caller ID.

The phone stopped ringing just as I walked into the bedroom.

I braced myself for an argument. "Late for a phone call…"

"Just Erin. I'll call her back tomorrow."

I nodded and went into the bathroom and brushed my teeth and filled up a glass with water.

I set the glass on my night table and settled into my side of the bed.

Jen turned the page of her book with one hand and reached over and took my hand with the other.

I wanted to check the caller ID myself, make sure it was really Erin. I wasn't sure I believed her. The very idea shocked me.

Abnormal. Unnatural.

Jen finished her chapter, turned off the light and was snoring within minutes.

I leaned over in the dark and looked at the caller ID screen. *Erin Matthews.*

It took me a long time to find sleep.

4

THE NEXT DAY, I started following Jane Cameron. I wanted to see where the best place was to have the conversation she was forcing on me.

Didn't take me long to figure out that there would be no opportunity to confront her during the day. She was all forward motion. She walked fast and drove fast. Meetings all over town with her various important clients. I couldn't afford to brace her in any sort of public way.

Nothing to stop me from wearing my uniform on my night off, though.

I had to make sure she was alone. I sat in my car across the street from her fifteen-story condo. She swept her Jag—what else?—into the underground parking garage just after nine that night. She was alone.

I pulled in four spaces down from her. I reached the elevator before she did.

In the shadowy light, she wasn't able to see even my faint resemblance to Michael.

"Did something happen here tonight?" she said.

She looked especially fine this evening in a silver suit, her golden hair pulled into a loose chignon.

"Happen?"

"When I saw your uniform, I thought maybe something had happened in the building tonight."

"Oh, no, ma'am. I'm here on my own. I'm just going to see somebody in the building."

She smiled. "Well, I love having a police officer around. Makes me feel safe."

The elevator door opened. We climbed in.

Then she said: "That's funny."

"What is?"

"Why aren't you in the lobby getting checked in by Lenny? He checks everybody in. Even cops."

I had been demoted from police officer to cop. She was smart. She knew there was something wrong with this situation.

I said, "I'll bet you didn't say that to my brother."

"Your brother? What're you talking about?"

A bit of panic—just enough to be gratifying—shone in those azure eyes.

She didn't know it, but she'd already lost control of the situation. It was almost disappointing. I thought she'd be a lot tougher.

AFTER SHE'D BROUGHT us whiskey sours, she sat on the divan across from my chair and said, "I hope you realize that all I have to do is pick up the phone and call my friend the police commissioner and your days as a cop are long gone, sweetie."

"And if that happens, 'sweetie,' then I'll get somebody to help me get a computer file of some of your messes we've had to help you with—especially a certain group of pissed off wives—and I'll download that file straight to a friend of mine who's a reporter at KBST. And I'll do the same thing if you don't agree to break it off with my brother right away."

She smirked. "You're going to blackmail me out of seeing your brother?" She didn't wait for me to answer. "I can't believe you two are brothers. Michael's so handsome and intense and you're so—" She hesitated. "I may as well be upfront with you. You scare me."

"Good. I should scare you. You've got good instincts."

She exhaled harshly. I tried not to notice the way her long sleek legs were stretched out on the divan or the sheer blouse she wore now, having discarded the coat to her suit. She kept a single shoe on a single big toe, dangling there. Like my brother's future.

"You'll dump him someday, anyway."

"I've been dumped, too, you know."

"Any tears go with this story?"

"It's true, you bastard, whether you believe it or not. I was dumped—twice in fact—and I got hurt just like anybody else would. You make me sound like some sort of professional heartbreaker. I have parents I see three times a month and I have a daughter I love very much."

"So much you put her in boarding school."

Her eyes narrowed. She just watched me for a moment, as if she was observing something in nature she'd never seen before. "Michael told me you were like this. So goddamned judgmental. He calls you 'The Pope.'"

"I'm judgmental about women who break up marriages."

She laughed. A harsh sound. "Michael told me you had an affair when you were about his age. Aren't you the hypocrite."

I felt my cheeks burn. "I made up for it. I've never touched a hand to another woman since."

"Mass three times a week? Confession every Saturday? Coach a Little League team? The perfect husband and father."

I finished my drink and set it down. "Thanks for the drink. I'll wait to hear Michael tell me that you've broken it off."

"What if I don't?"

"We've already discussed that."

"You'll ruin me."

I waited until I was on my feet. "I'll sure give it my best shot." I started walking to the door.

"I really do love him. I've never claimed to be anything other than what I am—a selfish, spoiled woman. But this time, with Michael, it's different—I really do love him."

I kept walking.

"I'm pregnant."

I stopped and looked at her.

"I never wanted to be owned by a man or by a child. But with Michael—I stopped taking my birth control. I went to the doctor's last week. I haven't even told Michael yet. I want this child. I want Michael, too. But if I can't have him, at least I'll have his child."

For once, I didn't know what to say. I was trying to make sense of all this. But there was no sense to be made of it, none of it. A little fling, every man did it once in a while. Back when it started it had seemed nothing more than that. But now I was listening to her tell me that she was carrying Michael's baby.

All I could think of was poor Laura and the kids. I walked to the door and stopped with my hand on the knob. I wanted to say something nasty. But then an old man's weariness overcame me. I didn't seem to have any strength left at all. Then words came: "I'll pay for an abortion. And Michael doesn't have to know about it."

She laughed. "You won't believe this, Mr. High and Mighty, but I don't believe in abortion. I may be a slut in your eyes but I'm still a good Catholic girl."

I turned my eyes back to hers and with the last of my strength, I said: "Then walk out of his life. He doesn't have the strength, but you do."

"That's the terrible thing," she said. "I don't have the strength, either."

5

THE NEXT AFTERNOON I tried to find my brother before his shift started. Sometimes he had coffee down the street at a luncheonette. He wasn't there. He wasn't in the precinct locker room, either.

"You didn't happen to see my brother, did you?" I asked Keller, who was spelling the watch commander while he was in Vegas at a police convention. Don't think there hadn't been a lot of jokes about holding a cop convention in Vegas.

"Bad sore throat and fever. Home sick."

"He call in himself?"

He gave me a sharp look.

"No, his wife did. Man, you gotta give the kid some breathing room, Chet. He calls in or Laura calls in. What's the difference?"

"Just curious."

He shook his head and walked on. It was clear that Michael had done a good job with the other cops at the precinct, letting them know that I was always interfering in his life.

Abnormal. Unnatural.

I called, but there was no answer at his house. I didn't leave a message on his machine. If he'd actually told Linda about his affair, this wasn't a hopeful sign. A number of paranoid ideas shook me, the loudest one in my head being the one where the wife, kids off at school, goes insane and kills her unfaithful husband. It happens.

I THOUGHT ABOUT asking Keller if I could take off early. Family emergency. But I knew how that would look.

Instead, I got in my car and did my job. I answered calls for a breaking and entering, a domestic, and a shop-lifting and assault at the big Wal-Mart superstore. I helped a little girl find her lost puppy and put a couple Band-Aids on a crying kid's skinned and bloodied knee. The whole time I was thinking of Michael and Laura. I tried to call three more times. No answer.

As soon as my shift was over, I got in my car and drove over there. A lone lamp lit the house, downstairs, the family room. Michael's car was gone. I went to the front door and knocked.

I could see her through the glass slat in the door. She was curled up in the corner of the couch. She wore a pair of faded pink cotton pajamas. With her short dark hair and sweet face, she could have been a sorority girl. The TV was on but the sound was off and she wasn't watching it anyway. Screen colors flickered across the living room.

I knocked again. This time she looked up. I walked over to the window and waved. She got up off the couch, buttoning the top of her pajama shirt and came to the door.

She let me in but said nothing. She went back to the couch and sat down. "You could've told me. Then this wouldn't have come as such a shock tonight."

I sat down in an armchair across from her. "It would've been just as much of a shock if I'd warned you."

She raised her head, closed her eyes, as if invisible rain was spattering her face. "This is so unreal." She opened her eyes, lowered her head, looked at me. "In case you don't think I got hysterical, I did. There's broken glass all over the kitchen floor. The kids are at my sister's house. I didn't trust myself enough to keep them here tonight."

"Don't do anything nuts."

She shrugged. "I never do anything nuts, Chet. You know that. I'm not dramatic. Or sexy. Or exciting. That's what he said she was. Exciting." Then: "Damn, I wish I had a cigarette."

"No, you don't. You quit five years ago. Keep it that way."

"And all my self-pity."

"You're entitled."

"I just keep thinking about all the people who have it worse than me. And here I am feeling sorry for myself."

"That never works. Believe me, I've been trying it all my life. Just because somebody's crippled or blind or has cancer doesn't help me at all."

She made a face. "We could always have sex."

"You frowned when you said that. Meaning that you know better."

"I have these fantasies that he walks in on me when I'm having sex with somebody and it makes him jealous and then he realizes what a good thing he's lost."

"You're in shock right now."

"That's funny you should say that. That's sort of how I feel. So shocked I don't know what to do with myself. I can't even get drunk. Two drinks and I throw up."

"You have any tranquilizers?"

"I've taken two already. This is the best they can do for me, I guess." Something changed, then. I wasn't sure what. The eyes were no longer vulnerable or sad. They were angry.

"I'm probably just lashing out here, Chet. But I need to say something to you, something I should've said a long time ago."

"Lash away. You'll feel better."

She took a deep breath and said, "This'll probably make you mad."

I was thinking she was going to tear into me for keeping the truth from her.

Instead, she said, "You didn't help my marriage any by constantly being on Michael's back."

Her anger was swift and sure. I was a little shocked, although I guess I shouldn't have been; I'd been told too often in too short a time how I was doing badly by my little brother.

"I don't think that's fair, Laura."

"I just had to say it."

"Did it make you feel better?"

"Maybe. But it made you mad."

"No, it didn't."

She smiled. "You're grinding your jaw muscles and your hands are fists. I'd say those are signs you're pretty pissed off."

"Irritated, maybe. But not pissed off." Then: "I was just trying to help you kids."

"That's just it. We're not kids, Chet. We're grown-ups. But you'd never acknowledge that. You were always checking on him at the precinct and giving him advice on handling his money and telling him who to hang out with and not hang out with and—God, I remember the time when your aunt died and you told him right in front of everybody at the funeral that he shouldn't have worn a tan suit to the wake. But that was the only suit he owned, Chet. And the time you saw our girls playing wiffle ball and you told him you thought they should be playing more feminine games. And when you got on his case about where we went to church, that it was better to go to St. Joe's because that's where the shift commander went. It just never ended, Chet."

I suppose, looking back, that's when it started, this black feeling. And that's the only way I can describe it. It was anger in such volume that I could barely breathe holding it back.

I said, "You ever hear the expression 'No good deed ever goes unpunished.' I used to think that was just a funny line. But it isn't. It's the truth."

"Now who's feeling sorry for himself? We're just talking here, having a conversation."

"Is that what this is, Laura, just a conversation?"

"All I meant was that you need to let him go. I hate that bitch he's in love with but even with them, Chet—you have to let them have their own lives. You can't be his father anymore." She hesitated. "He told me they're going to move away. He said he's giving notice to the commander tomorrow that he'll be leaving."

"Oh," I said, "just great." And the anger made my breathing short again. Gave me a sudden stabbing headache just above my left eye. Made every taut muscle in my body scream for release. "You know how hard I had to work to get him on the force? All the trouble he'd been in, and I had to promise that he'd straightened out and really wanted to be a cop. And now he's throwing it all away."

"It's his choice, Chet. His choice. He's a grown man. Right now I'd like to get that gun of his and empty it into his heart. And then I'd do the same to her. I hurt so much right now I don't know what to do. But it's his choice and you've got to let him make it."

"Right. I get him through high school, studying with him every night so he'll get good grades. And then I get him through a couple of years of college until he starts hanging out with punks. And then I get him on the road to recovery and introduce him to you. And you're everything a man would want in a wife. And he throws it all over for some slut. And I'm supposed to like it."

"You don't have to like it any more than I do, Chet. But you've got to let go now. He's in love with her and he's moving away and there's nothing we can do about it."

I stood up.

"Where're you going?"

"I'm not sure."

"Are you okay?"

I thought about it for a moment.

"No, I'm not. All the things I've done for you two over the years and this is what I get, this is what you say to me."

"I'm sorry, Chet. I didn't mean to chase you away."

I went to the front door, opened it. "You aren't chasing me away, Laura. *I'm* chasing me away."

6

I DIDN'T COUNT the beers. I was careful to stay under control, but that didn't mean I was sober.

A little bar near the old stadium. Dark, anonymous. I found myself salting my beer the way the old man had. He used to take me to the neighborhood tavern with him. Sometimes we played darts or talked football. Those were my favorites times, the few occasions when I got to be alone with my old man. I'd sit on the stool next to him and he'd pop peanuts in his mouth and sprinkle salt in his beer. I always wanted people to know he was a cop because I was so proud of him. But he never wore his uniform when he went drinking. He said it just caused trouble. I'd always wondered what he meant by that. If somebody gave him trouble, couldn't he just shoot him? That was how my eight-year-old mind worked. Nobody could insult cops. They were the good guys.

But I made the mistake he'd avoided. Early on I wore my uniform into a few non-cop bars and paid for it. No fights or anything but a couple hours of vague insults grinding into my ear canal. Everybody, especially drunks, has a good stock of anti-police stories.

I had one more beer than I should have and went out to my car.

And that was when it happened. A lot of it was the rain. It came down in such force—it sounded like hail by then—that it hammered the metal of cars and overflowed gutters within minutes. My wipers started straining after just a few blocks. I wasn't sure where I was going. But I was in a hell of a hurry to get there.

7

YOU CERTAINLY CAN'T call this first degree murder, my lawyer told the press the next day. *It was a terrible accident. A terrible, terrible accident. I doubt the D.A.'s even going to bring charges. You wait and see.*

I can honestly say that I wasn't even aware of where I was after I left the tavern. I just instinctively took the usual way home. I know that might be hard to believe, but it's true. I forgot entirely that I'd be passing by her condo. I just wanted to be home, in my own bed, slipping into darkness.

She could have been anybody. I don't expect you to believe that, but it's true. Wrong time, wrong place. For all of us.

They were coming from the yuppie bar across the street from her condo, covering their heads with newspapers they must have dragged along from inside.

I was driving too fast. The road was wet. I couldn't see.

And there was this person stepping into the beam of my headlights—and I was slamming on the brakes—and then there was this other figure reaching for her, jerking her back from the path of my car but in doing so he himself stumbled and fell into the way of my skidding car and—

DANIEL AHEARN, MY lawyer, says to me, "You wait right here and I'm going to let her have two minutes with you."

"You going to be here, too?"

"Are you crazy? Of course I'm going to be here. But she's been calling and coming up here all day long."

"I'm afraid to see her."

"Chet, listen, what happened was an honest accident, just the way you told me, right?"

He knew better and I knew better. But I had to keep repeating the story so eventually I'd believe it, too.

I'd seen her running out into the street and then I was back in that alley where I ran the killer down that time. All the misery she'd caused. Poor Laura and the kids. And ruining Michael's life after he'd tried so hard to be trustworthy and sober again and—

But then Michael had suddenly pulled her back and tripped in front of my car and by then I couldn't stop and the sound he made when the car hit him—I knew he was dead; I *knew* he was dead.

"So she's going to come in here and go all hysterical on you and accuse you of being a murderer and tell you you're going to the gas chamber. But you're going to do what?"

"I'm just going to sit here and calmly tell her that I'm sorry. That it really was an accident. That it was just this terrible coincidence that I happened to be driving by that night."

"And that's when I say, 'I hate to put it this way, Jane, but his loss is as big as yours, wouldn't you say? He accidentally killed his own brother.' So, you ready?"

I felt like I might get sick. "I'm ready."

"Remember, just keep taking a lot of good long breaths to keep yourself cool and steady."

I took a good long breath.

"That's right," he said, "just like that."

He patted me on the shoulder and then he went through the door to the reception area.

She was already screaming and sobbing when he brought her in.

She stood in front of me like an interrogator. She didn't talk. Between sobs, she shouted. "You think you're going to get away with this, don't you? Well, you're not. Not when the D.A. gets all the witnesses lined up. Even his wife's going to testify against you, you know that, Chet? Do you know that? As much as she hates me, she's going to testify against you?"

And that was when she slapped me. I couldn't tell if it was skill or luck but I sure felt it.

She touched her stomach. "Thanks to you, your brother's baby won't have a father. Maybe you think about that when you're in prison, Chet. His poor little kid without a father." She started crying again. "This was supposed to be so good, so happy for the three of us. We were gonna be a family. But you couldn't let that happen, could you, Chet? You had to make sure your little brother did just what *you* wanted him to, didn't you? So you killed him! Your own brother! You killed him!"

Abnormal. Unnatural.

She spat at me. It landed on my nose and immediately dripped down to my upper lip. My lawyer stepped in then and started dragging her to the door. She was still screaming in the outer office. I imagine the wealthy clients sitting in the reception room were wondering what was going on.

When he came back and closed the door, he said, "That is one nasty bitch."

"She said my sister-in-law's going to testify against me."

He waved me off, but I saw hesitation on his face. "She doesn't know what she's talking about, Chet. You think Laura wants her kids to hear about what kind of man your brother was?"

My brother.

"How about bond?"

"Just what I predicted. Judge said no bond. You're on your own recognizance. I brought along all your awards and commendations. Nobody thinks you ran Michael down on purpose. It was raining and dark and he just stepped too far out into the street. His blood alcohol was way over the limit. I'm not arrogant enough to call this a slam dunk. No serious criminal case is. But I can practically guarantee you you'll never see any prison. You'll be free."

That was the word that was supposed to make me feel better. *Free.* I kept thinking about it all the way home and all the way through our quiet dinner and even when we were in bed and when I couldn't respond to Jen as I usually do.

Free. But I knew better than that now, didn't I?

(written with Ed Gorman)

CEMETERY DANCE

ELLIOTT FOSSE, AGE THIRTY-THREE, small-town accountant. Waiting alone. Dead of winter. After midnight. The deserted gravel parking lot outside of Winchester County Cemetery.

Elliott stared out the truck window at the frozen darkness. His thoughts raced back to the handwritten note in his pants pocket. He reached down and squeezed the denim. The pants were new—bought for work not a week ago and still stiff to the touch—but Elliott could feel the reassuring crinkle of paper inside the pocket.

While the woman on the radio droned on about a snow warning for the entire eastern sector of the state, storm winds rumbled outside, buffeting the truck. Elliott's breath escaped in visible puffs and, despite the lack of heat in the truck, he wiped beads of moisture from his face. With the same hand, he snatched a clear pint bottle from the top of the dash and guzzled, tilting it upward long after it ran dry. He tossed the bottle on the seat next to him—where it clinked against two others—and reached for the door handle.

The wind grabbed him, lashing at his exposed face, and immediately the sweat on his cheeks frosted over. He quickly pulled the flashlight from his pocket and straightened his jacket collar, shielding his neck. The night sky was starless, enveloping the cemetery like a huge, black circus tent. His bare hands shook uncontrollably, the flashlight beam fluttering over the hard ground. Somewhere, almost muffled by the whine of the wind, he heard a distant clanking—a dull sound echoing across the grounds. He hesitated, tried to recognize the source, but failed.

Snow coming soon, he thought, gazing upward.

He touched a hand to the lopsided weight in his coat pocket and slowly climbed the cracked steps leading to the monument gate. During visiting hours, the gate marked the cemetery's main entrance and was always guarded by a groundskeeper, a short, roundish fellow with a bright red beard. But, at one in the morning, the grounds were long closed and abandoned.

Elliott's legs ached with every step. The liquor in his system was no match for the strength of the storm. His eyes and ears stung from the frigid blasts of wind. He longed to rest, but the contents of the note in his pocket pushed him onward. As he reached the last step, he was greeted by a rusty, fist-sized padlock banging loudly against the twin gates. It sounded like a bell tolling, warning the countryside of some unseen danger.

He rested for a moment, supporting himself against the gate, grimacing from the sudden shock of cold steel. He rubbed his hands together, then walked toward a narrow opening, partly concealed by a clump of scrubby thorn bushes, where the fence fell just short of connecting with the gate's left corner. Easing his body through the gap, Elliott felt the familiar tingle of excitement return. He had been here many times before…many times.

But tonight was different.

Creeping among the faded white headstones, Elliott noticed for the first time that their placement looked rather peculiar, as if they'd been dropped from the sky in some predetermined pattern. From above, he ruminated, the grounds must look like an overcrowded housing development.

Glancing at the sky again, thinking: *Big snow on the way, and soon.* He moved slower now, still confident, but careful not to pass the gravestone.

He had been there before, so many times, but he remembered the first time most vividly—fifteen years ago, during the day.

Everyone had been there. A grim Elliott standing far behind Kassie's parents, hidden among the mourning crowd. Her father, standing proudly, a strong hand on each son's shoulder. The mother, clad in customary black, standing next to him, choking back the tears.

Immediately following the service, the crowd had left the cemetery to gather at her parent's home, but Elliott had stayed. He had waited in the upper oak grove, hidden among the trees. When the workers had finished the burial, he had crept down the hill and sat, talking with his love on the fresh grave. And it had been magical; the first time Kassie had really talked to him, shared herself with him. He'd felt her inside him that day and known that it had been right—her death, his killing, a blessing.

High above the cemetery, a rotten tree limb snapped, crashed to the ground below. Elliott's memory of Kassie's funeral vanished. He stood motionless, watching the bare trees shake and sway in the wind, dead branches scraping and rattling against each other. A hazy vision of dancing skeletons and demons surfaced in his mind. *It's called the cemetery dance*, the demons announced, glistening worms squirming from their rotten, toothless mouths. *Come dance with us, Elliott*, they invited, waving long, bony fingers. *Come.* And he wanted to go. He wanted to join them. They sounded so inviting. *Come dance the cemetery dance…*

He shook the thoughts away—*too much liquor; that's all it was*—and walked into a narrow gully, dragging his feet through the thin blanket of fallen leaves. He recognized the familiar row of stone markers ahead and slowed his pace. Finally, he stopped, steadied the bright beam on the largest slab.

The marker was clean and freshly cared for, the frozen grass around it still neatly trimmed. There were two bundles of cut flowers leaning against it. Elliott recognized the fresh bundle he'd left just yesterday, during his lunch break. He crept closer, bending to his knees. Tossing the flashlight aside, he eased next to the white granite stone, touching the deep grooves of the inscription, slowly caressing each letter, stopping at her name.

"Kassie," he whispered, the word swept away with the wind. "I found it, love." He dug deep in his front pocket, pulled out a crumpled scrap of lined white paper. "I couldn't believe you came to me again after all these years. But I found the note on my pillow where you left it."

Sudden tears streamed down his face. "I always believed you'd forgive me. I truly did. You know I had to do it…it was the only way. You wouldn't even look at me back then," he pleaded. "I *tried* to make you notice me, but you wouldn't. So I had to."

The cemetery came to life around him, breathing for the dead. The wind gained strength, plastering leaves against the tree trunks and taller headstones. Elliott gripped the paper tightly in his palm, protecting it from the night's constant pull.

"I'm coming now, love." He laughed with nervous relief. "We can be together, forever." He pulled his hand from his coat pocket and looked skyward. *Snow coming, now. Anytime.* A sudden gust of wind sent another branch crashing to the ground where it shattered into hundreds of jagged splinters.

Two gravestones away from it, Elliott collapsed hard to the earth, fingers curled around the pistol's rubber handgrip, locked there now. The single gunshot echoed across the cemetery until the storm swallowed it. Bits of glistening brain tissue sprayed the air, and mixed with the wooden splinters, showering the corpse. His mangled head lolled to the side, spilling shiny gray matter onto the grassy knoll.

For just one moment, an ivory sliver of moonbeam slipped through the darkness, quickly disappeared. As the crumpled scrap of paper—scrawled in Elliott's own handwriting—was lifted into the wind's possession, the towering trees, once again, found their dancing partners. And it began to snow.

BLUE

THE AIR-CONDITIONER IN THE car is broken, and some idiot on the radio reports that the temperature is "98 degrees and the time is 10:47 a.m. Looks like today's gonna be another scorcher, folks." *Yeah, no shit, sherlock.* The tiny red needle on the gas gauge hovers just barely above the EMPTY line. The twins are arguing again in the backseat; someone throws a punch and they start to wrestle. I feel the itch of a headache coming on and have to use the bathroom.

But I couldn't care less.

I keep driving.

MY MOMMA'S NAME was Clarissa, but most folks just called her C.C. That's what Grandpa started calling her when she was just a little girl and the name stuck. *Come over here, C.C., my sweet little butterfly. Come on over and sit on your pappy's knee and listen to this here story...*

Momma's family was big on nicknames; we all had them. Sunshine. Slim. Spider. Big Bear. Little Bear. Gator. So many I can't even remember them all.

My name's Amanda, Amanda Leigh Parker, but for as long as I can remember, folks just called me Blue. *Like a summer sky and a mountain stream,* Grandpa used to tell me. God, I loved him. Miss him like crazy even after all this time. If Grandpa were still alive, things would've turned out different for Momma and me. You can bet the bank on that one.

I FILL THE gas tank in a dusty little town I can never remember the name of. I also buy two grocery bags full of snacks—potato chips and cookies and candy bars—and a six-pack of grape soda. The car is pretty quiet now—the twins stopped their squabbling hours ago—just the radio turned low and the lonely howl of the wind outside. At first, Jenny and Brad get excited when they see all the junk-food, but neither ends up eating very much. Neither do I. A couple hundred miles of this heat has worked its magic on all of us.

I open a candy bar and take a bite and steer the car back out onto the highway. I wiggle my backside to get comfortable, and I can feel the wad of bills in my jeans pocket. I reach down and rub my thumb over the rough denim. Just over three thousand dollars in there—the most I've ever seen close up, much less had tucked away in my very own pocket.

Thinking about the money makes me suddenly nervous. I can feel my face redden and my ears start to get warm. I glance at the rearview mirror and see nothing but empty highway and endless desert.

I speed up anyway.

MY FATHER'S NAME was Walter, and no one in the family thought well enough of the man to give him an official nickname. Or maybe they did. I heard them say it often enough: *that lousy sonofabitch.*

Of course, when I was real young, I couldn't understand why they said the things they said. He was my daddy after all—the one who tucked me in at night and read me bedtime stories about famous explorers and great adventures in faraway countries. He was the one who could talk in so many funny voices and walk on his hands. The one who showed me how to hook a catfish down at Hanson Creek and walk across a log without being scared.

When I was little, I loved Walter the way all little girls love their daddy. But then I got older...

And my vision cleared.

I started to smell the liquor on his clothes. On his breath.

Saw the bruises on Momma's arms and neck.

Heard the stories around town. About the drinking and the fighting and the women.

One day, when I was fourteen years old, I came home from school and found Momma crying in the barn. At first, she was embarrassed to look at me; she had a black eye and a cut on her forehead. She tried to tell me that she'd had an accident. That she'd fallen from the loft and darn near killed herself.

But she saw the way I was looking at her—and she knew I knew the truth.

For a long time, we didn't say much of anything. Just sat in the cool shadows of the barn and hugged each other. After awhile, I told her how sorry I was and how I hated Daddy for doing the things he did, and she told me not to hate him, that he was a good man at heart, but that he was under too much pressure with the business failing and all the bills piling up. She promised me things would get better.

She was wrong.

IT'S DARK OUTSIDE now, and the night air feels good on my face.

From time to time, I glimpse twin specks of light up ahead in the distance and moments later a car rockets past us heading in the opposite direction. Same thing in the rearview mirror—first it's pinpricks of headlights, then the sudden whoosh of air, and finally just the darkness again.

It's strange out here, driving in the desert at night. Almost like I'm dreaming.

The kids are sound asleep, Jenny's head resting on Brad's shoulder. I can't tell which one is doing the snoring; they both inherited that little trait from their father.

I check my watch. Stretch my neck and listen to it pop. I'm getting a little stiff, but not the least bit tired. Quite the opposite. With each passing mile, I feel more alive and excited…and there's also something else, something that takes a while before I realize exactly what it is.

For the first time in a couple of weeks, I don't feel afraid.

THINGS ONLY GOT worse after that day in the barn with Momma.

Within six months, Walter's store went bankrupt and he was forced to hire on with Jefferson's Trucking. The new job kept Walter on the road two weeks out of every month—I was grateful for this, and I know Momma was too, although she never said a word about it to me.

Between the store closing up and all the nasty stories floating around town—some folks were saying that Walter lost a lot more money gambling on card games than he ever did at the store—well, after all that business, people pretty much stopped coming around the house to visit. They even stayed away during the time when Walter was out on the road.

As young as I was, even I could understand the reason for this, and so could Momma—people just didn't know what to say anymore. Some folks were embarrassed and others were just plain frustrated. They had tried to help in the past, but Momma had turned them all away with nothing more than a polite thank you. Now things were at their worse, and Momma and me were on our own.

Every night I prayed for things to get better.

But I guess no one was listening.

Week before Christmas that year, Momma ended up in Arkansas County General with a couple of broken ribs. She spent four days in a hospital bed, and Walter spent thirty days in the county jail.

It was in the hospital that Momma first told me about her dream. I think it was the pain medicine that did most of the talking for her, because when she told me about it, she sounded so crazy and upset—so unlike my Momma—that I was frightened to gooseflesh just listening to her.

For the past couple months, Momma explained, she'd been having the same dream each and every night…

She's being held prisoner, locked away in the highest tower of a crumbling, ancient castle. The tower is made of rough blocks of stone and is so enormous that when she looks out the window all she can see are dark storm clouds and endless night sky. It's never daylight in her dream; always nighttime and always in the midst of a horribly violent storm, with rumbles of thunder marching closer and closer and jagged flashes of lightning stabbing the sky. As the storm grows more and more powerful, the stone tower begins to sway dangerously in its grip, enough to make her dizzy, and no matter how hard she tries she can never see the ground below. It's almost as if there is nothing out there to escape to, nothing left in the world to hope for.

But that wasn't the worst of it, Momma explained.

In the beginning of the dream, she is dressed in her wedding gown and high heel shoes, everything clean and pretty and white, her long blonde hair flowing down behind her back, braided so nice and perfectly...but when she finally turns away from the window and glimpses herself in the fancy gold mirror hanging on the opposite stone wall, there is nothing left of her but a bag of bones—a parched skeleton—grinning an awful grin and smelling of wet, graveyard dirt, and her hair is limp clumps of rotting string, her dress nothing but tatters of faded yellow cloth...

Listening to her tell me about the dream that day in the hospital made me realize something very important: it was the first—and only—time I had ever seen my Momma afraid.

WE DRIVE INTO Los Angeles early the next morning. I pass maybe twenty hotels before finding one I like the looks of. I tell the kids to stay in the car and I go inside to pay for the room. I hand the woman behind the counter cash in advance for a week and give her a false name. The fat man sitting next to her never looks up from his crossword puzzle.

Once inside the room, the kids immediately turn on the television and flop onto the bed. I lock the door and turn on the air-conditioner and peel off my clothes to take a shower.

Despite the weather, I run the water steaming hot and take my time.

It's the best shower of my life.

ON THE TWELFTH day of September that long ago year, two days short of my sixteenth birthday, Momma took Walter's deer rifle down from the rack on the den wall, loaded it at the kitchen table, walked back into the den, and shot Walter three times in the head while he was sleeping on the sofa.

She had discovered that Walter was raping me.

I'd never said a word to her, but she found out anyway.

Later that morning, when the sheriff's boys came by, they found Momma sitting on the front porch, rocking in her favorite chair, reading from the Bible. She held the front door open for the officers and told them exactly what had happened.

Walter was dead, of course. His brains splattered all over the wooden paneling and the antique cuckoo clock I used to love so much when I was a little baby. Still, the judge wasted little time in deciding that Momma was in no kind of shape to stand trial. "Prison is not the place for her," Judge Henderson stated for the record. "It seems that she has already served her sentence...for most of her adult life."

So, instead, they sent Momma to some mental clinic in Texas, and she lived there in medicated peace until the day she died...only three-and-a-half years later from a heart attack.

Soon after the shooting, my Aunt Charlotte, Momma's youngest sister, came down from Thornton and took me home with her on the train. Uncle Pete made me a bedroom in the basement of their house, and I lived there for the next five years...until I met Charlie.

OUR HOTEL ROOM is on the third floor. It has a tiny balcony—room enough for two adults to sit without much comfort—and a view of the main highway and the strip mall across the way.

After my shower, I put on clean clothes and sit outside with wet hair and smoke a cigarette; my first in a long couple of years. Charlie always hated it when I smoked.

I inhale one cigarette all the way down to the filter and light a second one right away. I notice the blood on my hand then. Dark smudges crusted in the swirls of my palm and around the knuckles. I stare at the blood, hypnotized by the sight of it. I thought I'd washed it all away, but I guess blood has a way of sticking to things.

History has a way of repeating itself, Blue.

Sitting there on the balcony, listening to the traffic pass, I can almost hear the whisper of my Grandpa speaking those words to me. It was one of his favorite sayings, and something I didn't much understand as a child. He was a dear old man—the gentlest and wisest I've ever known—and I miss him terribly right now.

I look at my watch. Run the numbers through my head.

Just over twenty-four hours ago, I killed my husband in the garage of our home. He was working on another one of his projects. Something for the garden, he told me earlier at the breakfast table.

I stood there in the doorway to the garage and watched him for maybe a minute. And then I did it. Carpenter hammer to the back of his head. Hit him maybe ten, twelve times until he stopped moving. Rolled him underneath the mini-van and left him there. Packed the suitcases, picked up the kids after soccer practice, cleaned out the checking account, and drove away into the desert.

I MET CHARLIE at a spring church picnic, and I knew I loved him by the end of our second date, two weeks later. I was twenty-one years old and had never been in love before—it was wonderful.

Soon enough we were inseparable, and to no one's great surprise, we married later that autumn.

I moved out of Aunt Charlotte and Uncle Pete's basement and we moved into a two-room apartment over by the lake. That winter, Charlie got promoted at the printing plant and I started working at the library. We spent most evenings taking long walks around the lake and talking ourselves to sleep. On our two month anniversary, we cut down our first Christmas tree together and, a week later, celebrated the holiday as happy as two people can be.

He was everything I ever dreamed a man could be: handsome, charming, hard-working, faithful.

We didn't have much in the way of material things back then, but we didn't care. We were in love. We were happy.

And we remained that way for close to ten years…through two miscarriages; the birth of the twins; a cancer scare (him) and a couple of other close calls (me); him getting relocated to Arizona last year and us having to pick up and move.

Ten long years, we were happy.

But then something went wrong…

I STARE AT the blood on my right hand for a long time and think of my husband.

It's noisy outside on the balcony—with all the morning traffic passing by on the highway—and my thoughts are spinning wildly inside my head. But I do know one thing for certain: I did the right thing.

CHARLIE WAS CHANGING…BECOMING a stranger right before my eyes. First, there was his job. Just last month, he'd mysteriously started working more and more late evenings at the office. And then, even more bizarre, he went in the last couple of Saturday mornings. He tried to explain all this by saying that the extra hours went along with his latest promotion, that he had additional responsibilities now. But I knew better.

Then there was the drinking. Where before Charlie had never touched the stuff, now he liked "a beer after dinner once in awhile." Those were his exact words. He insisted that he enjoyed it only a couple times a week, but he didn't fool me; I knew exactly what was going on.

And, finally, there was sweet little Jenny. My baby butterfly. Charlie had started spending more and more time with her lately. Reading to her at bedtime. Playing ball with her in the backyard. Helping her with her math homework. Focusing his attention solely on her and ignoring Brad almost completely.

But as soon as I brought up the subject, he looked at me with one of his worried expressions, came over and hugged me, and said that maybe it was time for us to call the doctor and have him check my medication again. God, I hated him when he got like that; so damn coddling and condescending. Then, just the other morning after breakfast, after the kids had gone to school, he'd made a big deal of saying that he was concerned about me, that I wasn't acting like my old self.

But he wasn't fooling me. No, siree, he wasn't.

He was the one who wasn't acting like his old self.

He was the one who was changing.

And then the other night it happened...

Momma's dream.

It came to me for the first time a week ago—and every night since. I couldn't believe it. After all those years, I had completely forgotten about it.

But there was no doubt in my mind. It was Momma's dream alright. Everything was the same. The tower, the storm, the skeleton...only this time it was *me* being held captive in that tower, *me* wearing that awful wedding dress.

And right away I knew what was happening: Momma had sent the dream to me as a sign—a warning.

Charlie was changing.

And, just like Momma, I knew what I had to do to protect my family.

I SIT OUTSIDE on the balcony and smoke the entire pack of cigarettes—twenty of them right down to the filter.

And then I get up and go inside to the family I love so much.

A CRIME OF PASSION

1

PAST MIDNIGHT. A DARK cabin nestled in the wilderness. Night sounds…invaded by the whisper of heavy tires. Doors slamming. The crunch of gravel under footsteps.

Many footsteps.

Instantly awake, Drake lifted the .38 from the nightstand and slipped out from beneath the bedsheet. He crouched to a knee, listening, staring out the open curtains at the front yard below. He glimpsed a flicker of sparks in the darkness, then the orange tint of flames, and thought: *My God, they're going to burn down the cabin.*

2

THOMAS DRAKE SOLD his first novel, *Nightlife*, on his thirtieth birthday. He celebrated both events with a carry-out pizza and a solo trip to the movies. The book—an urban crime thriller—sold well in hardcover and the paperback edition snuck onto the *N.Y. Times* list for three weeks. The resulting four-book contract allowed him to quit his job as a social worker and write full-time.

Despite the lucrative deal, Drake continued to live a comfortable, rather conservative life in the suburbs outside Baltimore. He was a bachelor by choice, rarely dated, and had never dated the same woman twice. Whose fault that was, he claimed he didn't know.

Drake did admit—and too often, his few friends scolded—that except for his bank account, he didn't offer a very attractive or exciting package. He was barely of average height, and at least ten pounds underweight. Receding hairline. Pale skin. A face of little character.

And he was far from daring or spontaneous, writing in an upstairs office six days a week, eight hours a day, preferring mornings and early afternoons, walking his two-year-old Labrador retriever several times a day, playing poker on odd Monday nights (more out of habit than actual enjoyment) and golf twice a week. And, no matter what the day had been like or what the next had to offer, he always read himself to sleep.

3

DRAKE SCRAMBLED CLOSER to the second-floor window, his heart pounding at his bare chest. Their van was parked at the bottom of the cabin's gravel driveway, parking lights still on. Cocky bastards. Surprised they didn't just toot the damn horn to announce their arrival. A small fire burned to the side of the van, a safe distance from the cabin. The flames threw distorted shadows across the lawn, and Drake watched as the figures took form. He counted all four of them, and found a hint of relief in knowing that no one was lurking beyond his view. They didn't appear to carry weapons, but Drake knew the firepower was there.

For just a moment, he contemplated opening fire on them from the window, but ruled against it. Despite an extensive book knowledge of weapons, he'd never actually fired a gun until a week ago. And a week's practice hadn't helped much; six bottles out of ten remained his best score. He knew his only chance was at close range.

The woman remained by the fire—it was now waist high and growing—while the others returned to the van. The back doors stood open and Drake could see several stacks of boxes inside. The men waited in turn, then carried armloads of what he immediately recognized as books—his own novel, *The Prey*, he knew—and took turns dropping them onto the fire. With a flush of surprise and anger, he realized that they were replaying the book burnings from New York and Chicago and the other cities they'd followed him to.

None of them made a move toward the cabin, content for the moment with the destruction of his books. He could hear them mumbling through the slightly open window. Nothing loud or clear enough to understand, but he guessed that they were congratulating themselves for finding him again, for destroying more of his evil work. Crazy fuckers. Probably thought he was cowering in fear. *Let them think it,* Drake thought. *It'll make my job that much easier.*

He remained at the window and watched, recognizing each of their faces in the glow of the fire. The woman named Jessie. Strikingly beautiful and clearly insane. She was their leader. And the three men. All large and equally crazy.

Six days. It had taken almost a week, but they'd somehow tracked him across hundreds of miles. Drake had known they'd eventually find him—in fact, he'd spent most of the six days at the cabin trying to prepare for this moment—but he couldn't help but wonder how they'd done it. He'd told no one where he was going. *No one,* because, quite simply, there'd been no one left. Drake shifted his weight and flexed the fingers holding the pistol. *Let 'em come,* he thought.

Outside, the fire spat gray smoke, and Drake imagined he could feel its warmth wash his face. He touched a finger to his cheek. It *was* hot, but only from anticipation…and yes, he admitted, from fear. As the three men returned to the van for another load, Drake pushed the curtains aside and thought, *That damn* Times *critic was right: I never should've sold it to the movies…"*

4

DESPITE HIS USUAL insecurities, the follow-up novels did well and continued Drake's success. His main character, Robert Steele, was an aggressive New York City attorney (by day); a street-smart vigilante with a penchant for breaking the law and serving his own brand of justice (by night). A rather trite theme, Drake admitted, but he'd added what proved to be an irresistible quality to his character. He had made the lawyer a hopeless romantic; a puppy-eyed tough guy with a heart of gold and a body to match. Steele chased criminals while gorgeous women chased him. Steele's audience grew into a wide and loyal one, and it showed in Drake's royalty statements.

By his fourth novel, Drake was a major force in the crime and mystery fields. A regular on the bestseller lists. Guest-of-honor at conventions. Major awards winner. Book club selections. Frequent appearances in the media: television, radio, newspapers.

Foreign sales from his first four novels had even allowed him to buy a lakeside cabin in the hills of Western Maryland. A place to escape the creeping closeness of suburbia, a place to really be alone and write. No neighbors. No telephone. No mail. Just a two-story cabin with spacious rooms, a double fireplace, and an office with a view of the lake.

Then…came trouble.

THE PREY, DRAKE'S fifth and most daring novel, drew more attention than all of his previous books combined. Part of the reason was that, for the first time, a Thomas Drake novel had debuted in the top five on both the *Times* and the *Publishers Weekly* best-seller lists. The other, more publicized reason, however, was the novel's controversial theme.

The Prey was darker—and more ambitious—than the typical Steele novel. Less romance and more gritty drama. The book followed Steele as he infiltrated the seedy New York underworld of child prostitution and pornography to search for the killer of his lover's teenaged sister. The world Drake described was ugly and dark and violent; his characters breathed hate and perversion. The writing itself was grim and graphically violent, and the ending was not a happy one.

Drake, his agent, and his editor all agreed that it was a risk, moving away from the popular Steele formula, but when the book debuted so high on the bestseller lists and stayed there, and when the critics lauded it as "chilling and thought-provoking" and "disturbingly real," their concern changed to delight.

So, when Warner offered close to seven figures for the motion picture rights to *The Prey*, no one was particularly surprised; and, despite his reservations about the book's graphic nature, the offer proved too much for Drake to resist. He signed the contracts, kept his fingers crossed…and waited anxiously for the movie's premiere.

The film was a disaster, bearing little, if any, semblance to its source material. Warner's final creation was a tasteless 98-minute, new-wave-director-on-speed's version of hell on earth, a thumbnail away from an NC-17 rating. The film was overly violent and obscene and grossly erotic. *Pornography for a mass audience*, the angry reviews shouted.

Concerned citizens protested the movie's showing in dozens of cities. The critics hated it, the public hated it, and Drake hated it.

And an underground group of fanatics who called themselves Mother Earth branded the movie "filthy" and "evil"—and hated it enough to kill.

5

ONE OF THEM was gone.

Drake leaned closer to the window and frantically scanned the yard. *Christ, he could only see three of them.* They were standing next to the van, watching the cabin, talking low. Drake squinted, trying to focus on their features. Too dark.

The fire had eventually weakened, thanks to a limited supply of books. *They must've bought out a dozen stores*, he'd thought, watching them dump the last load. Drake had suspected that, with the book burning nearly complete, they'd make a move for the cabin soon. So, he'd left the window momentarily and hurried back to the nightstand, grabbed a full box of ammunition, and then returned. The process couldn't have taken more than five or six seconds, but they must've known all along where he was watching from and taken advantage of his mistake.

He finger-tipped a flannel shirt from the chair near the window and slipped it on. Then he emptied the box of bullets into the pocket over his heart. Again, he considered opening fire from the window, surprising them, and hopefully taking advantage of the confusion. He tensed. It just might work…no! *Damn it!* Drake thought. It would just force their hand that much quicker, show them that he wasn't going to surrender so easily. *Damn it!* He thought he'd be ready for this. Ready for anything after what had happened back at home.

The roof creaked and Drake flinched, almost dropping the gun. He imagined one of them standing directly above him, motioning to the others and laughing. Then lowering his weapon and drilling machine gun fire through the roof.

The second-floor windows were unprotected, but the doors and windows downstairs were heavily boarded from the inside. They wouldn't withstand constant battering, but they'd prevent a quick and easy entrance and allow Drake the time to defend the breach. He'd begun transforming the cabin into a fortress during the second day, feeling, at times, both paranoid and silly. Now, he knew he'd been right.

Suddenly, he heard a crack of breaking glass and wood downstairs. Den window. Side of the house. Another crack followed.

Drake glanced out the window again, a chill tracking his spine. Only one of them remained by the van now; the others had disappeared. Another board cracked. Louder this time. Closer. He sprinted for the stairs.

6

MOTHER EARTH'S REIGN of terror had started two months earlier with a two-page letter to Warner Studios. The group had determined that *The Prey* was an "evil movie; a deranged portrayal of America's youth," and condemned the movie studio for making the film and blamed the book's author for producing such trash.

Over the course of several weeks, Warner and Putnam forwarded a total of twenty-three letters to Drake from the organization. None of the letters listed a return address, and the postmarks on the envelopes were from various states.

Shortly after, similar letters began arriving at Drake's post office box, an address he'd been certain only business associates were aware of. Finally, they began showing up at the house.

All the letters were written in the same handwriting and all carried essentially the same warning: *If you don't stop the paperback release of* The

Prey, *withdraw from your upcoming signing tour, and seek redemption for your sins we will have no choice but to punish you.* And each letter was always signed the same: *The faithful disciples of Mother Earth: Jessie. Carl. Randy. Willie.*

No one Drake spoke with had ever heard of the group and considering the apparent size of its membership, he wasn't surprised. His publisher ran a check through the research department and even checked with the F.B.I., but nothing turned up on either's computer files. The postal service tried but couldn't help, and the police claimed that they needed more to go on than a stack of crazy letters. Their only advice: *just ignore the freaks and they'll eventually forget all about you.*

But they didn't forget him.

They sent more letters. Then packages. Cardboard boxes full of black ash and charred copies of *The Prey:* burned, they claimed, to symbolize their contempt for the novel's author.

Mutilated publicity photos of Drake.

Mangled baby dolls, signifying the author's ill effect on the country's youth.

Then, during the signing tour that Putnam had arranged, he'd begun noticing the same face in the crowd in different cities. A tall, raven-haired woman. Thin and very attractive. Well-dressed. Intense. Always closely watching him.

He initially spotted her during a book signing, staring at him through the store window. Then…sitting alone at a corner table in a Detroit restaurant, walking in a Houston airport terminal, and in the passing crowd at several other signings. Only her professional appearance had kept Drake's suspicions to a minimum. *Perhaps she's a stewardess,* he thought. Curious and strangely attracted, he twice tried to follow her, but both times, she'd vanished.

The woman finally confronted him during a signing at a Midwest Kroch's & Brentano's. She waited her turn in line, unnoticed by the author, then while Drake scribbled a signature, she leaned over and quietly introduced herself as Jessie from the organization Mother Earth.

The words froze Drake and instead of grabbing the woman—as he would later wish he'd done—he was too terrified to even look up. After a moment, he dropped the pen and slowly lifted his head. The tall woman's red lips spread into a smile, and he immediately recognized her as the woman he'd been seeing in the crowd.

Before he could react, she doused the book-covered table with a container of clear fluid and set it afire. The crowd panicked and scrambled, and Drake knocked over two rows of paperback racks trying to escape the small fire. The woman disappeared in the ensuing commotion.

The woman did not appear again, but there were six more book burnings. Each time hundreds of copies of *The Prey* were set afire on the sidewalk in front of the bookstore in which Drake was appearing. And each time the culprits escaped without a trace. Witnesses in each city reported that there were four persons involved: three men and a woman.

Finally, after a bomb threat was phoned into a Washington D.C. mall bookstore, the tour was cut short and Drake was granted an early vacation.

He returned to Baltimore, where the county sheriff's office agreed to give him protection outside his home. But after a week passed uneventfully, the police left.

Then, the phone calls began…

THE FIRST CALL came late on a Sunday night, during the local weather broadcast on the eleven o'clock news. Drake had called it an early night and was reading an old Dean Koontz paperback in bed—half-listening to the news—when the phone rang. He picked it up after the first ring, startled and annoyed by the shrill interruption.

"Hello."

"Is this Thomas Drake?" A woman's voice.

He immediately knew who it was on the other end. He shivered and stared at the closed bedroom door, the drape-shrouded window. His number was unlisted. Always had been. Only his agent, two editors at Putnam, and a few relatives and friends had the number. He couldn't believe that they'd found it. He went to hang up the receiver, and then changed his mind. Just play it cool. Play their game.

"Yes, this is Thomas Drake. And who is this?"

"I think you know who this is. And I suggest that you listen very carefully to what I have to say."

"And if I don't?" He got up from the bed and began pacing the carpet.

"We are a very powerful organization, Mr. Drake. With resources beyond your comprehension. Trust me, we will find a way to make you listen. We always have in the past."

"You mean…Christ, you mean you're done this before? I'm not the first person you've—"

She laughed; an angry, ugly sound. "Oh, yes. There have been others. None as popular as you, of course, but there have been others." She waited, then said. "Alex Forrester wouldn't listen either. Do you remember him?"

Jesus, he remembered. It had been in all the newspapers. Alex Forrester. Rock and roll musician. Heavy metal. Accused of headlining a satanic movement; using his music to recruit devil worshipers. Paralyzed last year in a highly publicized automobile accident. Brakes failed. *Oh my God.*

"You…you were responsible for that accident—"

"Do you know why we chose Mother Earth as our title?" she asked, ignoring the question. "Because we live by nature's laws. There was a time when this earth was free of darkness and evil; it was pure. It is our mission to make this country pure again; to cleanse it of all filth."

"You're crazy," Drake whispered. "Absolutely crazy." He'd known from the start that this woman and her Mother Earth followers were a bunch of lunatics. But until now, the real danger of the situation had failed to sink in.

"The choice is yours to make," she said, her voice rising. She was enjoying it now, taking pleasure from the control she held over him. "You still have time to seek redemption for your sins."

"What sins? Have you even read my book? I haven't done anything. I'm not responsible for what ended up on the screen."

"Of course you are, you miserable man. The film is simply an extension of your vision. It is *your* message that must be stopped. Do you think the people see anyone else's name on the movie credits? No, of course not. Only yours. And yours is the only name on the book cover. It is you who is responsible."

"No, that's not true. Why are you doing this to me? You have no good reason to—"

"NO GOOD REASON!" She was shouting into the phone now, her voice trembling with rage. "I have a fourteen-year-old daughter, lying comatose in a hospital room because of…of filth like you."

My God, he thought, *she was crying.*

"My baby was once an innocent child, a pure person, Mr. Drake. But she was too trusting, too easily swayed. I didn't see the warnings. I failed her. Her group of peers were evil; they read the filthy books, watched the filthy movies, and they acted as characters from those evil worlds. They lied to their parents. They drank and partied and dressed like sluts. They did things with boys. My baby was high on drugs when the car she was a passenger in went over an embankment. Now, she just lays there in that horrible hospital."

"What is it that you want from—"

"The predators in this world," she continued, "the spreaders of evil like you, think they are powerful and strong, but under nature's laws, we know that evil breeds only weakness and purity offers eternal strength. Remember that, Mr. Drake. Remember that."

Drake sighed. "Just tell me what it is that you want me to do? We cut the signing tour in half. The paperback release is a week away. I couldn't stop that even if I wanted to."

"You must repent for your sins. Speak with your public, to your readers. Warn them. Tell them you have repented. Tell them that the book is wrong, full of filth and lies and evil messages—"

"I'm hanging up, lady. I can't listen to this anymore. And don't try to call back, because I'll have the police put a tap on the phone and—"

"Come now, Mr. Drake. We both know that the police will be of no help to you. They went through the motions for seven days and now you are all alone."

Drake shivered again and walked to the window, parting the white curtains with a finger. The side yard and street were empty.

"Besides, if you keep calling, the police will just think the whole thing is a publicity stunt for the book. They didn't believe Alex Forrester when he called, you know?" She was under control again, teasing him now, taunting. "Trust me, the police will be of no help. We are much stronger than you think."

"Fuck you."

"Such harsh words." She laughed. "The oldest rule of nature is that the strong shall survive and the weak shall perish. Don't be weak anymore, Mr. Drake. For your own sake, don't be weak."

He hung up, silencing the awful voice, and called his agent and told him of the latest incident. He didn't call the police. Afterward, he left the phone off the hook.

The next morning, Drake drove into town and bought an answering machine. He installed it that same morning and screened his calls the rest of the week. He counted over a hundred hang-ups before deciding to disconnect the line completely.

Things went downhill fast after that night.

SIX DAYS AGO, on the exact day of *The Prey*'s paperback release, Mother Earth went over the edge and took Drake with them. He found the dog on his way to fetch the morning paper. The black Labrador was sprawled on its back, legs stiff, mouth open, and definitely dead. A smear of blood on the walk revealed that it had been killed in the grass—single bullet to the head—then dragged onto the concrete front porch. Stuffed between the dog's teeth was a ball of glossy, colored paper—a wrinkled book cover.

He buried his companion in the back yard, then showered and packed a single bag. He didn't consider, even for a moment, calling the police.

After a trip to the grocery store for supplies and food, he drove downtown to a pawn shop and picked up a brand new—at least that's what the owner claimed—.38 caliber pistol and a dozen boxes of ammunition. Then he loaded the car and headed for the cabin.

An hour later, he stopped at a crossroads convenience store and phoned Colin at the office. But instead of hearing Colin's ever cheerful voice, Drake found himself speaking with one of Colin's literary partners. *"I'm afraid I have some tragic news to pass on to you, my dear Thomas."*

Drake immediately knew what had happened.

"The police were here this morning. It seems that poor Colin was...was shot to death in his apartment late last night. A foiled robbery attempt, the police suggested. There were signs of a struggle and the lock was damaged.

"There was something strange, though. It seems that the killer tried to burn down Colin's apartment by setting a pile of books afire atop his magnificent Persian rug. Now that makes perfect sense: the police think that the murderer was simply trying to cover his tracks. But what is so puzzling is that every single book on the pile was one of yours. I wonder where they all came from? Don't you find that queer? It's just so terrible—"

Drake hung up, cutting him off in mid-sentence. He felt nauseous and sat inside the parked car for almost an hour before his head felt clear enough to continue.

He arrived at the cabin late in the afternoon, an emotional mess. Anger. Fear. Disbelief.

He was sure they would search for him; they'd gone too far now to turn back. *The disciples of Mother Earth.* He didn't know who or what in the hell they were, but he was sure of one thing: they'd look for him and eventually find him.

And he prayed he'd be ready.

7

DRAKE CLEARED THE stairway in two strides and ran for the den window. He could hear the wooden boards groaning, surrendering under pressure. He crossed the kitchen and walked right up on the man who was climbing, legs first, into the cabin. The man's blue-jeans were pushed up above his shins, exposing thick, hairy ankles. He wore no socks, but a leather holster holding a small pistol was strapped to his right ankle. The man was obviously stuck—probably caught on a jagged piece of board or a nail—and was grunting with effort.

Drake stopped short of the den carpet, hoping the man hadn't heard his approach. *Close range. In the back.* He raised the .38, his arms shaking wildly, and took aim. *Steele would never do it,* he thought in a flash of sanity.

He lowered the gun. *Steele would just knock the bastard unconscious and tie him up.*

Drake looked up at the man again, at the gun hanging from his leg, and wondered if the same gun had been used to end his agent and long-time friend's life. He imagined the man breaking into Colin's apartment and pressing the gun barrel to Colin's bald head and firing. He imagined the man stuffing the tattered remains of a book cover into his dog's lifeless mouth, and…

…Drake raised the .38 and pulled the trigger twice in a quick, jerky motion. The man spasmed, his legs kicking at empty air, and a pair of red mouths opened near the center of his back. He went limp.

The adrenaline rush was overpowering and, for a moment, Drake felt as though he might faint. He steadied himself against the back of the sofa and brought the gun to eye level, as if he were unsure if he'd actually pulled the trigger.

A loud crash and a sudden flash of light in the next room snapped him back. He moved cautiously through the kitchen, searching the shadows for movement, turned the corner and froze at the base of the stairs. A pile of broken boards lay at his feet, and the bay window stood wide open, the van's headlights shining bright white into the cabin.

The lights were blinding, but Drake leveled the gun and forced himself closer to the window. Holding his breath, he leaned over the windowsill and peered around the right side. Nothing. Then, to his left. Again nothing.

He backed away from the window, shading his eyes with his gun hand. He was about to return upstairs when a long, silver canister flew through the window and exploded with a loud *pop* as it hit the floor. A second can followed, landing with an identical *pop*. A cloud of white smoke erupted with a hiss.

Tear gas, Drake guessed, his eyes already beginning to sting and water. *Trying to smoke me out.* He shaded his eyes and ran for the stairs…and tripped face-first on the pile of broken boards. The gun flew from his hand and slid across the floor, settling somewhere near the bottom of the staircase.

Drake crawled on all fours, fingers groping for the lost weapon. The gas was overpowering now; he could barely open his eyes. His throat felt on fire; he couldn't stop the coughs that racked his body. *No*, his mind screamed. *It can't end so easily. Don't panic now.* Suddenly, his fingers touched something metal and cold and he knew it was the gun. *Okay, get yourself together now*, he thought. *Find your way back upstairs.* His fingers closed around the rubber hand grip…

…and were crushed beneath an unseen boot.

He screamed with pain.

The boot released.

Drake sensed movement above him, then felt strong hands pick him up and fling him backwards out the window, onto the waiting lawn several feet below.

8

"IT IS NATURE'S way, Mr. Drake." The voice was soft and calm. Unbearably confident. "And it is our way."

Drake was stretched out on his back on the dining room table, his arms and legs bound with thick rope. A piece of tape covered his mouth. Jessie sat on a chair at the end of the table. Two men stood behind her.

They'd surprised him at the bay window, and he'd surprised them right back by fighting like a wildcat. It had taken both men to take him down. One of the men sported a two-inch gash across his forehead and the other man's lips were cracked and swollen. The third man was still inside the cabin, stuck in the window; he was dead.

The men rarely spoke, but the woman had spent the past fifteen minutes repeating the same crazy sermon she'd told him earlier over the telephone. "We live by nature's laws, Mr. Drake. It is our duty to make this earth pure again." She motioned to one of the men and he removed the tape from Drake's mouth.

Drake sucked in air, coating his dry lips with a sweep of his tongue. The back of his head ached from where he'd been struck, and he longed to massage it. His eyes were the worst, though; red and raw.

"Kill me now," he hissed. "Just get it over with."

"Oh, but we have no intentions of killing you. We only kill when necessary to achieve our final objective, and you, Mr. Drake, are exactly that. By allowing you to live, by allowing the world to witness our power, we will set the highest possible example and hopefully deter future sinners from walking your path. Mother Earth's message will be heard across the country very soon, thanks to you."

"You're...you're all crazy. My God, you killed Colin for no reason. You chased me all over the country because of a damn book."

"Ah, but a very popular book. A book that will, unfortunately, be read by millions. We told you, the film is only an extension of your vision. It is *your* message that must be stopped."

He spoke without thinking: "I'll never stop writing."

"But you will, Mr. Drake. We will make sure of that. I know we have met once before, but allow me to formally introduce myself. I am Jessie Moore. Doctor Jessica Moore. And these two gentlemen with me are…"

9

EXCERPTED FROM THE Monday evening edition of the *Baltimore Sun*:

BALTIMORE—Bestselling crime novelist, Thomas Drake, was discovered early this morning suffering from shock and severe dehydration at his country home in the Western Maryland wilderness. The local author was flown to the University of Maryland's Shock Trauma Unit, where he is listed in serious but stable condition.

Though officials declined to discuss details of Drake's condition, the father-and-son team of hunters who stumbled upon the gruesome scene, Jim and Jeffrey Cavanaugh of Cumberland, claimed that the local author was suffering from bizarre wounds and was close to death when they first found him.

"The first thing I noticed was that both his hands were missing, gone right at the wrist," said the elder Cavanaugh.

"There were bloody bandages wrapped over the stumps, but they were full of dirt and green pus and he didn't even seem to notice. He was crazy as a goat, eyes staring all big and wide, slobbering all over himself, mumbling about his Mother and the earth and something about nature's way. It was spooky as hell."

"And then we figured out why he was so hard to understand," continued the son, Jeffrey Cavanaugh. "Someone had cut out his tongue."

Ironically, Drake's latest novel *The Prey*, sparked by contro- versy over the recent film release, debuted at the number one spot on the *New York Times* paperback best-sellers list yesterday and...

10

"STUPID." ALTHOUGH WHISPERED, the single word echoed about the small hospital room. It was a small white-walled room; a private room with a washing sink, sitting couch, a single bed, and the usual tangle of hospital machinery. A skeleton of a girl lay stretched atop the white sheets, a clear mask covering her nose and mouth. Her long dark hair, its luster faded, snaked across the pillow. Her eyes were closed.

"How could I be so stupid? I failed you again, my dear Chelsea." Jessie, dressed in a conservative business suit, held a page from the *New York Times* vertically for her daughter to see. Thomas Drake's *The Prey* was still perched atop the paperback list: eight weeks and counting. After a moment, she lowered the paper to her lap.

"How could I be so stupid?" she repeated, as if insisting on an answer. "We knocked him out of commission, sent an important message, but our actions were merely counterproductive. The damn book is selling: even now his filth is spreading to the people."

She stood and unlocked the safety rail on the left side of the bed. "What shall we do, sweetheart?" she asked. "Help me see the light." The bar lowered and Jessie leaned down and cuddled against the cool side of her daughter's body. She slipped the mask down and softly kissed the girl's lips, then replaced the mask.

She sat down again on the stiff hospital chair and, as was her custom, began reading to Chelsea. Sometimes she read books or magazine articles, but always the newspaper first...to keep her daughter abreast of current events. Now, she read from the *Times* entertainment section. The lead arti- cle was about New York's revitalized publishing world. Industry numbers were skyrocketing. Hardcover sales were up forty percent; softcover sales nearing fifty. Companies were expanding.

She finished the article, dropped the newspaper to her lap, and watched her daughter's lifeless face for a reaction, for an answer to her plea for help.

Chelsea had targeted both Forrester and Drake, but Jessie knew it was *she* who had failed in the latter plan's execution. Now, as Chelsea told her what to do next, Jessie's pulse quickened.

"Yes, yes," she said, her enthusiasm mounting, a plan forming in her mind. "We won't fail you, baby girl. We'll go right to the top this time."

She ran a polished fingernail over the black-and-white photograph— of Putnam's CEO and Vice President, standing together, smiling—then slashed the photo to shreds with a sweep of her nail and said: "We'll go right to the top."

HOMESICK

TIMMY BRADLEY HATES HIS new house.

He hates the slippery, shiny floors and the long, winding hallways and the big fancy rugs. He hates the stupid, ugly paintings on the walls and all the weird looking statues that sit on the furniture. He hates just about everything.

Including the strange way that his father and mother have been acting ever since they moved here. To this house.

He sits alone in his bedroom—lights off, door closed—looking out the window at the darkened city. Crying.

Timmy misses his old house and the way things used to be when they lived there. He misses his friends and Sarah and he even misses his school. But he *especially* misses the way that his father—even though he'd been busy back then, too; after all, his father had been the Governor of Massachusetts for goodness sake—used to take time out to play with him each and every day. That's what they had called it back in those days—"time out." No matter what was going on, his father always found a few minutes to go out for a walk with Timmy or play a card game or watch some television. Sometimes he would even take Timmy along on a short trip when it didn't interfere with school and his mother said it was okay.

None of this happens anymore.

His father is always surrounded by people now. And on those few occasions when he *is* alone or just with the family, his father is always so quiet and serious. And distant. Nothing at all like the goofball who once danced around Timmy's bedroom with a pair of Jockey shorts on his head or the father who once bounced on his bed so hard that the frame broke and they laid there giggling for what had to be fifteen minutes.

This house has changed him, Timmy thinks.

He moves away from the window. He sits on the edge of his bed and stares at the back of the bedroom door. He is no longer crying.

Timmy knows that his mother is trying to make things better for him. She, too, is much busier now, but *still* she plays with him a lot more often than before and seems intent on kissing him on the cheek at least a hundred times each day. Or at least it feels like a hundred times.

And, of course, once or twice a week she gives him her little speech: "You have to understand, Timmy. Daddy's job was important before, but now he's the President. For the next few years he's going to be very, very busy with real important things. But you'll get used to it here; it's such a beautiful house. It really is…"

That is part one of the speech; some days he gets part two; other days, he gets both: "…And soon you'll meet new friends and find fun and exciting things to do. You just have to be more patient and remember, we *all* have to make sacrifices. Especially your father. Don't you think he'd rather spend time with us than go to all those stuffy meetings and dinners? Of course he would. He misses us, too. Just remember, sweetheart, he's the President now, and that's a very big deal…"

Timmy almost always comes away from these talks feeling sad and lonely and a little guilty. Jeez. What *can* you say to all that talk when you're only twelve years old?

Some days—usually on those days when his father smiles at him the way he used to or spends a few extra minutes with him after dinner—Timmy thinks that his mother might be right. That things might turn out okay after all. He thinks this because sometimes if he concentrates long and hard enough, he can remember not being so happy in their old house for those first few weeks after they'd moved it.

Back then, like now, there were so many adjustments to make. All the fancy stuff he wasn't allowed to touch. All the secret service men and the stupid security rules he had to memorize. The stiff, new clothes he had to wear and all the dumb pictures he had to dress up for. And, worst of all, he remembers, all those boring parties he had to go to.

When Timmy thinks back to all those things and how, over time, he'd learned to live with them, he sometimes thinks he is just being a baby. A big, fat crybaby, just like he'd heard his father whisper one night last week when he thought Timmy wasn't listening: "I've *got* to get going now, dear. I'll talk to him later. Besides, he's just being a baby again."

Timmy sits back on his bed and listens to his father call him a baby. (*He's just being a baby again. Being a baby.*) Just thinking about that night hurts his feelings all over again, makes his face red and hot and sweaty. And it also makes him angry.

Who is he to call me a baby, Timmy thinks. *He's the one who messed everything up. He's the one who made us come here in the first place.*

Timmy looks up at the picture frame on his dresser at the pretty smiling blond girl in the photo. His stare locks on the wrinkled pink envelope sitting next to it.

> *Dear Timmy,*
>
> *I got your letter and the package. Thanks so much; it's sooo beautiful. This letter is so short because I have to eat dinner in a couple of minutes. My mom says I have to stop mooning over you, can you believe that she actually said that...that I was mooning over you? Anyway, she said that I was wrong to promise you that we'd still go steady and she made me go to the dance with Henry Livingston this past weekend. I ended up having a lot of fun. Henry sure can fast dance. Not as much fun as I would have had with you, but what can we do?—you being there and me being stuck back here. Henry asked me to go to the movies with him on Friday and I told him yes. He's a bunch of fun, not like you, but what can we do? So, I guess we're not going steady or anything anymore. My mother's making me show her this letter before I mail it, so she'll know I "broke it off." Sorry. Those are her words, not mine. I miss*

you, Timmy, and I'll write again soon if my mom lets me. She said she has to think about it. Please write back as soon as you can and don't be mad, okay?

Love, Sarah

P.S. Henry said to say hi and don't be mad at him.

Timmy feels the tears coming and looks away from the picture. But it's too late. He's already crying. Again. Jeez, maybe he *is* a baby. Maybe his father is right about him after all.

But that doesn't matter now. Timmy no longer cares *what* his father thinks. Besides, he knows this is different than last time. Last time they moved he didn't get sick, he didn't cry, he didn't have nightmares. This time is different, he thinks.

He looks at the bedroom door and wonders what is happening downstairs. He figures it is just a matter of time now. If all goes according to his plan, he'll be back in Massachusetts in time for soccer season. Back holding hands and walking home from school with Sarah. Back playing video games and tag-team and roller-ball with all his friends (except for that back-stabber Henry Livingston).

Timmy looks at the clock on the wall. It is after seven o'clock—Sarah and Henry are probably inside the movie theater by now—and he wonders again why it is still so quiet outside his bedroom.

Just be patient, he thinks. Just like his mother always says, *you have to be more patient, Timmy.* To pass the time, he tries to imagine everything as it has happened. Inside his head, he watches himself as he…

…pours the poison directly into their coffee, careful not to get any on the edge of the cups or on the tray. Then he swirls it around real good with his finger until all the white powder disappears. Finally, he pretends to stretch out on the sofa and read a comic book but he really waits and watches them take their first sips, then tiptoes upstairs to his room.

He looks at the clock again. He can't imagine what's taking so long.

He walks to the window and sits down with his back to the door. He wonders what movie Sarah is watching. He thinks of her there in the dark, eating popcorn and sipping soda, Henry's fingers touching her hand. Closing his eyes, he whispers a quick prayer. He asks only that everything goes according to his plan. That soon it will all be over and they will send him home again. Back to Sarah. Back to his friends. Back to his old house.

A few minutes past eight, when he hears the loud, angry voices and the heavy footsteps outside his door, he knows that his prayer has been answered. He is going home.

DEVIL'S NIGHT

ONE

IT ALL STARTED ON a wind-blown Friday night in October. It was the night before Halloween, the night we always called Wreck Night or Devil's Night back when we were kids and Halloween was second in our hearts only to Christmas.

At least the newspapers got *that* much right. The day, I mean. They pretty much screwed up the rest of the story.

I was there that night. Let me tell you what *really* happened...

TWO

IN THE CHILL autumn months after my first child was born, I spent many late night hours driving the streets of my hometown. It practically became a routine. Two, three nights a week, around about midnight, I'd creep into the nursery one final time to check on the baby (a healthy boy named Joshua after my father) and then I'd kiss my amused wife goodnight and off I'd go, driving the streets in random routes until my eyes went blurry and my spine sprouted kinks the size of quarters.

Driving and thinking. Thinking and driving. Some nights with the radio. Most nights in silence.

That was a little more than four years ago, but I still go out and drive some nights. Just not very often now; maybe once or twice a month, tops.

My wife, Janice, is wonderful (and wise) and she's known me for more than half of my thirty-six years, so she innately understands the need for these trips of mine. We rarely talk about it, but she somehow knows that this town where we both grew up and still live today, this town—its streets and houses and storefronts and lawns and sidewalks and the very sky above—gives me a real sense of peace and understanding I could never hope to find elsewhere. I know how funny that sounds, how old-fashioned, but it's the best and probably the *only* way I know how to describe my feelings for this place.

When little Josh was born it was an event that thrilled me to new heights, but also deeply troubled me. That's actually a pretty big understatement, the part about it troubling me. You see...I worried about the baby. I worried about my wife. I worried *a lot* about myself. I worried *a lot* period. There were just so many new and important questions, and more and more of them seemed to be born with each passing day.

Could I be a good father?

Could I provide for the family with just a teacher's salary?

Could I protect the baby from a world so different than the one I grew up in?

Fact is, I never found the answers to most of the hard questions that arose during that period in my life—hell, most of them still exist today—but the answers that I *did* find usually came to me during those midnight drives. They got me through some rough times.

So, you see, that's the reason I went out for a ride on that windy Friday evening. There were budget problems at school to be dealt with the following week and budget problems at home to be dealt with that very weekend, and I needed a dose of cool night air to help clear my head. We were just recently a family of four, having added a terribly fussy but nonetheless adorable baby girl to the mix. Josh and the baby were sound asleep and Janice was upstairs resting, a few hundred pages into one of those romance paperbacks she loves so much. The house was just too damn quiet. It was seven minutes past nine o'clock when I steered a hard left out of our driveway.

THREE

I WAS SITTING in my car smoking a cigarette when the madness began.

It was just a short time later—sometime before ten—and I was parked off to the side of the road, halfway up Carson's Ridge, which overlooks the back of the old post office property. The place had been closed down for a number of years, but the town's braintrust had yet to figure out what to do with the large plot of land. The matter was quickly becoming a front-page item in our little weekly newspaper. There were two schools of thought: tear it down and build a mini-mall or convert it into a clubhouse and surround it with a couple of fancy swimming pools and an outdoor picnic area. Neither idea did much for me. We already had two shopping plazas, and what we needed a planned picnic area when we lived right smack in the middle of the North Carolina hills was a mystery to me. A better question, if you asked me (and no one ever did), was who the heck built a post office three miles out of town in the first place?

The ridge was one of my all-time favorite spots. I usually went there when I was feeling old and sappy and nostalgic. I'd park among the trees and think about the great Friday night bonfires we used to have deep in the woods after high school football games and all the sweaty nights that Janice had sent me home with a hard-on in my jeans, having let me touch her breasts, but never quite reciprocating with her own fingers.

I hadn't been a big sports star in high school—second string on the soccer team was the best I could muster—but my older brother, John, had lettered in three sports and made All-County in two, so I was automatically invited to most of the parties and was generally deemed okay to be seen talking to.

Those school years seemed so long ago now, and I looked back on them often (probably too often) and fondly (thanks, mainly, to Janice). And I remembered them as a time of such innocence. Compared to today, anyway. Sure, there had been some drugs—pot, mostly—and plenty of alcohol and more than a few drunken brawls. And, yes, there had even been a handful of sex scandals, like the time Tracy Anderson got caught sleeping with her boyfriend *and* Tammy Wright's boyfriend both on the same weekend. But it was nothing like today. Nothing like the big cities.

No crack cocaine, no guns, no fourteen-year-old mothers. Things had changed so much, so fast.

So there I was, smoking my cigarette and listening to *The Doors* on the radio, feeling every inch the crusty old high school English teacher when the red Mustang glided into the back lot using only its parking lights. At first, I thought it was just a couple of kids, sneaking back there to neck or maybe planning to do a little something more. But then when the Phantom of the Opera staggered out of the car—and I didn't care if it *was* almost Halloween—I knew something weird was going down.

Even from a distance, it wasn't a pretty sight. As soon as the car jerked to a complete stop, the guy in the costume was out the door and down on his knees. Throwing up.

I shook my head and laughed. The guy was royally plastered.

The Phantom stayed on his knees for record time and each time he dipped his head and convulsed I felt a little sorrier for him. He looked like a dog that'd gotten into a bad bowl of chili. Still, I had to admit it was pretty damn funny; the Phantom of the Opera down there puking in the parking lot, mask still in place, black cape flapping wildly in the wind. It was a grand performance.

After awhile he got to his feet and looked around self-consciously. He took a few wobbly steps, then stopped and stood *very* still. I figured the parking lot was probably doing cartwheels in front of him. Either that or the dead leaves swirling across the lot had suddenly taken on the appearance of a hungry swarm of giant, brown rats. Depended on how much he'd had to drink, I supposed.

I started to feel a little guilty for spying on the poor guy, but he obviously didn't see me parked snug against the treeline.

He obviously didn't see me because of what he did next.

He took a quick swipe at his chin with his shirt sleeve and slowly walked to the back of the sports car and popped the trunk. The trunk lid sprung open, momentarily blocking my view, then quickly closed again.

When the Phantom walked back into sight again, he was carrying a woman.

A very dead woman.

"Jesus," I whispered, pressing forward against the steering wheel, squinting for a clearer view. Suddenly, my heartbeat was very loud in the car.

The Phantom headed for the treeline, the body cradled in his arms.

I was parked a good fifty yards away and it was pretty dark, what with only a handful of lights still working in the lot, but I had a bird's-eye view and I knew right away that it was a body. Fairly petite. Long blond hair fanned out toward the ground. Slender white legs hanging limp from beneath some type of skirt or dress.

Suddenly, the Phantom stopped walking. He leaned over to the side a little and shrugged his shoulders, adjusting his grip the way a shopper might do to get a better hold of a particularly bulky bag of groceries. Seemingly content, he glanced over his shoulder once more, and then continued toward the trees.

It was like watching television. Maybe it was the fact that I was staring through a windshield and the picture before me was perfectly framed. Or maybe it was because suddenly everything seemed to move in dream-like slow motion. All I can tell you is that for those first few seconds after I saw that body, it didn't seem real. *Nothing* seemed real. I might as well have been kicked back in my basement watching *NYPD Blue* with a bowl of pretzels in my lap.

Amidst all of this, my fingers started burning, and I remembered my cigarette. I stubbed out what was left of it in the ashtray and clicked off the radio. When I looked up again, the Phantom had disappeared into the woods.

And it hit me then. What I had seen.

I sat there feeling scared and numb and excited all at the same time, fully understanding for the first time what it was that I was witnessing. I sat there and didn't move, didn't breathe.

He surprised me by returning so quickly—five minutes at the most—a time when, for some strange reason, the idea of leaving the scene never crossed my mind. At first there was only the night and the whipping wind. Then, a subtle shifting of shadows at the wood's edge. Finally, the Phantom appeared like a ghoul from a nightmare.

Empty-handed.

He hurried back inside the car, his stride more confident now. This time even the parking lights stayed off. And then he was gone, and there was only the wind and the darkness and the silver shine of moonlight.

I looked at the glowing red numbers on the dash. They read: 10:03.

FOUR

I FOUND HER maybe a hundred yards in. Buried beneath a tangle of dead tree limbs and a lumpy pile of wet leaves.

The Phantom had done a crummy job. If *I* could find her in the middle of the night with only a flashlight, trust me, *anyone* could.

I lifted a couple of the larger branches off of her and pushed them aside, careful not to make contact. And then I simply stood there in the darkness, staring. Just staring.

Dim flecks of moonlight filtered down through the trees, pleasing only the shadows. The wind lashed at the back of my neck, seeming to focus there, and the cold sting of the metal flashlight tickled my palm. It all seemed very real now.

No matter how hard I tried, I couldn't pull my eyes away from the body.

I'd been wrong earlier. She wasn't a woman at all. She was just a teen-ager. A girl.

And I knew her.

A part of me wanted to gather her up into my arms, brush the dirt and leaves from her hair, take her far away from this place. *But take her where?* Another part of me wanted to flee as fast as my legs would carry me—back up the ridge to the car, straight home and upstairs to bed. Back to where my family waited, where it was safe and warm and the wind couldn't find me.

I knew I was close to panic then; very, very close to losing whatever foolish courage still lingered within me. I could feel it building inside me like a scream. My mind, as if feeding the madness, turned traitor: I looked at the girl's dress, filthy and torn, and thought how amazingly pretty it would look on Janice. How it would be just perfect for our Sunday afternoon picnics at the creek. I looked at the girl's face, at the dark, angry hole centered in her forehead. I found myself wondering if my tiny daughter might grow up to look anything like her; if she would wear her hair in a similar cut, if she would dress anything at all like the girl. And then I thought of Josh and wondered, if he'd been a dozen years older, if this girl would have been to his liking; if perhaps they would have even dated, maybe gone to Homecoming or the prom.

These were the thoughts of a crazy man. I knew that. But I couldn't stop them from rushing over me. For the first time in my life, I was surrounded by madness. Drowning in it.

A gust of wind rattled the dark trees high above me.

I felt the scream coming...

I dropped the flashlight and ran.

FIVE

I DROVE ACROSS town with the windows wide open. It was chilly, but I needed the fresh air to breathe. Besides, my stomach was still doing jumping jacks and puking was definitely not yet out of the question. I figured better safe than sorry.

I drove slowly, with no clear direction, but somewhere in the back of my head I knew where I would eventually end up. It was just a matter of time.

As I passed through the neighborhood, I noticed that most every house on most every street had some type of Halloween display or decoration.

Glowing pumpkins rested on porch railings, smiling their jack-o-lantern smiles, slanted orange eyes winking at me in the wind. Mummies and ghosts and witches and goblins guarded shadow-webbed front yards, daring me to stop the car and trespass. Corpse-shaped mounds of leaves protruded from in front of countless homemade tombstones, silent remembrances of the dead and buried.

I thought of my own narrow strip of front yard—adorned with a glow-in-the-dark graveyard and a fishing line-suspended Grim Reaper—and I grimaced. Josh and I had had a blast setting the whole thing up two weeks ago, but it didn't seem very funny anymore. In fact, none of the houses looked like very much fun at all.

In less than twenty-four hours, Sparta—and towns just like it all over the country—would be celebrating Halloween. There'd be trick-or-treaters and costume parties, candy apples and haunted houses...

But that was tomorrow.

Tonight was Devil's Night.

A night for mischief, as my father used to say. *Yes siree,* he'd whisper, his eyebrows lowering, *Halloween may be a night for make-believe ghosts and goblins, but you'd better be sure to turn on all the lights and lock your doors on Devil's Night. Because that's when the real monsters lurk…*

And then my mother would hush my father with a swat of her hand and all us kids would giggle and we'd finish our dinners with smiles on our faces and nervous, thumping hearts in our chests.

A night for mischief…

HER NAME WAS Amanda Hathaway. The girl in the woods.

She was sixteen years old and a student of mine. One of my favorites. Not just from this year's class, but one of my *all-time* favorites.

She worked part-time over at the ice cream shop in the mall, and whenever Janice or I came in with Josh, she would always sneak him an extra scoop of chocolate and make him feel co-conspirator with a *sshing* finger to her lips and a wink of her eye. Josh loved it.

Amanda was in my last period English class. This was her first year at Sparta High, and the semester was barely two months old, but she'd already proved herself a model student. Not straight A's across the board, mind you, but certainly honor roll with more A's than B's.

But it wasn't her grades that made her my favorite. There were several other classmates, in fact, who regularly earned higher marks.

No, it was more than that—Amanda Hathaway was simply *special.* In a time when many teenage girls were openly disrespectful or arrogant or flirtatious, she was a teacher's dream. Extremely well-mannered and on the quiet side, she was much more serious-minded than most of the other students. I sensed it the very first week of classes: she gave you her full attention because she *wanted* to learn, not because she *had* to.

Yet at the same time, Amanda was popular with her classmates. She was quiet, but not invisible. Polite and smart, but not a geek. Pretty and well-liked, but not a snob. It was a precarious balance for a sixteen-year-old, but she carried it off in spades.

I guess that's what I liked the most about Amanda Hathaway: here was a very decent and beautiful young girl who could have moved among the school's elite, but instead she chose her own path. She traveled in a circle of one.

It was a rare thing to see nowadays, and I admired the hell out of her for it.

We often talked after class, usually after the other students had left, and she would tell me in that quiet, little excited voice of hers about a particular book she was reading or a short story or poem she was working on. Sometimes she would even let me read one.

That was another thing I liked about Amanda—she really trusted me. Besides her parents, I was the only one who knew about her "little secret" (as she often called it): more than anything else Amanda Hathaway wanted to one day become a writer.

WHEN I PULLED into the high school parking lot, I discovered that I was still gripping a quarter in my sweat-slicked hand. I stared at it for a moment and tossed it back into the ashtray.

Before tonight I had never dialed 911, so I hadn't known that it was a toll-free call. Of course, I should've guessed it—who had the time to make change during an emergency?—but I wasn't thinking straight at the time.

Looking back, I guess I was *never* really thinking straight. If I had been, I never would have gone looking for the body in the first place. I never would have hung up the telephone as soon as the emergency operator answered. And I sure as hell never would've gotten back into my car and zig-zagged my way across town to a high school Halloween dance.

No, I wasn't thinking straight at all.

SIX

I FOUND THE red Mustang in the side parking lot. I placed both my hands palm-down on the hood. Still warm. I cupped my hands together and took a quick look inside. Nothing much. A balled-up sweater or sweatshirt on the front seat. A Diet Coke can on the floor. Some cassette tapes.

I walked around to the back of the car and studied the trunk. No blood. No ripped clothing. Nothing.

I took a deep breath. Let it out slowly. And headed for the school.

IT HAD DAWNED on me just a split second before the 911 operator had answered—I had seen the car before. The red Mustang. I couldn't remember where, I couldn't remember when, but I had seen it. I was suddenly sure of it.

So, I'd hung up the telephone and walked quickly across the Safeway parking lot and started driving. A few miles later I was *pretty* sure of one more thing: the Mustang belonged to a student. Present student or former student, I wasn't sure. I'd tried to picture the Phantom in my mind—could he have been just a boy? Again, I couldn't be sure.

Then, I had remembered the Halloween dance—the *costume* dance— and I'd made my way toward the high school, not really expecting to find anything and not knowing what I'd do even if I *did* find something.

And all the while this was happening, the sane half of my brain— the part that balanced checkbooks and went grocery shopping and taught English class and changed diapers—screamed out at me in a shrill, panic-stricken voice: *What the hell are you doing? What are you thinking? Why haven't you called the police?*

But there had been no answers.

Only silence.

I CHECKED MY watch. It was almost eleven and the dance was in full swing.

The high school lobby and cafeteria (where the actual dancing was taking place) were decorated in traditional October fashion: bright orange and black streamers draped the walls and ceilings. Dozens of cardboard Halloween displays—black cats and pumpkins, mostly—covered walls and glass windows and display cases. And, of course, several menacing-looking scarecrows had been placed at various spots throughout the rooms. It was all very innocent and fun.

As I walked in, I smiled and nodded at Valerie Gallagher, a science teacher (and our faculty gossip) who was selling tickets just inside the door. She smiled back—a sleepy little grin that told me she'd already had her usual couple of sips back in the teacher's lounge—and I was grateful that she didn't stop me to chat.

But then, halfway across the lobby, Dan Sellard cut me off. He was a freshman-year English teacher and one of my Thursday night poker buddies. I had no choice but to stop.

"Hey, thought you weren't going to make it tonight?" he said.

I shrugged my shoulders and thought fast. "I, uh…was out for a bite and thought I'd drop in."

He laughed and arched his eyebrows disapprovingly. "Let me guess—large cheesesteak and fries from Frank's?"

"Right on both accounts," I said, faking a smile. "Anything going on here?"

"Nah," he said, shaking his head. "Same old thing. But hey, you hear about Thompkins leaving after this semester?"

Jeremy Thompkins was Sparta High's vice-principal. Like myself, he'd lived in Sparta his entire life. "Leaving where?" I asked. At the moment, I didn't really care what the answer was, but for the life of me, I couldn't figure out how to get out of the conversation.

And then, thankfully, I didn't need to.

Before Dan could answer, a chorus of loud voices rang out behind us. A shoving match had erupted in front of the girls' bathroom. A boy with a gorilla neck and a letterman's jacket had a smaller kid by the shirt collar. And he was starting to twist.

Dan shook his head and turned away. Over his shoulder, he said, "Talk to you later, McKay. Duty calls."

And, just like that, I was free.

I walked into the cafeteria and stood off to the side. Waited for my eyes to adjust to the darkness. There were maybe twenty or thirty kids dancing in the shadows. Others were standing around or sitting in groups of various sizes. A handful stood all alone, trying their hardest not to look miserable and embarrassed. One guy looked like he wanted to cry, and I wondered why the heck he'd come to the dance in the first place.

The DJ—a bald guy with the worst mustache I'd ever seen—was set up against the near wall. By sheer coincidence, he was also one of the skinniest men I'd ever seen and every time he bobbed his head to the music, I feared for his life. His neck appeared no thicker than my forearm.

I caught myself staring at the guy in silent wonder and quickly looked away.

And then I saw him.

The Phantom.

Standing across the room, on the other side of the dance floor, talking to three other boys. None of the others were dressed in costumes. I didn't know their names, but I recognized them as younger students.

I stood and watched them for a long moment...

Then, I started across the dance floor.

What in the hell are you doing? the voice screamed.

There was no response.

Twenty feet away.

Louder this time: *Have you lost your mind?*

Ten feet now.

You could get in big trouble for—

All four boys looked up at me. Stopped talking.

And the Phantom took off his mask.

"Hey, Mr. McKay. Cool dance, huh?"

My heart stopped.

The Phantom was Teddy Bogan. *The* Teddy Bogan. One of the most recognizable kids in school. Teddy, Sparta's best known Special Education student...who could barely catch a ball thrown to him from ten feet away, much less operate a car. Teddy, whose left hand was shriveled beyond repair, the result of a childhood accident. Teddy, who struggled mightily to keep up with even the Special Ed. Curriculum.

"You okay, Mr. McKay?" It was one of the other boys talking now. They all looked up at me with wide eyes and uneasy smiles.

I nodded and said, "Yes, I'm fine. Just checking to see...if you're enjoying yourselves."

I didn't wait for their response. Instead, I turned around a little too quickly. I could feel the heat rushing into my face, and I didn't need a mirror to tell me that I was flushed a dark, embarrassed red.

"Okay," I whispered to myself, taking a deep, calming breath. And then inside my head: *Enough is enough. Who did you think you were anyway, Sherlock Holmes? Barney Fife's more like it, pal. It's time to call the police and tell them everything. Tell them you were scared and panicked. Tell them—*

I blinked my eyes.

Swallowed.

Blinked some more.

The Phantom was right in front of me.

Slow dancing with Kerri Johnson, gliding past me now. If my arms had been working, I could've reached right out and touched his flowing cape. Grabbed him.

Kerri, dressed as a dark and exotic gypsy, giggled and tossed her long, black hair. It was a move that had doubtlessly given dozens of Sparta's young men any number of wet dreams. She laid her head back on the Phantom's shoulder, and they held each other close, spinning ever so slowly. Soon, they melted into the center of the crowd.

I couldn't believe my eyes.

The Phantom was here…

In my school…

Dancing with Kerri Johnson…

But…

Only one person *ever* danced with Kerri Johnson…

And it *couldn't* be…

A month-old memory slammed me in the face—hard and swift and crystal clear.

Last week of September. An hour or so after the final bell. I'd turned the corner and stumbled upon a red-faced and flustered Amanda Hathaway standing outside the assembly hall. The boy standing next to her, as polite and cool as ever. I'd said a quick hello and left them alone, sensing that I had interrupted something intense and private, but at the same time, thinking that it made no sense. Just my imagination was all. Hell, even all the teachers knew that he was going out with Kerri Johnson. Everyone knew that.

I stood in the shadows and watched them dance, thinking about that afternoon back in September. Even in a dark and crowded room, they stood out. They really did. If circumstances had been different, it would've made for a pretty picture indeed: two beautiful young people with the world at their fingertips; the Phantom dashing and mysterious in his mask and cape; the gypsy girl innocent yet alluring in her silk and beads. I watched them dance until the song ended and prayed that I was wrong.

SEVEN

A LONG AND winding hallway connects the back corner of the cafeteria with the Sparta High gymnasium (when the new school year began, the administration asked us teachers to start referring to this area as the "Physical Education Department," but it's really just a drafty, old gym, two ancient locker rooms, and a couple of glassed-in offices, so despite the request, most everyone still calls it by its most practical name: the gym).

During the day, this hallway is one of the busiest places in the school—there's an almost round-the-clock flow of students rushing in to dress before gym class or hurrying out to shower after gym class.

Or just hanging around.

You see, this hallway is also one of the few "cool" places in the school—along with the courtyard out back and the front lobby—so there's usually a pack of students clustered around each corner and outside each doorway. Standing, talking, waiting to be seen.

But that's during the school day.

After classes—day or night, it doesn't matter—this hallway is dark and quiet and deserted. It's a pretty scary place to be.

Unless you *want* to be alone, that is…

AFTER THE SLOW song ended, I watched Kerri Johnson walk right past me out into the lobby, probably on her way to the bathroom or the snack bar.

And then I watched as the Phantom slipped from the back corner of the cafeteria into the dark hallway.

I followed him.

Quietly.

Carefully.

After what felt like a very long time, I rounded the last corner and found him bent over, drinking from one of the two water fountains outside the boys' locker room. He must've heard my footsteps because when I was still a fair distance away, he looked up.

"Oh, hey, Mr. McKay. How's it going?"

He straightened up and wiped a dribble of water from his chin. His voice echoed in the empty hallway, and the familiar sound of it brought about an immediate transformation. Despite the mask and cape, he was no longer the Phantom. Now he was just plain, old Bobby Wilcox. Eighteen-year-old Bobby Wilcox. Hometown boy with the dashing good looks of a movie star. The scholarship officers—in two different sports, mind you—all lined up and waiting.

Bobby Wilcox—smart, popular, handsome…a killer?

Maybe you're wrong about this? the voice inside my head whispered. *You can't be sure—*

When I reached his side, I got right to it. "I think we need to talk, Bobby…I think maybe you're in some trouble."

I spoke softly, for I didn't want my words to carry, and for a long moment I was sure he hadn't heard me. But then:

"I know, I know," he said, looking at the floor. "You'd think I would've learned after last time. I just…I just…I guess I was just being stupid again."

I paused for a moment, genuinely confused. "Exactly what does that mean?" I asked.

"You don't remember? Sophomore year, I got caught drinking at the Christmas dance. Got suspended from the basketball team for five games. Got detention, embarrassed my folks…"

I smelled it then. On his breath. Hard liquor—whiskey, most likely.

I flashed back to him throwing up in the parking lot. *Jesus, he thinks I'm nailing him for drinking.*

My head started shaking back and forth. "No, no, no," I said. "I don't care about your drinking. That's not it."

The expression on his face told me that he didn't understand.

I sucked in a long breath of air. Blew it out. Thought about it for a second, then said very carefully: "Tell me about Amanda."

It was as if I'd pressed some invisible button: the color drained from his face. His entire body sagged. And he started shaking.

I placed a hand on his shoulder, finding it hard to believe that I was actually touching him. "Bobby, calm down. Take some slow and easy breaths and talk to me. Tell me—"

"You know about Amanda?" he said, shrugging off my hand. He looked like he wanted to run away.

I nodded.

"How?"

"It doesn't matter."

"But how could you—"

"I told you it doesn't matter. Now, Bobby, you need to tell me what happened, and then we need to go to the office and call the police. Just you and me. No one else needs to know—"

"But *everyone* will know, won't they? Everyone will know what I did."

He started crying then. Not the sniffle-type of crying and not the whimper-type of crying. This was full-fledged, tears-streaming-down-the-cheeks, sobs-racking-the-body crying. It sounded very loud in the deserted hallway. I checked over my shoulder. The last thing I wanted right now was company.

"You wouldn't understand," Bobby cried. "I had to take her there. I had to do it. I had to..."

His voice dropped off.

His mouth opened wide and, for a moment, he looked like he'd just swallowed a large insect. Then, he started making loud, wheezing sounds and his eyes fluttered open and closed, open and closed.

I moved quickly. Took off his mask.

"Easy, now, Bobby," I said. "Easy now. Just breathe, nice and slow."

I reached over and took him by the elbow. Guided him toward the wall. "You just need some air is all. Why don't we sit down for a minute? Why don't we just sit down and—"

But that's as far as I got.

Because that's when I felt something hard pressed into the center of my back and heard the voice say: "We're gonna walk out the side door and we're gonna do it quietly. Listen to me and no one will get hurt."

I listened.

EIGHT

"DAMN IT, I wish you would stop all that blubbering! You're nothing but a goddamn baby...

"I knew I shouldn't have trusted you. You always were such a wimp..."

It was like that all the way across the parking lot. White-hot anger, dripping with disgust.

And Bobby never said a word. Not one word.

WE WERE SITTING inside the red Mustang. The three of us.

Bobby in the back seat—curled up on his side, still crying, still lost in his own little world.

Me in the driver's seat—looking straight ahead, hands on the steering wheel, knuckles squeezed bone-white, heart pounding so hard I was afraid it was going to stop altogether.

Kerri Johnson in the passenger seat—turned sideways with her back against the window, facing me, a shiny black pistol in her hand.

She was still wearing her costume, but she no longer looked exotic and alluring. Now, she just looked dangerous. She leaned over and inserted the key into the ignition, and I smelled her perfume. It was sweet and airy and reminded me of summer afternoons and suntan lotion.

"Drive," she said.

"Where?"

She nudged me in the ribs with the barrel of the gun. "Just drive. I'll tell you where to go."

I started the car, turned on the headlights, and eased onto Route Nine. The high school disappeared behind us. Thick treeline crept up close on both sides of the road, blocking out the moon. It got very dark and—except for Bobby's sobbing—it got very quiet. Moments later, as we neared the turnoff into town, she said, "Take a left here."

I turned and kept my eyes on the road. I took this as a good sign—we were heading *into* town and not away from it. A million jumbled thoughts were ricocheting around inside by head but nothing was making any sense. More than ever, I just wanted to go home. Back to Janice and the kids. The baby would be waking up soon. She'd be hungry and cranky and—

"Too bad you had to get mixed up in all this, Mr. McKay," she said.

I said nothing.

She looked over the headrest into the backseat and said, "Jesus, Bobby, can't you shut the hell up! Enough is enough. This is all your damn fault, anyway. You and that goddamn Amanda—"

Bobby surprised her (and me) by responding so quickly and so loudly. I jumped in my seat. "You can just go to hell, Kerri Johnson! Straight to hell where you belong! Don't you *ever* say—"

She hit him in the face. Hard. With the gun.

There was a wet smacking thud, and Bobby stopped yelling.

I couldn't stop myself from taking a quick peek at the rearview mirror. Bobby was sitting up, holding the side of his head, his face red and puffy and glistening with tears and saliva. His eyes were wide and panicked; they looked more scared than angry.

Kerri laughed, and it was a hideous sound.

"Keep your eyes on the goddamn road," she said, poking me in the shoulder with the gun.

I nodded. Kept my mouth shut.

We rode in silence for several minutes. Except, of course, for the sniffling sounds coming from the backseat. I was actually thankful for the quiet. I used the time to think, to run everything through my head. The whole thing was beginning to make sense to me now. The pieces were slowly falling into place, and they were forming a very ugly picture.

We turned left onto Longley Road.

Then right onto Baker.

A few blocks later, I broke the silence. "Why are you doing this, Kerri?"

She looked over at me. Sneered. Her upper lip practically did a dance. "Why don't you ask loverboy back there? He'll tell you all about it, won't you, loverboy?" She paused for effect, and then said, "No? What's the matter? Not in the mood to talk right now?"

"How long has he been cheating on you?" I asked. I skipped a beat for my own effect, then added, "With Amanda, I mean."

She didn't answer for a long time.

"Ever since school started," she said quietly. "Ever since the first week of classes."

"That's not true," Bobby said from the back seat.

"SHUT UP!" she screamed. She whirled around and pointed the gun directly at him. Her hand was shaking wildly. "No more lies, loverboy, no more of your fucking lies."

"Stop calling me loverboy," he wailed. "Please, please stop all of this."

And just like that, her hand stopped shaking. Her finger caressed the trigger. Her lips pulled back into a snarl. "You're nothing but a lying, cheating bastard—"

"Easy, Kerri," I said, slowing the car and hoping she didn't notice.

"You shut the hell up, too. None of this is your goddamn business, anyway. You poked your nose in the wrong place at the wrong time, and now you're gonna pay for it."

"Kerri, listen to me—"

"No, you listen to *me*! I said shut up and drive. Not even one more word." She stabbed the gun in my direction and cold steel kissed my cheek.

I looked at her and shuddered. I couldn't help it. There was madness burning in her eyes. She was afire with it.

Once, back in college, I'd watched a film about predatory jungle cats. Nothing special, but there'd been several minutes of footage showing a pack of adult male cats in a blood-soaked feeding frenzy. At that moment, driving across the darkened streets of Sparta, that's precisely what Kerri Johnson's eyes reminded me of: pure bestial hunger and rage. Uncontrollable and without conscience. There was nothing human left inside those eyes. Nothing at all.

I shut my mouth and followed her directions.

A left, then two more rights.

It was seventeen minutes before midnight when we pulled into the parking lot behind the old post office.

NINE

"JESUS, NO WONDER you found the body," she said.

The wind had died down considerably, and the woods were ominously still and silent. Nothing seemed to move. Overhead, the cloud cover had mostly blown away and now thick shafts of moonlight fell from between the treetops. Amanda's body laid in clear view.

"Send a boy to do a man's job and this is what you get," Kerri snickered.

Bobby elbowed me and said, "He already told you that he found her and uncovered her. I swear I did a better job than this. I buried her real good."

"Oh, shut up and stop whining," she said. "I'm so sick of all your goddamn whining."

Kerri stood on one side of Amanda's body. Bobby and I stood on the opposite side. She held the gun in front of her. I could tell she wasn't sure what to do next.

I didn't look at the body. Not once. Instead, I searched for a way out. I considered making a run for it, just sprinting off into darkness, but quickly decided against it. I've never been the most coordinated man, and call me a coward if you wish, but it was pure and simple fear that stopped me. The fear that I would stumble and fall before I got even ten or twenty or thirty yards away; the fear that I would roll over onto my back and have to watch as she stood above me and smiled and slowly pulled the trigger...

No, it would have to be something else.

"Tell me, Bobby." Her voice was sweet and mocking. "Exactly what was it about dear little Amanda that made you want to leave me? What... could...it...be? She do your homework for you? Rub your back after practice? Was she good in bed, Bobby?"

"Shut up."

"No, tell me. I really want to know. She had everyone else fooled, but I bet she was a real slut in bed, wasn't she? Was that it?" She was enjoying this. Getting louder. Her voice was frantic. "Did she suck your cock the way I used to, Bobby? Did she fuck you the way I used to? Come on, don't be shy. Tell us."

"Stop it. Just stop it. The only thing we ever did was kiss. And talk. It wasn't the way you said it was. I swear."

"You were going to leave me," she said, and it wasn't a question.

"I loved her, Kerri. Damn it, I didn't mean for it to happen, but I fell in love with her. Can't you understand—"

"Love!" she spat. "What the hell do *you* know about love? You fell in love with *me* after only a month. Remember that, loverboy? Calling me day and night. Writing me all those letters. You remember that?"

Bobby hung his head. Said nothing.

"Hell, I should have killed you right along with her," she hissed.

There was a long stretch of silence then, maybe one or two full minutes. Bobby stared at the ground; Kerri stared at Bobby; I stared at Kerri. No one spoke. No one moved. And then:

"You know, it was a lot easier than I thought it would be," she said. "Killing her, I mean."

"Stop it," Bobby said.

"No, really. It was a piece of cake."

"Stop it!"

"I mean all I did was push her down and squeeze the trigger. Didn't even aim. Just pointed and shot her right in the goddamn head."

"STOP IT!"

"And the blood. Jesus, it was—"

Bobby lost it then.

He let out a scream that wasn't quite human and dove over Amanda's corpse. He crashed onto Kerri's chest, and they fell hard to the ground and rolled into the shadows. There was the unmistakable sound of flesh striking flesh, but I couldn't tell who was hitting whom. Then, I saw it—a glint of metal in the moonlight. The gun. Lying in the dirt. I dove toward it. And then we were all fighting for it. Rolling. Scratching. Kicking. Punching.

A finger gouged my eye.

Kerri screamed in my ear.

Someone pulled my hair.

I felt a hand grab me between the legs and squeeze.

A wave of nausea hit and my vision went spotty...

A gunshot roared in the night.

Then another.

Two sharp cracks.

I rolled free, onto my back, and felt something hot and sticky running down my arm.

High above us, a barn owl screeched and took flight from the treetops, and I watched as it flew across the face of the moon...

TEN

I WAS THE only survivor. I suppose I should tell you that right up front. And, although I survived to tell this story, it doesn't have a happy ending. At least, not in the traditional sense.

They took me to Parkton General Hospital with a bullet wound to the shoulder. A clean wound, the doctor called it. No muscle or nerve damage. He said I was very lucky. Nonetheless, Janice cried so hard I thought they were going to have to admit her into the next bed. That afternoon, her mother drove down to stay with the kids, and Janice and I spent Halloween night watching *Twilight Zone* reruns on the hospital television. After a few days, the doctors sent me home.

In deference to the families, Sheriff Cain tried to keep the story out of the press, but he should have known better. It was the biggest news story in the history of Sparta, and it even made the newspapers as far up north as Boston. There was a rumor floating around town for a couple of weeks that one of those tabloid television programs was coming down to do a story. But they never did show up, and I (and a whole bunch of other folks) were grateful for that.

Predictably, the out-of-town newspapers and television people went hot and heavy on the love triangle aspect. The headlines ranged from SEX-CRAZED CHEERLEADER GOES ON RAMPAGE to TEENAGE LUST LEADS TO BETRAYAL AND MURDER. They used yearbook photos and maps of Sparta and one channel even used videotapes that had turned up missing two weeks earlier from the high school.

For a few weeks—right up until around Thanksgiving—it was a real mess. Reporters all over the place, asking questions, badgering folks for comments. Curious strangers running loose around town. People calling the house at all hours. Knocking on the front door. Taking pictures. They even had to block the entrance to the parking lot behind the old post office. And when that didn't keep the reporters and the sightseers out, they had to string up a barbwire fence, for God's sake. Seems like a waste of money to me, though. I heard they're planning to start construction in a month or two on the brand new shopping plaza. I also heard Wal-Mart is moving in, so at least that's something.

Just for the record, in case you've been on the moon and haven't heard, here's the story exactly as they reported it (some were racier than others, but all the reports essentially said the same thing): a seventeen-year-old cheerleader from a small town in North Carolina kills her classmate in a jealous rage and convinces her unfaithful boyfriend to dispose of the body. Then, after overhearing the drunken and remorseful boyfriend confess to a teacher at a high school dance, the girl kidnaps them both at gunpoint and forces them to drive to the woods where the body is hidden. Once there, she shoots the boyfriend to death, wounds the teacher, and finally is killed herself in a struggle for the gun. The shaken English instructor is the only witness, and he's not talking to the press. His only statement, issued through the local sheriff's department: "A tragedy. Plan and simple. A dark night for this town. A night best forgotten…"

And that's pretty much it, the story I told the police after they rushed me to the hospital—all summed up, nice and neat.

They called it self-defense. A clear-cut case.

The police and the lawyers agreed. Without question.

Even Kerri Johnson's mother and father took the time to send over a card to the house. They scribbled inside that they'd heard at the church that I was having problems coming to grips with what had happened. Reassured me that I was not to blame for their daughter's death. That it had been "self-defense," and that she had brought it upon herself through "unholy actions." The bottom had been signed LOVE, RICH & TERRY. Like a Christmas card.

You know, self-defense is a nifty little concept when you really stop and think about it. It can mean an awful lot of things to an awful lot of people.

Truth is, if I do just that, if I stop and think about it long enough, I can *almost* bring *myself* to believe in it. Just like all the others.

But then the dreams come.

And I see only truth…

MY SHOULDER IS bleeding pretty badly, but strangely enough, it doesn't hurt. Not even a twinge of discomfort. I'm standing in the shadows with the gun in my hand. I'm not sure how the gun got there, only that at some point during the struggle I'd rolled onto my back and there it was.

Bobby is behind me, face-down in the brush, dead or dying from a point-black shot to the back of the head. And there, lying at my feet, is Kerri. Smiling up at me.

I stand there for a long time, staring down at her. At her smile. At her eyes.

And, once again, I think of Janice and my children. I think of this town I call my home. I think of my school and the kids I have taught there. Finally, I think of Amanda Hathaway and, from the corner of my eye, I glimpse her still body.

I look back to Kerri—in one night, this girl has taken away so much from me. And still she lies there smiling. Unhurt. Unremorseful.

I take a step forward and raise the gun. Her smile turns into a sneer.

One step closer.

And I pull the trigger.

Kerri jerks once on the ground and immediately starts groaning.

It's an ugly sound, and I want it to stop.

I kneel down next to her and look into her eyes…and see nothing. Nothing worth saving.

So I pull the trigger once more…

IT'S SUMMER NOW and Sparta is a magical place once again. The grass is thick and green. The hills are alive and sparkling with nature's touch. Every day the sun seems to shine a little brighter.

Just yesterday, the four of us went on a late morning picnic down to Broad Creek. There was no one else there and, for a time, it felt like we were the only ones living and breathing in the entire world. Josh caught three catfish and a sunnie before he got tired and took a nap on a stretched-out blanket in the shade. We took off the baby's shoes and dipped her tiny feet in the cool, bubbling water and marveled at the smiles it brought about. After lunch, Janice picked a bouquet of fresh flowers and they now decorate our dining room table.

For the longest time, I sat in the sunshine and watched my family. And thanked God for blessing me with so much.

Janice smiles more often now, and she says I do the same. She thinks I'm finally leaving the bad memories behind, and I have to agree with her.

Still, sometimes my sleep is troubled and I find myself dreaming of that terrible night back in October.

And in these dreams, I see their faces.

Amanda Hathaway, eyes closed forever.

Bobby Wilcox, weeping and afraid.

And Kerri Johnson…smiling at me with the eyes of a monster.

I don't dream as often now, and I'm thankful for that. One day I hope to stop completely. One day I hope to forget.

But in the meantime, I'm still father and husband and teacher. I've also become a celebrity of sorts around here—albeit a reluctant one. And I still go out and drive some nights. Just not very often now; maybe once or twice a month. Janice still understands, but she worries about me.

I worry about her, too.

And the kids.

I worry about a lot of things.

BRIDE OF FRANKENSTEIN:

A Love Story

CLASSIFIED MATERIAL
The following are excerpts from a journal found in the suspect's residence:

June 3

THE TIME HAS FINALLY come and I can barely contain my excitement. After weeks of careful planning and preparation, I am almost ready to proceed. I brought in the final load of equipment and supplies from the university early this morning, and I found what I needed from the hospital clinic yesterday. Everyone at the hospital acted delighted to see me, of course, but I could tell they were uncomfortable with having to face me after all this time. They were stiff and serious, and so careful with their words; even the expressions on their faces were fragile masks. I know they were laughing behind those masks. They have always laughed at me. The final piece of equipment is due to arrive here at the house some time tomorrow after lunch. UPS has been very good to me. The basement looks wonderful and is well on its way to becoming fully operational. I must remember, though, to buy a couple of big fans later this week; I'll have to scrub the floor some more, too, to keep the dust down. The air downstairs is much too musty to work in for long stretches of time, but that should clear up. The overhead lights I picked up were a good fit, but I'll need at least one more. It's all finally coming together.

June 6

IF I AM discovered, they will surely think I am mad. Of that, I am quite certain. But they do not share my vision, and they do not feel my pain. Of that, I am also certain. I do not concern myself with the danger of discovery; I plan to be painstakingly careful. Besides, there are so many other things that call for my attention. Strangely, I find myself wondering what my peers would think if they could take a peek into my secret world. I think of that arrogant bastard Fred Benson, his tiny rat face squinting in the bright basement light. Eyes flashing wide when he finally realizes exactly what it is he is seeing, grabbing his heart and swooning the way he does when he wishes to make one of his dramatic scenes. I especially like to envision what the ice princess Jennifer Taylor's reaction might be. I crack up just thinking about that! She would probably take one look and drop stone cold to the floor. What a sight that would be! But all of this is harmless curiosity. Of course, I do not care for their opinions. They never did understand. Sure, they acted compassionate for a time. Expressed what seemed like genuine sympathy. Told me to keep my chin up. But, then, when I didn't bounce back to their idea of a normal functioning human on their own damn timetable, they sent Charlie Cavanaugh—as if that moron knew anything at all about the pains of lost love—out to the house to give me the old "life goes on" speech. No, sir. They know nothing of my misery. Nothing of the darkness that has enveloped my heart.

The lab is complete now. Everything seems in fine order. Tomorrow is Saturday. I will make my move in the morning.

June 8

IT WAS SO easy! So damn easy! If a single sliver of doubt that my vision was true and honorable existed before yesterday's events, it is certainly gone now. This must be my destiny! I am so filled this beautiful spring morning with hope and wonder and the tingle of sweet, sweet memories, I feel I could burst! Yesterday was as mentally numbing and physically exhausting as any day I have ever known, but after just a few hours of sleep, I feel more than sufficiently rested. Indeed, I feel rejuvenated, enlightened. Body and spirit.

I found her only miles from here. A dear, sweet woman. A classic beauty with thick, flowing hair the color of sun-sprinkled wheat and the lean, tan body of an athlete. After I did what I had to do—the hardest part—I gently placed her in the back of the van and covered her with the flannel blanket Marilyn and I always used to spread for picnics. Drove carefully home and backed into the garage. Carried her in through the breezeway and down into the basement. Spent most of the night checking and rechecking the system, then hooking her up. Today will be a busy day.

June 9

SPENT THE PAST eighteen hours with her. I'm drained, but not at all discouraged. If I am to break new ground here, I must remain strong. Looking at her, I can't help but daydream about Marilyn—wonder what we would be doing if she hadn't left me...what our lives would be like. I find myself thinking of one day in particular...back when I was very young, the first semester of my final year of undergrad school, I think. We'd awakened that Saturday morning in each other's arms, eaten a light breakfast outside on the back porch. Spent the afternoon downtown, walking hand-in-hand, munching soft pretzels and snow cones, browsing in the book and record shops, playing video arcade games in one of the sidewalk mini-malls. Hours later, our legs begging for mercy, we stopped for dinner at one of our favorite Fells Point seafood restaurants and watched the boats cruise the harbor, their white and blue and red lights dancing a private show for us as we enjoyed our meals. We slowly walked the streets home, her head on my shoulder, and made wondrous love for over an hour before finally falling asleep. It had been a truly magical day, full of life's simpler pleasures. The kind of pleasures you had to be in love to understand and fully appreciate. The kind of pleasures Marilyn blessed me with each and every day for over 35 years…and then took away so cruelly.

June 12

SOMETHING IS WRONG. It's not working. I checked and rechecked the entire system and cannot locate a problem anywhere. I wonder if, perhaps, I am the problem. I'm not thinking clearly enough, I know that much. My vision is blurry, and I keep hearing Marilyn's voice down there, but now I can't understand her sometimes. It's almost as if she's going farther away from me instead of coming closer. And I keep seeing things…a wave of a finger, a blink of an eye, a twitch of a nose. But it's not possible…not yet. I just need some rest tonight. That's all. I will keep at it in the morning.

There has been no mention of the missing woman on the television news. I've watched the Channel 11 spot every day, and taped the other two channels. Nothing. There was an article in the *Sun*, but this is the city, so something like this merits a mere three paragraphs of mention on page 9. Off to bed now. But first I'll say a prayer that I dream of Marilyn and that I find the problem tomorrow.

June 19

I HAD NO other choice…I had to go out and find two more. It wasn't as easy as the first time. I had to drive out to the country this time, but I did it anyway. I made it back safely, and they are waiting for me in the basement. I should have known that Marilyn's sweet voice was telling the truth— that the first woman was not the one. I was not the problem; *she* was. She had been telling me that all week, but I wouldn't listen. Wouldn't listen to anything she was saying. Now I know better and have two specimens to choose from; I only pray that one of them will work out. I'm starting to feel the pressure now. Things are going to heat up in a hurry, I'm sure. Three incidents in just over two weeks will make this big news by the morning paper. I can't risk the chance of going out and finding another...please let one of them be the one!

June 20

SUCCESS AT LAST! The third woman is perfect! She's so much like Marilyn that it's almost spooky. And her voice is so strong and clear now; so chipper and cheerful, just like when she was here with me. Before I hooked her up today, she begged me to carry her upstairs and let her sit in her favorite old chair for a while. I obliged and promised her only fifteen minutes, but ended up rocking and humming to her for over thirty. She's safe and sound in the basement now. Finally, all the pieces are in place. Soon we will be together again!

June 21

MUST KEEP IT brief tonight. I haven't felt this drained since residency, when the thought of a good night's rest was a fool's dream. The procedure is progressing magnificently, if a lot slower than I expected. It seems the only matter I overlooked was the lack of an assistant, and the delays that could possibly arise because of that. Nonetheless, I am supremely confident, and will continue in the morning when my strength allows. Soon, my love.

June 23

MY GOD, IT'S over! I've failed! They have come for me! The alarm is sounding upstairs, and I can hear the angry shouts of the men and the hungry cries of their dogs. They are pounding on the door and I fear they will break through at any moment! It rips my heart that I am so very close to eternal love but I will never feel her tender lips on mine ever agai—

EXCERPTED FROM THE June 25 press statement issued to all media by the Baltimore City Police Department:

At approximately 9:25 a.m. on Monday, June 23, state and local authorities arrested Doctor Francis Einstein at his home in the 1400 block of Federal Hill and charged him with numerous offenses, including trespassing, theft, and graverobbing.

Evidence seized at the scene indicates that Dr. Einstein, 35, is responsible for the three "body snatchings" that have taken place in city and county cemeteries over the past three weeks. In each incident, cemetery personnel reported that they were surprised by a white male and knocked unconscious with what was thought to be a rag soaked in ether. Each time, when the employee regained consciousness, the casket lay open and the body was missing.

Additional evidence found in the residence indicates that Dr. Einstein is also responsible for several robberies at the University of Maryland's School of Medicine, including the theft of a human brain from a Neurology research lab.

As you will all soon see (the residence is still an active crime scene and will not be released to the media until 9 a.m. tomorrow), the basement of Dr. Einstein's home has been constructed into a makeshift laboratory facility, with twin stainless steel operating tables, a functioning life-support system, and various other unidentified medical equipment. Dr. Einstein was found hiding in the basement and placed in custody, and all three bodies were discovered on the property.

After extensive questioning, police psychiatrist Donald Gaines reports that Dr. Einstein's only official comment is: "I did it all for love. I did it for my Marilyn."

Gaines explains: "The woman he is referring to is Marilyn Caroline Einstein, his deceased mother. For reasons unknown, she took her own life six months ago (gunshot wound to the head), and according to his former partners at his medical practice, Einstein never recovered from his loss. He was still on emergency medical leave at the time of his arrest. Neighbors and friends report that Einstein was extremely close to his mother (his father died when he was seven years of age) and had never left the home he grew up in, even after he earned a national reputation as a surgeon.

"I'll try to have more details for you all on this later, but the initial story at least is that Dr. Einstein claims he saw a vision and heard a voice inside his head some time ago that told him he could bring Marilyn back if he found the right body and a functioning brain...that he could somehow reanimate her. Apparently, he believed the voice to be that of his mother because, he claims, it told him things no one else could know about himself. The voice also told him that she was as sad and as lonely as he was and that she was sorry she had committed suicide and that she longed to return to life again. When Einstein's initial reaction was one of doubt, the voice became angry, told him that it was his destiny and that it was for this reason that his mother originally named him Francis. The voice told him that his given name was Doctor Francis Einstein...then repeated over and over and over again that his common name was FrankEinstein...FrankEinstein... FrankEinstein.

"After a short time, Dr. Einstein became convinced that he was indeed the Frankenstein of myth and legend, and he set out to recapture his mother's love."

Dr. Einstein is currently under police guard at City Hospital's Psychiatric Department, where he is awaiting further testing.

PAGE ONE HEADLINE of June 26 evening edition of the *Baltimore Sun*:

FRANKENSTEIN LIVES!

THE SEASON OF GIVING

I WAS STILL THINKING ABOUT the deuce of hearts when the little girl with the face of an angel yanked on my coat sleeve.

It was the first weekend of December, six inches of new snow blanketed the city, and we were already pulling double shifts at Parker's Department Store. Management had settled on the usual preholiday security setup—four guards spread out over each of the three floors; one man per floor in a regulation United Security uniform, the other three working plainclothes.

Only one of us had to wear the suit.

Earlier, as per our new daily routine, we'd cut a deck of cards in the guard lounge. I'd felt pretty confident when Eddie Schwartz, who had worn the suit three days running, pulled the black three. And I'd gone on feeling pretty confident until I turned up the stinkin' deuce of hearts.

Eddie ho-ho-hoed like Santa when he saw it—something he hadn't done once during his tenure in the suit. The others had a good time with it, too. Cracking wise, speculating about my relationship with the reindeer as they watched me dress. Giving me a standing ovation as I left the lounge, my middle finger extended as stiff and proud as the candy-striped pole in front of Santa's workshop way up north.

I wasn't laughing, though. I'd avoided wearing the suit since the season started, and after hearing the complaints from my co-workers—"God, that thing's hot. It smells like my old closet. Christ, it's embarrassing."—I'd been hoping my luck would hold.

Well, I'd never had much luck. But now, a few hours into my shift, I could almost see that the whole thing was pretty funny. *Almost*. Me, of all people, dressed up as Santa Claus. Me, a bearer of gifts, when my usual commodity was misery. Mr. Sunshine in a bright red suit and cap. Shiny black boots. Pillow stuffing for a belly. Fluffy white beard. Everything but the red nose, which I'd lost for good when I stopped drinking.

On top of all that, the guys were right. The suit *did* smell like an old closet, and it *was* hot and heavy as hell. But it also had its advantages. Working the front of the store was a relatively easy job. Not much to do, actually. Stand behind an old Red Cross kettle, smack dab in the middle of the mall's main intersection, just south of a North Pole display featuring jungle gyms disguised as Victorian houses, slides, and plenty of not-so-inconspicuous toy advertisements. Ring a rusty old cowbell every few minutes; but mainly keep an eye out for trouble on the North Pole, because Parker's didn't want to handle any personal injury suits involving kids at Christmas. Still, compared to chasing shoplifters and pickpockets up and down the clothes aisles and arguing with irate holiday shoppers, the Santa gig was a cakewalk.

Anyway, that was the setup. Back to the little girl.

I'd noticed her as soon as I returned from my break. A little angel moving slowly through the crowd, head down, getting bumped and nudged with every step. She looked about seven or eight, a tiny thing wearing a faded winter jacket at least two sizes too big for her. The frayed collar was flipped up, and you could just see the top half of her pale face as she bobbed and weaved, eyes telling anyone who bothered to look that she was on her own.

The crowd swept her along like a strong wind pushing a tiny leaf, and I feared that she might be trampled. Instead, as if sensing my concern, she looked in my direction and our eyes locked momentarily.

Thinking for an instant that I was wearing my security uniform instead of the Santa suit, I mistook the look of glee in her eyes for desperate relief.

I could play the rest of the scene out in my head. She was going to tell me that she was lost: could I please help her find her parents or her brother or sister?

That happened all the time, but sometimes the scene took a scarier turn. Plenty of parents these days used the mall as a free baby-sitter— dropping off their underage kids for a few hours while they ran errands. In these tough times, too many people thought it was cheaper and easier to give a kid a five-spot for pizza and video games than to spring for a sitter. They were the kind of parents who thought everything would always be okay. With them, with their kids, with their spouses.

I used to think that way, but now I know better. We all do a hundred little things every day, without even thinking about them. But one thing I've learned—little things have a way of becoming big things before you even have a chance to notice.

As the girl approached me, I decided she was a definite candidate for a drop-off. Reason number one: her eyes told me that she was alone. Reason number two: she looked scared. Reason number three: her appearance—clothes that were hand-me-downs or garage sale bargains; the pale, unhealthy cast of her otherwise beautiful face—spoke of a family that couldn't afford a baby-sitter, let alone three squares a day.

The girl stopped in front of me, her eyes lonely but somehow still as blue and bright as a summer sky. She smiled suddenly, and my own mouth twitched into a grin.

I was unused to that particular expression.

"You have to sit down," she said, very seriously.

"Huh?"

"You have to sit down so I can sit on your lap."

The Santa suit. Of course. I crouched down to her level. "Sorry, sweetie," I said. "You're looking for the real Santa. He's over on the second floor, sitting next to the carousel."

"I *know* you're not the real Santa." She rolled those lonely eyes, branding me a first-class dope. "And neither is the other one. But you work for Santa, right?"

The only thing I could do was nod.

"Then you can tell Santa what my wish is."

I had to laugh then, and the thick elastic band on the fake beard knifed into my cheeks. It didn't matter though. I didn't care. I mean, it wasn't a raucous ho-ho-ho worthy of good old Eddie Schwartz, but it came from a part of me I thought I'd forgotten about. There was something special about that, just as there was something special about this serious, sad-eyed little girl.

Change rattled into the kettle, and I waved my thanks to a shopper, but the little girl didn't have patience for my manners. "Well?" she asked. "Are you going to sit down, or what?"

"Here's the deal." My voice was low, conspiratorial. "You're right about me being on Santa's payroll. But I still think you'd better talk to the other Santa." I crossed my white-gloved fingers. "He and the big guy are just like *this*."

I expected a smile out of her, but what I got was a frown. Her blue eyes puddled up, and the brightness leeched from them. "You don't understand. I can't wait. The line for the other Santa is way too long." She pointed over her shoulder, and her tiny finger was actually shaking. "M-my mom will be done shopping any second. And then we gotta go home."

Okay, I thought, *now we're getting somewhere.* "Your mother is in this store? Does she know where you are?"

"Yes…well, kinda. I told her I was going to the bathroom and that I'd meet her by the North Pole." She pointed over to the playground where other kids were sliding and charging around and having a good time.

"Sure about that, sweetheart? You know, it isn't nice to fib to one of Santa's stand-ins."

She nodded furiously. "Can't I please tell you now? Can't I, please?" Her eyes were beyond desperate. "*Pleeaazzze…*"

God, she was a cutie. Fragile as the expensive dolls in Parker's toy department, and with the same porcelain complexion. I watched her tiny lips move as she talked. Noticed the patch of freckles on her nose, the perfect shape of her ears, the way her hair was tied back with a long red ribbon.

Realized with a sudden jolt why the girl had captivated me so.

Realized exactly who she reminded me of.

I hadn't seen my daughter in almost seven years. Not since she was eight years old. Not since that rainy December morning Sheila had chosen to make their break for freedom. Talk about your basic holiday hell. Divorce papers had followed a week later. Merry Christmas. Not that I noticed at the time.

It was an easy decision for the judge. I was a drunk then, didn't care that I had a wife who needed me, a daughter who needed me even more. Didn't care that the alcohol was killing my spirit and turning me into a man my family genuinely hated. And then when I finally did realize what I had lost, and what I had become, it was much too late.

I spent a full year in a stupor, trying to forget the look on my daughter's face when she summed the whole thing up so beautifully: "You're not my daddy anymore," she said the last time I saw her, "because you're a bad man."

I emptied hundreds of bottles in her memory after she spoke those words, savoring the simple truth of that baldly elegant statement. And when I finally got tired of emptying bottles, I broke one and carved up my wrists with a sliver of glass. Pathetic, if you want to sum it up bald and elegant.

The little girl tugged my sleeve again, and I jerked away, imagining her fingers brushing across the scar tissue on my wrists, imagining that the red material of the Santa suit was stained with my blood.

"Please let me tell you my wish."

"Okay." I pushed away my memories, feeling a strange combination of sorrow and glee. "But you have to tell me something first. Have you been a good girl this year?"

Her forehead wrinkled in deep thought—and my heart melted a little more because I'd forgotten all the perfectly genuine expressions that kids have—and then she gave me a very serious nod. "I think so. Mommy says that I'm a good girl all the time."

"I'm sure your mom wouldn't lie," I said. "Now, you give me the word, and I'll give it to the big guy at the North Pole."

She moved closer, and her voice became a whisper. "I don't want any toys." She paused and looked around, as if someone might be listening to her little secret, as if an eavesdropper could render the wish null and void in Santa's eyes. "I just want Santa to bring me a brand new daddy for Christmas. And I want him to make my real daddy go away."

My heart skittered, then started beating faster. I looked at the little girl and suddenly saw my daughter, and a hot sheen of sweat dampened my face.

You're not my daddy.

My mouth was running before I knew what to say. "Now, sweetie, I'm not so sure that Santa Claus can bring you that type of present. Wouldn't you rather have a pretty new dress?" *Or a coat that fits?* I thought, looking again at the tattered thing she was wearing.

She didn't say anything, but that didn't keep me from hearing the other voice in my head. *You're not my daddy, because you're a bad man.*

And then I was apologizing, alibiing for a man I didn't even know. "Look," I continued. "I'll bet your dad will get you something nice. I'll bet he already has a great big present for you right under the tree. I'll bet—"

"No!" A tear rolled down her cheek, and she wiped it away before anyone else could see it. "I don't *like* my daddy's presents. I want a new daddy, someone to make me and mommy happy. I just have to get one. You gotta help me."

Suddenly the Santa costume felt as heavy as a suit of armor, all the weight centered on my chest and stomach. And for the first time since going straight three years before, I thought of just how lucky my little girl was to have a real father now, someone to watch over her and protect her and love her. Someone who wasn't a *bad man*...even if he was a damn chiropractor.

My eyes misted over and I closed them. I didn't know what to say. I sent my own wish to Santa, FedEx. All I wanted for Christmas was the right answer for this little girl.

"Julie, what in the world have you done to Santa?"

I opened my eyes. The girl's mother was younger than I would have guessed, late-twenties probably. A mirror image of her daughter, another waif in faded jeans and a worn jacket, carrying a single Parker's shopping bag.

I grinned. This time it was a reflex. I really didn't know what to do.

"I sure hope Julie hasn't been bothering you," the woman said. "I got held up in line and—"

The woman smiled and tousled Julie's hair. She was every bit as beautiful as her daughter, and every bit as tragic. Her eyes held the same sadness, but they never flashed bright the way her child's sometimes did. They were the eyes of a woman who had faced too much pain in her time and had given up the fight. Someone who was merely existing, not living.

Someone just like me.

"Well, I'll apologize anyway," the woman said. "Julie's a good girl"—Julie nudged my leg, as if to say *I told you so*—"but she can be a bit headstrong." The woman made a polite show of checking her watch. "Julie, honey, we really have to get going. We're already an hour late. You know how your father gets when his dinner isn't waiting for him."

"Okay. In a minute, Mom."

I smiled at the friendly mother-daughter battle waging before me, recalling the occasions when my wife and daughter had done the same.

But those days were gone.

You're not my daddy...

"Well, thanks again for being so nice to Julie," the woman said. "And have a Merry Christmas." She took Julie's hand. "Let's go, honey."

They were swallowed by the crowd and, just like that, the incident was over. Or so I thought.

A few seconds later, the little angel reappeared. "I almost forgot," she said, panting. "Please tell Santa this is where I live."

She handed me a piece of paper. The lined kind you tear from a small tablet. Three short sentences in careful block print. A street address that wasn't far from the mall.

Her hand drifted away slowly. Brushed my big black belt. Brushed the front of my red pants.

Her fingers lingered for just a second against my crotch.

She looked at me with those lonely eyes. "I'll do anything," she said. "Tell Santa I'll do anything if he gives me what I want."

Then her hand was gone, and she was gone, and everything was very clear.

I just want Santa to bring me a brand new daddy for Christmas. And then I want him to make my real daddy go away...

You know how your father gets when his dinner isn't waiting for him...

I don't like my daddy's presents...

I'll do anything...tell Santa I'll do anything if he gives me what I want...

I stared at the slip of paper with Julie's address on it, thinking about the fierce determination on the little angel's face and the sad quiet beauty of her mother, knowing with complete clarity how life had molded them.

Understanding, for the first time, how life had molded me.

I CALLED IN sick more than I should have, made use of my days off, didn't sleep much. You can always find time to do things if you really want to, and I found that I wanted to do something for the first time in years. Besides, it wasn't like I had a ton of unfinished Christmas shopping or invitations demanding my presence at holiday parties hither and yon. No airplane ride to visit the relatives out west. No drive in the country to visit friends. No Christmas in Connecticut for me.

No, my social schedule was clear. I spent my time with Julie and her family, though they never knew that I was around.

The rusted mailbox in front of the house said COOPER. The house itself looked like any other in the neighborhood, just another old ranch-style thing that needed work—new gutters, energy-efficient windows, some paint. There were no Christmas lights hanging from the eaves, no tree in the window. That wasn't unusual—more than a few of the Cooper's neighbors seemed to be getting along without the prescribed signs of sea-sonal cheer. The neighborhood was definitely not upwardly mobile, more like *we're-holding-on-by-the-skin-of-our-teeth*. But Julie's was the only house on the block where the snow mounded unshoveled on the walk, the only house where a television antenna stood in for a cable hookup.

None of that really surprised me, not at first. I'd seen the way Julie and Tina—that was her mom's name—dressed. I'd followed them to enough discount markets and cheap gas stations to know that things were tight with them.

I wasn't really surprised until I saw Julie's father for the first time. He glided past my parked car late one evening, lounging behind the wheel of a black Cadillac Seville that shone like a new eight ball. He parked next to the rattletrap Datsun that Tina drove, a hunk of Japanese metal that looked like Godzilla had had his way with it.

A couple days passed before our schedules meshed. Then I followed Mr. Cooper instead of Julie and Tina.

I hated him instantly. For one thing, he worked for the phone company. He was a big enough fish to warrant his own parking space, and he made a habit of taking the bigger fish to lunch and picking up the tab. I followed him into places where I could barely afford the price of a Diet Coke and a bowl of soup. I watched as he left generous tips for the waiters, and I don't think I'll ever forget the satisfied little smirk that crossed his lips when he gave his boss a pen-and-pencil set from Parker's, a shoplifter's favorite that would have set me back several day's pay. After work, Cooper stopped off for drinks at a bar near the highway, a dive called the High Hat Club. Dropped more tip money, though he kept to himself. Didn't spare the booze, either. He was always pretty well tanked by the time he headed home.

All this while his wife and daughter lived like paupers.

That wasn't the only reason I disliked Julie's dad, though.

His first name was Adrian. That went right along with the little smirk.

And Adrian Cooper liked to rape his daughter.

It happened on weekends as far as I could tell. Tina actually had a job on Saturday and Sunday at a run-down florist shop over by the mall, but I knew the job was just a ploy to get her out of the house.

I sat in my car on two consecutive weekends, trying not to be noticed on that gray little street. Four days, and every one of them was the same. Tina would leave for work. Shortly thereafter, the drapes would whisper closed, and the lights would be extinguished. The last drape to close and the last light to dim were always in Julie's bedroom.

Several hours passed each time. Then the lights came on and the drapes were opened, after which Adrian packed the sullen little girl with the porcelain complexion into his big black car and treated her to an ice-cream sundae at the mall. I'm sure that in his sick little mind that trip to the mall made everything okay with him. The son of a bitch couldn't even see it. Slurping up his ice cream, fingers drumming so innocently on his pale daughter's knee.

Four days of that, and I saw everything as if I had x-ray vision. I sat there in my old car, watching the minutes tick by on the dashboard clock. It was all I could do to stay behind the wheel while it happened.

And then the last Sunday came, the Sunday before Christmas, and suddenly I realized I was done sitting.

The Caddy pulled out and headed for the mall. I made a U-turn and parked in front of the rusted mailbox that said COOPER. I got out and walked up the drive, and I didn't even bother to knock because no one who lived on the gray little street was paying attention.

I kicked in the door. Like I said, there wasn't a Christmas tree, but there were a few presents. It didn't surprise me that most of them were addressed to "Adrian" or "Daddy." I collected a stack, took them out to the car, and dumped them in the backseat, just to make it look good. I waited to hear the sirens, but there was no sound at all.

I returned to the house, and this time I closed the door behind me. Adrian and Tina had separate bedrooms. Adrian, of course, occupied the largest in the house.

It was a fairly boring room. Dull—if tasteful—furniture, stupid little Sharper Image gadgets, uninspiring prints on the wall, and a bed with a very hard mattress.

A stout, masculine dresser stood to the right of the bed. I searched the drawers and found stiff pin-striped shirts and argyle socks and other clothes that seemed designed especially for a phone company fast-track kind of guy. Other drawers housed Ralph Lauren clothes for fast-track-kind-of-guy weekends.

In the bottom drawer, beneath Adrian's Polo sweaters, I found a pistol.

So, the bastard was smart enough to be a little paranoid.

I figured the pistol was a sign that I was getting close. I pulled up the lining paper glued to the bottom of the drawer. A large envelope was hidden underneath, along with a few kiddie porn magazines.

I dumped the pictures on the hard bed and saw the little girl with the face of an angel doing the things her daddy made her do.

But I only looked at her eyes.

AFTER I LEFT the house, I drove over to the florist shop and parked next to the battle-scarred Datsun with four balding tires.

Tina was inside, busily misting some ferns that hung near the cash register. I thought that she looked good in the cheap pink blouse with her name stitched over the pocket, and then our eyes met and I found myself remembering Julie's eyes in Cooper's secret pictures.

"Can I help you?" she asked, and it sounded like she'd break apart if I refused the offer.

"I hope you can." I tried to make it light, but I was a bundle of nerves. "I guess I'm just not a white Christmas kind of guy. I want something green. You know, something nice. Not a fern or anything. Something with flowers."

Her eyes narrowed. "I don't mean to sound weird or anything," she said. "But your voice—it sounds really familiar. Have we met?"

"Picture me with a long white beard."

"What?"

"Santa Claus." I smiled and found the expression was becoming a little more comfortable. "Parker's Department Store version, at your service."

She laughed, and it was a good sound. "I thought we'd met."

"Yeah. I guess there's something about a man in red that makes a lasting impression."

We stood there for a moment, staring at each other, and then she went into florist-shop mode. "So," she said, looking around, "we've established that you're not a fern kind of guy. Is this for a gift?"

"No. It's for me. I just want a little something to, y'know, brighten things up."

"If you want bright, maybe you should get another string of lights for your tree."

I shrugged. "I don't have a tree. I live alone." The statement sounded too blunt, so I tried to lighten it. "It's a real small apartment. I need all the oxygen for myself."

That fell flat.

"Sorry," Tina said. The word slipped out as a sigh, and she left it at that. I recognized the ploy. She didn't *ask* any questions because she didn't want to be *asked* any questions.

"So?" I said.

"How about this?" She was smiling now, holding a little pot with some kind of miniature bush in it.

"I don't know," I said. "I'm looking for something with flowers. And this looks like one of those Japanese bonsai things—"

"No." Her voice brightened. "It blooms. It's a miniature rose."

"What color?"

"White."

I nodded, and we moved over to the cash register. The top button of her blouse was undone, and I could still see the porcelain skin of her neck...and the bruise that began at her collarbone and ran God knows where.

She cringed a little, raising her arm, working the register buttons. I didn't say anything, even though the picture of her husband's little smirk was locked up tight in my head without possibility of parole. *Fair trade*, that smirk said, *a little pain for a late dinner.*

She took my money, and I started for the door. Then something inside me switched gears, and I stopped short. "I've got a question for you," I said.

"Shoot."

"Miniature roses—if you treat them right, do they grow up to be regular roses?"

She shrugged. "I really don't know."

I stood there a moment, just to let a beat pass, and then I shrugged. "Well, I guess I'll just have to wait and find out for myself."

"You'll let me know?" Tina asked.

"I'll let you know," I said.

I didn't realize then, but it was the first promise I'd made in years.

THE BLACK CADDY with the billiard ball shine pulled away from the parking spot marked A. COOPER, and I followed it into the night.

Adrian had worked late—three hours overtime by my estimation—but that didn't matter to me. Now that his day was over, everything was going to go smoothly. Adrian was going to hit the High Hat Club. I was going to join him. Belly up with Mr. Fast Track and strike up a conversation. If that was possible. Order a beer, my first in three years, and hold myself to just one, if *that* was possible (and I prayed that it was). Maybe we'd talk about the kind of magazines that came in brown paper wrappers, or trade tips about how to find camera shops that were willing to print pictures of naked children if you were willing to shell out some of the cash your wife and kid never saw. In short, I wanted to watch old Adrian sweat a little bit, just so I would know what that looked like. I wanted to see him loosen his expensive tie, and I wanted to sniff the air and learn just how effective his expensive deodorant was.

But if he was all chatted out after a tough day shilling 800 numbers, that was okay too. I could wait. I could bide my time. Either way, when Adrian left the High Hat, I planned to be right behind him, closer than he could imagine. Closer even than his own shadow.

The Caddy eased onto the freeway and dipped into traffic. I followed. I was signaling for the exit near the High Hat when Adrian changed lanes and headed south. Sweat beaded on my forehead, and a hole seemed to open up in my guts. This wasn't right. This wasn't supposed to happen.

And then Adrian's turn signal was flashing. He took the Briarwood exit, traveled a road I knew by heart, and made the same turn I'd made morning after morning for the last three years, ever since I'd gotten sober.

There weren't many empty parking spaces, it being the Monday before Christmas, so Adrian Cooper parked his Caddy in a handicapped spot near the big glass doors of the mall that housed Parker's Department Store.

I STARTED TO worry when closing time came and there was no sign of Mr. Adrian Cooper. Then I remembered what kind of guy he was. Cooper certainly thought he held a paramount spot in the universe. Such an important personage wouldn't think anything of holding up a few working stiffs so he could get what he wanted.

The thought got under my skin and stayed there. As if on cue, Adrian exited the mall's smoked glass doors. A slash of bright light knifed across my feet, and then the door whispered closed and the light was gone. I stood to one side of the door, just some nobody Adrian had to step around, and I welcomed the shadows and the soft green light that painted the snow-covered parking lot.

Adrian's expensive loafers crunched over the fresh snow. He balanced a stack of boxes which were wrapped in the signature silver-foil wrap of my employer.

The Caddy was one of two cars parked in the first row.

Adrian noticed what I'd left for him quicker than I'd expected.

"Shit," he muttered, setting the boxes on the hood of the Caddy and snatching something from under the windshield wiper.

It wasn't what he had expected. It wasn't a parking ticket.

His knees actually quivered. He nearly went down. I enjoyed seeing that.

I walked over and took the little picture of Julie out of his hand.

"This is what it feels like," I said.

He didn't seem to hear me. I took the keys out of his hands, opened the door before he could protest.

"We have to talk," I said, lowering a leather-gloved hand on his shoulder, pushing him into the car.

THE FIRST THING Adrian did was loosen his tie. Then he started to sweat, and the Caddy was choked with a scent both raw and spicy.

We were parked at the edge of the mall lot, next to a chain-link fence that rimmed a Christmas tree lot. The hour was late and the lot was closed. All I could see was a sprinkling of dim white Christmas lights; a giant inflatable Santa, arms bobbing under the weight of fresh snowflakes; and the stark, spindly silhouettes of the cheap, dead trees.

"I bet Julie would like a tree," I said.

Adrian Cooper nodded.

I laughed, kicked at the silver paper around my feet, and shifted the boxes so my hands were free. "You know, she still believes in Santa Claus."

Adrian sputtered, "I—I didn't realize that."

"And you know what else?" He didn't reply, but our eyes met, and it killed me that even in this moment his blue eyes held more spark than either Tina's or Julie's. "No," I continued, "you don't know, so I'll tell you. Julie knows something most seven-year-olds don't know. She knows how to come on to Santa Claus. She's a little kid who had to learn how to whore just to survive. And you taught her that. You're the one who twisted her."

Cooper's hands were tight on the steering wheel. He didn't say a word.

"Aren't you going to offer me money?" I asked.

"I...I don't think...you want money."

"You're right about that." I reached into my coat, and my fingers closed around the pistol I'd taken from Adrian's stout, masculine dresser. "You know, I had a wife and kid once. A little girl, just like Julie. A woman just as pretty as Tina. I blew it with them. Oh, not as bad as you. Not nearly as bad as you. But I blew it. See, I was a smash-up-the-family-car kind of guy, a come-get-me-out-of-jail kind of husband. A sorry-I-missed-Christmas kind of dad.

"With me it was the bottle. That's a sickness. But I woke up and saw it. I faced it down until I memorized every ugly scale on the monster's hide. And I learned how to control it. Things are better now."

Adrian's voice was very quiet. "Maybe I can..." He hesitated, searching for the right word.

I found it for him. "Change? Maybe you can. I'm not saying it's impossible. But I don't think that it's going to happen. And I don't think Julie and Tina can count on the odds you'd give them."

One hand stayed on the pistol. The other hand drifted over one of the boxes from Parker's Department Store. My gloved fingers brushed the wisps of red silk nestled in tissue paper. I hooked the spaghetti straps, lifted the teddy, and watched it dance in the shadows. It didn't seem any bigger than a handkerchief, really.

"Amazing," I said. "I didn't know that they made these things so small. What did you tell the salesgirl, anyway? You tell her that your wife was Vietnamese?"

"Look," Adrian said, "if you're going to do something—"

I slipped the gun from my pocket. I could hardly feel it with my hands sheathed in heavy gloves.

"Wait a minute." His blue eyes were focused on me instead of the gun. "I know this is going to happen. I know I can't stop you. But I think it would be easier on both of us if you give me the gun. I'd rather do this myself."

I thought it over. I really wanted to believe him.

But I couldn't, and that was sad. "I can't play those odds, Cooper," I said.

He closed his eyes. I stared down at the Christmas card, which had been covered by the skimpy teddy. On the front, a cartoon man wearing a goofy grin, saying, "You're invited to trim my tree." On the inside flap, same man, naked and grotesque. "All it takes is two red balls."

Under that, scrawled in expensive ink from a Parker's Department Store pen:

Love My Little Girl,
Daddy

Adrian Cooper said, "Are you sure—"
He never finished the sentence.

WHEN THEY LOWERED the coffin into the grave, I was thinking that it should have been wrapped with a big red bow.

Tina and Julie buried Adrian Cooper on Christmas morning. I interpreted that as a good sign, a sign that Tina wanted to lay the past to rest and move on. No one else attended the funeral but the minister, and he was in and out in a matter of minutes. Everyone's busy on Christmas.

Everyone but me.

I stayed in the shadows, standing over the grave of a man I didn't know with flowers in my hands. It looked like Adrian's death would be ruled a suicide. I had been pretty careful—I'd worn gloves when I pulled the trigger, and then, after Adrian was dead, I'd twisted his fingers around the weapon and fired a shot through the open window. And if there wasn't a suicide note, the ripped up greeting card, torn photos, and lingerie seemed to stand in pretty well in the minds of the homicide detectives.

Still, I wasn't willing to take any unnecessary chances by getting too close to the ceremony. Cops love to watch funerals, I'm told. So I viewed the proceedings from a distance, and I saw a little girl and her mother standing over a dirt grave rimmed by a meadow of snow, their faces show-ing nothing, but their fingers interlocked.

I guessed it was as good a start as any. God knows there have been worse. But the real start came a moment later, when the two of them turned and walked toward Tina's Datsun.

I had to stop myself from chasing after them, and it was probably the hardest thing I've ever done. I stood there in the cold, flowers gripped in my gloved hands, remembering the deuce of hearts I'd drawn on the day I met Julie. I thought of her father and his black heart, and I wondered what color my heart was after all I'd done.

The Datsun took off under a cloud of smoke. Four bald tires left black lines in the snow.

And everything was very quiet.

Snow dusted the gravestones, so very white. I thought about the white rose sitting all alone in my apartment, and the gray little neighborhood where Tina and Julie lived. All those houses that no one seemed to care about. Maybe one of them was waiting for someone to come along and give it some special attention.

I found, to my surprise, that I was making plans again, but this time they were the kind of plans that were meant to be shared.

And standing there in the snow, I began to wonder how soon my min-iature rose would flower.

(written with Norman Partridge)

A CAPITAL
CAT CRIME

CLASSIFIED MATERIAL (FILE 33)

The following transcript contains excerpts from the tape-recorded interrogation of suspect Michael Lee Flowers, conducted on April 12, 1994. Interrogation duties handled by Special Agent Jay Ryan (A3323) and Special Agent Frank Cavanaugh (A4194). Side B of the first of two tapes (Files 31 and 32) begins with the following statements:

RYAN: State your name again.

FLOWERS: Michael Flowers.

RYAN: Age?

FLOWERS: Forty-nine.

RYAN: Occupation?

FLOWERS: I told you…I'm unemployed…I used to be a sixth-grade teacher, but that was a long time ago.

RYAN: Residence?

FLOWERS: (*laughs*) Washington, D.C. Downtown mostly.

RYAN: Okay, then let's get back to where we were before the tape ended. I'd just started to ask you who else you'd shared this information with. Can you tell me now exactly how many people you told about the cats?

FLOWERS: Humph, that's kinda tough to answer. Maybe six…seven…ten people. A dozen if you count the two cops who caught me this morning.

RYAN: (*directed at Agent Cavanaugh*) Jesus, that many.

FLOWERS: I don't know for sure. Maybe more, maybe less. Spend a few years out on the street and you become a storyteller. Everyone out there's got a story to tell—

RYAN: Names. We'll need the names of every person you told in case we need to talk to them later. When we're finished here, we're going to give you some paper and a pen, and what we need for you to do is this: write down the names and where we can find each and every person you told about this. If the senator decides to press charges, it'll be a damned sight better for you, if we can verify your story. A couple of witnesses who'll swear you told them this same story *before* today's events will prove that you didn't make up the whole thing on the spot just to save your ass…or as an excuse for what you were doing to those poor cats.

FLOWERS: (*pounds fist on table*) Christ, a city full of the damned animals and I have to pick a senator's daughter's cat. (*several seconds of silence*) Do you really think he'll press charges?

RYAN: Relax, Mr. Flowers. It's like I said, if you cooperate with us, tell us the complete truth, we'll do our best to make sure there are no charges. Agent Cavanaugh has known the senator for many years; if anyone can take care of you, he can.

FLOWERS: Well…I can give you the names, but it won't be easy to find these guys. Most of them are like me; they have to move around a lot.

RYAN: That's okay. It's really just a precaution we're taking for your own protection. Hopefully we won't have to bother with any of them. Now, listen, what we need to do right now is go over your story one more time.

FLOWERS: And then can I get something to eat?

RYAN: (nodding) When we're finished here we'll get those names down on paper and then you can eat anything you want.

FLOWERS: Do I start from the beginning again?

RYAN: Yes, from the beginning. But this time, instead of listening to the entire story at once, we're going to run through the short version. We're going to ask you specific questions and we'd like for you to answer each question to the best of your ability. We understand that the day in question took place almost a year ago, but remember, we're looking for details here. The more you can remember, the better. So take your time and think carefully about everything you say.

FLOWERS: Not really much more to remember, but I'll tell you again just the same.

RYAN: Okay, let's go back to that day again.

FLOWERS: One more time, huh? (clearing his throat) Let's see…it was a Monday, the day after Easter. I remember that because my stomach was still full from the big dinner we'd had the night before down at Patterson's Shelter over on L and Tenth. Fresh Virginia ham, potato salad, hot rolls, the works. It was one helluva feast. Don't remember the exact date—

CAVANAUGH: Did you have anything to drink that night?

FLOWERS: Don't drink alcohol. Never have. I told the police they could test me but—

CAVANAUGH: Drugs?

FLOWERS: Never have.

RYAN: Are you certain about that—?

FLOWERS: —was early in the morning, somewhere between six and seven. I remember it was raining. A breeze was blowing in from the Potomac and it was cold. Real cold for April. I had just come from the wall...the Vietnam Memorial, you know? I go there a couple of times every month to visit some old friends of mine. I spent two tours in Vietnam...and I know maybe fifteen, twenty of those names on that wall. I know too many of them. Also know that I was damned lucky to come home from there, so I go and see my friends as often as I can.

The workers and guards don't like it when we come around during the day, though, because the tourists don't like to see us close up. It's the same way all over this city. Go right ahead and live and die on our streets, but for Godsakes, don't come near our national monuments, and whatever you do, don't do it when someone else can see you. You're too dirty, you stink, you're animals, you're dangerous. They've got plenty of reasons. Not too many good ones, though. The volunteer workers are a whole lot nicer, but they don't start up until the summer.

Anyway, back to the story. After I finished at the war memorial, I cut across the recreation fields near the river and walked over to one of the abandoned row homes over on Preston. You know, the ones they closed down last winter? Some of us used to go there from time to time to play cards or to get out of the cold. The basement was too messed up to be of any good use and was usually flooded anyway, but the top floor wasn't so bad. Corner unit had a sofa and a table and some old chairs. We tried to keep the place in decent condition and keep it quiet so not too many others would find out about it. But it didn't work. A few months ago, a bunch of crackheads burned the place down, fried themselves in the process.

So, anyway, that's where I was—on the top floor of that old row house on Preston Street, reading a paperback next to the window—when it happened...

RYAN: There were how many men?

FLOWERS: There were two men and—

CAVANAUGH: And you're sure they didn't come together?

FLOWERS: Positive. I watched them pull up on opposite sides of the street. I only read for about an hour or so that morning, and then I got tired and put the book down on the windowsill, checked out the view. It was still pretty early and the rain was getting heavier, so the streets were empty. I know what you're thinking...Preston Street is never empty, but it was that morning.

Both cars pulled up within a few minutes of each other. First, one of those long dark sedans with blacked-out windows circled the block, then parked across the street. I couldn't tell how many people were inside, but the man got out of the back door, so there was at least someone else inside the car doing the driving. The man who got out was black. Black skin, black coat, black pants, black umbrella. That's the best look I got of him and that's all I can remember about the way he looked. That and the fact that he was tall, very tall.

A minute or so later, a green van pulled up almost directly beneath my window, and the second man got out.

RYAN: —so you're certain that you never saw a third person?

FLOWERS: Yeah. I never saw the driver leave the limousine, and I don't think there was anyone else inside the van.

CAVANAUGH: Why do you say that?

FLOWERS: Well, the guy driving the van wasn't very big and he didn't look very strong, either. After he opened the van's back doors, he struggled with that box for quite some time before he got a good hold of it. The black guy was still standing across the street, and I just figured that if someone else was inside the van, the little guy would've asked them for some help—

FLOWERS: —almost had myself a heart attack when I heard their footsteps on the stairs. I thought for sure they were coming all the way up to the top floor, and I swear, I've never been so scared in my entire life. I didn't know what was going down—big-time drugs, a payoff, something—but I didn't think they'd be real happy to find me waiting up there. So I crawled into the corner behind the sofa and tried my best to stay real quiet. When they stopped on the second floor, I thanked the Lord and sat perfectly still, praying that they'd take care of their business in a hurry and be on their way.

But what I'd forgotten about that particular corner was that there were two holes—one about four inches across and one about half that size—in the floor behind the sofa where pipes used to run up from the basement. Not only could I hear most of what they were saying, I could actually see a small portion of the room.

CAVANAUGH: You say you saw only one of the men clearly?

FLOWERS: That's right. The man who was driving the van stopped right in my line of sight, at a perfect angle for me to see through the big hole, and that's where he put the box down. They talked for a minute or so, they might've shook hands, and then he started pacing back and forth as they spoke...so I could only see him for a few seconds at a time before he disappeared from my sight, but I must have glimpsed his face twenty or thirty times.

RYAN: Okay, one more time, what did he look like?

FLOWERS: Well, he sure wasn't anything special to look at. That's what I remember most about him. He was no taller than me and probably just as skinny. And he had white hair. I remember that real well. I'd thought he was blond when I saw him outside, but it must have been the rain and the window glass, because his hair was as white as snow—

FLOWERS: Christ, I've already told you all this!

RYAN: I know this is terribly repetitive, Mr. Flowers, but that's the idea here...to see if we can help you to remember something you forgot about the first time. Now, please be patient with us. This next part is extremely important. What else can you tell us about the box he was carrying?

FLOWERS: (*several seconds of silence*) I'm telling you the truth, I don't remember anything else. The box just about came up to the man's waist. It was covered with a cloth or a blanket or something, which the man removed once they were inside. The box or cage or whatever it was looked like it was made of glass and metal, and it looked like it must have been pretty heavy. When I saw it, I remember thinking: no wonder he'd had so much of a problem getting it out of the van. And when the man removed the blanket, I got a clear view of what was inside the box—

FLOWERS: That's right. There were cats inside the box. Nothing else, I'm certain. The glass looked thick and heavy and practically bombproof, but it was crystal clear. The box was divided right down the middle by a clear partition and there were two cats inside one section and a third cat inside the other. I saw them clear as day. No question about it. And all three cats looked the same; I remember thinking that they looked like Halloween cats because they were orange and black—

CAVANAUGH: —and you're absolutely certain you heard them use those exact words?

FLOWERS: I told you, I couldn't hear everything clearly because it was raining so damned hard and the rain was making too much noise on the roof. But I heard enough. Snatches of conversation here and there. Words. Sentences.

The black man spoke kind of softly, so I didn't hear him much. I don't think he was American, though. He spoke pretty good English, but the words came out slow and stiff, like it was a learned language. The man from the van had a surprisingly strong voice, though, and I could hear him talk the majority of the time. I think he might've been nervous because—

CAVANAUGH: But let's be perfectly clear here, you do submit that you heard them talk about some type of rabies and you heard them mention those particular countries by name?

FLOWERS: Yeah, I heard all of that. I swear to it. I didn't hear the specifics, but I heard a word here, a word there, and it all fit together. They were talking about some kind of disease, some kind of new rabies strain or virus or something or other, and how dangerous their business at hand was. I remember they kept pointing and leaning down and looking at the cats, and the man from the van made a big show of explaining that the single cat was pregnant. Then they started talking about all those medical terms and foreign countries and they lost me in a hurry—

CAVANAUGH: But you recognized the names of those countries, huh?

FLOWERS: Sure did. I taught history for two years before switching over to social studies, so I knew exactly what countries they were talking about, knew where they were located too. But it all happened so fast...I just couldn't piece everything together...until I read that newspaper last month—

RYAN: And you came to this conclusion as soon as you read the newspaper article?

FLOWERS: No, not *the* newspaper article; there were many articles. You see, papers are easy to get around here. Even for the homeless, because so many people throw them away, leave them in the park, on the subway, wherever they please.

I read the first article last month in the *Washington Post*. The second story a week later. Then, two more ran last week, in both the *Post* and the *Washington Times*. Each story almost identical. Two tiny countries across the Atlantic, nearly a quarter of Central America, even somewhere in Cuba for Christsakes...all suffering from the same deadly virus. Thousands dead, thousands more dying, scientists and doctors baffled. A disease of unprecedented danger and unknown origin, the officials claimed. And the names of those countries...well, I could have told you them almost a year ago. Jesus—

FLOWERS: —was scared and that's the how and the why I got caught this morning taking off with the senator's daughter's cat. I freely admit it...I was gonna take the cat somewhere and kill it. Just like I did to all the others. All I can think about now is that I knew all this time. All those people dead...and I knew.

I'm not sorry for what I did to those cats, either. I mean, maybe our cats *are* safe, maybe it was just those three in that glass box. Who knows? But, for Christsakes, Cuba's awful close to the coast of Florida...and, besides, what if—

CONFIDENTIAL MEMORANDUM

To: Royce Larkin, Commander-in-Chief
From: Jay Ryan, Special Agent
Date: April 13, 1994

Matters Regarding the Michael Lee Flowers Case as of 10:30 A.M.—Immediately following his interrogation, Flowers identified (from an employee file photo) government researcher Jeremy Blevins as the man he observed in the green van. Blevins was apprehended at 4:54 A.M. and remains under guard at CIA Headquarters. After listing the seven names and approximate locations of those other persons he'd shared this information with, Flowers was sedated and efficiently terminated. Special agents were dispatched immediately and as of nine this morning, only one of the seven persons remains at large. We are continuing to question the two police officers who brought Flowers in, although we have their full cooperation and the full cooperation of their home district. At this time, they appear to present no problem to this investigation. The senator is unaware of any problem other than that of the homeless catnapper. Please post further instructions at your convenience.

THE SINNER KING

"But then the times
Grew to such evil that the Holy cup
Was caught away to heaven and disappear'd."
—*The Holy Grail*

1

I STOPPED FOR A DRINK of water at the bottom of a grassy knoll and, when I finally caught my breath, I heard the dogs. Muffled barking off in the distance. A mile or so away. The frenzied, hungry sound of the hunt.

I returned the canteen to my knapsack, swung the bag over my shoulder, and started up the hill, picking up my pace. No need to panic, I told myself. I'd known from the start that my absence would not pass undetected, but I *had* hoped they wouldn't pick up the trail so quickly. The odometer on the Jeep had recorded sixty miles of progress before the terrain had forced me to abandon it, so I thought I'd had a decent jump on them. I'd even hidden the bright red vehicle under a copse of trees, in case they searched from the air. Now, I was certain they'd found the Jeep and were close behind.

I moved carefully down the opposite side of the hill, scanning the ground. If I lost my footing and turned an ankle or a knee, it would all be over in a matter of hours. I reached the bottom of the hill and ran for the treeline. The Canadian wilderness was beautiful in early autumn, and it served as both a curse and a gift for my cause. Unfortunately, it was one of the last remaining true wild-lands on the continent and if I had been anywhere else at the moment I could have reached civilization—and help—by now. On the other hand, considering the motives of the tracking party behind me, there were no better surroundings to hide in if forced to do so.

I moved deeper into the wilderness. Forty minutes later, chest heaving, legs feeling like rubber, I reached the summit of a rocky ridge. I resisted the urge to take another drink, and instead, leaned against a boulder the size of a mini-van. The rock felt cool and smooth against my shoulder and I rested my cheek against it, closing my eyes, savoring its touch. Within seconds, a vision of snarling dogs snapped me back, and I quickly unshouldered the pack and eased around to the backside of the ridge, which was lined with a cluster of smaller but no less impressive boulders.

The view was truly awe-inspiring. Miles of bright, sun-speckled autumn forest stretched before me like a quilt sewn with the richest fabric from every color of a rainbow. I could see acres of healthy woodland, peaks and valleys, streams and rivers snaking across the land like the pulsing veins of a giant, scattered lighter-toned green patches of rolling meadow, the occasional dark blemish of rocky bluffs similar to the one I was standing on. Not a single sign of civilization as we know it.

God's country, indeed, I thought, remembering one of Lucas Ransom's favorite expressions. He was such a dramatic bastard.

Somewhere in the distance, I heard the dogs. Impossible to determine if they were drawing closer, or if I was making ground on them. I searched the landscape but could not spot any movement. Suddenly, I thought of the camp—the evil place I was fleeing—and what they'd done to pitiful Francis. A shiver tickled my spine. No way were they going to take me. No way.

I reached down and touched the heavy cloth of the backpack, feeling the rough edges of the Grail inside. And as my fingers caressed the material, a dark realization came to me: taking the Grail had been a mistake. If

I had just snuck out of camp, they might not have followed me, thinking a city man could never cross hundreds of miles of wilderness. But they would never give up now. They would never stop searching until they'd found their Holy Grail.

I slung the knapsack over my shoulder and jumped to my feet, inspired, actually energized, by the horrible thought. Drawing a deep breath, I ran—a bit too fast for the rocky terrain—up the slope of the ridge, pushing blindly through the heavy foliage ahead, out into—

—nothing.

The ground beneath me suddenly disappeared.

Replaced by clear, blue sky.

A sheer cliff laughed at me as I fell—

—deeper into the hungry ravine—

—toward the rushing white water below—

Slow motion, spinning, arms flailing, knapsack feeling impossibly heavy, the sky so brilliantly blue it hurt my eyes—

—and then there was only darkness.

2

DARKNESS…FLAMES DANCING dangerously close burning my face my body with their heat a screaming man inside the flames his face and mouth bubbling melting into a mask of blood his arms dripping black and yellow and red as he reaches for me he wants to take me with him into the fire a flame touches my hair my lips and i beat it out before it can taste me then the sound of singing a sickening evil sound then a gigantic cross jutting up into the air a white sword cutting the pure sky hundreds of men and women kneeling below the cross in flowing white robes singing chanting…

Slowly, the darkness fades, is replaced by a dimly-lit room with a single small window, a sweet-smelling breeze kissing the air around me. I think I am safe until I try to move and cannot, my arms and legs restrained, until I hear soft music on the air, until I see a golden crucifix hanging on the wall, and then I know I am not safe. I must be back at the camp. They found me. I try to scream, but the pain is too much…and then there is only the darkness again.

3

I CAME TO some time later to the sound of chirping birds and wood being chopped. Early morning sunlight streamed into the room through an open window. I stared at the empty walls, recalling the crucifix from my nightmare, the music, the flames. All horrible memories I'd taken with me from the encampment.

I moved my head and a wave of pain and nausea washed over me. Bits and pieces slowly floated back to me. The dogs...the cliff...the river... falling! I was afraid to look down at my body. A dark vision flashed in my mind: *that of a sideshow freak with no limbs. My arms and legs were not restrained at all; they just weren't there anymore.* I lifted my head slowly, moaning, and caught a glimpse of two feet under a white blanket.

The bad news was it felt like I had a broken bag of bones for a body and was strapped to a bed in the middle of nowhere. The good news was I didn't think I was back at the camp.

From what I could see, head perfectly still, eyes still blurry, the room looked like it was part of a larger log cabin. The walls were undecorated, a single naked light bulb dangling from the ceiling. I could just see the top half of a fireplace against the far wall, and I couldn't help but think of the flames. Real flames—like the ones back at the camp—not the kind that frightened me from my dreams.

"Hello," I croaked, mouth impossibly dry, not recognizing the sound of my voice.

The chopping stopped outside the window.

Footsteps.

A door opening and closing.

A long, breathless moment.

"Well, I'll be," a man's voice came from somewhere beyond my vision. "My friend has awakened."

I didn't know the voice, so I kept quiet.

"Don't be afraid, partner, I imagine you're wondering where you are and how you got here." Movement in the room. "Let me pull this chair up and get you a sip of water." A man's grinning face appeared directly above me and, for just a moment, I thought I was staring at the face of my long-dead father. The man had to be damn near seventy—the same age my father would have been—his face a friendly ball of wrinkles, a balding brow, deep tan, eyes the color of clay, a smile enough for two men.

"You just relax yourself and take this water down real slow like." He lifted a paper cup to my lips and I tasted the nectar of the gods. "Whoa, partner. That's enough for now. Too much will do you more bad than good. Trust me."

"Where am I?" I managed, water running down my chin. I wanted so much to lick my lips, but my tongue wouldn't cooperate.

"You're in the home of the honorable Lewis Perkins, that's me, halfway down the south side of the Levathian Valley. Where should you be?"

"How...where did you find—"

"I didn't exactly find you, partner. The river brought you to me. I was heading upstream, and instead of fish, I found you. Thought you was dead at first."

I swallowed and said, "*I feel* like a corpse."

The old man chuckled and whistled loud enough so that it hurt my ears. "Partner, you are one beat-up individual. Near as I can see, you got a broken leg, broken wrist, bruised ribs—don't think you broke any of them though cause you ain't been spitting no blood—and probably one whopper of a concussion."

I groaned.

He shook his head and real concern crept onto his face. "I fixed you up best I could. Cleaned the cuts. Set the breaks. But you were out cold for more than two days, partner. And when you finally started coming to last night, I had to tie you down to keep you from hurting yourself worse. You kept hollering about flames and crosses and other crazy stuff, sounded something like singing. Heck, I had to turn my music off, and yank that there crucifix off the wall just to keep you calmed down. Weirdest thing, it was."

"My God," I said, a tear slipping down my cheek. "You saved my—"

"No reason to thank me yet, partner," he said, loosening the ropes from my legs and arms. "You could die on me next hour for all I know."

I tried to smile. "Well, in that case, I'll hold off on the gratitude." He smiled back and gently patted my arm. He had rough, weathered hands, the hands of a good, hard-working man. I decided right then that I would have liked this man even if he hadn't saved my life.

"Listen," I said, "this is very important. Could I use your phone?"

"Sorry, no phone this far out. Lines don't run anywhere near here, and I ain't never had one of those satellite jobs; too expensive, and who would I call anyway?"

"Anyplace nearby I could call from?"

"Closest place would be, ummm, over near Rockton or in Riverdale. It's a toss-up as to which is closer."

Riverdale…the camp was just north of Riverdale. "Has anyone…anyone come around here looking for me?"

Another look of concern, mixed with suspicion this time. I didn't blame him. "No, no one comes around this side of the valley except for hunters from time to time. But my land's posted so they don't come in this far if they know what's good for them."

He paused, as if considering his next words carefully. "I found a knapsack that belongs to you."

My heart skipped; I'd forgotten about the backpack.

"And judging from what's in that there sack, I think you've got some kind of story to tell. And, if I'm gonna be caring for you, I reckon I've got a right to hear it."

I opened my mouth, but he "*ssshed*" me quiet.

"Not today, partner. You're a sight. You get some rest right now, and we'll get some food in you soon."

"Thank you," I said, feeling helpless and foolish. A strong man like myself transformed into a child.

He patted my arm again, turned and left. A moment later, he returned. "You don't worry, partner. If anyone does come around here looking for you, as long as it ain't the law, I'll tell them I ain't seen a sign of you. I'll get rid of them real quick like. You don't go worrying about that, hear?"

I nodded and whispered a hoarse "thank you," suddenly exhausted from the conversation.

The old man winked at me and closed the door.

4

A FULL DAY passed before the old man mentioned the backpack again.

He'd spent the past twenty-four hours pumping food and drink into me and tending to my injuries best he could. The pain in my leg and arm was just bearable, but I counted myself lucky that neither injury had broken the skin and neither limb appeared terribly deformed. The old man sure wasn't a doctor and he wasn't the best cook in the world either, but his genuine concern and gentle manner of care more than made up for it.

There *was* one thing the old guy—Lew, he asked me to call him—was good at though, and that was talking. I was his first company in years, he told me, and he was making up for lost conversation. By that first day's end, I'd learned everything I needed to know about him, even though he still knew nothing about me.

Lewis Perkins. Sixty-two-year-old retired Air Force man. Aircraft mechanic. Living on just under 600 acres of his father's land. Wife, Carmella, deceased. Cancer. Buried in a meadow a few hundred yards behind the cabin. No phone. No communication with the outside world. Had supplies flown in four times a year to a lake a mile-and-a-half north of the cabin. If the weather was bad, and the flight had to be aborted, they flew in exactly a week later. Last shipment came in less than a month ago. Spent his days hiking the countryside. Fishing. Hunting. Some watercolor painting from time to time. Most nights spent reading. Smoking his pipe.

It was during dinner on that second night—deer meat, green vegetables, and hot bun rolls—that Lew brought up the knapsack again. He did so in a sly, roundabout fashion, and as usual, it was some time before he stopped talking.

"You know, Bill," he said around a mouthful of deer meat, "you're not the first fella that river brought to me."

I stopped pushing my fork across the plate and leaned my head back on one of the pillows he'd propped under me on the bed. A fire crackled in the corner of the room, its warmth mixing with the cool night air coming through the window. The painkillers Lew had given me before dinner (he told me that he used them a couple times a winter for his arthritis) were taking the desired effect. My stomach was full, and I was ready for a good story.

"No, sir. 'Bout two years ago, I found a man about a mile from where you washed up. But this fella was still in the river, hooked on some fallen brush like a trapped beaver, and he was deader than dead. Had been that way for a few days. But, you see, this guy had a full pack with him. Looked like he belonged out here. I even found his camp some ways upstream. Probably slipped on the rocks or, heck, he could've had a heart attack for all I know."

He stopped, and looked away, plucking a strand of meat from his teeth with pinched fingers. He swallowed a drink of beer and looked back at me. It was obvious that he was waiting for me to talk, and when I didn't, he continued.

"What I'm getting at is this. After I found you, I didn't find no camp and, believe me, I looked. And the only thing you had on you was some old backpack, all tangled around your arm. Just a few pieces of food, a canteen, a little old .38, some waterlogged notebooks, and a fancy-looking gold cup all wrapped up in a flannel shirt. No supplies, no warm clothes for the night. It looked like you'd lit out from somewhere in a big hurry and—"

"I'm a journalist," I said, pushing the dinner plate further down on my lap. I knew it was time for *me* to do the talking now.

Lew shook his head. "A writer, huh? I knew you were something special. I sure did."

I couldn't help but smile. "I'm not from around here."

"Oh, no kidding," he said with a smirk. "I thought you were a mountain man or something. Maybe a fur trapper."

I rolled my eyes and continued. "I live in Philadelphia. Have all my life, all thirty-nine years. Write features for a few of the national magazines. Public interest stories. I spent the last three weeks on an undercover assignment over near Riverdale, at the New Order camp. You heard of it?"

"Those religious folks?"

"Yeah. Exactly."

Most people *had* heard of the New Order. Founded three decades ago by New York business tycoon Lucas Ransom, the highly publicized cult of religious fanatics had built their own village—their camp—in the Canadian wilderness, where they worshiped a Holy God of Nature and lived almost completely off the land. Many of their methods and practices were controversial and the group itself was under investigation by several law enforcement agencies.

"What were you doing there?" Lew asked.

"Last month I got an assignment to go undercover and infiltrate the New Order. Pose as a new member, a convert. Take a good look around, take a few pictures, talk to some people, and then disappear. We'd checked the area out pretty good and there was a spot close to the camp where a helicopter could land. I was to stay in camp for five weeks, then sneak out in the night and rendezvous with the chopper pilot and escape with my material."

"Five weeks, huh? That's a long time," he said, looking up at the cabin ceiling, thinking. "Then that's who you were running from. Something went wrong, huh?"

"Oh, yeah. Something went wrong all right. Murder went wrong. I watched them kill a man in that holy camp of theirs." My breath hitched and I reached for my glass and took a drink.

"Take it easy, Bill. Take it slow and start over again."

I took a few even breaths and asked, "Lew, are you familiar with the myth of the Holy Grail? Have you ever heard of the Sinner King?"

He shook his head.

"Okay, bear with me here. This'll take a few minutes but, when I'm done, I think you'll understand everything."

"Take your time," he said. "Ain't got no place to go."

I nodded. "According to history, the Holy Grail is the cup from which our Saviour drank at His last supper. He was supposed to have given it to Joseph, who took it with him to Europe, along with the spear, which the soldier had used to pierce our Saviour's side. Well, the Grail and the spear were supposedly handed down from generation to generation and the men who watched over these treasures were supposed to be men of great purity. But one of these men failed and thus began a terrible myth, that of the Sinner King. This man was supposed to have looked at a partially disrobed female and, according to legend, the sacred spear then fell upon him, inflicting a fatal wound, thus crowning this man as *Le Roi Pescheur* or the Sinner King. Do you follow me so far?"

The old man nodded, clearly entranced by my little history lesson. "Yes, yes. Go on."

"Well, soon after arriving in camp, I discovered that the members of the New Order have their own Holy Grail for worship. Certainly not the Grail of historic legend, but a fine substitute with an undeniable power over the congregation.

"Now here comes the ugly part. You know the saying: history often repeats itself. Well, it certainly did in this case. One of the four guardians of this Holy Grail—a fella named Francis—was discovered to be having an affair with a teenaged girl in the camp. This man was brought before the holy men of the New Order and sentenced to death. I…I watched helplessly as they burned him at the stake."

"My God."

"It was horrible. Barbaric. I've been a journalist for twenty years and I've never seen anything like it. They held a ceremony and every person in the camp was there. It was like a celebration, singing and dancing…it was incredible."

"So you decided to run?"

"No, I wanted to wait the final two weeks for my pick-up. But a few days later, while cleaning inside the chapel, I overheard two of the high priests talking in the confession room next door. It seems that somehow, one of the congregation had discovered my true identity and the priests were going to, that very night, spring a little surprise on me. On impulse, I grabbed the Grail from the altar and took it with me. I'm still not sure why I did it. Then I got my backpack and my story notes from my room, stole a Jeep and drove as far as the airfield road would take me."

"And they came after you? Is that why you fell?"

"No," I said, smiling despite the serious nature of the conversation. "I'm a klutz. Always have been. I just ran out of ground to walk on and fell into the river. Thank God, you found me."

"Yeah, no kidding." He let out a long whistle. "What an experience."

"Lew, I gotta tell you, you may be putting yourself in danger by keeping me here. In case you haven't guessed by now, that thing in my backpack is their Holy Grail, their highest treasure, and they're not going to stop looking for it."

"You can stop worrying about that. This is my land and I'll defend it against anyone who crosses the wrong line." He scratched his head, thinking again. "You know, there's a hunting cabin on the western border of my land. It's empty most of the time, but hunting parties use it from time to time to rest, grab a quick meal, or sometimes stay the night in bad weather. I could get out there in a few weeks, when you're up and around a bit, and leave a note for someone to send a plane up to the lake, get you out of here."

"Jesus, a few weeks—"

"You won't be up and walking for at least another week, and that's gonna be with the help of a crutch. Someone's gotta be here to cook for you, take care of you."

Again, I felt as helpless as a child. "I know, I know. Just thinking that a few weeks is a long time."

"Yeah, but you're lucky. Death's even longer."

I shut up. He had a good point.

The next hour passed quickly, both of us running our mouths until our throats were sore. I told him more about my experiences at the camp, about my life in Philly. He told me about how he'd met his wife, the time spent overseas while in the military. At twenty minutes past ten o'clock, we said our goodnights, and soon after I was asleep.

5

TWO WEEKS LATER...

"All right!" I yelled. "That's the biggest one of the day." I watched Lew as he slowly walked to shore, the clear water moving swiftly around his rubber waders. He plopped the fat trout to the ground—where it flipped from side to side—and gave me a big smile. In the weeks I'd been here, under Lew's care, a bond had formed between us. It was as if the dire circumstances had allowed us to forgo the usual stepping stones of friendship, and progress directly to the strongest of relationships.

"I think I'll nail three or four more keepers and we'll call it a day, okay?"

"Sounds good to me. I'm going back and grab us a couple more beers."

He looked at me, the worried expression that I had already learned to dread creasing his face. "Maybe I'd better—"

"Now, don't go looking at me like that, Lew. You know damn well I can walk just fine with the crutch you made." I picked up the heavy pole and waggled it in his direction. "It's a two-minute walk to the cabin."

"Well, you be careful," he said, dropping his trout into the cooler with the other fish. "Look out for holes and rocks. And watch out for all those tree roots. There's some monster roots around this river. I've tripped on them a few times myself."

"I'll be careful. I promise."

"And, hey, some of those roots are hard to see."

I could still hear the old guy chattering away with his warnings when I reached the cabin. I took two frosty bottles of beer from the kitchen cooler and a pack of Oreo cookies from the counter and limped into the den, looking for Lew's pipe. He allowed himself two smokes a day, and I thought he'd probably enjoy one after all his hard work. I spotted the old bulldog pipe on the bookshelf next to a stack of thick aircraft reference books and what looked like a photo album. I grabbed the pipe, and absently flipped open the album cover.

Four rows of small black-and-white photos covered the first page. Each picture, faded and yellowed with age, was attached by tiny adhesives on the corners. The first three pages of the album held childhood memories—images of a young boy with a baseball cap on backwards, riding the shoulders of an older man. A child atop a painted horse on a merry-go-round. On a tire swing. In a cute little dark suit, holding hands with a smiling mother and father.

The middle pages held memories from older years. Bare-chested men crouched on the wing of a WWII bomber. A young Lew trying to look street-tough in full dress uniform. A smiling beauty who must have been Carmella. A simply wonderful shot of Lew and Carmella, arm in arm, on their wedding day...

I heard something behind me and whirled, almost losing my balance. Nothing.

Suddenly, standing there looking at the pictures from years long past, I felt guilty for probing into my friend's life without being offered an invitation. Hurriedly, I snapped the photo album shut and as I turned to leave, a single picture fell from its pages and fluttered to my feet. I pushed the photo across the floor with my crutch until I had a better angle at which to retrieve it, bent slowly, and pinched the picture with two fingers. I wiped the dust from the print and almost put it back in the album without looking at it. I spun it very slowly in my fingers, like a playing card, brought it to my face, and almost fainted dead to the floor.

Oh...

my...

God!

My heart trip-hammered.

Had to be a mistake.

Had to be.

I stared at it for a breathless moment, then stuffed the photo back into the album and started for the river, barely using the crutch, grunting in pain. Act as if nothing has changed, I thought. It *could* be a mistake. It truly could. But if it's not, I need to buy some time to think this over. Just act as natural as possible.

But I knew that was going to be damned near impossible because all my thoughts—sad and very frightened thoughts—were centered on that photo. The small black-and-white picture which had showed a horrifyingly clear image of a smiling, few years younger Lewis Perkins, standing next to New Order's founder, Lucas Ransom, in front of the congregation's holy temple.

6

DINNER THAT NIGHT was a pair of fat trout and baked potatoes out on the front porch. Autumn twilights this mild were rare for the valley, and Lew wanted to take advantage of the pleasant breeze.

After the meal, I sat back on the step with the night's last beer and stretched my leg. Lew rocked himself in his chair, smoking his second pipe. We sat mostly in silence, which was rare for us. Finally, Lew broke the quiet.

"You been thinking of home today?"

"Huh?"

"You been mighty quiet all evening. Thought you might've been thinking about back home, missing your friends."

"Yeah, I guess I have been. Wondering how much longer it's going to be."

"Shouldn't be too long now. A hunting party's bound to see my note anytime soon. Just keep hoping."

"It's all I can do."

"You know…I'm really gonna miss you like the dickens when you leave here. Hate to say it, but it's almost gonna feel like when Carmella passed on. Like I lost a part of me. Just all quiet again."

I wanted to say so many things, wanted to say that he was like the father I never knew, wanted to stand up and embrace the old man right there on his front porch in the middle of the dark wilderness, wanted to ask for a simple and clear explanation for what I'd seen. Instead, I just took another swig of beer and watched the stars dance their lonely dance in the endless night sky.

7

I COULD TELL by the sun that it was mid-afternoon when I finally regained consciousness. Bright sunlight usually streamed through the window until just after lunch, when, at that time, the trees blocked the rays. The room was in warm shadow now. I tried to blink the fog from my eyes, but it didn't help. My head pounded, no doubt from whatever had been in that final beer the night before.

It had been pretty easy to figure things out after I came to and found my legs and arms bound to the bed once again. He'd fooled me good, he sure had; I just hadn't figured the old guy was going to make a move so soon.

Footsteps.

"It's not what you think, Bill."

I laughed and it came out harsh and angry. "And just what the hell am I supposed to think, friend? You drugged me, knocked me cold, and strapped me to my damn bed. What am I supposed to think, huh? I'm being punished for leaving the toilet seat up?"

"I know you saw the pictures."

"I saw one damn photo, you bastard."

"Please don't be angry with me." His voice trembling now.

"If you're a part of their crazy clan, why didn't you just turn me in? Get it over with. Why didn't you tell them I was here with you?"

"I'm not a member of the New Order…not anymore. Haven't been for years. I lied to you. I lied to you about a lot of things…I never left a note in the hunters' cabin. Never went there at all."

"Jesus," I whispered.

"And I *do* know the story of the Sinner King, the story you told me about the Holy Grail. I know it all too well.

"Ten years ago, Carmella and I lived at the camp. Worshiped there. We had been there for four years and both of us were held in high standing by the priests. Carmella was an educational leader, and I was one of the guardians of the Grail. But I made a terrible mistake, misunderstood the improper advances of a neighbor's wife. Accidentally encouraged these advances."

He stopped, loud sobs shaking his body. "I, too, am what you call a Sinner King. I, too, like the man you watched them burn at the stake, failed in my duty to the Lord. But that was ten long years ago. I have *never* heard of the sacrifice you described, thank God. They excommunicated us, forced us to leave the camp and abandon the practice of their faith. My dear Carmella died three years later, worn down by grief and shame."

My journalist's mind working full speed, I spotted a ray of hope. An opportunity. "That's okay, Lewis. It's all okay. Help me get back to Philadelphia. Help me find someone to fly me out of here. I can write a story that will change the New Order forever, a story that will avenge both of our losses—"

His eyes widened in surprise…in fear.

He shook his head rapidly, silencing me. "No, no, no. Don't you see what all this means? Can't you see? It became so clear to me last night. You. The Grail. Falling to me from the heavens. It's a second chance. A second chance to prove that I am worthy. That I am pure enough to protect and watch over the Holy Grail."

I saw the madness in his eyes then. Eyes no longer tired or sad. Eyes that danced with desperate insanity. He brushed a strand of hair from my face, gently, lovingly, stroking my brow, and I thought I might be sick.

"You must stay here with me, Bill. I'm old and will not live forever. Don't you see? You and the Grail—you were sent to me. The Grail will need a guardian when I pass away, and you…"

8

SIX WEEKS LATER…

The restraints are no longer necessary. Even if I still *wanted* to escape, it is not possible. I know that now…after two failed attempts. My leg still bothers me, and I don't know the land well enough to survive a single night, much less an entire journey. To leave now, in the midst of winter, would be suicide. The cabin is my home now.

It's all rather strange. We still talk into the long hours of twilight. Comfortable, easy conversation, spotted with much laughter. We are rarely apart. Eat our meals together. Fish and hunt together when the weather allows. Read or play cards by the fire.

Lew keeps the Holy Grail on the mantle, balanced on a fancy wooden stand we spent the better half of a week carving and sanding. He kneels and prays before it each morning, and then again in the evening. He keeps after me to join him, like a father badgering his son to go to mass each Sunday. He swears that the Grail speaks to him in the voice of God, comforts him. That if I join him, I too will hear.

What he doesn't know yet is that I *already* hear. As each day passes, the voice inside my head grows louder, clearer, stronger. Tomorrow morning, I will join him before the Grail, and I will listen.

It is night now, a beautiful winter sky blankets the valley, but I anxiously await daybreak. Lew will be so happy with my change of heart. He never lost faith in me. He tells me each morning, without fail, arms outstretched, that this will all be mine one day soon: the cabin, the valley, the Holy Grail.

And I think he may be right.

A SEASON OF CHANGE

1

IF IT WASN'T FOR the headlights, I never would've seen it.

The house was a spiderweb of shadows, the porch and front lawn lost in darkness. It was after one in the morning, and I was a little drunk and a lot tired. Four hours of Loughlin's Pub entertainment was all I could handle for one night. Despite a soft spray of moonlight, I never would've seen the broken paper clip if a car hadn't slowed and turned the corner as I reached for the door, its headlights sweeping across the lower half of my home, sparking a tiny glint of silver in the keyhole.

I reacted predictably at the sight of the tampered with lock. I cussed—not once, but twice—and kicked the door. Made me feel better, too. I knew the key wouldn't make a fit but, seeing that I was pissed off and pickled and the all-too-familiar combination formed a good enough excuse, I tried anyway.

I felt the key push the paper clip further into the hole and immediately wondered why the bastard who'd jammed the lock hadn't stuck around to do the job right. Dog-tired and drunk, and I gotta deal with a goddamned prank. No justice in this world.

I started to turn around and in midturn, my mind flashed: *Or maybe they just didn't have time to finish the job, maybe they're still nearby.*

To my right, under the bay window, one of the shadows moved, and instinctively I moved away from it, knowing that my last thought had been a correct one. A second shadow, to my left this time, elongated and the rosebushes exploded. I heard clothing tear and a grunt of pain. And then I felt my head explode and heard nothing at all.

<h1 style="text-align:center">2</h1>

THE FIRST THING I saw when I came to was the moon. And the pointy son of a bitch was laughing at me.

I was flat on my back, underneath the den window, a few yards to the right of the porch. Taking deep, slow breaths, I reached down and touched the emptiness in my waistband.

"Son of a bitch," I whispered. Wasn't gonna look good. Over ten years on the street, and a couple of damn thieves kick my ass, take my gun, and roll me under a bush like a dead bird. No sir, wasn't gonna look good at all.

My head roared when I moved to check the time. The familiar glow-in-the-dark dials told me that only fifteen minutes had passed. And the fact that I still had the two-year-old Seiko on my wrist told me that the guys who'd nailed me weren't petty crooks.

I felt the back of my skull and my fingers came away wet to the knuckles. "Son of a bitch," I muttered again, shaking my head.

I struggled to my feet, after a couple of sad attempts, and walked very slowly to the porch. My keys were gone, of course, and the door was still closed. Didn't mean the bastards weren't inside, though. With another flash of pain, I bent and checked for the paper clip. It was still in place. This time I didn't bother to try the lock. I'm not *that* stupid.

I crept around the house and found the extra back-door key that I keep hidden underneath the plastic birdbath. The sliding glass door looked untouched; I unlocked it and stepped inside. In addition to my gun cabinet, which I showcase in the den, I keep an extra 9mm in the garage. I swung right in a crouch, slipped through the cluttered breezeway, and retrieved the gun. Then I searched the rest of the house, hitting the downstairs first.

I'd turned on just about every light in the house and checked every room except the bathroom when, as I crossed the hall, I itched my forehead and my fingertips came away smeared an obscene red. Too glossy for blood. I flipped the bathroom overhead on and stepped in front of the mirror.

The harsh light stung my eyes, but I could see my reflection clear enough to start my entire body shaking. My hair was slicked with sweat and blood and a patch near the back was spiked and tangled from where I'd rubbed it. My eyes were wide and nervous, my cheeks flushed with pain and adrenaline. I'd looked worse before—hell, I'd looked worse *without* having my ass kicked—but what scared the very crap out of me was the word that had been written, in smeared lipstick, across the length of my forehead.

The word that read: MAILMAN

3

IT TOOK ALL of six seconds for my brain to register what the word meant and another six for me to reach the phone. I punched the number and waited. Dead air. Nothing.

"Shit." I hung up and hurried down the stairs, falling on my ass the last six or seven steps. I grabbed a backup set of keys from the kitchen, pushed the back door open, and staggered across the side yard. I unlocked the truck door and had the radio transmitter in my hand before my ass hit the seat.

It was worse than I had feared. Much worse. They didn't even have to run a check for me. They'd been trying to call, but there'd been problems with my phone. Bastards must've cut the line. I flashed my lights and hit the I-95 exit at a clean eighty.

Ray York, my partner for the past six years, lived one exit south of me, ten minutes closer to Baltimore City. He was a good cop and a good friend. A big bear of a man, he was always happy, always smiling, always seeing the bright side of a situation. Downright unnatural for a cop. We spent plenty of off-duty hours together, but Ray was a big-time homebody, and most of the time we watched videos or ball games in his basement. His family consisted of his beautiful wife Connie—I'd been the best man at the wedding three years ago—and a pampered golden retriever named Cowboy.

Cowboy was an only child, but it wasn't likely to stay that way, Ray always joked. He claimed that as soon as Connie got promoted, they were going to start working on a family. He wanted five kids. Just the thought made me cringe.

The call had come in at 12:41. Anonymous, of course. *You'll find him in the back* was all they'd said, along with the street address. The operator ran a check on the address and rushed a call through when she recognized the name.

They'd found him in the backyard. Shot twice in the midsection. Still alive. Barely. Asking only for me. They were waiting for the medivac copter.

4

A PAIR OF patrol cars appeared behind and followed me off the Hanson exit, through an empty intersection, and onto Tupelo, the secluded dead-end street where Ray and his wife lived. An officer recognized me and waved me through the line. He stopped the other two cars and directed them to the curb.

The area was abuzz with activity: officers standing in small groups talking, others shuffling to and from the backyard. I parked at the end of the asphalt driveway and waded through the crowd. A young state trooper side-stepped from my path, looking terrified and sick and embarrassed. Jerry Higney, a fifteen-year vet with a locker near mine, called my name and pointed toward the back. I looked at him and his eyes told me the same thing the rookie's had.

The ambulance was parked far back in the yard, near the open field that bordered Ray's property. Its overhead lights were flashing, the twin back doors standing open. A ring of on-duties surrounded the scene, shielding all the activity. I slowed to a jog, pointing at my badge, when a cop I didn't recognize stepped out to intercept me. He nodded and moved out of the way, and I saw Ray on his back on a stretcher, surrounded by paramedics.

I stepped closer, moved over him. His eyes flickered open and when he saw me…he smiled.

I froze.

His face was perfect, untouched, and smiling. I tried to smile back—I honestly did—but couldn't. Two paramedics knelt at his side, fist deep in his open stomach. I reached for his hand. He took it and squeezed; his grip so very soft, almost nothing. I squeezed hard enough for both of us and leaned closer.

A man with a blood-smeared jumpsuit and a nose the size of Cleveland touched my shoulder. "You'll have to stay back so we can—"

I shook my head and interrupted, "He's my partner."

Someone called him and the paramedic glanced over his shoulder, then looked back at me and said, "Okay, but if I tell you to move, you damn well better do it."

I felt Ray's fingers twitch, and he whispered in a voice that made my heart hurt and my eyes water. "You get a look at his nose? Sucker's almost as big as your's." He smiled again, but this time it hurt him, and he gritted his teeth and groaned.

I think I did smile then, despite his pain. His goddamn nose jokes got me every time. I pressed closer. "Take it easy, buddy. Bird's on the way; everything's gonna be all right."

A paramedic knocked me off balance momentarily and when I looked back at Ray, his stare was savage. "Mailman," he hissed.

"I know," I said. "Couple of his boys were waiting for me at the house tonight." I rubbed the back of my head instinctively. "The sons of a bitches surprised me."

He shook his head and said, "They were waiting...waiting outside. They..." He rolled his head to the side and vomited. I cleared his mouth with my fingers.

"Don't talk anymore. Just try to—"

"Listen to me," he whispered, his voice almost gone. "Connie's at her mother's. They were gonna...gonna go shopping tomorrow. You tell her, okay? Tell her..."

I shook my head, knowing what was coming but not wanting to hear it, not wanting to be there anymore.

"Tell her..."

I waited for more, but he just stared at me, eyes pleading for an answer to this mess. "I will," I managed. "Don't worry about that now. I'll take care of it."

And then he closed his eyes and said, "I'm sorry."

I didn't know what the hell he meant, and didn't have much time to think about it before two paramedics pushed me aside, both yelling, "Code Red," and the rest of the crew went bat shit.

It was ugly. The backyard looking like a scene out of one of those high-tech science-fiction flicks. Lights everywhere, big white skylights shining brightly upward. Police red-and-blues flashing through the darkness, a bizarre laser show for the onlookers. Police officers and medics scurrying across the lawn. The paramedics pushing and poking and breathing into Ray, until the one with the big nose is standing up in disgust, snatching the radio, telling the copter to turn around. And then it gets very quiet and the lights blink out like in a stage play, only this act is real, and my partner is dead.

I FOUND CONNIE'S mother's phone number inside the house and called. Connie answered after the fourth ring, sounding sleepy and irritated. A few minutes later, she sounded worse. Her mother took the phone and told me they'd be leaving in a few minutes. The courageous bastard that I am, I left before they arrived.

5

I SPENT THE next couple of days inside. Alone. Took the phone off the hook. Didn't dress or shave. Nibbled at something when I got hungry, which wasn't often. Sat staring out the back-porch window. Thinking.

I don't think they meant to kill Ray, just knock him down a lick or two, like they'd done with me. A warning. Ray and I had spent the past six weeks heading up a special task force designed to crush the Mailman and were finally, after a month of drawing blanks, making some progress.

Mailman's legal name was Reggie Scales. Black male. Twenty-four. Skinny and ugly. A cold-blooded killer. A self-proclaimed mastermind, he employed others to do his dirty work. Kept his own hands clean. Scales ran Baltimore City's drug trade: heroin, cocaine, crack. Of course, there were still chump-change dealers on the street—always would be—but Scales handled the main traffic. His gang numbered over thirty. And they called him Mailman on the street because he always delivered.

We'd been getting closer and closer—one of his street sellers was starting to get nervous and talk—and he must've figured it was time for a warning. Something nice and subtle, like a little too-close-to-home-for-comfort ass-beating to soften the hard-ons we had for him.

Judging from evidence found in and around Ray's house, I guessed that it had happened like this: Mailman's men were creeping around the house when Ray opened the back door and let Cowboy out for his final shit break of the night. The dog spotted one of them and attacked. They'd found Cowboy with a bullet in his neck about twenty yards from the back door. A guy I know who works K-9 told me that he'd probably died quickly, and I know that would've made Ray feel a little better. Another officer told me that Cowboy had a chunk of human flesh the size of a golf ball in his mouth. Good for him.

Mailman's men must've either panicked after Cowboy attacked or Ray must've fought like a bastard and forced one of them to gun him. Nothing else I can think of. I know that seeing Cowboy gunned down right before his eyes would've made Ray crazy, so I'd bet on the latter. Christ, he really loved that mutt.

6

WE BURIED RAY on a Sunday. A seasonably cool morning, the sky stretched a crisp, clean blue. A thin layer of fallen leaves blanketed the cemetery grounds. There was no wind, no rain. Didn't feel like funeral weather.

I wore my dress blues and if I wasn't in such a deep funk, I would've felt ridiculous. The entire precinct—and over two hundred other officers from as far away as Ohio—were in attendance. And, of course, the media showed up. Reporters, a shit load of camera crews—the whole damn circus. They tried their best to look sincere, but just looked hungry. I found out later that the funeral was the lead news story on all three networks. As usual, I declined all interviews, and threatened several reporters with bodily harm. Off camera, of course.

I stood behind Connie during the service and felt like a real bastard. Not only had I left before she arrived at the scene, but I'd only called her once over the past three days.

She'd sounded as well as could be expected on the telephone. Said both her parents were staying with her and that she'd been taking some pills to help her sleep and that they were working. She'd asked me a lot of questions—about Ray and that night, about the Mailman—few of which I had answers for. The conversation lasted barely fifteen minutes; it was all either of us could stand. Before I hung up, I told her what Ray's last words to me had been—*I'm sorry*—and asked if she knew what he'd meant. She'd answered me with silence; I told her to forget it and hung up.

After the funeral service, I spoke briefly with Ray's parents, then wandered around aimlessly for a few minutes, afraid to get in my car and drive away, but more afraid of staying and saying good-bye to my partner. Connie spotted me, excused herself from the main group, and walked over. We hugged without exchanging words—there was really nothing either of us could say—and she slipped a piece of paper into my hand before we parted. I talked to a few other officers, and then snuck away before the media freaks got brave again.

I unfolded the paper and read what was written, once in the parking lot and again in the car. Then I went home and got drunk. I read it a third time the next morning and got drunk again.

7

BALTIMORE'S INNER HARBOR is a contradiction of humanity.

If you sit on Federal Hill and look straight ahead out over the harbor, you can see the truth in that statement.

The harbor attracts money—all kinds. Well-dressed tourists, bored locals, hand-holding couples, businessmen and businesswomen doing lunch. Families wait in line at the aquarium, the science center, the shops and food joints. Catch a show on the Bay Lady, ride a miniature motorboat or paddleboat, eat and drink on an outdoor patio, listen to a concert. Summer, winter, hot, cold, it doesn't matter; they flock here like ants on a corpse.

Two blocks away, in the harbor's shadow, it's a different story. Barefooted kids run the streets; uneducated, undernourished, underloved. Doors and windows are open—no air-conditioning. Too many people are on the street; it's a weekday and they should be at work. A whistle sounds from a second-floor window, and the dealers disappear into the cracks. Seconds later, a dented police cruiser turns the corner. The officer inside is hot and bored and anxious to go home to his swimming pool. The squad car passes—the officer never glancing in any direction other than straight ahead—and the dealers reappear with smiles on their faces. Business is good.

Two city blocks...two different worlds.

And it's impossible to prevent these two worlds from clashing. Beggars line the store and restaurant fronts. Drug dealers and pimps wait in line next to visiting suburban schoolchildren. Street people sift through trash cans while spoiled teenagers hunt for the latest fashion rage or cuss the slow-walking elders in front of them. Yuppie women complain because no one notices their new outfit or haircut, while real people die a block away and no one notices or even cares.

Coming to the Inner Harbor always depresses me, and when I get depressed—which is more often than I like to admit—I tend to preach. But I preach to an audience of one, so I offer no apologies.

Connie had called late last night to arrange this morning's meeting. Ten in the morning at Federal Hill. I was early, unusual for me. I sat back in the grass and thought about the note while I waited. I supposed I could play dumb, ask her what she meant or just try to change her mind. The problem was I knew exactly what she meant and wasn't sure that I *wanted* to change her mind.

Kill him.

The words were handwritten in black ink on lined tablet paper, probably the same pad and pen Connie used to record her grocery list every week. But instead of fruit and vegetables, this request was a little less healthy.

I hadn't been able to accept Ray's death yet—hadn't said good-bye to him at the funeral or returned to work and faced the job alone—but I wasn't sure if taking out the Mailman would allow me to. And I wasn't sure how I felt about Connie. Compassion and pity and...disappointment?

Revenge was a primitive and intense emotion, one that I experienced fairly often. Hell, I had no *moral* problems with her request. The badge certainly wouldn't stop me. I'd been a terrible human long before I became a cop, and unless you listened to Ray, I'd never stopped being one. But, for some reason, I'd never expected it of Connie. At least, not to this degree. I'm a pompous bastard, I know.

She finally showed at 10:04, walking gracefully down the stone path, looking beautiful in a schoolgirl way, blond ponytail swinging from side to side. I didn't see her swollen eyes until she drew close and kissed me softly on the cheek. She sat beside me in the grass, and we talked for several minutes before silence overtook us. Somewhere in the middle of the quiet she looked at me, green eyes wide and moist, and I nodded. Her body wavered, all her breath leaving her at once, and she smiled sadly. Then she touched my hand and left me alone.

8

TWO WEEKS LATER and I'm on the street. Past midnight. Light rain falling. Cruising the city, west side, in my beat-up Mustang. I hadn't driven the junker for months—ever since I'd bought my truck—and the clutch was kicking my ass. I was wearing an old army jacket over a sweater and blue-jeans. Had a wool cap pulled low over my forehead with some fake hair sticking out the back. I looked pretty damn stupid, but, hell, I valued my life more than my pride.

I had a 9mm in my shoulder holster, a shotgun under the dash, and a plastic baggie of cocaine underneath my jacket on the front seat. Earlier, I'd jumped a dealer on Fayette Street, out by the hospital, and cleaned out his stash. Knocked out two of his teeth in the process. Didn't feel good doing it, but I needed the stuff and wasn't about to pay for it.

After fifteen minutes of driving, I spotted who I was searching for on a dark corner and pulled to the curb. I leaned over and rolled down the passenger window.

"Hey, old man. Hey, Snowman. I'm looking for some information."

The man didn't look up. He was sitting on a crumbled porch, chin resting on his hands, oblivious to the rain. He looked close to sixty, but was actually in his mid-forties, a well-known veteran of the street. Because of his round belly and choice of drug habit, the street called him Snowman. He was wearing a filthy wool cap and a recycled trench coat down to his knees. I noted the hat and felt a little better about my disguise.

I called him a second time, this time offering to pay for the help, and again he ignored me. A young redneck couple, voices raised, obviously arguing about something, turned the corner, and I leaned back into the driver's seat. I waited for them to pass, then placed the clear bag of cocaine in my lap and poked a hole in the top with two fingers. I scooped a small amount of the powder into my other palm and exited the car, leaving the bag on the seat. Our undercovers had tried unsuccessfully to pry information from the Snowman several times before, usually using small amounts of money as bait.

The man heard the car door slam and slowly opened his eyes. Dull. Expressionless. Before he could close them again and return to his dream world, I opened my hand in front of his face.

"It's all yours," I said, motioning for him to take the drug.

He eyed me cautiously, and then craned his neck up and down the street, eyes scanning.

"This isn't a setup," I said. "All I want is some information. I'm looking for someone and if you can help me find him, there's a bag of this stuff in the car that's yours."

I crouched to a knee and offered my hand again. He lifted a filthy, scarred hand, and I poured the cocaine onto his palm. He touched a finger to the powder, lifted it to the tongue, then, seemingly satisfied that it was the real thing, emptied it onto a scrap of newspaper. He carefully folded the paper and stuffed it under his hat.

"Who?" he asked, not looking at me.

"Mailman."

"Uh uh. Can't help you."

I walked back to the car, checking the street for wandering eyes. I lifted the coke from the seat and held it level to the man's face, feeling guilty as hell. His eyes widened, showing human emotion for the first time. Showing hunger. "All I want to know is where he is," I said. "And all this is yours. No tricks. Otherwise I find someone else to do it."

He stared at the bag, eyes unblinking, tongue snaking out to lick cracked lips. "One hour. Wait here."

I stuffed the bag inside my jacket and smiled. "I'll be waiting."

I WATCHED THE old man disappear down the street, then pulled the car around the corner and turned off the engine. I checked the time, then opened a paper bag and pulled out a ham-and-cheese sandwich and a candy bar. Damn if I wasn't prepared.

I had actually packed the same snack, dressed in the same pathetic disguise, and loaded the car twice before, false starting both times. I didn't even leave the curb the first time, and I did a U-turn on I-95 and returned home the second time.

There was no turning back tonight. I knew that.

Premeditated murder. Two words that I'd heard and said hundreds of times before; they haunted me now. Since the meeting on Federal Hill, I'd found myself thinking of the Mailman less and less, and thinking, instead, of Connie and the note. Ray's death had triggered something inside of her—eaten away something good and pure—and she'd turned to me for help. I didn't know whether to feel honored or ashamed.

EXACTLY FORTY-FIVE MINUTES after he had left, Snowman returned. He walked to the driver's side of the car and waited for me to roll down my window. Without a word, he held out his hands.

"Give it to me first," he said.

"You know where he is?"

He nodded.

I handed him the bag, and it disappeared inside his coat.

"Mama Lucia's," he said, turning to leave.

"Little Italy?"

"Yeah." Then he was gone, humming as he went.

IT WAS EASIER than it should've been. Easy and quick.

There were only two men guarding him. Both standing outside, hiding from the rain underneath the awning. I popped up behind the first one and forearmed his head a couple of times until he went to sleep, and the second one—a muscle-bound teenager—actually took off running before I could get to him. Guess you can't buy loyalty.

Mama Lucia's was a corner restaurant at the north end of Little Italy. Vine-covered red brick. Two stories. A relatively quiet section of the city. Only three blocks away from the harbor, it attracted plenty of suits and other expensive clientele and served as one of many tourist attractions. And if it was like most of the other ethnic restaurants on the block, there were living quarters on the top floor. Mailman probably had something on the restaurant owner—like an overdue coke bill—and figured it was the last place anyone would look for him.

It was close to three in the morning when I walked in the front door, gloves on, gun in hand. The downstairs dining room was dark and deserted. I headed for the stairs, moving carefully through the cramped maze of tables and chairs. Considering the Mailman's healthy ego, I was surprised that the place wasn't crawling with armed guards. A few seconds later, as I reached the last step and entered a narrow, carpeted hallway, I heard squeals of pleasure, then a deeper-toned groan, and immediately knew why security was minimal. The Mailman was getting laid.

The animal sounds—they sounded like they were mauling each other—were coming from the end of the hall. There was a single door and it was cracked open, a sliver of dim light escaping into the hall. No wonder his men had been waiting outside in the rain.

I had no brilliant plan of action and instead of formulating one now, I simply walked into the room, yanked the flabby woman off the Mailman's lap, and shoved the barrel of my gun under his nose. "Don't move or I swear to God I'll pull it."

"Be cool, man," he said, gold teeth flashing. He was nude, slicked with sweat, sitting up on a tangle of sheets. He held his arms up and I could count the ribs sticking out below his scrawny chest. Christ, he certainly didn't spend his money on food. I'd seen enough pictures of Scales to recognize his face, but still I couldn't believe this was the guy we'd been looking for. He looked like a damn kid.

The woman was hysterical behind me. She screamed and cussed me and started clawing my back, so I reached back and pistol-whipped her across the forehead. She hit the carpet, and shut up real nice after that.

"Listen, man, I—"

"Just shut up and sit your ass right where you are, and we'll have no problems. I'm just gonna take you out of here and talk to you."

His eyes widened and he nodded his head spastically, looking like a broken puppet. He even smiled, as if to show that he trusted me. It was a sad sight.

I moved quickly, hoping that the downstairs was still clear. I pulled a set of handcuffs from my coat, yanked the Mailman's arms behind his back, and snapped them on his wrists. There was a pair of ugly yellow jockeys on the floor, and I slipped them on him, myself. Wasn't my idea of a good time, but I'd seen his naked body long enough.

I guided him down the hall in front of me, shielding myself, in case anyone was waiting. I knew the gorilla downstairs wouldn't be waking up anytime soon, but I wasn't sure if the other one had called for help or grown balls in the meantime and returned.

For once, the horseshoe was up *my* ass, and the downstairs was exactly as I had left it. I escorted the Mailman down the block, shoved him in the front seat of the Mustang, got in, and drove away.

"BE CAREFUL, MAN. I told ya I can't swim."

"And I told you to shut your mouth. We're almost there."

We were inside one of the abandoned shipyards outside of Fells Point. Walking single-file down a narrow concrete path above the water. The docks had long been taken out, leaving a sheer drop from the concrete into the black water. The rain was falling harder now, and the walk was dangerously slick. A row of dark, abandoned warehouses stretched several hundred yards in both directions, blocking the view from the street. On the way, I'd told him that someone was waiting in one of the buildings to talk to him. I figured I could waste him down here, and nobody would ever find him. It was almost over.

I studied his silhouette closely as we walked, itching to pull the trigger. He was so damn thin, his body took on an almost elastic appearance. He was a full ten inches taller than me, but I probably outweighed him by twenty pounds. It was too dark to see clearly, but I could hear the squeak of his bare feet on the pavement and the slap of thick gold chains against his chest. Wearing only underwear, he shivered badly in the cold rain.

We passed an ancient loading platform, broken and uneven now, and the pathway widened a bit. I looked back over my shoulder; we were far enough from the street now.

"The building's right up here," I said. He slowed his pace, and I pushed the 9mm's barrel into the center of his back, nudging him forward.

"Damn it, man. Keep me the fuck away from the edge. I can't swim, I tell ya. I can't fuckin' swim."

Suddenly, a flash went off inside my head. My heart hammered.

I can't swim.

I pushed him over the edge to see if he was lying.

He wasn't.

I watched the bubbles until they disappeared.

9

I HATE ANSWERING machines. The only reason I finally bought one is because I kept missing calls from my bookie. Now I get messages all the time from a Mr. Pony. Clever guy.

I always screen my phone calls, with an emphasis on the *always*. I pick up maybe one time out of every three or four dozen calls. That's it. But, and it never fails, the single call I answer in the flesh is always the one I wanted most to avoid.

That's how Connie finally tracked me down, a week and four messages later. She didn't ask me why I hadn't returned the calls, so I didn't make up a sorry excuse. I had a feeling she knew, anyway.

"Is it over?" she asked, skipping any casual bullshit.

I'd rehearsed this moment over and over again, but my mouth felt dry and sticky. "Yes," I finally said.

"How are you?"

"Fine," I lied.

Silence. Then she said matter-of-factly, "I'm expecting my sister and her family tonight, but if you'd like to come over and talk—"

"No, no, that's okay," I said. "I've got a lot to catch up on downtown." Another lie.

"Okay, if you're sure." Long pause. "Listen, I've been thinking about what Ray said to you that night."

"Uh, huh," I said, knowing precisely what she was talking about.

"Well, you know Ray thought of you as a lot more than just a partner. I mean…he really admired you. He loved you."

Her voice was strangled and soft, and I knew she was starting to cry.

"He thought of you as a brother…as family. And I think he was saying sorry because he was leaving you alone. He worried about you, you know? He used to talk about it a lot. No wife, no family, not many friends. Just your work. He always told me that if something happened to him, he knew I could go on. I had family members close by, good friends, a job I enjoyed." She sighed. "You were the one he worried about. I think Ray was apologizing for leaving you alone. That was just like him, wasn't it?"

I didn't answer. Couldn't. Just thanked her after a moment and hung up, knowing that what she'd said was the truth.

Later, I made myself a sandwich and ate it outside on the back porch. I watched the leaves dance across the lawn, and the late-afternoon sunshine and the whisper of a breeze felt good on my face. Autumn was in full swing now, and for the first time since I was a teenager, I remembered that it was my favorite time of year. A season of change.

I sat there for a long time nibbling at that sandwich, thinking about Ray. About his unshakable spirit and outlook on life. About the big mouth that had given me so many headaches during so many workdays—his stupid jokes, his boring family talk, his childhood adventure stories. And I thought about the many times when we'd sat, shared a beer or dinner, and just talked. About nothing in particular, about everything that was important to us.

As the afternoon passed, I could feel the heavy weight of guilt slowly ease away. What we'd done wasn't right, but it had cleaned the slate. It had allowed us—Ray's survivors—to survive.

And to start over again.

When the sun finally lowered and the chill set in, I took my empty paper plate and went inside. It was the best damn sandwich I ever ate.

10

LATER THAT EVENING, while reading the newspaper, I found myself staring at the classified advertisements. I turned to the section for household pets and circled a phone number for purebred puppies. I thought about it a bit longer and decided to call in the morning. Someone to keep me company, I thought. One of those shiny gold ones…like Cowboy.

I know Ray would've liked that.

MIDNIGHT PROMISES

SHE PEEKS AROUND THE edge of the door. Tiptoes inside the room and kisses him good morning. A soft peck on the cheek.

He doesn't stir.

She walks over to the window and pulls open the curtains. It's June and the sky is rainbow blue with lazy white clouds swimming by. The view is a pretty one—distant trees swaying in the breeze, a bed of flowers blooming in the foreground—and she wishes, as she does every morning, that she could open the window just a crack.

She places her bag at the foot of the bed, takes off her windbreaker and sits down in the chair. She gently takes his right hand and begins stroking each of his fingers.

Later, when he wakes up, she'll move over to his left side so that he'll be able to see outside the window.

But for now she sits with her back bathed in golden sunlight.

THE CANCER IS taking him away—inch by inch.

Every day, a little more of him disappears.

And she sits and watches.

Always she watches.

She leaves at night now but only because they make her.

"You need your rest, Mrs. Collins."

"We'll take good care of him."

"I promise we'll call you if your husband needs you for anything."

"You remember what happened last time, Mrs. Collins. We don't want a repeat of that, now do we?"

So now she goes home each night. Precisely at ten o'clock with the other visitors.

A silent elevator ride to the lobby. A slow walk to the parking lot. And the lonely drive home.

Home...where there is nothing left for her.

Just a quiet, cold house. A mug of hot cocoa in the dark kitchen. The day's mail. And an empty bed.

Home is like a stranger to her now. Or perhaps *she* is the stranger. She can remember a time when this house smiled at her each time she walked through the door. Whispered in her ear as she crossed the foyer that everything was safe and sound and wonderful.

Now there is only silence.

Not even a whisper of life there: no lights or television or radio. No laughter or idle conversation. Nothing.

Just the same damn thing, night after night after night.

Hot cocoa. Mail. Bed.

And, of course, the nightmares.

They come more often now.

Sometimes—very, very rarely—she dreams happy thoughts: *A close-up of his smile. The sound of his laughter. The feel of his lips on her mouth. The touch of his hand as they walk barefoot on a moonlit beach.*

But most nights she dreams darker thoughts: *an x-ray view of his torso... showing nothing. Absolutely nothing inside—just a hollowed-out husk of a man. Surviving on nothing but air.*

Or her standing alone in a cold, driving rain. Standing above his open grave. Dropping a single red rose onto the shiny black casket...

Or the apple dream. This one is the worst of all—sheer, breath-stealing terror. *She sees the two of them sitting in front of a large desk of dark, polished wood. Holding hands. Listening to a doctor. The doctor's face is grim. His lip is trembling. He tells them that the first reports were wrong, that the cancer has spread and he holds up an x-ray...and the image is that of an apple tree. Tumors everywhere, hanging there like fat, ripe apples. Dozens of them. Dark and moist and plump. Waiting to be picked...*

Thank God, this dream doesn't come very often.

Because when it does, she almost always wakes up screaming.

IT'S LUNCHTIME AND the hallway is buzzing with activity.

She gets up and closes the door.

He's sleeping again, but she isn't worried about the noise disturbing him. It's the smell—he can't stand the smell of the hospital food. It makes him nauseous.

A lot of things do that to him. Food. Flowers. Perfume. Even some liquids. They all smell funny now. One of the drugs is responsible, but she can't remember which one.

He doesn't eat the food, anyway. Not anymore. They use a tube for that now. A shiny, little clear thing that snakes right into his stomach.

She remembers that as a particularly bad time—the week he stopped eating.

But even worse was when he stopped talking.

It's been thirteen days now. And barely a whisper in all that time. Too weak, the doctors explain. Too many drugs.

So, most days, they just sit there and hold hands and stare into each other's eyes. Sometimes they smile and make silly faces, sometimes they just sit there and cry.

With the door closed, the room is very quiet except for the constant beeping of the I.V. She turns the volume down a notch—she knows the machines as well as any nurse on the floor—and starts to read again, a letter she'd written him just before they were married. Her voice cracks several times and there are tears in her eyes, but still she keeps reading. She has a stack of letters in her bag, tightly-bound with a thick rubber band, and she is determined to get through them all.

THE MORNINGS ARE no kinder than the nights. Same routine every day—up by six-thirty, out the door by seven-thirty.

She starts each morning with a long, hot shower and she always tries her hardest to think of something nice, something cheerful to start the day with. But she never can.

She forces herself to eat a good breakfast most of the time. Toast. Fruit. Juice. For energy. She knows this was the reason she'd gotten sick last month and needed to see the doctor—not because she was sleeping in his hospital room every night! Not because she was overtired, for goodness sake!

She had simply forgotten to eat. For three or four days. She can't remember which.

So now she takes the time to eat most mornings. And when she's done, she washes the dishes and wipes down the countertop. Then she grabs her keys from the foyer and locks the door behind her. She gets into her car and pulls away from the curb. And never once looks back.

DINNER IS SERVED at quarter to six.

She closes the door as soon as she hears the familiar squeaking of the tray-cart working its way down the hallway.

He's awake now and they're looking at photos.

High school. College. Summers at the beach. Even pictures of the wedding. She brought them all.

He smiles at most of the pictures. Points and grins and raises what's left of his eyebrows. It's the most animated—and alert—he's been in weeks, and it does her heart wonders to see him this way.

When she gets to one particular photo, he really surprises her. His face lights up like a child's and he takes it from her with trembling fingers.

It's an old photo. From the very first summer they spent together. A narrow strip of three small black-and-whites from one of those cheap, little booths you sit inside. In the first two, their faces are pressed together cheek-to-cheek and they're grinning like goofy kids. In the last one, they're kissing.

He lifts the photo to his face and tries to kiss it. But the tubes get in the way.

So she takes it from him and kisses it herself, then lays it on the sheet atop his chest.

He smiles at her and closes his eyes.

She does the same and moments later when she hears the whisper—"*thank you*"—she thinks she must be dreaming…

Until she opens her eyes and sees his stare and the tears streaming down his cheeks.

And at that exact moment, she knows with complete certainty that she is doing the right thing—the letters, the photos…

In her heart, she *knows*.

Just after eight o'clock, he falls asleep again and she returns the photos to her bag. Except for his favorite one—she leaves that right where it is.

She holds his hand and watches him sleep until ten. Just like so many times before.

Then she kisses him goodnight and heads for the elevator.

SOMETIMES, WHEN SHE'S away from the hospital, she tries to convince herself that he's improving. That he's looking better. And that she'll walk through the door the next morning and he'll be sitting up and talking and maybe eating some scrambled eggs. And she'll bounce over to the bed and say, "Hey, kiddo, I *thought* you had some color in those cheeks last night—"

But she knows none of this is true. She knows what's really happening.

Fourteen hours a day is enough to convince anyone.

He'd lost his hair during the second cycle of chemo. By the end of the third, he was thirty pounds lighter.

A month later—halfway into the final cycle—they knew it wasn't working.

So, they'd switched to different drugs and a different program.

And it had worked for a while, too. For a few weeks, at least, he seemed to stabilize. His energy crept up a few notches, his weight maintained.

But then, as if the whole thing had just been some sort of cruel joke, it all went downhill and fast.

He stopped eating.

His skin turned a sick combination of yellow and green.

He started to sweat so much and the smell...oh God the smell...

And then, almost overnight, the pain doubled. Then tripled.

And then it got so bad that he started to cry—something she had never seen before. Not when his mother died, not when they first learned about the cancer. Never.

So the doctors had immediately injected him with the heavy stuff...

...and most of the pain had gone away...

...almost overnight, just as fast as it had come, it had gone away...

...and her husband had gone away with it.

Now he sleeps most of the time.

And when he *is* awake—well, it isn't much different than when he's still sleeping. Or at least it seems that way to her. His eyes are so milky and unfocused, he barely moves a finger, he doesn't talk...

She feels miserable and guilty for thinking this way. Of course, she's glad he no longer feels the pain. Of course, she's grateful to the doctors for making him so much more comfortable.

But God, she can't help it—she misses his voice, his laugh, his charm; she misses the way he once looked at her.

Without those things, she is not only afraid, she is all alone.

SHE SLIDES THE ring onto his finger and closes his hand into a fist. His fingers are skinny and gnarled—like an old man's—and she's worried that the ring will fall off. Tumble down to the floor and no one will find it.

She lets go of his hand and stares at it for a long moment, then walks over to the window.

It's almost midnight and a full moon is shining far away in the distance, coating the trees with a silver luster, making everything look wet and slick like just after a rainfall.

She parts the curtains slightly and a sliver of moonbeam enters the room.

She looks at her bag on the floor. Thinks about the letters and the photos inside. Wonders why she didn't leave the bag in the car.

She knows she's stalling, but she can't help it.

She turns and looks into the shadows: at the blinking machines and the tangle of tubes and the clear, dripping bag with the big red sticker that reads: CHEMO: *Do Not Handle Without Protective Gloves.*

She stares at the man she loves so dearly, the only man she has *ever* loved.

Thirty-four years of life and he's been there over half of them, she thinks.

Just you and me against the world, kiddo…

She puts her hand inside her jacket pocket.

Walks to his bedside and leans over.

Kisses his sweaty forehead.

Closes her eyes and whispers: "I'll forever love you, my darling."

And her words will live in this room forever.

She places the gun to his forehead and makes good on her promise.

There's a sudden explosion of sound and light, and she falls hard to the floor.

She looks up involuntarily and shudders.

And then, for the first time in all their years together, she breaks her word to him. She opens her mouth wide, slides the cold barrel inside and pulls the trigger.

A promise kept.

A promise broken.

And the unending silence of night.

THE
NIGHT
SHIFT

"HEY, WHERE THE HELL you been? I've been calling..."

"Traffic was a friggin' mess. Backed up halfway down the interstate. And I left the phone at home in my other jacket. My kid finds it sitting there, he'll be calling cross-country again. Cost me a fortune."

"You're a cop. Haul his ass in."

"I might just have to when the bill shows up. You shoulda seen last month's."

"You do it. Scare him a little. Teach him to respect authority and all that jazz."

"Yeah, right. Respect authority, just like your kid, huh? Mr. I-Got-Busted-My-First-Week-At-College-For-Smoking-Dope."

"Hey now...you know damn well he said *he* wasn't the one smoking it."

"I know, I know, he was innocent as a newborn and he didn't even inhale the second hand smoke."

"Let's just drop it, okay, Logan? Anyway, we got a bad one in there tonight. Real bad. You hear?"

"Yep. Thompson was out there in the parking lot doing his usual routine. Eyes big like silver dollars, face all red and sweaty, talking faster than a preacher on speed. He put on a helluva show."

"You gotta admit, he's got reason this time. How much he tell you? Jesus, partner, this one's bad…"

"HEY, BEN, I just thought of something. Why no press in on this thing? They should be all over this—"

"And they will be. Give it another hour or two and that parking lot'll be packed. The thing went down real quiet. Middle of the day. Everyone's at work, at school. Team was in and out in less than an hour. No leaks yet, I guess."

"They're still over there, huh?"

"Where? The house, you mean?"

"Uh-huh."

"Oh yeah, they'll be there thru the night, I bet. Bennie from Morning said it was like a House of Horrors. Like something from one of those true crime books he's always reading."

"Press'll love this shit."

"You're not kidding."

"I guess they're keeping a real low profile at the house. Maybe we'll sneak over that way later tonight. Take a look around for ourselves."

"Sounds good to me."

"THE PLOT THICKENS."

"Huh?"

"The story gets worse."

"Yeah?"

"The strange grows even stranger—"

"Dammit, Logan, just spit it out if you got something to tell me. I got paperwork to do and—"

"I just got off the phone with Jerry Hammond's kid. He works over the lab—"

"I know where he works."

"Well, he said something pretty darn weird to me."

"What'd he say?"

"Well, he said there was something wrong with one of those heads they found."

"Something wrong with it? No shit, Sherlock, it was cut clean off."

"Nope, that ain't it."

"Tell me then, dammit. What'd he say was wrong with it? What's so weird about the head they found?"

"He said it ain't exactly *human.*"

"JESUS, YOU GET a look at it? A *close* look?"

"The head?"

"No, the foot. The hand. Yes, the damn head! Thing was creepy as hell."

"Yeah, I checked it out. It was…interesting."

"Interesting? You call that thing *interesting*…hell, you're just as nuts as the sicko who did it, if you think that thing's interesting."

"It is though. You saw it."

"I'll tell you what's interesting, partner. We got us a freak living two streets down from an elementary school, he goes out and kills seven people over a fifteen month period and this is the first we catch a sniff. I mean, Jesus, we get lucky on a damn traffic stop and catch the guy. Freak's got heads stuffed in an old freezer in his basement. Body parts in the garage. And then this damn thing…whatever the hell you wanna call it."

"It's a head."

"Not like any head I've ever seen."

"Still a head though."

"I guess so, you wanna get technical about it. I ain't trying to argue here."

"Gotta admit, it *is* interesting."

"I don't give a flying fart what you think. I think it's weird, and I think it's sick."

"No need to argue about it."

"HOW BIG YOU think that thing was?"

"The head?"

"Yeah, the head, dammit. Don't start that shit again."

"Hammonds said it was seventeen-and-a-half inches top to bottom. Don't remember how wide he said it was."

"Thing was huge, I know that much. And creepy as hell. You see the mouth, those weird teeth? And those crazy eyes? Weren't shaped like no eyes I've ever seen. And just what in blue blazes were those things on the back of the head?"

"Couldn't really tell."

"Did you look?"

"Yeah, I looked. But his hair was still half-frozen all crazy like that and—"

"You know what they looked like, don't you?"

"I'm not gonna say."

"C'mon, you saw, you know as well as I do."

"Maybe…but I'm still not gonna say."

"Why? You scared? You scared to say what they looked like?"

"Yes. As a matter of fact, I am."

"I'M STUFFED."

"Me too."

"Can't eat another bite."

"Same here."

"You wanna head on over to the house?"

"Your call. What time you got?"

"Just past midnight. Hey, where's your watch?"

"My kid borrowed it for the prom last weekend. Lost it."

"Jesus."

"You're not kidding. That was a good watch."

"Big-time detective like you needs a watch. How you gonna log in all that paperwork you don't know what time to put on the form?"

"How about I just borrow yours?"

"Ain't gonna happen."

"Hell, I *knew* that. Okay, let's get outta here. The house or the station?"

"Ahh, let's head on in, I guess. I got a lotta—"

"Paperwork."

"Exactly."

"HEY, LOGAN, THE Captain wants to talk to us. In his office. Right now."

"Uh-oh."

"Uh-oh is right. And it gets worse. I think I saw some Feds in there with him."

"Jesus."

"You're not kidding."

"NOW *THAT* WAS weird."

"You're not kidding. Weirdest thing I ever been a part of."

"Hell yes it was. Me too."

"Straight outta that show *The X-Files* or something."

"That's *exactly* what I was gonna say."

"Great minds think alike, I guess."

"I mean, Jesus, what's the odds of that? A freak goes out and kills seven people, stuffs their heads in a freezer and one of 'em turns out to be—"

"A million-to-one, partner. A million-to-one."

"Gotta admit what they said in there gave me the creeps big-time. Never heard anything like it. And to think...that thing was just walking around here...man, that's nothing I want to *think* about, must less *talk* about. Hell, I was happy to sign those papers."

"Me too."

"Captain said we all gotta sign 'em. Almost twenty of us. You think anyone'll bitch?"

"I dunno. You never know with some guys. But they won't if they're smart. Those guys in there looked pretty damn serious."

"You bet they are."

"Besides, what's the point in bitching?"

"Exactly."

"Hey, you hungry?"

"Christ, Ben, we just ate."

"That was almost three hours ago."

"How you know? You ain't even got a watch."

"I just looked at yours."

"Well, you can stop staring at my wrist, thank you very much. Just ask me what time it is from now on like a normal person would. Next damn thing you know, you'll be trying to hold my hand."

"Jesus, c'mon, Benny, my stomach's growling."

"You're a sick puppy."

"I'm a hungry puppy is what I am."

"Alright, alright, lemme grab my hat, it's gettin' cold out there."

"Meet you in the parking lot?"

"Give me five minutes. Gotta pee."

"Pizza?"

"Sounds good to me."

ONLY THE STRONG SURVIVE

FINGERS OF DENSE FOG caressed the shadow that emerged from the abandoned rowhouse. Across the street, two drunks scuttled into an alleyway, oblivious to the miserable cold and wind and the sudden appearance of the mysterious figure. A wall of gray mist immediately swallowed them, muffling their footfalls, erasing their existence.

The shadow moved silently across the littered walkway, its face shifting with a subtle metamorphosis. Arrogance, loathing, and disdain bled away like flowing lava; quickly replaced by a mask of compassion, tenderness, and understanding.

The facade, uncomfortable though necessary, fit like a favorite glove. The face, once gaunt and callous, was now chubby—even cherubic. The face wasn't pretty or pleasing to the eye, wasn't meant to be; but it exuded a vulnerability that cried out for protection against a hostile world. It was the desired effect.

A full moon watched the shadow's progress from above, its brilliant luster defeated in the heavy fog. The night phantom crossed yet another filthy intersection, gazed skyward. Another change would soon come; a change once dreaded more than anything, but now welcomed like the winter's first snowfall.

The boy—he'd been on the street for three years now and considered himself a man, but was nonetheless barely sixteen—sat shivering in the back seat of the police car. Earlier in the evening, juiced up on crack, he'd wandered down a side alley, a shortcut to a friend's house. He'd heard someone screaming up ahead of him, the most awful screaming he'd ever heard, and in the heavy fog that had enveloped the city, he was certain he'd seen two people struggling. Instinctively, he'd turned tail. Hauled ass. Ran headlong into a patrol car responding to an anonymous call, and here he sat, a prime suspect.

He lowered his head, feigning sleep, as he listened to the detective and the beat cop who'd grabbed him.

"No way the kid could've done that," the detective said. He was a fat, ugly man. His face all flab and scar tissue. Oddly though, in stark contrast, he spoke with a soft, almost melodic voice. The boy didn't know why, but he sure liked the sound of it.

"He's strung out on crack," the cop said. "You can't predict what they'll do when they're on that stuff. And he was fleeing from the scene." In comparison, the cop was handsome and young. Very young.

"Scared away, more like it. I wish we could arrest him and wrap it up, but it's more complicated than that."

"More complicated?" the cop asked.

"Looks like the victim was attacked by a pack of wild dogs or something. Chunks of meat gouged from his neck and torso. No way Junior over there could have inflicted those wounds without being covered with blood."

"But the kid's on crack, sir—"

"Ahh, fuck the crack, will ya? Not a speck of blood on him. Nothing." The detective started pacing. "No way we can take the easy way out on this one. Trust me, I wish we could. But there're other factors involved. And besides, that stiff ain't no John Doe. It's Judge Langford. Judge Miller Langford."

"Jesus," the cop whispered. "What was he doing out walking on a night like this? Shit, I'd have thought he'd be all cozy cruising around in a limousine or something."

"Don't read the papers much, do you, son?" It was a statement, not a question. The detective was a street-wise veteran. Close to fifty, he had two dozen years under his belt, along with too much booze and too much pasta. He used his hand to rid his thick gray hair of a sheen of rain.

"The good judge helped deliver food to the homeless," he continued. "You know, the ones who pollute the streets rather than hole up in a shelter. Went out twice a month; just him and another volunteer. Way I figure it, he'd finished up for the night and was on his way home. It's only two blocks away, you know. Decided to cut through the alley to save time and ran into a pack of street dogs. Trust me, the only perp we're going to get from this is one who barks."

The cop laughed, adjusted his cap. "What about the kid's story? He said he saw a fight going down. Two people struggling. Didn't mention no pack of wild dogs."

"Like you said, the kid's stoned. Take him in to the station and get a statement, but don't include it in the official report. Unless the ME says otherwise, he was offed by a pack of dogs. No reason to further complicate matters, if you get my drift."

The detective waved and started to head back to his car, stopped in mid-stride and motioned the policeman to his side. His voice low, he said, "Listen, Charlie, when I said there were complications involved here, I meant it. Maybe I shouldn't be telling you this, but I've got a feeling you know something's a little weird here. This is all I can tell you right now..." The detective wiped the moisture from his brow, lowered his voice another notch. "...this ain't the first killing we've had like this. Mutilated. Chewed up. There's been others. Quite a few, actually. Homeless bums and drunks mostly. But a few law-abiding folks, too. Enough to make some important people nervous, if you know what I mean. The ME says it's gotta be some kind of wild dogs, but we ain't never seen 'em or heard from anyone who has seen 'em. The bottom line is this: if there's some nut out there doing this, we sure as shit don't want it getting in the papers. So...keep a lid on this until I tell you otherwise. Got it?"

The cop nodded and mumbled a response. Shook the older detective's hand and started back toward the patrol car.

The boy breathed a sigh of relief. He couldn't hear what they were talking about now, but he'd heard enough of the earlier conversation to know that he was off the hook. Damn sure wasn't no pack of dogs, he thought, but as long as he wasn't being charged, it was no skin off his back if they believed him or not. He hadn't told them the whole truth anyway. That poor old man hadn't been fighting with just anyone back in that alley. He'd been fighting with, shit, no way to get around it—a goddamned werewolf. And not one of those big dumb hairy things he remembered seeing on the tube, either. This werewolf had fur all right and teeth the size of switchblades. But it also had knockers. No fucking way they were going to believe that. A werewolf with tits! Jesus!

He settled back, rested his head. No use making waves, he thought. Just keep your mouth shut.

He had more important things to worry about, like getting some more cash before his stash ran dry.

THE TWO-LEVEL RED brick building known as the Hope Street shelter actually sat on the corner of Bell Street and Third Avenue. The "Hope Street" part of the name was the brainstorm of one of the founding sponsors; a cheerful reminder, she'd explained, that no matter how desperate things appeared, there was always hope. Not many of the people who worked or lived at the shelter gave the name much thought, though. Their business at hand was far too important for such concerns.

The morning after the murder was typically busy. Breakfast, clean-up, wash-up. Duties for everyone. Sandwiches to be made and distributed to those still on the street. Second-hand clothing and blankets to be collected. Various housecleaning details to complete.

Shortly before lunch, one of the staff coordinators introduced Frank Lofton, a brand new volunteer, to Thera Waterston, and assigned them both to the "box city" on the Broad Street subway concourse.

Kinda old for a new volunteer, Thera thought, smiling cheerfully at the quiet newcomer. *But still green behind the ears, I'm sure. Just like all the others.*

Loaded down with sandwich-filled paper sacks and thermoses of steaming coffee, they slowly made their way through the city streets, toward the subway concourse. From time to time, Thera stole a sidelong glance at Frank, and she found it amusing that he appeared visibly nervous. *First day on the job jitters?* she wondered. But then when he finally spoke up and said what seemed to have been perched on his lips for some time—"I, uh, heard you were with Judge Langford last night, before he was attacked."—she understood why.

"Terrible tragedy," Thera said. "Imagine with all the crime in the streets, he gets attacked by a bunch of dogs." She shook her head. "Such a nice man, too. You know, he had just about everything, but twice a month, no matter what the weather, no matter how busy he was, he'd still be out here helping those less fortunate than him. Poor guy." She shook her head in pity. "Hey, you mentioned earlier that you're an attorney, right? Did you know the judge?"

Frank laughed, a deep, husky echo. "Oh, we tangled some. I'm a defense attorney, semi-retired. Judge Langford and I are about the same age, matter of fact. To answer your question directly, yes, I did know him." He hesitated, still following Thera, seemingly more relaxed now. "You see, I've always been a bit unconventional. Eccentric. Whatever you want to call it. A royal pain in the ass is what Judge Langford called me on more than one occasion, I'm proud to say. You see, I never made it easy on him. Sometimes just one step away from contempt. Controversial, but effective. He didn't think too highly of my tactics, if you know what I mean. But he was a very decent man."

They reached the entrance and descended the steps to the subway platform. Thera saw that Frank—his nose wrinkled, forehead creased—was clearly revolted by the smell.

Thera breathed in deeply, savoring the sweet aroma that enveloped them at the entrance to the box city. Human feces, rotten food, and vomit greeted her like an old friend as it assaulted Frank's senses. She saw him blanch and wondered if he would puke like so many of her other "protectors" had at their first taste of man's descent into hell.

"How can they live in this squalor?" Frank asked.

She shrugged and said, "Most do so out of choice."

"I don't understand. Why…why don't they come to the shelters? This place is horrible…at the very least a breeding ground for disease."

She shook her head and explained patiently: "These people long ago abandoned the system. To get into a shelter there are forms to fill out and questions to answer, a time when you must be in at night and a time when you must leave each morning. In many cases, it's the same old bureaucracy, that drove them out onto the streets in the first place."

"But they're little more than animals here."

She shrugged again. "Free to come and go as they please."

"Are they transients or...regulars down here?" he asked, searching for the right word.

"Depends. This particular group here has formed their own little community. To most this is their permanent residence for the winter. They discourage those who come uninvited to crash for just a day or two or to get free sex or rob someone for drug money. This is their turf, as they say, and I've known some to protect it to their death."

"You make it sound almost noble," Frank said. "Like you're proud of them. I'm sorry, I know I'm naive, but I think these people are sick and need help."

"Some are. And others..." She let the statement dangle. "Is that the only reason you volunteered; to make sure they get the help they need?"

"Yes, isn't that why you're here?"

"Sure, we're here to help—a sandwich, some coffee, and a healthy dose of sympathy and compassion. But we can't force them to accept our help and we shouldn't. If we tried we'd be no more than a shelter on wheels. The 'man' telling them what to do again, which is what they walked away from in the first place. Assert your superior attitude or values here, and they'd just as soon slit your throat as accept your food."

Frank squinted in confusion. "Are you saying you turn a deaf ear to their suffering?"

"This is *their* city, Frank," she said with growing impatience. "They make all the rules...*and* enforce them. If someone is sick, you do what you can, but you always ask first. If someone doesn't want to be helped so be it. If you see someone shooting up, look the other way. If a man beats his woman, turn a deaf ear. Trust me, don't become personally involved in their despair. It will suck you under like a whirlpool."

"You make it sound so callous."

"Maybe, but I'm also being realistic. You know how long I've been doing this?" She didn't wait for an answer.

"A long, long time. And I leave here in one piece each night. I'd like to keep it that way."

She picked up her pace, momentarily leaving Frank trailing behind her on the concrete stairs. Suddenly, she stopped and turned. "Listen, if you want to live with these people, *then* you can interfere. But, just like Judge Langford, after a few hours you'll go back to your posh home, your wife, and your cute little grandkids. You'll have a good meal, maybe even seconds before dessert, and you'll sleep in a comfortable bed with too many covers. And, pardon me for being blunt, but you'll be telling your cronies down at the courthouse how fulfilled you feel helping those less fortunate than yourself. Don't get me wrong, I'm not condemning you for volunteering. That would be silly. But let's face it, you're not here for the duration. My job, so to speak, is to make sure you make it home in one piece. Like I said, some of those down here would be just as happy to slice and dice your throat as they would be to accept your offer of a sandwich, all depending on their mood. That won't happen with me around to guide you. A few months down here and you'll understand. But for now, just observe."

Frank simply nodded, startled by the eloquence of the woman's speech, stunned by its stark truth. They reached the bottom of the steps and took in the tableau that lay before them. It stretched a good city block; dozens of boxes, from Amana refrigerator cartons that housed two, even three persons, to boxes no bigger than a doghouse with a lonesome soul curled up within. Fires of various sizes burned in metal trash cans or on the bare concrete. Clotheslines stretched in every direction. The forty or so tenants of the cardboard condo took no visible notice of the interlopers, but Frank could tell they were aware of a foreign presence. A quiet hum sounded across the concourse—a hush of whispering—and soon tensions eased as word of Thera's presence spread.

Thera smiled, instantly forgetting the frustration the conversation had filled her with. She felt at home down here, in total command. These were *her* people, *her* disciples. She swept the concourse with her eyes, sensed an undercurrent of lingering fear and loathing and confusion... and she knew her powers here were strong. But there was still—always— so much to do...

Pretending to trip, she reached out and grabbed Frank's hand. Rubbed his skin. Felt his very soul. As they touched, Thera probed his mind much like a computer searching for data.

What do you fear most? she asked, using the strongest and darkest of her powers.

Suffocation, he answered automatically, though no words left his lips, though no thought entered his conscious mind.

Why? she asked.

My brother used to put a pillow over my face at night. At first, he was just clowning around, but all the same a part of him wanted to rid himself of competition for our parents' affection. He seemed to know just how long he could keep the pillow over my face without killing me. Once or twice I passed out. Worst of all, he seemed surprised each time when I woke up. Relieved he hadn't gone too far, yet a bit disappointed, too.

You never told on him?

My father despised weakness. Demanded we fend for ourselves.

Satisfied with what she had learned, Thera led Frank to a GE air-conditioner box. A man's face swathed with scarves peered out at her approach, his eyes darting from Frank to Thera. His eyes locked with Thera's, and terrified by what he saw, he scampered from the box, moving as fast as he could on a gimpy leg down the subway platform. He was soon lost among the maze of cartons.

Frank grimaced and said, "What was that all about?" But before he could finish, Thera grabbed his hand and led him—controlled him—into the opening of the now vacant box.

You're back in your bedroom, Frank, with your brother. He's putting a pillow over your face. Don't struggle. He'll only press harder. Sleep.

Frank slept.

Freed from the shackles of her companion, Thera emerged from the box and surveyed her flock. Suddenly, she felt unexpectedly sapped of her strength. Tired beyond belief. A wave of nausea coursed its way through her body, and she felt strangely disoriented. She bent to a knee, rested her head.

Several minutes later, her head cleared and she felt fine again. But before she had the chance to dwell on the cause of her sudden weakness she sensed an intruder; a new inmate who had committed himself to this asylum without her permission.

A fury so great welled within her she had difficulty maintaining her benign facade. A predatory animal, she prowled the clapboard village. A tiny trickle of urine snaked its way down her pants leg and sizzled when it hit the cold concrete, as she laid claim to her territory. Halfway down the platform she felt his eyes bore into her, felt the man's sexual frenzy take hold at the sight of a vulnerable woman.

She made her way to a battered moving storage crate and saw the transient. She peered at the hardened face, the face of a man used to getting his own way. Stubble from a week's growth couldn't hide his boyishly handsome features. A real ladies' man, she thought. She knew his kind. They took what they wanted, through deception, and discarded the fragile psyches when they were finished. No emotional involvement. All he wanted was a vessel for his carnal desires.

"Where's Walter?" she said.

"Who the fuck is Walter?" His eyes were all over her.

"You're in his box. He was an older man with gray, almost white hair. Real skinny. Had a problem with one of his eyes. Wore a patch."

"That guy? You could say I convinced him to find other lodging."

The rage surged in Thera. "You had no right. He was one of mine."

"Well, now I'm one of yours. Better yet, you're one of mine."

As he spoke, his hand wandered up Thera's leg. She ignored his touch and he grew bolder. His hand was on her thigh, moving upward; a snake seeking heat on a crisp night. She scanned his mind. *Fire—he feared fire.*

Why? she asked.

I used to like fires, his mind responded, his hand inching still closer toward its goal. *I used to set animals aflame and watch them swat themselves silly, roll around like crazy, but...*

Now you don't like it anymore? She probed deeper, searching for answers.

I set fire to my parent's house when I was fifteen. I was pissed at my old man. No one was home...rather no one was supposed to be. But when I was watching it burn, I heard someone scream. My sister. She was supposed to be on a date. She couldn't get out, and the firemen couldn't get to her in time to save her. She jumped through the top-floor window—a spinning ball of fire—and landed at my feet. I watched her flopping around, her skin melting, her hair burning, beating herself silly, like one of those damn animals.

Thera looked down at him and smiled. He screamed in anguish.

He withdrew his hand and stared into his own private hell. His hand was ablaze, the flames racing up his arm. Boils formed, blistered, and burst; bubbling pus coursed down his arm, dripping like wax through his fingers. With his good arm he flayed at the flames with a blanket, to no avail. The unchecked fire snaked around his body, tentacles of flames clawing at his face.

He bolted for the tracks, jumped off the platform, all the while swatting at the invisible flames that clung to him like molasses. Within the cardboard city, dozens of eyes watched the crazed youth running helter-skelter down the tracks beating at some invisible demon.

Thera watched until the screams faded to silence, then she waded among the boxes, distributing coffee and sandwiches to her charges. She worked in an ordered pattern, until she came to a big wooden box leaning perilously to one side. She had something special today for Randall, a bum who seemed to be escaping the blue funk that had enveloped him the past three months.

"You're looking mighty chipper today, Randall."

"Haven't had a drink in three days," he said, before a racking cough shook his body. He wrapped a tattered blanket he wore like a shield tightly around him before he continued. "There are times my mind starts to clear. You know, times when an end to my nightmare is almost within my grasp. So close…I can almost touch it."

Sobbing, he rested his head on Thera's shoulder. She consoled him, caressed the back of his neck…

…and went to work on him.

"Remember coming home and finding your wife had left with your children, Randall? Fled your tantrums and beatings. You're alone, Randall. You listen for them, but all you hear is silence. They're gone. Forever." She pulled a flask from her purse and gave it to him. "Have a drink. You'll feel better."

The craving for alcohol struck him like a kick in the groin. He gulped down the liquor she offered.

Thera smiled. He had almost made it out. Made it to freedom. He'd gotten to the front door, she mused, but now he was back in the basement; the door locked. He was trapped with only bottle after bottle of cheap wine to offer solace.

She pressed some money into the man's hand. She didn't have to tell him what to do with it. Randall was an easy one. Satisfied, she moved on to the others.

She was administering to Sophie, thirty minutes later, when Frank surprised her. Sophie had been the first person she'd transformed many years ago, and the old woman held a special place in Thera's heart. Sophie had once been a doctor who spent three nights a week tending to the homeless—her way, though she'd deny it to her death—of displacing the guilt she felt at having a chauffeur, maid, cook, and a huge house empty now that the children were grown and her husband was dead.

Thera, who had been new to the city at the time, had marveled at the woman's total command of the downtrodden. Sophie had known when sympathy was the right tonic; known when to badger, cajole, or chastise to get her way. She had taught Thera everything she knew about the urban underworld, and was unknowingly responsible for showing Thera just how much potential working with the homeless possessed for a woman with her unique powers. Thera's final test was turning the old woman into one of the legion of dispossessed herself, and she had passed it with flying colors.

Ultimately, it had been Sophie's greatest fear that was her downfall— rape. Gang rape, at that.

After discovering her fear, it had simply been a matter of fabricating the horrible act…A cry for help at the end of the platform. Sophie rushing to comfort a poor soul. A hand placed over her mouth. Dragging her into a maze of boxes that housed vermin who wanted more than coffee and a sandwich. One of them shoving himself inside her, another stuffing his hardened penis into her mouth. Bugs that had nestled in the man's crotch awakening and scampering all over her face, past her lips, into her mouth…between her legs…

Sophie now spent her days trying to rid herself of the phantom parasites that wended their way through her body. Thera almost felt sorry for the once-proud woman who now sat scratching her crotch, oblivious to the stares of others, her face pitted with oozing sores, rubbed raw.

Absorbed in the reverie of her first conquest, Thera was startled by the hand on her shoulder.

"Do you, uh, think we could go now? I...I think I've had enough for one night."

Thera stared unbelieving at Frank. It wasn't possible, she thought. No one she put under her spell had ever awakened on their own. She'd always had to rouse them after she'd completed her work.

She studied Frank with renewed interest.

He was tall and lean, his skin black as tar; his lanky frame topped by a fleshy face that seemed almost out of proportion with the rest of his body. White, almost iridescent teeth poked through a mouth that seemed unable to contain them. Brown eyes sat deep in his skull, alive and alert, but too old to be dangerous. Certainly nothing special about him, Thera thought. Just a typical face in the crowd.

"Are you all right?" he asked.

"Yeah. Sure. I'm just...surprised to see you is all. You passed out, you know. I left you in one of the boxes while I tended to their needs," she said, holding up her near empty bag of sandwiches.

"I'm terribly sorry. And embarrassed. I was afraid that's what happened. I'm feeling a bit queasy, but I'll stay if you—"

"No, no. I've done all I can for tonight. Let's go. By all means, let's go."

Leading him away by the hand, she probed his mind but came back with nothing. A swell of nausea attacked her. Suddenly feeling hot and stifled, she picked up her pace. She had to get away from this dungeon, this man. Needed fresh air. Needed to toss off her camouflage.

Needed rest.

She was so very tired.

THREE WEEKS PASSED, and Thera and Frank made several return trips to the subway concourse. During these outings, Thera continued to probe Frank's subconscious, searching each corner for weakness.

Eventually, she found what she was looking for when she learned of Frank's overwhelming desire for revenge against his brother. How he wished to put a pillow over his brother's face, smother him, scare him. Only *he* wouldn't be content just to render him unconscious.

These probes, though, continued to trouble her. There were nights when she'd pick up nothing at first, as though Frank were an empty vessel. Then, quite abruptly, images would form; his life would unfold. And too often there were the strange bouts of light-headedness and nausea, similar to the one that had attacked her during that first night's work with Frank.

Tonight, with the moon glowing almost full in a star-lit sky, all of her senses were on edge, as fine-tuned and ready as any weapon. Thera knew there would be pain when the change occurred tomorrow night; there always was. But unlike the days of her youth when she had feared—and misunderstood—her monthly transformation, the pain no longer held dread for her. In fact, she now longed for the change, wished it could happen more often.

Unlike many of her kind, Thera had been born into a large family of werewolves. Born and raised in the backwoods of North Carolina, her family and generations of werewolves before her, had remained safe for many years. As a result, she'd lived a peaceful, uneventful existence for most of her growing years.

Uneventful, that is, until shortly after her seventeenth birthday, when she'd learned of the special powers she possessed—the ability to read another's mind, the ability to control it. Her mother told Thera many wonderful tales about other wolves in the past who were said to possess these same powers, wolves who grew to do great things in this country. These tales inspired Thera, made her want to see the world, do great things of her own. And her mother also warned her of the dangers associated with such powers. The temptations they presented.

For over three years, Thera remained the toast of the country village she grew up in. But eventually she'd grown bored with the life and people around her. She'd tired of playing mind games with animals or dumb-as-dirt country folk. She'd longed for challenges, a way to really test her power. And she eventually found it in the city of Philadelphia…

Making her way through the clapboard village, having already placed Frank to sleep in a nearby box, the sensation of weakness and disorientation returned to Thera once again. She steadied herself against a wall and rested for a moment. Her thoughts turned back to Frank. Maybe he would prove to be a real challenge after all, she thought. These past few years, everything had been so easy for her and she'd learned to take her powers for granted. For years now she'd brought her valiant protectors to the bowels of humanity, probed for their weaknesses, and magnified them completely out of proportion, driving them past despair into insanity, until they lost all hope and became, themselves, one of the homeless. Thera knew her mother would not have approved, but she no longer cared. It was the ultimate symbol of her power: she controlled all in this, her special world.

Nine of the three dozen or so lost souls down here were solely her doing. *Her children.* She fed them with an ounce of guilt, a cup of pain, and a morsel of degradation whenever they appeared ready to escape their stupor. And once a month, she would literally devour one, to satiate her other appetite. It had been Sophie who had unwittingly given her the idea. The woman's words still echoed in Thera's head: *"No one cares about these people. They could disappear one by one and no one would ever notice."*

She had been right.

And now there was the newcomer, Frank Lofton. He was so different from the others, more resilient, more complex—a most welcome challenge.

Her sandwiches exhausted, she scanned the concourse and was alarmed to discover that Frank had awakened and was standing at the other end of the platform, not only alert, but attending to Lamar...*one of hers.* As she watched, Lamar bellowed in pain, his scream echoing like the chimes of a grandfather clock in the cavernous subway tunnel. She ran to them and saw the once-proud banker writhing on the ground. The man's stomach was bloated, as if he were pregnant and in the midst of a contraction. His skin was sallow and mucus oozed from his nose in a steady stream.

"What happened?" she asked, as Frank stared benignly at the suffering vagrant.

"He said he was feeling poorly. I gave him some coffee. He complained of cramps and—"

Lamar's howling cut Frank off in mid-sentence. The screaming man's eyes flashed wider than Frank thought humanly possible, blinked spasmodically, then froze in place, no longer seeing. The screaming stopped. His body drew very still and an audible *wheeze* sounded from his mouth, followed by a stench so rancid even Thera fought the urge to gag.

Thera stared in horror. She had never lost one like this before. She'd always taken them when *she* was ready. She felt robbed, violated. Lamar was one of *hers*, dammit! He didn't dare die without her consent!

As Frank consoled her, Thera made plans. Tomorrow Frank would take Lamar's place in her colony. Tomorrow she would make Frank kill his brother in his mind, and suffer the torment for the rest of his life. Tomorrow he would join the ranks.

AS THERA ENTERED the concrete catacombs the next night, her senses were charged with anticipation. Eyes darting, she marveled at the absence of color in the subterranean jungle. Everything was a different shade of gray. With winter winds raging above, these dwellers of the dark were content to remain below ground. Without sunlight their complexions resembled those of mushrooms. The rags and tattered clothing, worn day and night on unwashed flesh, had faded until they, too, seemed devoid of color.

While her own transformation wouldn't take place for several hours yet, Thera had already undergone various changes. Her sense of smell was more pronounced than before; a fine down covered her body; her already long black hair had grown as well, and she wore it in a bun so as to not attract attention.

Lacking her usual patience, she immediately led Frank to an Allied Van Lines storage box—Lamar's former home—and began to probe. She employed her utmost concentration—knowing that tonight was the night—but his mind came back an empty shell. Panic rose in her as she searched like a child who couldn't find a prize in a Cracker Jack box. But no matter what she did, there was nothing to be found.

"Who are you? *What* are you?" Thera asked, exasperated. She expected no answer and none came. She sat down next to him inside the box, weary beyond belief at the toll her fruitless exploration had taken. Somewhere in the back of her mind, she recalled feeling equally drained the last several times she had probed Frank's mind. But before she could give the thought full consideration, Frank opened his eyes...

...and smiled at her. In a flash, she felt *his* mind locking on and surveying *hers*. She felt *his* fingers picking at the locks of *her* brain, seeking to open the vault of *her* memories, as she had done so often herself.

And then the truth hit her.

"I...I thought I was the only one. But...but, you're like me, aren't you?" she asked.

"Like you and then some," he said, his voice soothing, hardly above, a whisper, yet with a malevolence he made no effort to conceal. "How could you be so arrogant as to think you were the only one of your kind? The only one in this city. In small towns we are hounded, hunted down, and destroyed. But in cities such as this, there is so much abnormality, no one is even aware of our existence."

She noted that his gray beard was darkening even as he spoke; and he no longer appeared old; the wrinkles had been erased from his skin; and his eyes twinkled with a youthful, almost feverish, exuberance.

"What do you want with me?" she asked, playing for time. "With all the places in this city why do you invade *my* domain?" She felt him searching, lusting for the key to unlock some dreaded secret that would render her powerless to him. She felt herself slipping. *Stall him,* her mind screamed. *Get him out of your head!* "Why here? Why them?" she blurted.

"Because they're *yours* and what's yours is mine. You see, I've been at this longer than you have, child. I didn't need this petty subway platform. My domain was once the entire Thirtieth Street Train Station. But the city council spent thousands of their precious dollars to clean the area out. So, quite simply, I'm here to take what I want. That is our nature, too, but you know that, don't you? We take, even from one another. When all this is mine, later tonight, I will shed the ravages of age and prowl the world above. Like you, I will stalk and have my kill, but I will let the hunger beckon until I can resist no more.

"Imagine how I lust for this night of freedom. An old man whose body betrays him day in and day out, tonight I no longer will be confined to this withering body; no longer servant to the whims of muscles that break instead of bend. It is truly wondrous." He stopped and a wide grin split his face. "And tonight I not only get my cake, I get to eat it, too."

"There's no need to quarrel over this squalor," Thera begged. "I'm willing to share." She didn't mean a word of it. She didn't know why, but sharing was not in her nature. Survival, though, most definitely was. She would agree to anything, do anything, accept any humiliation to escape his grasp. There'd always be another day, another time, another confrontation, and she'd be better prepared the next time; the element of surprise would be gone then.

"Good try, but no sale. Sharing is not a part of our vocabulary. Conquest. Dominance. Destruction. But sharing? I'm afraid not."

At that moment, beneath the mattress of her mind, he found her greatest fear; the dread of becoming one of *them*, one of the controlled. And as he spoke, Thera knew she was doomed.

"You're one of them, now. Tired, so tired of fighting all the time. This is your home. This is where you belong. You will be safe here…"

FRANK LEFT HER after a few minutes passed, a surge of happiness swelling in his heart. For the first time, he tended to *his* flock. A dose of guilt here, a spoonful of pain there, a taste of degradation—something for everyone. A short time later, he was keenly aware of eight figures making their way toward the Allied Van Lines box. The stench of blood hung thick in the air. He stopped his work long enough to watch as they dragged Thera out; hummed to himself as they tore at her with nails and teeth; laughed deep within as they stripped the bloody carcass of its few valuables.

The cycle of life and death in this cardboard cavern reminded him of the deep, dark jungles he had prowled long ago…

…where only the strongest survived.

(written with Barry Hoffman)

THE
INTERVIEW

"GOOD MORNING, SIR. MR. Thompkins, is that right?"

"Yes, yes, Bernard Thompkins. Come in, come in. Please."

"My name is Detective Ryan. I'm sorry to disturb you but we're interviewing everyone in the area."

"Of course, yes, of course you are. It's terrible. I can't believe this has happened."

"Did you know Brent, Mr. Thompkins?"

"Please, sit down. Right there on the sofa. And call me Bernie."

"Thank you."

"Can I offer you something to drink? A snack perhaps?"

"No, nothing for me. I've just had my breakfast."

"Well, let me know if you change your mind, Detective Ryan. I have some wonderful cookies. Homemade chocolate chip. My daughter visited just yesterday."

"Thank you, I will...now I was asking if you knew Brent Warrick very well."

"No, I didn't. Hardly at all, in fact. I knew his parents from passing them on the street; a wave here, a wave there. But we weren't friends, really. I remember Brent came over sometime in the spring and knocked on the door and asked if he could cut my lawn. But I'd already hired the Parker boy for the summer."

"So you didn't speak with him very often?"

"Just that one time. Maybe a hello now and then, just like with his folks. I remember now that his mother sent a very nice card when my Marion passed away last November. I bet I still have it around here somewhere."

"I'm sorry to hear that, Mr. Thompkins."

"Please...it's Bernie."

"Bernie it is."

"And thank you...but Marion was seventy-seven when she passed and not well at all, so it was a blessing really."

"Yes, I can understand that. It was the same way with my mother. Okay now, Bernie...did you *see* Brent very often?"

"You mean out in the neighborhood? That sort of thing?"

"Yes."

"Oh sure, plenty. Saw him playing outside with his friends most days. They played baseball in the park across the way. Tackle football in the autumn. Sometimes I saw them ride their bikes past or run by in their bathing suits dragging wet towels behind them on the sidewalk."

"Never any trouble with Brent or his friends?"

"No, never. Nothing like that. They were good kids."

"Ever hear of them getting into any trouble out in the neighborhood?"

"No, nothing I can think of. But I don't attend the community meetings anymore, so I don't hear much neighborhood business. Just what I see myself."

"Have you seen or heard anything suspicious lately? Anything at all out of the ordinary?"

"No, I...I don't believe so."

"Are you sure, Bernie? You seemed to think of something for a moment there."

"It's nothing, really."

"Well, you're probably right but, just in case, why don't you tell me."

"Oh, alright. I'll probably just sound like a senile, old man...but here goes. I don't sleep well, Detective. I'm almost eighty years old and I'm alone. I have arthritis something terrible in my legs and a bad stomach on top of that. I get maybe three, four hours a night. And a nap after lunch, if I'm lucky. When the weather's warm, I spend a lot of time sitting out on the front porch. I throw on a sweater and I sit out there in my old chair and watch the stars and the trees and I listen to the wind and the night sounds. Used to smoke my pipe, but the doc put a stop to that a couple months back."

"And you saw something one of those nights, did you?"

"Like I said, it was probably nothing..."

"Please, go on, continue."

"Well, the neighborhood pretty well goes to sleep around eleven on most nights. Even a little earlier when the summer months pass. After eleven, the streets are nice and quiet. *Hushed* is the word I always think of. Of course, you get some kids running around, teenagers out having fun with their friends. Pretty innocent stuff mostly. The worst I've ever seen is some firecrackers and a six-pack or two. One night someone broke a bottle across the street out there but it could've been an accident for all I know. Sometimes there are couples out walking their dogs, holding hands. A jogger or someone on a bike once in a while. And, of course, there's always a handful of cars driving past...some of them a little too fast and some of them a little too slow. It's the slow ones that I always pay special attention to. I'm afraid I have what Marion used to call an 'active imagination,' Detective. And so when I notice a car pass by much slower than is necessary, I automatically imagine that the driver is cruising these dark streets to check out houses for potential break-ins. Master thieves at work, you see. And there I sit, hidden on my front porch, neighborhood chief of security."

"Unfortunately, you're probably right on target about *some* of those drivers being up to no good."

"Well, maybe...but nine times out of ten, I end up recognizing the car as one that belongs to a neighbor down the street and my theory goes right out the window. And the other cars—the ones I *don't* recognize—I usually never see them again. I figure they were lost and looking for a familiar landmark, maybe had too much to drink and couldn't find their way home. But there *was* one car—a truck actually—and I saw it three nights in the same week. All three times about two or so in the morning. And slow, very slow. Thought that was *mighty* strange but nothing ever seemed to come of it."

"When was this?"

"Let's see…had to be about a month ago. Maybe a little less than that."

"What can you tell me about the truck? Did you see anyone *inside?*"

"Driver was alone all three times, I saw that much. But that's *all* I can tell you. It's just too dark out there on the road. Couldn't say whether he was black or white or yellow. Heck, couldn't say if it was a *he* or a *she*, for that matter."

"How about the truck?"

"It was an old one. Faded red, I think. And not one of those fancy new ones. Just a plain old pick-up."

"Didn't happen to notice any stickers or decals or the license plate?"

"No, sir, I'm sorry, I didn't."

"No reason to be sorry, Bernie, this is good. This is very good. Now tell me, what exactly did the truck do?"

"Just came crawling down the road. It didn't drive along and *then* slow down, nothing like that. It just maintained its speed like it was in no hurry to get anywhere in particular. Passed by the house and disappeared around the bend. Same thing all three nights."

"And you say this was about a month ago?"

"Best I can remember, yes. Like I said before, maybe a little less. You think the truck might have something to do with what happened to Brent?"

"It might and it might not. But we have to check out every possibility."

"Did anyone else in the neighborhood see anything?"

"I'm not sure. You're my first stop of the morning. I still have the rest of this street and one other. And who knows what the other detectives will come up with."

"Well, I just hope you find whoever did this. It's an awful awful thing. Things like this didn't use to happen when I was growing up. Never even heard of such things. But it was a different time then…a different world."

"That it was."

"Terrible, just terrible…my heart goes out to that boy's mother and father."

"Okay, Bernie, I think that's it for now. I hope you won't mind if I come back again if I need to."

"Of course not. You come back anytime, anytime at all. Now let me get that door for you. It's old and kinda cranky sometimes, just like its owner."

"It's okay, no need to get up. I can see myself out."

"No trouble, Detective, I'm already up. Time for me to get the newspaper anyway."

"Oh, one last thing, Bernie."

"Shoot."

"How about some of those chocolate chip cookies for the road?"

"I knew it, I knew it. And you won't regret it either, Detective. My daughter can cook up a storm."

"I bet she can."

"Here's a handful for the road and a couple napkins so you won't make a mess."

"Tha...thank you."

"Is something wrong, Detective? Is there anything else?"

"I'm afraid so, Bernie. I'm afraid you're going to have to come with me."

"With you?"

"Mr. Thompkins, I'm placing you under arrest for suspicion of murder..."

"GOOD WORK TODAY, Ryan. Very good work."

"Thanks, Lieutenant. Dumb luck is more like it, though."

"Hey, sometimes luck is our best friend."

"Poor old guy."

"Thompkins?"

"Yeah."

"He murdered that little boy, Ryan. Don't you forget that."

"I know, I know."

"Doc Reyes said that Thompkins probably lost it sometime after his wife died. They'd been together over fifty years and the loss was too much for him to bear. His daughter told us that he practically became a hermit after that, barely left the house these past few months. Stopped talking to his neighbors, stopped going to church, quit the Senior Center, that sort of thing."

"It's a shame. Probably a great guy before all this happened. Truth is, he reminded me a little bit of my Pop."

"Ahh, those are the tough ones."

"So what do we have for a timeline so far? Thompkins' daughter stops by for a visit sometime yesterday morning. Stays until just after lunchtime. Later in the afternoon, Brent Warrick shows up, probably asking about odd jobs. According to his mother, he was saving for one of those new video games. You figure he invites the boy inside for some of those cookies, maybe the promise of a job around the house, and then something happens to make him snap?"

"That seems about right."

"But it had to go down slowly, Lieutenant. Slowly enough that Brent knew something was wrong with Thompkins, knew he was in trouble. Slowly enough to give him time to write his name on that napkin. Time for him to write the word *help* right next to it—"

"And then time enough for him to place the napkin back with the others."

"Smart kid."

"Not smart enough."

"His parents didn't call the station until almost nine o'clock. They thought he was at a friend's house all day. That leaves about six, seven hours—"

"Six or seven hours for Thompkins' mind to fry...for him to kill the kid, and then sneak the body out of the house and into the woods."

"The body was discovered...let's see...at eleven-fifteen p.m., a five minute drive from Thompkins' house."

"They're searching the garage and car as we speak. Still nothing from the next-door neighbors?"

"Nope. One's on vacation at the shore. Other one was gone visiting relatives all day and didn't return until after all the commotion started. About ten-thirty last night."

"So what do you think went down in that kitchen, Ryan? What do *you* think happened?"

"Jesus...I don't know, Lieutenant. Maybe...maybe he gives the kid some cookies and then just starts babbling, saying crazy things, scares him. Or waves a knife in his face. Or maybe he starts crying for his dead wife and then *pow*. Hell, I don't know. But I'll tell you this much, it makes me sick to think about it."

"Amen to that."

"Still nothing from Thompkins? He still not talking?"

"Oh, he's talking alright. Your sweet little old man...he swears he doesn't remember a thing..."

"HELLO. ANYBODY HOME?"

"Upstairs, honey."

"I'll be right up."

"Hang on, I'm coming down. I'll meet you in the kitchen."

"Okay."

"Grab yourself a beer. I'll reheat dinner and you can tell me about your day."

"Sounds good to me. And, boy, do I have a story to tell you..."

THE
POETRY
OF LIFE

I'M FORTY-EIGHT YEARS OLD and have been a music teacher for twenty-seven of those years, and I still believe there is no sweeter sound in this world than the sound of a child's laughter.

Sometimes, when I hear it, I stop and listen and almost wish I could somehow bottle it up to save for later. This might happen when I am teaching a class or shopping for groceries or walking past one of the two playgrounds that bookend the neighborhood in which I live. I'll pretend to find a reason to stop—my shoelace is untied or perhaps I need to check the price on a particular can of soup—and I'll stand there and close my eyes and just drink it in. That beautiful melody.

Regrettably, I've never had any children of my own. Never married. Never found that kind of love.

I came close once. A long time ago when I was attending university. But it wasn't to be.

I say regrettably, but only because of my deep affection for children. I have never once complained or second guessed my lot in life, not even during those infrequent long sleepless nights that sometimes come to me when I have no choice but to lay there and stare at the dark ceiling and fight my troubling thoughts.

People often worry about me, that I am secretly sad or lonely or depressed. No shortage of pity for the spinster. But they needn't be concerned.

I have my books and my television and my students. An older sister in Florida who emails me jokes and cute videos of kittens. A four-year-old Border Collie named Ginger. No cats, yet.

And then there is Shirley, my best friend and next door neighbor.

Shirley is a beautiful black woman. Sixty. Widowed. Mother of two adult boys who live out of state and rarely visit. We take turns at each other's houses several times per week. Playing cards and watching our shows. Sometimes we cook or share Chinese delivery. And while she will never warm my bed on a cold winter night, she warms my heart in a different way. I love her very much.

Shirley is also a kind woman and always smiles when I talk about how hearing a child's laughter fills my heart, how it fuels me. She is the one who first started calling it the poetry of life. We were sitting on the front porch one summer evening, drinking lemonade and doing crossword puzzles, and I fell in love with those words the moment she said them.

The poetry of life.

It was the perfect description of not only the sound itself, but also how I felt when I heard a child's laughter. It was *poetry*. It was *life*.

I even started using it in my classes. I invented a lesson plan where each student would think about what constituted the poetry of life for them and then they would write down those thoughts. Then I would help each student turn those thoughts into a song.

Of course, many of the boys wrote about basketball or football or video games. And, of course, many of the girls wrote about their best friends or Taylor Swift or Justin Bieber. They were ten years old, after all.

But there were also some surprises.

Some *poetry*.

One little girl wrote about sunrises and how they reminded her of the little sister she had lost a year earlier to cancer.

Another girl wrote about flowers and how they helped her forget all the sadness and ugliness in the world.

Yet another wrote about spider webs and how if she stared at them long enough they looked like maps to her, maps to imaginary worlds.

And then there was my favorite: the little boy who wrote about thunderstorms and how they sounded like music inside his head, how they filled his heart to the point of bursting.

The poetry of life.

But I will never hear another song now.

Not after the message I received on my phone an hour ago.

Not after what the school board has decided.

I'd tried to call Shirley right away. Shirley had a way of calming me when my mind went dark and troubled. I called her twenty-two times, but she wasn't answering.

So I'd gone to the playground next. Thinking that if I could just hear that sweet sound one more time, it might bring me peace and guidance.

But it hadn't worked.

The poetry was gone.

I'd felt nothing.

This not only confused me, it terrified me.

And for the first time in my life, I felt truly alone.

I have time to think all this as I pull into a parking spot and turn off my car and listen to the ticking of the cooling engine.

I have time to think all this as I walk across the parking lot and into the school.

I have to walk slow.

The guns are heavy.

A LONG
DECEMBER

Tuesday, December 3

I WOKE TO THE SOUND of slamming car doors outside and saw flashing lights reflected on my bedroom window and ceiling, and thought one thing: Grant.

But Grant was at school in Richmond, two hundred miles away, and the logical part of my brain, which was obviously a lot more awake than the rest of me, told me to relax: if something had happened to Grant, they would have called to tell us, not shown up at the house in the middle of the night.

Besides, there were too many car doors slamming out there, and muffled voices now. Whatever was going on involved a lot more than just one vehicle.

I rolled over in bed and looked at the clock on the nightstand—11:53pm— then glanced at Katy, snoring quietly next to me. She was usually a light sleeper, and I was amazed she was still out. I guess a couple glasses of wine and three hours of late night reruns of *The Office* will do that to you. Good for her.

I eased out of bed, feeling the cold shock of hardwood floor against my feet, and made my way over to the window. The December night had left a thin coating of frost on the outside of the glass, and I used my hand to wipe away condensation from the inside.

There were three police cars parked in my neighbor Jimmy's driveway, two of them with their bar-lights still flashing. As I watched, an unmarked sedan and a police van pulled up to the curb. Two people quickly exited the sedan and walked across the front yard, disappearing from my sightline.

I craned my neck for a better look, but I couldn't see whether they had gone into the house or were merely gathered out on Jimmy's front porch. Wide awake now, I could feel my heart thumping in my chest. *What the hell was going on?*

As quietly as possible, I crept out of the bedroom and was halfway down the stairs when someone knocked on the front door. A single knock, not very loud.

I didn't even bother to look out the peephole. I unlocked the dead bolt and pulled open the door—

And found a smartly-dressed woman standing on my front porch. She was tall and thin and had the reddest head of hair I had ever seen. She held up a badge and an identification card, and it took me a moment to realize she was talking.

"...Anderson. I'm sorry to bother you."

I pulled my focus away from the shiny police badge and blinked at her. "I'm sorry."

"Are you Robert Howard?"

The use of my name caught me off guard. "Yes...I am."

"My name is Detective Anderson, Mr. Howard. I'm sorry to bother you at this late hour, but it's important I talk to you."

I leaned forward and looked past the line of shrubs that lined my porch. Jimmy's front door was wide open, and officers were coming and going with focused intent.

"What happened? Is Jimmy okay?"

"Jimmy is your neighbor James Wilkinson, is that right?"

"Yes. Is he okay?"

Another police van glided to the curb, this time directly in front of my house. I noticed other house lights coming on up and down the street.

Neighbors wearing robes and winter jackets starting to appear on front porches and gathering on the sidewalks.

"When was the last time you saw James Wilkinson, Mr. Howard?"

I had to think about it for a moment. "Let's see...he was here at the house all day Thursday for Thanksgiving, and then I saw him Friday evening when my wife and I got home from shopping. He said he was going to visit some friends for the weekend."

"And you haven't seen him since that Friday evening?"

"No."

"Heard from him? A phone call maybe?"

"No. Nothing."

"Did he mention where he was going or the names of the people he was planning to visit?"

I shivered in the cold air and shook my head. "No, he didn't. Can you tell me what's going—"

"We're serving a search warrant, Mr. Howard. Your neighbor, James Wilkinson, has been charged with two counts of murder. He is presently a fugitive on the run."

I couldn't help it—I laughed. "This has gotta be some kind of mistake, detective."

"Unfortunately not. I know this comes as a shock, but Mr. Wilkinson has been under surveillance for some time now. It was only through a combination of bad luck and incompetence that he escaped arrest this weekend. We've been watching his house for the past forty-eight hours in the hope he might return, but that hasn't been the case."

"This is crazy. Who did he supposedly murder?"

She ignored the question. "You have any idea where else he might have gone, Mr. Howard?"

I pretended to think about it. "I have no idea. I still believe this has got to be a mistake. Jimmy's a good guy."

The detective reached into her jacket pocket and came out with a business card. Handed it to me. "We're going to need to ask you some additional questions, Mr. Howard. Tomorrow will be fine. Please call the office first thing in the morning. We'll set up a time." She turned away to leave.

"Wait a minute. Talk to me about what?"

She stopped and looked back at me. "It's my understanding that you're James Wilkinson's best friend, Mr. Howard. Is that correct?"

It suddenly made me nervous to admit the truth. "I guess so, maybe."

"That's why we need to talk to you, Mr. Howard."

She turned and walked away in the direction of Jimmy's house. I watched her go, then stared past her at the glow of the Henderson's red and green Christmas lights across the street. Their twinkling reflections blended with the flashing police lights, washing the frozen trees and lawns in festive, holiday colors. It felt like I was dreaming.

"Hey, what the hell's going on?"

I snapped out of my daze and looked down at Ken Ellis, my neighbor from down the street. He was wearing flannel pajamas and a robe. He stepped up onto the porch next to me.

"Cold as a witch's titties out here. What that cop say to you? Something happen to Jimmy?"

I don't know why I lied, but I did. "She just said that she wanted to talk to me tomorrow. Didn't say what was going on."

Ken lifted his eyebrows. "*She*, huh? Chick cops are hot. She a looker?"

"Umm, I didn't really get a good look, Ken. She was in a hurry, I think."

"Well, I hope Jimmy's okay, buddy. I know you two are thick as thieves."

You're James Wilkinson's best friend, Mr. Howard…

Ken glanced back at the street. "Hey, there's Marcus. Fat bastard finally woke up." Already headed across the lawn, "I'll catch you later, Bobby."

I flipped a wave, walked inside and closed the door, relieved to be out of the cold and alone again.

I started up the stairs, then hesitated and walked to the front window. I realized I couldn't stop watching what was going on next door. And I couldn't stop thinking: *it has to be some kind of mistake. It has to be.*

I was still thinking those same thoughts fifteen minutes later when I watched the police officers walk out of Jimmy's front door carrying two black body bags.

"THERE'S JUST NO way," Katy said, her expression incredulous. "Jimmy can't even watch scary movies! You remember how he acted when we put on the *Poltergeist* remake Thanksgiving night?"

I nodded.

"He was so spooked he made an excuse to leave early! No way. Jimmy couldn't hurt a fly."

"That's what I told the detective."

We were sitting across from each other on the bed. It reminded me of the early years of our marriage. Sitting in bed together, eating pizza and talking for hours and watching crummy late night movies on cable television. It was about all we could afford, but it was enough. It was a pleasant thought to have on an otherwise shitty night.

I had awakened Katy a half-hour earlier when I finally came upstairs. Feeling numb, I told her everything the detective had said to me, but I left out what I had seen from the downstairs window. After all, it was dark outside; maybe it had been a mistake.

"You're sure she said two counts of murder?"

I nodded again. "I'm sure."

She looked down at her crossed legs, thinking, shook her head intently. "No, it's got to be a mistake."

"That's what I—"

"Oh my God, honey, you're going to have to call Grant in the morning. Tell him before it gets on the news. You know how much he loves Jimmy."

I *did* know. Jimmy was Grant's godfather. His friend. His mentor. "I'll call him first thing."

Katy got up and went to the window. Peered outside for a moment. Turned around and said, "If Jimmy's a murderer, I'm Jack the Ripper."

I was too exhausted to laugh, but I managed a smile. "Come back to bed, you nut."

She listened and crawled in next to me. I covered us with a blanket and we held onto each other in the dark.

"It's a mistake," she whispered, and a short time later she was snoring again.

She's right, I thought to myself. *It has to be.*
But then what was inside those body bags?
Sleep was a long time coming.

Wednesday, Dec 4

WE SAT AT the breakfast bar and watched the morning news on television in stunned silence, our food going cold on the plates in front of us.

The story was everywhere. The announcers, with their oh-so-serious expressions and suitably grim tones of voice, had to work extra hard to keep their excitement in check. Every once in awhile, one of them would slip and you'd see the joy in their sparkling eyes or hear the glee in their giddy voices; they just couldn't help it.

The sound bites came at us one after the other:

James Wilkinson, age 60, a fugitive...

Charged with multiple counts of first-degree murder...

Body parts from multiple victims discovered in his basement workshop...

Authorities working to find out the victims' identities...

Multi-state manhunt under way...

Their words expertly interwoven with the stark images:

A close up of Jimmy's house in the early morning light.

A long panning shot showing a comfortable, middle class neighborhood, including our own home.

Jimmy's faculty headshot from the university, a bold black headline centered above it:

LOCAL MAN POSSIBLE SERIAL KILLER?

"Jesus, so now he's a fucking serial killer," Katy said, pushing her plate away in disgust and getting up from the bar stool.

I gave her a minute, and then I followed her into the den where I found her standing in front of the fireplace, staring at the framed photographs on the mantle.

I came up behind her and hugged her, resting my chin on her shoulder. She wrapped my arms in her own arms and squeezed. Neither of us said a word.

There were three photos on the mantle: the first of Katy and I on our wedding day, youthful and smiling and scared to death; the second of two young boys, my brother and me, both of us bare-chested and tan and trying to look tough; and the third of Jimmy and Grant and me, standing on a pier somewhere in the Chesapeake Bay, each of us grinning like a fool and holding up a stringer full of rockfish.

"I feel numb," she finally said, breaking the silence.

"Me too."

She took my hand in hers and turned around to face me. "Do you still think it's all a mistake, Bobby?"

I couldn't read her expression. I didn't know what she wanted to hear, so I just told her the truth. "I don't know."

I USED THE remote control to open my garage door and warily drove out into the circus that had sprung up overnight.

There were cops everywhere next door. Some still filing in and out of the house, while others searched the garage and the shed out back. Two officers were using what looked like metal detectors in the flower beds and on the back yard lawn. Another was busy doing something on the roof.

Jimmy's entire yard had been lined with yellow police tape, and two big tents had been erected in the side yard. More cops gathered in and around the tents doing God knows what. The usually quiet street out front was crammed with nosy neighbors and reporters and television cameras. More police officers stood in the road, doing their best to control the crowd and direct traffic.

I slowly drifted down my driveway, trying to attract as little attention as possible, but as soon as the reporters noticed my car, they swarmed toward me in a hungry pack. Panicked, I sped up, trying to escape, but had to stomp on my brakes when I discovered a WBAL news van was blocking my exit. I started blowing my horn.

Cameras and microphones slammed against my car windows. Frantic, sweaty faces pressed against the glass and screamed my name, machine-gunning questions at me:

"*Robert…!*"

"*Did you have any idea?!*"

"*Bob…!*"

"*Do you know where he's hiding?!*"

"*Robert…!*"

"*Did you know?!*"

"*Bob…!*"

"*You had to know something…!*"

"*Robert…!*"

"*C'mon, give us two minutes…*"

"*What did you tell the police…?!*"

"*C'mon, don't be an asshole, Robert…*"

"*You were his best friend, you had to know something…*"

A pair of baby-faced troopers finally arrived and corralled the reporters out of the driveway and away from my car. An older man with long, greasy hair climbed into the WBAL van and moved it out of my way.

I nodded my thanks to the troopers, turned right out of the driveway—"*You were his best friend, you had to know something…*"—and headed for police headquarters.

(TRANSCRIPT 17943C)—THE FOLLOWING TRANSCRIPT CONTAINS THE COMPLETE, UNEDITED INTERVIEW WITH WITNESS ROBERT JOSEPH HOWARD CONDUCTED ON DECEMBER 4, 2016. INTERVIEW CONDUCTED BY DETECTIVE LINDSAY ANDERSON (A3343). CORRESPONDING VIDEO FILES LABELED AS FILE 104A AND FILE 104B.

DETECTIVE LINDSAY ANDERSON: State your name for the record please.

ROBERT HOWARD: Bob…Robert Howard.

DETECTIVE: Age?

ROBERT: 49.

DETECTIVE: Occupation?

ROBERT: Regional Sales Manager at Stark Industries.

DETECTIVE: Residence?

ROBERT: 1920 Hanson Road, Edgewood, Maryland.

DETECTIVE: Marital status?

ROBERT: I'm married...to Katy Holt Howard. I don't know if you wanted her name or not.

DETECTIVE: That's fine, Mr. Howard.

ROBERT: Sorry. I'm a little nervous.

DETECTIVE: I understand. I want to first thank you for coming in today under such unfortunate circumstances. We certainly appreciate your cooperation.

ROBERT: You're welcome.

DETECTIVE: Do you have any children, Mr. Howard?

ROBERT: A son. Grant. He's a sophomore at Richmond University.

DETECTIVE: You are currently acquainted with a Mr. James Lee Wilkinson?

ROBERT: Yes...I am.

DETECTIVE: And what is your relationship with Mr. Wilkinson?

ROBERT: We're friends. He lives next door to me. At 1922 Hanson Road.

DETECTIVE: How long have you resided on Hanson Road?

ROBERT: Let's see...we bought the house in '05...so it'll be 12 years this spring.

DETECTIVE: And when did Mr. Wilkinson move into the house next door?

ROBERT: Oh, boy...I don't remember exactly...my wife probably does...I would say somewhere around eight years ago. I know Grant was in middle school at the time.

DETECTIVE: So Mr. Wilkinson moved into the residence at 1922 Hanson Road somewhere around 2008?

ROBERT: That sounds about right.

DETECTIVE: And that was the first time you had ever met Mr. Wilkinson? There was no prior relationship?

ROBERT: That's right. My wife and I met him on the day he moved in.

DETECTIVE: What was your first impression of Mr. Wilkinson?

ROBERT: He seemed like a real nice guy. Older and a little quiet at first. Maybe even a little shy, like he wasn't used to being around people a lot.

DETECTIVE: You say that he was older. Can you provide any other background information regarding Mr. Wilkinson?
ROBERT: I know he was eleven years older than me and a widower. It felt like we didn't have a lot in common at first...but that changed with time.

Ummm, what else? He said he and his wife had never had any children; she wasn't able to. She had died a few years before he moved to town. A heart attack in her sleep. He grew up in a small mill town in upstate New York; I can't remember the name. Lived there until he joined the Army and then lived all over the place until he got out. He ended up going to college to get a teaching degree.

DETECTIVE: Any specific family background?

ROBERT: Nothing very specific. He told me both his parents were deceased; he didn't talk about them very much, didn't have pictures of them around the house or anything like that. And he'd lost a younger sister to cancer right before he went into the Army. Her name was Mary, and he took her death very hard, I know that. They had been very close growing up.

DETECTIVE: You mentioned that at first you didn't have very much in common with Mr. Wilkinson...but this changed in time?

ROBERT: It did. We became close friends.

DETECTIVE: And what do you attribute this closeness to?

ROBERT: Well, a lot of things, I guess. Proximity. You see a guy every day, even if it's just a wave hello, or the occasional beer shared across the fence, you get to be friends with the guy. And, the more we talked, the more I think we realized we had a whole lot in common after all. We both liked fishing and golf. Photography. I taught him how to kayak; he taught me how to fly fish and play chess. We both liked history and documentaries. The first time he told me he was going to be teaching history part-time at the university, I threatened to enroll in all his classes. He laughed about that. Let's see, what else? We both came from broken homes and we had both lost a sibling when we were younger. It was...something we didn't talk about a lot, but it was *there* between us...like an unspoken bond, I guess you could say.

DETECTIVE: I'm sorry, Mr. Howard. Did you also lose a sister?

ROBERT: No. (pause) My older brother drowned when I was ten years old.

DETECTIVE: Again, I'm very sorry. (shuffling papers) Okay, you say you both liked to fish and play golf and had an interest in photography. Did the two of you participate in these activities together? If so, how often and where?

ROBERT: Mostly, we just went fishing together. Usually over by the dam or we'd rent a boat and go out on Loch Raven Reservoir. Grant used to come with us a lot before he went away to school. He liked Jimmy a lot, and the feeling was mutual.

DETECTIVE: I understand that Mr. Wilkinson is your son's godfather.

ROBERT: Who told you that?

DETECTIVE: Some of your neighbors, I believe.

ROBERT: He is…but not in the traditional sense. Grant was never christened in a church or anything like that…but yeah we all agreed a couple years ago that Jimmy was Grant's de facto godfather. It's almost like an inside family joke.

DETECTIVE: So you all went fishing together. How often did this occur?

ROBERT: Maybe three or four times a month during the summer. Less in the spring and fall.

DETECTIVE: No secret, secluded fishing spots for you and Mr. Wilkinson? A cabin tucked away in the woods somewhere?

ROBERT: No, nothing like that.

DETECTIVE: Okay, you mentioned golf and photography next.

ROBERT: Golf maybe once a month from spring to fall. He joked that we were better at watching golf on television and talking golf than we were at actually playing it. And photography was just something we talked about and traded books about. He was a lot more experienced than I was. He had a little darkroom in his basement and played around with developing his own photos. That's about it.

DETECTIVE: Did Mr. Wilkinson have any other friends? Any romantic ties? A dating life?

ROBERT: He played a lot of chess online, and poker with a regular group from the college. The game rotated from house to house, and I usually joined in when it was Jimmy's turn to host. But those were the only guys I ever saw over there. He liked his privacy, I know that. And women? No, I never saw any women at his house, nor did he ever really talk about women with me.

DETECTIVE: Why do you say Mr. Wilkinson liked his privacy?

ROBERT: He just seemed very set in his ways. Never unfriendly or anti-social, I don't mean that. My wife would tell you those words describe me a whole lot more accurately than Jimmy. He just…had his routines. He cut his lawn on Saturday mornings. He went to the grocery store on Thursday nights. He visited the library every other Friday. He liked to be home by a certain time in the evenings. In bed by a certain time. Lights out by a certain time. He guarded his reading and writing time very closely.

DETECTIVE: (shuffling papers) What kind of writing was Mr. Wilkinson working on? Did you ever read any of his writing?

ROBERT: Actually, no, I never did. I think it was too personal to share. He said he was keeping a journal, about his life, his experiences and travels, and I know he worked on it every evening.

DETECTIVE: Did he write on a computer? Notebooks? An actual journal?

ROBERT: I couldn't tell you.

DETECTIVE: Okay, you said Mr. Wilkinson never discussed other women with you. Did you get the feeling this was because he still felt loyal to his deceased wife?

ROBERT: I honestly couldn't tell you. Katy asked me the same question one day. All I know is that he rarely talked about his wife, and he never talked about other women to me.

DETECTIVE: And Mr. Wilkinson never saw other friends except for the occasional poker game?

ROBERT: I know he played an occasional round of golf with friends from the college, but I got the feeling it was more of an obligation than a good time. And I believe he had some acquaintances from the library, but not like a regular book club or anything.

DETECTIVE: Did Mr. Wilkinson drink alcohol? Take drugs?

ROBERT: The strongest drug I ever saw Jimmy take was Nyquil and even then he put up a fight. But you don't win many arguments with Katy, trust me. Drinking...in all the time I've known him, I probably saw Jimmy drink a total of fifteen, twenty beers. Never any hard liquor. And, remember, that's over a period of like eight years. Jimmy took good care of himself; he was in great shape for a sixty-year-old.

DETECTIVE: Would you say Mr. Wilkinson was a religious man?

ROBERT: Not so much religious...I would say he was...spiritual. He was a pretty deep thinker. He could come up with some pretty heavy thoughts. He claimed to be a reformed Catholic. Had a big crucifix hanging in his den over the television.

DETECTIVE: Did he travel much?
ROBERT: Rarely. Maybe once or twice a year, he would visit an old Army buddy for the weekend or go on a solo fishing trip up north. He was excited last week at Thanksgiving, talked about going to see a couple guys from the old days.

DETECTIVE: Those were his exact words? A couple guys from the old days?

ROBERT: I think so, yeah. (pause) Maybe it was a couple Army guys from the old days. Or a couple guys from the old Army days. I'm not a hundred percent sure.

DETECTIVE: I want you to think very carefully about this next question, Mr. Howard. In all the years you lived next door to James Wilkinson, did you ever witness anything suspicious or alarming or disturbing?

ROBERT: (pause) No. Nothing.

DETECTIVE: Mood swings? Unusual displays of temper? Sneaking around?

ROBERT: Nothing.

DETECTIVE: Ever notice Mr. Wilkinson attempting to change his appearance in any way?

ROBERT: Never.

DETECTIVE: One final question, Mr. Howard. If you had only three words to describe James Wilkinson to me, what would they be?

ROBERT: (pause) Kind. Practical. (pause) Smart.

DETECTIVE: (shuffling papers) Well, that's all I have for now. I want to thank you again. I'll want to speak to your wife at some point, but we can do that at your home. No need for her to make the trip downtown. And I may want to ask your son a handful of questions over the telephone, but that can certainly wait.

ROBERT: That's it? I can go now?

DETECTIVE: Yes, sir, you're free to go. Oh, it's my understanding you had a little run-in with the press this morning. I'd prefer if you didn't talk to any reporters about this interview.

ROBERT: I definitely don't intend to.

DETECTIVE: Perfect. And be sure to let us know if any of them bother you or your wife.

ROBERT: I sure will. Thank you.

END OF TRANSCRIPT 17943C

AFTER I CALLED Katy and told her about the interview, I stopped at the McDonalds drive-thru and shot my diet all to hell. Two quarter pounders with cheese, large fries, and a chocolate milkshake. *Comfort food*, I told myself, and drove to the creek to eat in peace.

Winter's Run was a winding stretch of muddy water that ranged in depth from a couple feet to maybe ten at its deepest point. It mostly held catfish and carp and sunnies, but if you were lucky and knew what you were doing—pretty much the same thing when it came to fishing—you could pull the occasional largemouth bass or yellow perch out of its belly.

I had fished the Run since I was a young boy myself, and once Grant was old enough and patient enough to hold a pole, it soon became our favorite spot. I credit nostalgia and location for that little favor; Winter's Run was only a few miles away from our house.

I steered onto a gravel road that paralleled the creek for some distance and followed it until it turned into rutted, frozen dirt. Once I reached an enormous dead tree that looked like it had been struck by lightning, its bark blackened and peeling, I pulled over onto the grass and turned off the car.

I had come to this spot with Jimmy several times, when we were both in the mood to cast a line but didn't feel like driving very far. I remembered that we had used corn and cheese balls for bait, hoping for a fat cat or carp. Mostly, we had just talked and laughed and enjoyed the breeze and each other's company.

I sat there and ate my lunch and, despite the ninety minute interview I had just completed, it felt like this was the first time I'd had to take a deep breath and *really* think about my friend and the things he had been accused of.

Jimmy a murderer? A serial killer?! How was that even possible? This was a man I considered a part of my own family; a man I had seen almost every day for the past eight years. Wouldn't I have known...*something*?

I finished eating and made a mental note to throw away the trash before I got home and Katy saw it. The last thing I needed right now was another lecture about my cholesterol. I took a last look at the slow-moving water and started the car. As I backed up onto the dirt road and pulled away, I realized that I'd forgotten to mention this particular fishing spot to the detective.

"THE DETECTIVE SAID they could either come tonight or tomorrow night. I said tomorrow."

"They?"

Katy was in the kitchen, making a salad at the big granite island she liked so much. The entire house smelled of her homemade tomato sauce.

"Her and her partner, she said. I felt like I was in an episode of CSI or something."

"That's what this morning at the station felt like. Like I was in a bad movie."

Sensing my exhaustion, Katy came over and hugged me, resting her head against my chest. "You should've heard Grant when I told him. He was so upset. He said he's going to call you tomorrow morning."

"I keep thinking about some of the questions she asked. Did Jimmy travel a lot? Did I ever see anything suspicious? Did I ever see him sneaking around?"

"You poor baby." She gave me a good squeeze and returned to her salad. "I'm not looking forward to tomorrow night."

"It'll be okay, I'll be with you." She smiled and quickly looked away, and I could tell there was something else on her mind. "What are you thinking?"

Her hands started working faster, and I realized she was nervous. "Honey?"

She stopped and looked at me. "It's nothing, really."

"Tell me."

Deep breath. "I know how you feel about Jimmy…how we *all* feel about him."

"But?"

"No buts, nothing like that. It's just…when you said that, about the questions the detective asked you…"

"Which one?"

She glanced down at her hands for a moment, then met my eyes. "About if you had ever seen him sneaking around."

I pushed off the counter where I was leaning and walked closer. "Did you?"

"Just…once."

"Jesus, honey, what did you see?"

"It's probably nothing." She shrugged, but I could see the tension in her face. "I was raking leaves in the back yard and the rake broke."

"I remember. Last fall"

"Well, I went next door to ask Jimmy if I could borrow his rake to finish the job, and his garage door was open. I guess I was kinda quiet about it because he didn't hear me walking up. He was down on his knees, stretching to reach something behind his work bench. I coughed to get his attention, and when he turned and saw me…"

"Yeah?"

"It was…just the look on his face, Bobby. He looked so angry and… mean. It was like he was someone else for a second or two, and then it was gone, and he was Jimmy again."

"That's all?"

"Yeah, I told you it was probably nothing…but it was weird. It *felt* weird."

It was my turn to shrug my shoulders. "Could've been any number of things. A shitty day, or probably you just scared him."

She started to answer, and the phone rang. She grabbed the cordless from the counter behind her. "Hello? Hello?" She clicked it off. "No one there."

The conversation broken, she went back to finishing the salad, and I went back to salivating over her homemade pasta and sauce.

···✳···

THREE HOURS LATER, fat and sleepy, I laid in bed waiting for the eleven o'clock news to come on, and pretended I could understand what Katy was saying as she tried to talk and brush her teeth at the same time.

"Yes, dear. You're right, honey."

She rinsed her mouth and spit into the sink. "Oh, hush it. You don't even know what I just said."

I smiled. It was a nightly game we played, and it felt like a nice, warm, safety blanket after all that had happened recently in our world.

Katy turned off the light in the bathroom and settled into the bed next to me, taking her book from the nightstand. She had just enough time to finish a couple pages before the news came on.

Jimmy, of course, was the lead story.

As the Channel 11 anchor, a skinny, blonde with the unlikely name of Jessica Jones, did her best to sound intelligent, a photograph flashed on the screen behind her. It was a photo I had never seen before, most likely from a college faculty picnic: Jimmy, dressed casually in shorts and a t-shirt, captured in mid-throw, a Frisbee in his right hand. His arms looked strong and muscular, his face tan and intense, and I knew that was why the station had selected the picture.

Jessica Jones smoothly threw coverage to her reporter on the street, and a tall, black man with a microphone in his hand took over. I resisted the urge to look out the window and watch it live.

"Police, today, are reporting that evidence found inside James Wilkinson's house now indicate that there are at least three victims. That's right, three. Police officials refused to say whether this new discovery stemmed from human remains or any additional forensic findings, but…"

"Jesus," I whispered, and Katy reached for my hand.

"Earlier this afternoon," the reporter continued, "I talked to one of James Wilkinson's colleagues at Washington College."

The screen flashed to a daytime shot with the college administration building framed in the background. The reporter towered over a middle-aged, bald man dressed in a tan sport coat.

"I'm standing here with Professor Jeremiah Robbins, head of the Washington College history department. Professor, I guess this has all come as a huge shock to you and your department…"

The Professor shook his head to demonstrate the severity of his disapproval. "That would be an understatement, to say the least. We are shocked and outraged at these findings."

Reporter: "And before this, how was Mr. Wilkinson viewed by his fellow teachers and students?"

Robbins: "I think it's very important to remember that James Wilkinson was merely a part-time employee of this institution. He did not carry a full class load and was actually only here on campus three days each week…"

Katy sat up in bed. "Those bastards are scrambling to distance themselves in any way they can."

"It's gonna get worse," I said.

Jessica Jones was back on the screen now: "After a quick commercial break, we will talk to one of James Wilkinson's neighbors about the latest findings…"

"Ugh, turn it off, Bobby. I bet you anything it's that bitch, Frannie Ellis. She must've called me five times today. I don't know who's worse, her or her perv of a husband."

I grabbed the remote control—and the telephone rang.

"Speak of the devil," Katy sighed. "I bet she's calling to tell us"—mimicking a high-pitched, annoying voice—"*she's going to be on television.*"

I laughed at my wife's antics and muted the television. I picked up the phone. "Hello?"

No response.

"Hello?"

No one there.

"Last time. Hello?"

I hung up.

"Thank God for small blessings," Katy said.

And then Frannie Ellis's chubby face was filling our television screen, eyes as big as quarters, mouth moving with superhuman speed.

"Ugh," Katy groaned, and rolled over to go to sleep.

···✳···

Thursday, Dec 5

THE NUMBER OF reporters in front of the house was down by at least half, and I made it to work the next morning with little trouble.

For the first half of the day, I distracted myself with catch-up phone calls and purchase orders, and it worked just fine. Co-workers interrupted a few times to ask questions—*"Don't you live on Hanson Road, Bob? How well did you know the guy?"*—but they were easy enough to blow off.

Grant called during his lunch break, and I talked him out of coming home early. Finish your exams and then come home, I told him. We'll catch up then.

But, by lunchtime, I found myself glancing out the second floor window at the park below, daydreaming about Jimmy. And, as the afternoon passed, I found myself surfing the internet in an attempt to answer the questions I had bouncing around inside my head.

I clicked the mouse and studied their faces carefully.

Jeffrey Dahmer.

Click.

Ted Bundy.

Click.

Arthur Shawcross.

Click.

John Wayne Gacy.

Click.

Dozens of victims. Murdered. Tortured. Butchered. Sometimes even eaten.

And the killers all looked so normal.

I found none of the answers I was searching for, and when four o'clock rolled around, I couldn't sign offline and get out of there fast enough.

As I was pulling out of the parking lot, a news teaser came on the car radio, promising another update on the hour about "the James Wilkinson Murders"—*"more victim information and an alleged Wilkinson sighting in Virginia"*—and I switched it off and drove in silence.

At a stoplight, I glanced in the rearview mirror and noticed a blue car behind me. I saw it again ten minutes later on the interstate. I wondered if it was following me.

Christ, it's getting to you, I thought. *Making you paranoid.*

I exited the interstate and drove the several miles home checking the rearview. I didn't see the blue car again.

"I UNDERSTAND THAT you're often at home during the day, Mrs. Howard. Have you ever noticed any strange or unusual comings or goings next door?"

The four of us were seated in the den. Katy and I side by side on the sofa. Detective Anderson and her partner, Detective Hynd, on matching chairs centered in front of the fireplace. Detective Hynd looked like he'd just walked off a television cop show: tall, stocky, crew cut, with a first class poker face. The guy made me nervous.

Katy had poured a cup of coffee for each of us. I had gone through mine in the first five minutes. Katy sipped at hers as she answered their questions. Neither detective had touched theirs.

Katy shook her head. "No, I really didn't. Jimmy was a creature of habit. I used to tease him about it all the time. I knew the days he worked at the college, and when he left the house on other days, I usually noticed his return within a couple hours."

"He never said anything inappropriate to you," Detective Anderson asked. "Even joking?"

"Never. Not once."

Detective Hynd this time: "Did he ever have any visitors that perhaps your husband didn't know about because he was at work?"

"Not that I saw, no. I mean, it's possible, I guess. But pretty unlikely."

"I asked your husband to take his time and really think about this next question, and I'm asking the same of you, Mrs. Howard. In all the time that James Wilkinson was your next door neighbor, did you ever witness anything at all out of the ordinary, anything unsettling or suspicious?"

Katy glanced away from the detectives, toward the large bay window that looked out over our front yard, body language I recognized as "leave me alone for a second, let me think."

When Katy finally looked back at Detective Anderson, she surprised me with her answer. "No. I can't think of anything. I'm sorry."

I felt her leg press against mine with the slightest of pressure.

"Well, that's all we really have," Detective Anderson said, getting to her feet. Detective Hynd followed suit, and I could feel him towering over me, even after Katy and I both stood up from the sofa.

"We appreciate your help, especially at this hour and in your home." Detective Anderson switched off her mini tape recorder and stuffed it into her jacket pocket.

"You're very welcome," Katy said, and walked the two detectives to the front door.

I KEPT WAITING for Katy to tell me why she hadn't told the police about what she'd seen in Jimmy's garage, but I'd waited too long, and now she was sound asleep beside me.

I watched her snore for a while, then rolled over on my side, trying to get comfortable. Sleep felt a long way off for me.

My brain wouldn't stop thinking. Why hadn't she told the detectives? On one hand, I was glad she hadn't told her story. It was probably nothing worth giving attention to. On the other hand, it bothered me—

—because I had remembered something, too. A moment in time that I'd completely forgotten, a moment that perhaps never even registered in the first place...until I listened to Katy's story about Jimmy in his garage... and then it all came back to me tonight.

Jimmy and I had been sitting in the center field bleachers at Camden Yards watching the Orioles play the Red Sox. It had been a cloudless Sunday afternoon, and the O's had been up by three runs in the top of the eighth inning. Six more outs and it went in the Win column.

The only blemish on an otherwise perfect day had been the pair of redneck drunks sitting behind us. We had tolerated their loud, slurred voices and cursing; we had put up with their catcalls and x-rated harassment of the Red Sox centerfielder; and we'd even turned the other cheek to a spilled beer that had soaked the game program I'd carelessly left on the ground at my feet.

But when one of them had spilled a full beer down the back of Jimmy's shirt and reacted with laughter instead of an apology, we'd had enough. I'd shot to my feet and started to turn around, but before I could say a word, Jimmy was standing next to me, his face a mask of barely contained rage, the drunk's neck grasped in Jimmy's right hand.

Before anything else could happen, two ushers were there to break it up and escort the drunks out of their seats. I remembered that the Orioles ended up blowing the lead, but won it in extra innings, and Jimmy and I had stopped at Chilis on the way home and stuffed ourselves sick with barbeque ribs.

It's funny the things you remember—and forget.

Friday, Dec 6

THE SKY WAS nothing but slate gray clouds, and it was starting to flurry as I drove out of my garage the next morning.

I stopped at the bottom of the driveway and took the newspaper from the paper box. It was safe to do now; most of the press was gone at this early hour. The television crews would be back later this evening to report live from in front of Jimmy's house, but when the around-the-clock police presence diminished so did the news vultures, as Katy now referred to them.

I glanced at the newspaper on the way in and wished I hadn't. Most of the front page was taken up by "the James Wilkinson murders" and the boldest headline read:

KILLER STILL AT LARGE:
POLICE PREDICT MORE VICTIMS

I tossed the paper in the back seat. At least I had a busy day ahead of me at work. More than anything, I needed to redirect my brain away from images of Jimmy hiding something in his garage or losing his shit at an Orioles game. Both of which most likely meant nothing.

I pulled into the office lot twenty minutes early and parked in my usual spot. Only a handful of other vehicles had arrived ahead of me. I grabbed my briefcase and got out of the car—and nearly slipped on my ass.

A thin coating of snow had already accumulated on the grassy surfaces, and was just now starting to stick to the pavement. I looked around to see if anyone had witnessed my near acrobatics, but I was alone in the parking lot. It was almost a peaceful sight with the falling snow and the hush of early morning stillness.

Already thinking about my morning conference calls, I grabbed my briefcase from where I had dropped it and started to walk toward the entrance doors—

—when a hand grabbed my shoulder from behind.

"Bob."

I nearly screamed and did a cartwheel, my feet pinwheeling beneath me. Spinning around, I held out my briefcase protectively in front of me.

"Hey, hey, I'm sorry. I didn't mean to spook you."

It was a man I had never seen before. My height. Curly hair. Glasses. Wearing an old Army jacket and holding a mini tape recorder.

"My name is John Cavanaugh. From the *Baltimore Sun*. I just have some—"

"No," I said, unable to say more, trying to breathe again.

"It'll only take a minute, I promise."

I shook my head and started walking away from him.

"According to neighbors, you were Wilkinson's closest friend," he said from behind me, hurrying to catch up. "I just want to know what he was like. The person inside the monster."

I stopped and turned on him. *"The person inside the monster?* Jesus. Leave me alone."

I started walking again, faster now.

"Are you cooperating with the police, Mr. Howard? I understand they brought you in for questioning."

Questioning?

I kept walking.

"Your neighbors said you two were as thick as thieves. Is that true?"

I reached the entrance to my building and walked inside, praying he wouldn't follow. He didn't, but just as the front door was swinging shut, I heard his final question: "Why are you protecting him?"

ONCE I GOT over the shock and anger (and maybe a little embarrassment) of my run-in with the reporter—a thirty minute phone call with Katy helped a lot—the day turned out pretty damn good.

Two of my morning phone conferences went off without a hitch, and the third, which I was dreading, ended up being postponed. I talked to Grant on the phone while I ate lunch at my desk, and spent the afternoon reviewing purchase orders and a sales presentation that wasn't due until mid-January.

By the time I said goodbye to Janie at the front desk and walked outside, the skies had cleared and the parking lot had been plowed. Maybe two inches of new snow blanketed the grass.

I didn't think the reporter would still be waiting, but I wasn't taking any chances. I looked everywhere as I walked to my car, and I'll be damned if paranoia wasn't working its wicked charm on me again, because it felt very much like someone was watching me.

I hurried into the driver's seat, locked the door, and started the car. I didn't wait for the engine to warm up. I drove quickly out of the parking lot, that nagging feeling of being watched still itching at the back of my neck.

DINNER WAS A nice surprise—tacos and Katy's special margaritas. We ate at the coffee table in the den and watched the remake of *The Road Warrior* on pay-per-view. It was just what I needed, and I had Katy to thank for that.

As the end credits rolled on the television, I untangled myself from the blanket we were cuddling under and started clearing the dishes from the coffee table.

Katy sat up and yawned. "Just leave it, honey. I'll get it in the morning."

"I'm just gonna dump it all in the sink. It'll still be there in the morning."

She laughed. "Gee, thanks."

"Any time, babe." I gave her a wink and carried the dishes into the kitchen. I scraped the plates and bowls into the trash, and left them in the sink.

"There is *something* you can do tonight, honey, if you're up to it."

I smiled and puffed out my chest. "And what might that be?"

She got up from the sofa and dramatically swung her hips as she walked upstairs. Over her shoulder: "You can take the trash out so the whole damn house doesn't stink in the morning."

I slumped. "Oh."

"HA, HA. YOU can take the trash out. *Real* funny."

I opened the lid on the garbage can sitting next to the garage and dropped in the zip-tied plastic bag. I replaced the lid and shivered in the frigid night air. The weather folks were calling for lower temps and more snow in the coming days.

Headlights flashed on the street below, and I watched as Ken Ellis's Escalade slowed and turned into his driveway across the street. He got out and hit the auto-lock on his remote and it chirped twice. He looked over at me and I gave him a wave. He stared for a moment, and then walked into his house without acknowledging me.

"Okay, that was weird," I mumbled to myself and headed back inside.

And then I heard something.

I stopped and listened—and heard it again.

A rustling in the bushes that bordered the front porch.

I glanced at the wide open front door of my house, light spilling out onto the porch, and moved to put myself between the door and the noise I had heard.

As I came around the side of the porch, I heard the sound again, and this time I could see the bushes move ever so slightly. There was no breeze.

I walked closer, stooping down, preparing for fight or flight, but mostly wishing I had my cell phone on me.

I stopped and held my ground, listening.

Nothing.

I took another step—

—and was flung back on my ass on the snowy ground—

—as Mrs. Watkin's orange tabby sprung from underneath the bushes with a hiss and scampered past me, disappearing into the shadows.

"Fuck me," I hissed back at the cat, quickly pushing myself to my feet, embarrassed and pissed for the second time in a day.

I brushed snow off my pants and looked around—thinking Katy's gonna love hearing about this one—and my eyes settled on the dark window at the side of Jimmy's house.

With little understanding of why I was doing it, I walked over to the window and peered inside. It was too dark in the house to see much, but I could make out enough details to see that the room was a mess. Furniture moved. Drawers and shelves emptied. Papers and books and knick-knacks strewn all over the carpet.

I flashed back to the many times we had played poker in that same room...

Jimmy's buddies from the college complaining about the fatty snacks Jimmy had provided and that they'd had to bring their own beer. Jimmy joking that, despite all their degrees and teaching experience, I was the smartest guy in the room. All of us talking and laughing and farting—enjoying each other's company.

I stood there for a long time, remembering, until I couldn't feel my feet anymore because of the cold. Then I went inside.

Saturday, Dec 7

WE SPENT THE majority of Saturday out of the house. Out of town, as a matter of fact.

It was Katy's idea to drive up to Middlebury for lunch and some Christmas shopping. She scolded me for ordering onion rings at lunch, and I told her we were even an hour later when she bought herself two new pairs of dress shoes. How many shoes does one woman possibly need? It's one of life's great mysteries.

All in all, it had been a near perfect day, and Jimmy's name hadn't come up even once.

We got home long after dark, just in time for the early evening news and a tray of cheese and crackers in the den. Katy joked that we were celebrating: it was the first night in a week that there hadn't been any reporters camped out in front of Jimmy's house for a live broadcast.

When the news came on at ten o'clock, we were surprised for the second time that evening: Jimmy wasn't the lead story.

There had been a shooting at a New Jersey playground earlier in the day. Two adults and three children had been killed. Four others wounded. When it was over, the gunman had turned his weapon on himself. It was awful, and while I couldn't help but wonder why anyone would be outside at a playground in the middle of December, I didn't say anything. People were dead, kids for Godssake, and my heart ached for their loss.

After a commercial break, Jimmy was the second story. There had been another possible sighting, this time in southern Pennsylvania, coincidentally where Katy and I had just spent most of our day.

Police officials were also planning a news conference for sometime next week.

Then, a brief interview with another concerned neighbor, an elderly Korean gentleman who lived at the end of our block and who rarely ever spoke to any of us. But he sure had plenty to say to the camera, very little of which was probably the truth.

And, then, finally, they saved the biggest surprise for last:

Because there I was in full techno-color, a terrified look on my face as I sat inside my car blowing the horn at the frenzy of reporters blocking the driveway.

I almost choked on my cheese and crackers.

Katy put a hand to her mouth. "Oh my God."

I sat there in shock as a close-up of my face filled the screen, and a television audience listened to me yell, "No comment!" in a pathetically shaky voice.

"According to several sources," the news anchor explained, "Robert Howard is not only James Wilkinson's closest neighbor, but also his closest *friend*. Up until this point, Howard has declined to comment, but sources report that Howard *is* cooperating with authorities and will be…"

Katy clicked off the television. "Fucking vultures. I told you." She turned to me. "Are you okay?"

I nodded. "I'm fine…just a little surprised is all."

"I guess until the cops have that news conference they're scrambling to come up with any story angle they can find."

"I guess so." I got up from the sofa and started turning off the lights.

Katy carried the tray and plates into the kitchen. "Uh, oh, your staff is gonna be buzzing at work tomorrow."

I groaned. "I hadn't even thought of that." I switched off a floor lamp by the den window—

—and froze.

A shadow was moving in the bushes outside—and it was a lot bigger than a cat this time.

"Just tell them you didn't want to get into it with them and—"

I dropped to a knee in front of the window and "*sshhed*" Katy.

She looked confused. "What is it?"

"I think there's someone outside," I whispered.

She started walking toward me.

"No, no, stop right there."

I peered over the windowsill—and there it was again. A dark shadow creeping closer now. Definitely a person.

"Call 911. Tell them to hurry."

She rushed back to the kitchen, and I could hear her voice cracking as she talked to the emergency operator. She hung up, and said, "Three minutes."

"I'm sure it is, but go double-check the front door's locked." I listened to her footsteps grow fainter, and then I snuck another peek over the windowsill—

—and found myself face to face with the curly-haired reporter from the parking lot. He looked as surprised as I did.

This time, I screamed. I couldn't help it.

So did Katy.

And then the front yard was flooded with flashing lights and loud voices and swarming with cops, and the reporter was turning around and holding his hands up in the air.

"AND YOU'RE SURE you don't want to press charges, Mr. Howard?" The officer stopped scribbling in his notepad long enough to give me a questioning look. I glanced at Katy, and she shrugged her shoulders. We were both exhausted.

The three of us were standing in the foyer, the front door closed to the chaotic scene outside.

The reporter, John Cavanaugh, was handcuffed in the back seat of a patrol car parked at the curb. Up and down the street, neighbors stood in small and large groups, drawn by the flashing lights and the hope of more drama. And, of course, the vultures were back, television cameras rolling, microphones humming, hairspray clogging the chill air. It was a circus again.

"I don't think so. I just want to be done with it."

The officer flipped his notebook closed. "Okay, but if you change your mind, call us in the morning." He opened the door and grinned at us. "We're gonna hang onto him overnight, let him sweat a little bit."

I smiled back at him. I liked that idea a lot.

Monday, Dec 9

SUNDAY PASSED IN a blur of football games and naps and ignored phone calls and emails. I never set foot outside the house the entire day, and the only time Katy left was to deliver sandwiches and drinks to the two police officers camped out in their patrol car in our driveway. By late evening, with the temperature plummeting to single digits, most of the press had gotten the hint and cleared out. We'd managed to avoid the news all day and were in bed by eight o'clock, asleep before nine.

So, when the alarm clock buzzed this morning at 6:30, we'd hit the ground running, feeling rejuvenated and hopeful.

After a busy morning of cleaning house and paying bills, Katy was spending the afternoon at a friend's house, playing Hearts and binge watching *Game of Thrones*.

All morning, I had faced a barrage of questions from my co-workers—"*Why didn't you tell us? What was he like? Did you have any idea? Do you think he's still alive? Are you sure you're telling us everything?*"—but eventually the questions had run dry and the office had returned to some semblance of normality.

I was able to eat lunch in peace, and now I sat at my desk, adjusting fourth quarter purchase orders and answering nosy emails from friends I had ignored yesterday.

There was a knock at my office door, and I looked up and saw Janie coming in with a file I had requested earlier this morning. "This what you needed, boss?"

I glanced at the name on the file. "Bingo. Thanks for finding it for me."

"Tis my job." She remained standing in front of my desk, and I knew she had more to say.

"Something on your mind, Janie?"

She shook her head. "I just couldn't believe when I saw the news yesterday. I couldn't believe it was you they were talking about."

"Yeah," I said, fidgeting. "It's been an interesting week to say the least."

"Well, listen, if you ever need someone to talk to…I read a lot of true crime books, dozens of them, so if you ever need to share, I'm right here."

"I appreciate the offer, but I'm—"

My cell phone rang. I gestured to it apologetically and Janie whispered, "Talk later" and scurried out of my office.

My cell phone rang again, and I picked it up from the desk beside me. Looked at the caller ID: *Unknown Caller.*

"Hello?"

No response.

I suddenly remembered the hang-ups at the house from the week before. "Hello?"

Nothing.

"Hel—"

Click.

I pushed the OFF button and stared at the phone.

KATY TURNED OFF her light and rolled over to face me in the dark. Outside, a strong wind howled in the trees and buffeted the upstairs windows.

"Do you remember our first apartment?" Katy asked. "Up on the fourth floor."

"Of course, I do. Brittany Place, Greenbelt's finest apartment complex."

She laughed. "The wind tonight reminds of back then. We were so young...scared and fearless all at the same time."

"Things haven't changed that much, have they?"

She thought about it for a moment. "I guess not."

"I think we're hanging in there pretty darn—"

The phone rang.

Katy groaned and reached for it on the nightstand.

"Hello?"

She waited.

"Hello?"

She hung up.

Neither of us spoke, and I knew she was thinking the exact same thing I was.

"Do you think it could be him?" she finally asked in the darkness, and I found myself wishing I could see her face.

"Him? Jimmy?"

"Yeah. Sometimes it happens during the day, too, when you're at work."

"Probably just reporters, honey."

"I don't know. Maybe. Can I ask you something?"

"Anything."

A long pause.

"Do you think he did it?"

I laid there, thinking.

"Bobby?"

"I don't know."

Thursday, Dec 12

THE GPS TOLD me to turn right in 200 feet, so I turned right, but I remained skeptical. The damn thing had had me driving in circles for the past half hour and now I was in danger of being late for lunch. A lunch I couldn't afford to be late for. I was scheduled to meet with the vice president of Canton Industries, something that had taken nearly two months to arrange. The proposal I had put together was maybe the best work I had ever done; now I just had to get my ass to the restaurant.

The past couple days had been relatively peaceful, which was a godsend after what had happened Saturday night. Katy was finally starting to feel relaxed in the house again. The press had quieted down, and there had been no more phone calls. I had actually slept soundly last night and was energized to close this deal.

The GPS told me to turn left in eight-tenths of a mile. I told it to "kiss my ass" and changed lanes—and that's when I noticed the blue car in my rearview mirror.

Instinctively, I slowed down—and the blue car slowed down behind me. I studied the mirror, trying to determine if it was the same blue car I had seen the week before.

"Your destination is located one-tenth of a mile on the right."

I looked up and, sure enough, there was the restaurant. "I'll be damned." I checked my watch: four minutes to spare.

"You have reached your destination."

I switched on my turn signal, glanced in the rearview mirror—and the blue car was gone. A silver mini-van had taken its place.

I swung into the Giovanni's parking lot and hurried inside exactly one minute early.

TWO-AND-A-HALF HOURS LATER, I was kicked back in my office chair with my feet up on my desk, feeling like the king of the world.

The meeting had gone well.

The meeting had gone *very* well.

Charlie Kennedy, Canton Industries VP, had shook my hand in the Giovanni's parking lot after lunch and promised a sizeable order no later than Monday afternoon. And if that wasn't blessing enough, he'd also called my boss at Corporate from his car and praised my sales proposal as one of the smartest he had ever seen.

Janie and several co-workers had greeted me like a conquering hero upon my return to the office. I couldn't wait to get home tonight and surprise Katy with the news.

I adjusted myself in the chair and closed my eyes, letting the feeling of success wash over me. It felt good to feel good about something again.

Before long, I felt myself dozing and didn't fight it.

THE BUZZING OF my cell phone woke me a short time later. I dropped my feet to the ground and sat up, wiping sleep-slobber from my chin. I snatched up my phone and saw that I had received a text message.

I tapped the screen and read: I KILLED THEM.

My heart trip-hammered in my chest. I read it again to be sure, then typed: *Who is this?*

I KILLED THEM ALL.

My hands were shaking. *Who is this?*

YOU KNOW WHO THIS IS?

Jimmy?

YOU KNOW.

What do you want?

WHAT DO YOU THINK I WANT?

???

YES YOU DO.

Tell me what you want.

I WANT YOUR BLOOD.

My finger froze over the phone screen.

OR MAYBE...

What?

KATY'S BLOOD.

The sight of Katy's name broke the paralysis of fear that was gripping me and spurred me to action. I grabbed my briefcase and headed for the parking lot, ignoring Janie's concerned questions as I hurried out of the front office.

As I jogged toward my car, I tapped HOME on the cellphone screen and listened to it ring. Once. Twice. Three times. "C'mon, pick up." It rang two more times, and I hung up and called Katy's cell phone.

She answered after the first ring. "Hey, baby, I was just thinking about you—"

"Where are you?"

"What? What's wrong?"

"Where are you?!" I started the car and peeled rubber out of the parking lot.

"I stopped at the grocery store on the way home from Kelly's. I'm just now pulling into the neighborhood."

"Listen to me very carefully. The first thing I want you to do is look around and make sure no one is following you."

"Following me? What—"

"Do it, Katy!"

"Okay, okay!" A pause, and then: "There's no one behind me at all. And I can see all the way to both ends of Bayberry."

"You're sure. No blue cars? Nothing at all?"

"I'm sure, baby. Now tell me what the fuck is going on."

I hit the interstate and cranked my speed to ninety.

"I want you to stay on the line with me and stay in your car when you get home. Don't pull into the garage. Park at the curb and wait for me there. I'll be home in ten minutes..."

DETECTIVE ANDERSON SAT across from Katy and me at the kitchen table and listened to someone talking on the other end of her cell phone. After a moment, she said, "I want it faster," and hung up without saying goodbye.

She looked up at us, face grim, all business.

"We're working with the phone company to trace the texts. Most likely it was a burner phone, but there are ways to track down where the phone was purchased and activated. It's not foolproof, but it's what we got."

She pulled several sheets of paper from a file folder. "Sign these and we'll put a trace on your phone. He calls or texts again, we'll find him. We'll also be able to record anything he says to you."

I picked up a pen and signed the papers.

Friday, Dec 13

I HEARD KATY crying before I reached the bottom of the stairs. Panicked, I rushed into the kitchen and found her slumped against the dishwater, her face buried in her hands. Everything felt like a bad dream again.

I sat on the floor beside her and wrapped her in my arms. "It'll be okay, I promise."

She cried harder, trembling.

"That's it, let it out."

She looked up at me, her face smeared with tears and snot. She pointed a finger at the television on the kitchen counter. "It's all over the fucking news. They even know what the texts said."

I opened my mouth to say something, but nothing came out.

"My mom called three times. She's worried sick."

"We'll go over there later today and talk to her. We'll make it okay."

"And Heather called and said everyone in the neighborhood is talking about us…saying things."

"What kind of things?" I asked.

She started crying again. "That…that we're playing up to the press, trying to get attention. First being all mysterious and then accusing a reporter of being a stalker and now the texts."

"That makes no Goddamn sense."

"I knowwww." Sobbing again. "She also said Ken Ellis was telling people you were a suspect, that you and Jimmy were thick as thieves."

I remembered the curly-haired reporter using those exact same words. *Ken, you lousy, big mouth son-of-a-bitch.*

"I'm scared, Bobby."

I brushed my wife's hair out of her face and used my hand to wipe her cheeks, and then I sat there on the kitchen floor and rocked her in my arms until the tears stopped coming.

I CALLED OUT of work for the day. Paced around the house. Checked on Katy to make sure she was resting. Looked out the bedroom window to make sure the patrol car assigned to guard our house was still parked at the curb. Talked to Detective Anderson on the telephone. She apologized for the leak to the press. She had no idea where it had come from, and I could tell she was as angry as we were.

After lunch, I went out to the garage and looked for something to do. I felt lost. I felt like my brain wasn't working the way it was supposed to.

I straightened the tools on my work bench (the work bench Jimmy had helped me build). I moved cases of bottled water from one spot on the floor to another spot on the floor. I hung a snow shovel on the wall hook where it belonged. I swept the floor.

I noticed a couple boxes of Grant's old school papers on the floor and cleared space on a shelf for them. I bent over to pick up the first box and on my way back up, I nailed my head on the blade of the snow shovel.

"Goddammit!"

I flung the box away, papers scattering everywhere, and swiped an angry hand at the wall, sending the shovel clattering to the ground. I lunged forward and kicked the cardboard box, sending it flying against the opposite wall of the garage. I spun around to look for something else to hit—

—and Detective Anderson was standing at the top of the driveway, staring into the garage at me.

"Everything okay, Mr. Howard?"

I touched a sore spot on the back of my head, checked my fingers for blood. "I'm fine," I said, embarrassed. "Hit my head, lost my temper."

She looked like she wanted to say something else, then changed her mind. Instead, she held out a file folder and said, "Do you mind if we go inside? Few things I want to talk about."

I LEFT DETECTIVE Anderson sitting in the den and went upstairs to get Katy. Once again, we sat together on the sofa across from the detective and waited for her to tell us why she'd come.

"First thing, I have some good news. The texts were a prank."

Katy sat up straight beside me. "A prank?"

"That's right. College kid over at Morgan State. Wannebe film director. Making a slasher film for his senior project. Thought it would be 'cool' to try to scare you."

"It worked," Katy said.

"He paid for the phone with his parents' American Express card. Was easy enough to track. The kid's remorseful, and stupid. Up to you if you want to press charges."

I looked at Katy, but she didn't say anything. I could tell she was relieved. I just felt angry.

"I also came to show you these," the detective said, spreading four glossy photos across the coffee table.

The photos were of three young women and a man who looked in his late 20's. Based on the clothing and hairstyles, the pictures looked at least five or ten years old.

"Recognize any of these people? Ever seen any of them next door at the Wilkinson's?"

I studied the photos and shook my head. "Not me."

"Me either," Katy said.

"You're positive?"

We both nodded. "Yes."

Detective Anderson collected the photographs and returned them to the folder. Looked at me. "The *real* James Wilkinson hasn't tried to contact you, has he, Mr. Howard?"

"What? No." I could feel Katy staring at me.

"If he does, you would never try to help him, right?"

It felt like the temperature in the room had gone up ten degrees. I didn't trust my voice to answer, but I knew I had to. "Of course not."

"That's good to hear."

The detective got to her feet. I thanked her for bringing us good news and walked her to the front door, anxious for her to leave. She walked out onto the porch, stopped and turned around. "By the way, what was your brother's name, Mr. Howard?"

"My brother?"

"The brother you lost when you were young. What was his name?"

"What does that have to do with anything?"

Her face remained blank. "Just doing my job, Mr. Howard."

I glanced back at Katy sitting on the sofa. She was watching us. "My brother's name was James."

Saturday, Dec 14

ADHERING TO THE kind of unspoken agreement that only decades-long married couples can employ, Katy and I never discussed the people in the photographs, and the next time we saw their faces, we were in bed watching the news—and a fifth face had joined them. Another young woman, pretty, with glasses and a scattering of pale freckles across her nose and cheeks.

The headline above the faces read:

POLICE NOW IDENTITY FIVE VICTIMS

Francis Lund, Teresa Thompkins, and Susanne Worthy were from Pennsylvania, Karen Hunter was from Delaware, and Frank Hubbard was from western Maryland. They had been identified from DNA remains found at both Wilkinson's home and a storage unit he'd rented in nearby Fallston. The oldest victim, Lund, had been killed approximately nine years ago, and the most recent victim, Hunter, just over two years ago. An unnamed police source indicated that several additional victims could soon be identified.

The telephone on the nightstand rang, and we both ignored it. After four rings, it stopped.

Katy turned off the television, and we laid in silence for a long time. I listened to the rhythm of her breathing soften and thought she was asleep—but then she surprised me and spoke in a whisper, "Shouldn't we tell the police about the hang ups?"

I pretended to be asleep—and didn't answer.

Sunday, Dec 15

THE TEMPERATURE WAS in the mid-30's, and a sheen of ice glittered in the bird bath at the corner of the back yard, but the morning sun felt good on my face. I was supposed to be repairing one of Katy's rose trellises out by the shed, but I couldn't stop myself from thinking about the five faces I'd seen last night on television (something about those freckles had really stuck with me), and my eyes kept wandering past the fence to Jimmy's back yard.

Streamers of police tape fluttered in the breeze. His shed was wrapped in the bright yellow tape and padlocked. I had helped him build that shed five summers ago, and he had recently helped me pick out mine from Home Depot.

My cell phone rang in my coat pocket. I considered letting it go, then thought better of it: *what if it was Katy calling from inside?*

I put down the hammer and took out my phone. Looked at the caller ID: *Unknown Caller.* I hit the ACCEPT button, ready for another hang up.

"Hello?"

Nothing. Of course.

"Hello."

I started to hang up and heard: *"I'm sorry."*

Startled, I almost dropped the phone.

"What? What did you say?"

"I'm sorry, Bob. You have no idea how sorry I am."

This wasn't a prank: I knew Jimmy's voice.

"Then…why?"

*"I couldn't help it. I wish I had a better answer, but I don't. I owe **you** the truth at least."*

"You have to turn yourself in, Jimmy."

"Believe me, I've thought about it."

"All the calls and hang ups…it's been you?"

"I missed hearing your voices."

"I have to tell the police you called."

"Hell, they probably already know after that texting fiasco. I was sorry you had to go through that."

"Where are you?"

Jimmy laughed. *"Do you remember that day we went fishing out by the dam? Caught all those fat channel cats and you fell in trying to unsnag your line? And on the way home you almost ran over that baby deer and we ended up chasing it into the woods so it would be safe, laughing and yelling and acting like a couple of idiot kids?"*

"Yeah, I remember."

Deep breath. *"That was a really good day, Bobby. I almost felt okay that day."*

My heart felt like it was breaking. "We can get you help, Jimmy."

"Nah, there's no help for me, old friend. There never was. Nothing left now but my penance."

"But if you turn yourself in, if you cooperate, maybe there's a chance—"

"My chances were all used up a long, long time ago, Bobby." Deep sigh. *"It's such a beautiful day outside. I'm glad you're spending it in the yard."*

"How did you know I was—"

The phone went dead in my hand.

I DIDN'T TELL Katy about the phone call. I didn't want to worry her, and I guess if I was being honest with myself, I didn't tell her for other reasons, too; I just couldn't quite figure out what those other reasons were.

I made an excuse to leave the house for a short time, and arranged to meet Detective Anderson at the diner down the street. She was waiting for me when I got there.

"And how can you be so sure it wasn't meant as a threat?"

"I just don't think it was," I said, sipping my coffee.

"He was obviously close by. Either watching you while you talked or he'd seen you in the yard a short time earlier."

"Right." I shrugged. "And if he'd wanted to do something to me, he would have had ample opportunity."

Detective Anderson's face hardened. "I know this is still difficult for you to process, Mr. Howard, but this man is *not* your friend. He is *not* the man you believed him to be."

I didn't say anything.

"He is the subject of a multiple jurisdiction manhunt, and he risked capture to see and talk to you. That fact speaks pretty loudly to me."

"I don't know what to tell you," I said, trying to make my voice not sound defensive.

"I want you to look at something."

She slid a stack of glossy photographs across the table. I picked them up and flipped through them.

They were murder scene photos: numerous angles of a young girl laying naked on the ground, her face hidden beneath long, blonde hair, her body and the floor around her smeared with blood. She almost looked like a Barbie Doll. Like she wasn't real. The last photograph took care of that: a close up of her face, probably a school picture, smiling and happy, looking very real, indeed.

"Lisa James. Seventeen-years-old. From Leesburg, Virginia. A straight 'A' student headed to Dartmouth later in the fall. She was killed eight years ago in a utility shed outside the community pool she lifeguarded at."

I swallowed and slid the photographs back to her.

"Her case had been unsolved until yesterday, when forensic evidence linked James Wilkinson as her killer."

She gathered the photos and got up from the table.

"You remember that next time Wilkinson calls you...or you start thinking of him as your old fishing buddy."

Monday, Dec 16

AN UNMARKED POLICE car followed me to work this morning, and then followed me home again just over an hour later, after a brief meeting with my boss.

"You hit it out of the park, Bob. Charlie Kennedy couldn't stop singing your praises, and trust me, that old bastard doesn't even like his own kids."

"Then why not let me work straight through Christmas Eve, like everyone else?"

"Everyone else isn't dealing with the mess you're dealing with. Besides, you deserve the time off after this sale."

I knew better than to argue with him. I was becoming a distraction. It was easier to give me an extended, paid vacation than deal with tapped telephone lines and undercover cops roaming around. Not to mention my panicked exit from the office the other day. Janie said I'd nearly given her a heart attack running out the way I did.

"So I'm not back until January 6?"

"That's right," he said, slapping me on the shoulder. "New year, new quarter, new time to kick some ass!"

Sometimes, I hated my boss.

THE HOUSE WAS too quiet. I couldn't stand it.

Katy was spending the day with her mother, and I didn't want to interrupt their time together just to whine about my job. I figured I could whine plenty to her tonight when she got home.

I tried to watch one of the afternoon soaps I always heard Janie raving about at the office, but gave up by the second commercial break. I got up and poured myself a drink. Katy would've been shocked—hell, I was pretty surprised myself—but I thought I deserved a drink after the past couple weeks. Maybe I would even take a nap.

I carried my drink back into the den and stopped in front of the fireplace. Took down one of the photos from the mantle. I could hear the ticking of the miniature grandfather clock behind me in the foyer.

"The brother you lost when you were young. What was his name?"

I heard the detective's voice in my head as I stared at the old photograph. My brother and me at the lake on a hot summer day. Bronzed by the sun. Crooked, trying-to-look-tough smiles. His arm around my shoulders. Wearing his favorite Baltimore Orioles floppy hat and his good luck lightning bolt pendant around his neck.

We looked like young gods. We looked like we would live forever.

Tuesday, Dec 17

BAGELS AND COFFEE at the breakfast bar—and admission time. I would've rather swallowed shards of broken glass.

"He called you?" Katy's voice shrill; the expression on her face incredulous. "When? What did he say?"

I started to answer, but she interrupted. "And why in the hell didn't you tell me?"

I put my hands up. "Calm—"

"Don't you dare tell me to calm down."

I slid off the stool and started pacing. Like a twelve-year-old boy, which is exactly what I felt like.

"I didn't tell you right away because I didn't want you to worry. I knew how stressed you were."

"When?"

"Sunday morning. When I was working out back on your trellis."

Shaking her head. "Oh my God."

"Honey, I didn't want you to worry. I even told Detective Anderson that I was—"

"You told the cops, but not me?" Her voice rising again.

I stopped pacing. "I had to…to be safe. They searched the neighborhood. Quietly, so no one would be alarmed. They even put up roadblocks in case he was still in town."

"Jesus, Bobby, what did he say to you?"

"He said he was sorry, he said—"

"He said he was *sorry*?" A mocking look on her face I had never seen before.

"He said he was sorry and was thinking about turning himself in. You can listen to the entire phone call. Detective Anderson has the audio file."

"And you didn't tell me because you were worried?"

"That's right, baby. But I knew I couldn't keep it from you for long."

"Did you ever think that I'm worried about *you*, Bobby?"

"Worried about what?"

She looked away for a moment, then met my eyes again. "Your state of mind for starters."

"What are you talking about?"

"Why aren't you scared, Bobby? Why aren't you worried about yourself in this whole thing? I know you loved him like a brother. I know you looked up to him like a brother. But you saw the pictures. You heard the reports."

"If he was gonna hurt us, Katy, he would've done it a long time ago."

"How do you know that? How do you *know*?"

"C'mon, he lived a hundred feet away from us for the past eight years."

"You don't know that, Bobby. You don't know *him*. None of us did. He's not who we believed he was. He's a monster."

Thursday, Dec 19

GRANT DUMPED HIS duffle bag and knapsack in the foyer and hugged his mother. "Sorry I'm late. Again."

Katy laughed and hugged him tighter. "That damn car of yours."

"Nothing wrong with that car a brand new engine and muffler won't fix."

We all laughed, and it was music to my ears after the last couple days of strained conversation and uncomfortable silence in the house.

Grant kissed his mom on the cheek, and then it was my turn for a hug. I noticed that he held on to me a little tighter and longer than usual.

"Good to see you, Pop."

"You, too. You, too."

He gestured out the window at the police cruiser parked at the curb. "What are they doing here?"

Katy glanced nervously out the window, while I gave him my best brush off. "Nothing important. Tell you after dinner."

He tilted his head back. "Speaking of dinner, what is that amazingly wonderful smell?"

Katy picked a fuzz ball off the shoulder of Grant's sweater. "Why don't we all head to the kitchen and you can see for yourself?"

"Don't have to ask me twice." And off he went.

Katy and I laughed and followed Grant out of the foyer. It felt good to be a family again.

LATER THAT EVENING, we all sat in the den watching *Meet Joe Black* on HBO. We had probably seen it a half dozen times already, but it was one of Grant's favorites.

Some time early in the movie, Katy reached over and took my hand in hers—and I knew I was forgiven.

I leaned over and kissed her on top of her head. Whispered: "Thank you. I'm sorry."

She squeezed my hand. Whispered back: "No more secrets."

"Promise."

She rested her head on my shoulder.

Ten days later, I broke my promise.

Saturday, Dec 21

THE MALL PARKING lot was a zoo. Grant carefully maneuvered his way around tired pedestrians overloaded with shopping bags and cranky, aggressive drivers looking for an open parking space.

If there was an undercover cop following us today, he was impossible to spot in the long line of traffic behind us. *Or maybe they had given up,* I thought. It had, thankfully, been a quiet couple of days; even the press seemed to be taking a breather.

"Right there," I said, pointing at an SUV with its reverse lights on.

Grant flipped on his right turn signal and eased to a stop. The car behind us immediately blew its horn. I glanced in the passenger side mirror, but it was impossible to see because of the duct tape that was wrapped around it, keeping it attached to the car. The SUV backed out of the space, drove away, and we pulled in.

"Piece of cake," Grant said, smiling.

Our annual Christmas shopping trip had been a longstanding tradition—ever since Grant was in middle school and he'd started using his lawn mowing money to buy us gifts. Once he became old enough to drive, Grant had assumed driving duties for the day. It was usually an adventure.

"You know I could've driven today," I teased.

"Now what fun would that've been?"

I reached down and released my seat belt, and my hand brushed against something cold and metal between the seats. Concerned, I held up a wrench for Grant to see. "Ummm, protection? You worried about something, son?"

Grant just laughed and took the wrench from my hand. Without a word, he turned to the driver's door and used the wrench to hand-crank his window halfway open. I hadn't noticed until now that his window knob was missing. He looked back at me with a smirk, and then cranked the window closed again.

"Impressive," I said, shaking my head and climbing out of the old Subaru. "Mom's right. You *really* need a new car."

IF THE PARKING lot was a zoo, then the inside of the mall was a jungle. I had never seen that many people crammed into one space before, except maybe an Orioles game.

We had been shopping for over three hours and had purchased exactly two gifts. *Two.* How was that even possible?

On the plus side, it had been nice to have some alone time together. We talked about school and life and football. We talked about my job and Katy; he agreed that her mood was brightening and she was acting more like her old self every day. Having him home from college and a couple quiet days had worked wonders for her.

And we talked about Jimmy, of course. He told me about his ten minute phone call with Detective Anderson before he'd left campus; she had been very nice to him, Grant said, for which I was grateful.

I'd had a scare early on when I thought I'd seen Jimmy watching us from behind a kiosk, but it turned out to be a false alarm. The guy was there with his grandchildren, pushing them around in one of those fancy double strollers. I saw him up close a short time later, and he didn't really resemble Jimmy at all.

WE ATE DINNER in the food court, after a fifteen minute wait in line for pizza and French fries, and another five minute wait for an open table. Afterward, when I came back from washing up in the bathroom, I saw a smiling Ken Ellis shaking hands with Grant.

"Here he is," Ken said, when he saw me walking up. "How's it hanging, Bobby?"

"Lot better once I get out of here," I said, glancing around at the surging crowd.

"Grant's looking good," he said, slapping him on the back. "Big man on campus with the ladies, I'm sure."

Grant didn't say anything; just stood there looking embarrassed.

"Well, we better get going. Still need to buy a couple things and—"

Ken leaned in close. "Anything new about Wilkinson?"

I remembered what Katy had said: about Ken telling the cops that Jimmy and I were thick as thieves, and how he'd been spreading gossip around the neighborhood that maybe I was a suspect, too. I decided it was time for some payback.

I leaned in and lowered my voice. "No one is supposed to know this, not even the press, but…"

Ken's eyes widened. "But what?"

"The police…there's gonna be another big press conference tomorrow morning. 8am sharp. Right out front of the Fallston Police Department."

Ken's chubby, little face nodded up and down. "I knew there was more coming, I knew it." He looked around conspiratorially. "Thanks. I won't tell a soul." And he was gone.

Grant looked at me in surprise as we walked in the opposite direction. "Did you just do what I think you just did?"

"And what would that be?"

"You just totally punked Mr. Ellis and sent him on a wild goose chase at eight in the morning."

I shrugged. "Karma's a bitch, son."

A FEW MINUTES later, browsing in a Barnes and Noble, Grant brought up the day he and Jimmy had spent in Gettysburg, walking the battlefield.

"It was probably my favorite day I ever spent with him," he told me.

I nodded. "I remember when you got home that night. You were so excited and couldn't wait to go to the library the next day to check out some books."

"I really loved walking around Gettysburg and learning about the battle, but it was more than that. I think it was because he treated me like a grown up for the first time that day. I was only fifteen, but the way he talked to me, the way he explained things…it made me feel special."

I knew what he meant. Jimmy had that way about him; a way of making you feel like the most important person in the world at any given moment.

"Something I've thought about a lot since all this happened…" He fidgeted with his jacket zipper, and I could tell he really wanted to get this out.

"When we were walking the field where General Pickett led his famous charge...he went on and on about the ghosts of the past and how he could feel them there on that battlefield. Each fallen soldier's hopes and dreams and fears and regrets. The way he described it to me...it gave me chills... and I swear it made me feel *something* there, too."

I nodded again, encouraging him to continue.

"The more you and Mom told me about what was happening...and the more I listened to the news reports...it really made me wonder what kind of ghosts Mr. Wilkinson has been carrying around with him all these years. I mean, if he did all the things they claim he did...it's almost like there has to be another person inside of him...a ghost that none of us ever really knew..."

Sunday, Dec 22

THE MOOD WAS a lot lighter the next morning, as the three of us busied ourselves in the kitchen, getting ready for an afternoon of watching football with some of Grant's old high school friends.

A radiant Katy danced around the granite island, making her pepperoni bread and singing along with the radio. Grant stirred a big pot of chili on the stove and cut up chicken wings on the counter. I sat at the breakfast bar, watching and laughing, as I peeled a bowl of jumbo steamed shrimp for pregame cocktails.

"I think we're gonna need more wings," Grant said. "Mark's coming, and that boy can eat." He started rinsing his hands at the sink.

"You stay and finish. I'll go," I said.

Katy rolled her eyes. "The master escape artist gets out of doing his work yet again."

I plopped a fat shrimp in my mouth, chewed it up, and started talking with my mouth open. "Not true, Miss Know-It-All, and highly offensive. Grant needs to remain here in case his friends show up early. You know how they get when there's free food on the table."

They both laughed, and Katy shooed me out of the kitchen.

I WAS STANDING in line at the register with three more packs of chicken wings and a family size bag of Doritos when my cell phone rang. I fumbled it out of my pocket, expecting it to be Katy asking me to pick up something else: chips or pretzels or maybe another jar of salsa.

Instead, the caller ID flashed a familiar message: *Unknown Caller.*

I answered, thinking: *No way it's him.* "Hello?"

I was wrong.

"*I know they're tracking the call, so I have to be quick, Bobby. I've been thinking a lot about you and Katy and Grant. I just wanted to wish you all a Merry Christmas.*"

I didn't know what to say, so I didn't say anything.

"*...and say how sorry I am again. You've been my one true friend, my entire life.*" The connection wasn't as clear as the first time. *Was he farther away?*

"*Grant was like a son to me. I'm sorry to have put you all through this.*"

"You would never hurt us, right, Jimmy?" I asked, finally finding my voice.

A burst of static.

"Right?"

Another loud crackle of static, and was there something else? *Was he laughing?*

"Jimmy? Jimmy!"

The line went dead.

LATER THAT NIGHT in bed:

"I think we were right not to tell Grant," Katy said. "He was so happy today."

I handed her the television remote. "No reason to worry him over nothing."

"It's not nothing, Bobby." The look of wariness was back on her face.

"I didn't mean it that way."

"Are you sure he was laughing?"

"No, I'm not sure. I told you, there was too much static to hear clearly."

She placed the remote on the nightstand without turning on the television. "What time are you seeing Detective Anderson tomorrow?"

"I told her I'd come down to the station around ten."

"Do you want me to come with you? We could tell Grant we were running to the store."

I shook my head. "It's not necessary. Just stay home with him."

"Bobby?"

"Yeah, baby?"

"You swear you aren't hiding anything else from me?"

I leaned over and took her face in my hands. Looked into her eyes. "I promise you."

Monday, Dec 23

GRANT CAME DOWNSTAIRS after his morning shower, took one look at us sitting at the breakfast bar, and said, "What's wrong?"

I guess our faces gave it away.

The television was on: a Channel 11 Special Report that had interrupted Katy's regular viewing of *Good Morning, America*.

The news wasn't good. Three more victims identified. Three more photographs of the deceased. Two women and a young man this time. Police sources described "souvenirs"—jewelry, articles of clothing, even a driver's license—found under a floorboard in 1922 Hanson Road that had helped connect James Wilkinson to the murders.

Grant stood and watched in silence; he looked as if he wanted to cry.

Katy got up and put her arm around him. "Honey…"

"That's eight now," he said, looking at her. "And they're still saying there might be others."

"We just have to try to block it out. We have to try to—"

"*Block it out?*" he said, pulling away from her. "He was my Godfather for Christsake." Tears spilled from his eyes now. "I loved him."

"Grant—"

He waved her off and walked out the side door and into the garage. Katy looked at me with a helpless expression I'd rarely ever seen on her face.

"I'll go talk to him," I said, and took off after my son.

"HE OBVIOUSLY FEELS very strongly about you," Detective Anderson said.

We were sitting in the same dinghy interview room as the last time I had been at the station. The same camera was recording our conversation.

"He knows we're watching you and tracing your calls, yet he still risked contact."

"He sounded lonely. It's Christmas."

"We have someone trying to clean up the audio right now. Do you really think he was laughing at the end of the phone call?"

"I don't know. For one second, I thought maybe I could hear him, but it was probably just static."

"Have you ever considered that he might be playing a game with you, Mr. Howard?"

"Why would he do that?"

"Why would he torture, mutilate, and kill eight innocent people?"

I had no answer for that.

"You said that Mr. Wilkinson liked to play chess. We found several other strategy games downloaded on his laptop."

"Okay…"

"We also found a hidden collection of video tapes in his garage. It seems Mr. Wilkinson was stalking and filming some of his victims ahead of time."

"Why are you telling me this?"

"Because I think it's important that you realize a couple things about James Wilkinson: he is very smart and he likes his games."

"Okay. I'm hearing you."

"Anything else at all you can think to share? It's important you tell me, no matter how small or trivial you might consider it."

I shook my head. "Nothing."

She stared directly at me. "And you would never keep anything from us, right?"

I almost said *You sound like my wife*, but held it in. Thank God. "No, I wouldn't."

"Still think you have nothing to worry about, Mr. Howard?"

She was looking for a reaction, and she got one.

"Do I think Jimmy would hurt us? No, I don't. Do I want you to find him and put him away? Yes, I do." Deep breath. "Look, he was my friend. A part of my family. And, yeah, he has the same name as my brother, but that doesn't mean a damn thing. It's hard to think about everything we shared—Christ, just three weeks ago, he sat at my table and carved our Thanksgiving turkey—and it's even harder to think that it wasn't real. But it wasn't. I know that. None of it was real."

"Well, it's good to hear you say that, Mr. Howard. Because it appears that he isn't quite finished yet. Last night, Pennsylvania police discovered a local florist murdered in her home and her car missing. They believe that James Wilkinson is responsible."

IT WASN'T REAL.

The words echoed in my head the entire drive home from the police station. I suddenly felt so tired. Beaten.

None of it was real.

I thought about all the times we had talked about the meaning of life and death; if there was a God or not; all of Jimmy's Army stories; the laughter-filled conversations about history and politics and football and the Orioles.

I thought about the countless times he'd helped me with odd jobs around the house and how he was the one who taught me how to use half the tools in my garage. The time he loaned me money so I could afford to send Grant to summer camp. And the time he counseled—and talked sense into—me after I confided in him that I was thinking about having an affair with a co-worker; my one near-slip in over twenty years of a happy marriage.

And I remembered the night, just the two of us sitting out back on the deck, watching a meteor shower, when he put his beer down and turned to me and said:

"Don't ever lie to yourself, Bobby. People lie to themselves all the time. To survive. To get by. But you look those people in the eye—even the toughest of the bunch—and you ask them, 'What do you think about when you see a shooting star in the night sky? Better yet, *who* do you think about?' Because that right there is their truth, and in that moment even they can't deny it. Maybe the saddest thing of all is those same people are usually the ones who stop watching stars that fall from the sky. They learn to just turn away from the magic."

It was beautiful and poetic and maybe the wisest thing anyone had ever said to me.

And none of it was real.

Tuesday, Dec 24

SURPRISINGLY, CHRISTMAS EVE turned out to be a wonderful day for all of us.

Despite the latest news reports about Jimmy and my trip downtown to the police station the day before, it was almost as if the three of us had made an unspoken family agreement to wake up fresh and not allow any of it to interfere with us having a great holiday.

Katy and I had been worried at first. Grant had slept in late, and we'd feared that he was still hanging onto his dark feelings from the day before.

But he'd shocked us by bounding down the stairs starving for a big breakfast and already dressed to go get a Christmas tree.

When Grant was still living at home, we would always pick out our tree the first weekend of December and set it up the second weekend. Now, that he was away at college, it had become tradition to buy it on Christmas Eve morning, and set it up after dinner and a nighttime walk around the neighborhood to look at Christmas lights.

We'd decided to skip the walk this year—after a quick discussion confirmed that none of us were particularly anxious to see or talk to any of our neighbors—but dinner had been amazing, as usual (Katy's homemade lasagna, rolls, and salad), and the tree took us until almost ten o'clock to finish decorating.

We'd watched the end of *White Christmas* together on television, and then hugged Grant goodnight as he went up to bed. Once we were sure he was asleep, Katy and I had made love in the comforting glow of the Christmas tree and dozed in each other's arms afterward.

For just a moment, everything had felt okay in the world again.

I LISTENED TO Katy's footsteps climbing the stairs, and finished rinsing our wine glasses in the sink. I turned off the kitchen lights and returned to the den to close up.

I couldn't take my eyes off the Christmas tree. It's twinkling lights and wintergreen smell brought back so many pleasant memories. Grant, as a boy, leaving cookies and milk and a handwritten note on the mantle for Santa; chopped-up carrots on the floor for his reindeer. Katy and I sneaking presents under the tree once Grant had fallen asleep.

I bent down and rehung an angel ornament, which had fallen down through the branches—and another memory washed over me.

Every Christmas Eve as a boy, after evening mass, my brother and I would walk hand-in-hand to the top of Tupelo Drive. Once we'd reached the crest of the hill, we would stand at the crossroad and look down Juniper Street at the carnival of twinkling lights decorating the houses along both sides of the road. Jimmy always used to say that it was like our own personal Christmas parade—and he was right.

After taking our time on Juniper, Jimmy and I would return home to change into pajamas, drink Mom's hot cocoa, and open one early Christmas present each. Then Mom would tuck us in, and we would whisper to each other across our cramped bedroom until we finally fell asleep.

It was the clearest and most favorite memory I had of my brother—and it filled my soul and made my heart hurt, all at once.

I unplugged the Christmas tree lights and walked upstairs in darkness.

Wednesday, Dec 25

I GAWKED AT the huge present wrapped in *Frosty the Snowman* gift paper. "I have *no* idea what it is!"

"And that's enough to drive you crazy, isn't it?" Katy beamed.

Grant laughed, and high-fived his mother.

"Whatever," I said, sounding very much like a pouting child.

I was notoriously difficult to surprise when it came to gifts, and that was somewhat of an understatement. If constant badgering—*"What'd you get me? What'd you get me? C'mon, just give me a hint."*—didn't work, then I usually resorted to sneaking around the house, searching high and low for hidden caches of presents or store receipts.

One year, I even snuck downstairs and used an exacto knife to carefully slice open the wrapping paper of one of my gifts under the tree. Once I had determined the gift's identity, I'd used scotch tape to reseal it.

I would have gotten away with it, too, if it hadn't been for Katy being such a light sleeper. Suffice to say, she no longer put presents under the tree until late on Christmas Eve.

"Go ahead, open it," she said, still grinning.

I didn't have to be told twice. I tore open the wrapping paper with a couple quick swipes of my hands—and my mouth dropped open in surprise.

"You got me a snow-blower!" I tilted the box for a better look at it, and then gave Katy a big thank you hug and kiss. I couldn't stop smiling.

"Well, well, better write it down on the calendar, folks. Bobby Howard has finally been punked!"

Still smiling, I took something from the pocket of my flannel pjs. Handed it to Katy.

"What's this?"

"You're not the only one who likes surprises." I looked at Grant and winked.

Katy slowly unwrapped—*My god, who takes their time opening Christmas presents?!*—the narrow box and lifted the lid. A string of pearls shined like miniature angels in the morning light coming through the windows.

She held them up in one hand and put the other hand to her mouth. "Oh...oh...oh my God..." And then she squealed and practically tackled me in a bear hug.

"And mark those calendars again, folks. Katy Howard has just been rendered—surely for the first time ever in her life—speechless."

And then it was my turn to laugh and high-five Grant.

AFTER THE THREE of us fawned over our gifts some more—Grant was especially enamored with his new iPad—and cleaned up the wrapping paper mess on the floor, we had just enough time to enjoy bagels and coffee and get dressed before Katy's parents arrived for the day.

Her parents were *never* late, and today was no exception. Within minutes of their arrival, Katy's mom was buzzing around the kitchen, helping with dinner preparations, and her father was camped out in front of the television in my recliner with his shoes off.

A short time later, Katy's sister, Anne, and her husband and two little girls arrived from Ohio. We had kept their trip a secret from Katy's parents, so after a brief and tearful reunion, we all retreated to the den for an afternoon of catching up, food, college football, food, board games, food, more gift opening, and more food.

The only time I heard Jimmy's name was during a local, television newsbreak at halftime of one of the football games. Pennsylvania State Police had arrested a former employee for the murder of the florist. Here in Maryland, a trucker thought he'd spotted Jimmy driving a late model Mustang on I-95 south of Baltimore, but he'd been unable to get a license plate. And that was it—back to football.

By seven o'clock, I felt more like a stuffed Thanksgiving turkey than a Christmas elf. I dozed at the end of the sofa, my swollen belly hidden beneath a pillow.

By nine o'clock, Katy's parents had left for home and her sister and family had gone back to their hotel for the night. We were alone again, and happily exhausted.

KATY WALKED INTO the bathroom as I was brushing my teeth. I rinsed my mouth and spit into the sink. "Today was nice, wasn't it?"

"Today was perfect." She lifted herself up on tiptoes and kissed me on the cheek. "Thank you."

"You're welcome, honey. Thank *you*."

Another kiss, this time on the mouth. "Can I ask you something?"

"Of course."

"Should I feel guilty reacting the way I did to your surprise this morning?"

I looked at her, confused.

"I mean, with everything going on. Jimmy. The poor families of the victims. And I was so happy..."

I took her gently by the shoulders. "No, no, no, you should *not* feel guilty, and either should I. We've worked hard to get where we are. We deserve to be happy once in awhile."

"Okay, good," she said, and I could tell she was relieved.

I walked into the bedroom and climbed under the covers. "It was nice to see your mom and dad today. They were actually a little better than I thought they'd be."

"They both stopped watching the news and reading the newspaper. That's helped a lot."

"Mark offered to lend me a gun, can you believe that?" Mark was our brother-in-law, an avid hunter and outdoorsman.

"I hope you told him no," she said above the water running in the bathroom.

"Of course, I did. Told him I'd probably shoot myself in the dick the first time I tried to use it."

Katy laughed and turned off the water. "Well, then I'm glad you told him no," she said, appearing in the doorway wearing her new string of pearls—and nothing else. "Because I really like your dick."

She turned off the light and came to bed.

Friday, Dec 27

"THERE YOU ARE," Grant said from inside the garage.

I was kneeling at the top of the driveway, trying to assemble my new snow-blower. It was slow going, parts scattered everywhere, and I couldn't help but think of Jimmy and how he would usually be the one helping me do this.

"Mom wants to drive by the mall to return the sweater Grandma gave her—of course—and then we're meeting Uncle Mark and the girls at Chili's for lunch. You wanna come?"

I stood and brushed dirt from my jeans. "Sure. Give me ten minutes to finish here and wash up."

He glanced at the mess I had made and flashed me a skeptical look.

"Okay, okay, maybe twenty. But they're calling for snow tomorrow night, and I want to be ready."

"I'll tell Mom a half hour," Grant said with a shit-eating grin and walked back inside.

"Nobody likes a smartass," I called after him, and just like that, I was blindsided by an unexpected surge of fatherly love and pride. For reasons I couldn't even begin to explain, I felt sudden tears in my eyes.

A dog barked on the street behind me, and I turned around just in time to see my neighbor, Aaron, picking up his newspaper and walking into his garage with his old German Shepard, Sarge, in tow.

I wiped a tear from my eye and walked down the driveway to my own newspaper box. I needed a moment to compose myself.

I grabbed the rolled-up newspaper from inside the box and opened it while I walked back to the house.

Halfway up the driveway, I stopped in my tracks, my heart skipping a beat. I stood perfectly still, the rest of the world melting away to nothing around me, and stared down at the paper. I read the words again, slower this time.

Then, I carefully refolded the newspaper and slid it into my back pocket—and went inside.

Sunday, Dec 29

IT WAS JUST after midnight, and I was sneaking out of the house like a teenager.

Katy and Grant had been asleep for almost an hour, and the house was dark and silent. Snow was falling outside and had already blanketed the lawns and streets. The forecast called for six to nine inches by morning.

Dressed in dark pants and sweatshirt, I crept down the stairs, made my way through the den, and out the kitchen door into the garage.

I grabbed a heavy jacket and Grant's keys from the workbench, where I had left them earlier in the evening, slipped into my freezing cold boots, and eased open the door to the side yard.

Snow and wind lashed my face, and threatened to yank the door from my hand. I tightened my grip and carefully pushed the door closed. If the wind had slammed it shut and awakened Katy, I was a dead man with an awful lot of explaining to do.

I marched around the side yard, through a couple inches of fresh snow, to the driveway and Grant's Subaru. I would have much preferred to take my own car or even Katy's, but Grant's car was parked in its usual spot, blocking the garage door, and with snow in the forecast, I hadn't been able to think of a single good excuse to ask Grant to park in the street.

I had spent the past thirty-six hours doing my best to not raise any suspicions, and it had been an exhausting task. Saturday had passed like an eternity. So many thoughts ricocheting around inside my head—and heart—and I had changed my mind a half-dozen times before finally settling on my decision.

I used my bare hands to clear snow from the Subaru's windshield, then climbed inside and eased the door closed. The interior of the car smelled like old pizza and dirty socks. I inserted the key in the ignition, unlocked the steering wheel, put the car in neutral, and released the parking brake.

Holding my breath, I drifted silently down the driveway and into the snow-covered street. The slope of Hanson Road carried me most of the way clear of my house, and only then did I attempt to crank the engine.

It wheezed and sputtered several times before it finally caught. I strapped on my seatbelt and drove carefully out of the neighborhood.

At least this piece of shit has four wheel drive, I thought, turning right onto Edgewood Road and cruising past the all-night Dunkin' Donuts and Texaco station.

THE NOTE HAD been hidden in the Friday morning edition of the *Baltimore Sun*.

It had been scribbled on a sheet of torn-out notebook paper, and I had recognized the handwriting before I'd even had time to digest the contents of the note.

After I'd read it the first couple times in the driveway, I'd hidden the note in the pocket of my jeans and read it twice more at the mall when Katy and Grant had been off on their own. I'd read it again a short time later in the bathroom stall at Chili's.

Later that Friday evening, after everyone had gone upstairs, I'd read the note one final time—and then I'd burned it in the fireplace. Once I was certain there was nothing left but ashes, I'd gone upstairs to bed and lay awake for hours.

THE STREETS WERE empty—except for the occasional snow plow lurking past me like some kind of prehistoric monster—and once I hit Route 22, I was surprised by how quickly I got there.

Not even twenty minutes after drifting down my driveway, I slowed and pulled to the side of the road—at the exact spot where Jimmy and I had once chased a baby deer into the woods, laughing and carrying on like carefree teenagers. It seemed like a lifetime ago, now.

I swung around and did a U-turn, so the car would be parked on the correct side of the road, and as I did, my headlights swept across a snow-covered field, exposing a staggered line of boot prints in an otherwise pristine blanket of fresh powder. The prints disappeared into the distant treeline.

I OWE YOU ONE FINAL TRUTH, BOBBY. PLEASE MEET ME.

I adjusted and zipped up my heavy jacket. Pulled on a winter hat. Took a couple deep breaths to calm myself. Then turned off the car and got out.

The snow was coming down harder now, the flakes fatter and wetter, and the wind had picked up. I adjusted my jacket collar and stuffed my hands in my pockets.

SUNDAY. 12:30AM. BABY DEER WOODS. I HAVE SOMETHING I NEED TO GIVE YOU BEFORE I GO AWAY FOREVER.

I started across the field, following the quickly disappearing boot tracks in the snow. I felt bulky and sluggish, like an overdressed snowman. The wind slowed my pace even more and stung my eyes. I squeezed them shut for a moment and saw Lisa James's bloodied face—just as she had been appearing in my dreams—the seventeen-year-old, Dartmouth-bound beauty who had been killed in the utility shed at her swimming pool.

PLEASE MEET ME, BOBBY. PLEASE DON'T BE AFRAID.

That's right, Bob, nothing at all to be afraid of, I thought, as I lowered my head and kept on walking.

Hell, I wasn't afraid. I was scared shitless.

I CROSSED A small creek, using ice-slippery rocks as a pathway, and slowly stepped into the woods, my eyes moving everywhere. Most of the wind was blocked here, but it moaned even louder high above me in the treetops. It took my eyes a moment to adjust to the deeper darkness.

"Jimmy?" My voice sounded like a stranger's.

I walked deeper into the woods. It felt like I was watching someone else in a movie. Someone very foolish.

"Jimmy?"

I thought I heard the snap of dead branches to my right, and I stopped moving, listening.

"That you, Jimmy?"

Nothing, but the wind.

I started walking again, and—

"I'm right here, Bobby."

From directly behind me.

I JERKED LIKE I'd been hit with a taser and spun around—and there was my old friend.

Standing next to the tree I had just walked past.

He was wearing dark pants and a sweatshirt with the hood up. No jacket. I couldn't see his eyes at all, and could see just enough of the rest of his face to see that he hadn't shaved in awhile. I had never seen him with a beard before.

"I didn't mean to scare you, Bobby."

We were maybe fifteen feet apart.

"Just an old pair of underwear. I can throw them away when I get home."

Jimmy laughed, and I hated that the sound made my heart feel something. "Same ole Bobby. God, it's good to see you."

He took a step forward, but I held my hands up to stop him. "That's close enough...please."

Jimmy froze, and I watched his shoulders sag. "I'm not gonna hurt you. I would never hurt you like that, Bobby."

"I told the police that. They didn't believe me, either did Katy, but I told them."

"I guess you can't really blame them for that. I've done some terrible things."

And there it was—an admission.

Wasn't that what I'd come for?

"Why, Jimmy?"

Jimmy lowered his head, and I saw his chest rise and fall. "It's like I already told you, I couldn't help it." He looked up at me again, and his face was sick with the truth of it. "It's a compulsion...a sickness...a kind of fever...I fight it and I win for awhile...but then I'm weak again..."

He inched closer to me while he was talking, and I suddenly heard Detective Anderson's words inside my head: *He likes to play games, Mr. Howard.*

"I have something I need to give to you, Bobby." Another step closer, and his hand disappeared into his sweatshirt pocket. "Something very special."

I took a careful step backward, hoping he wouldn't notice—and prayed that the snipers could see well enough in the dark and snow to have a clear shot.

I DIDN'T KNOW where the snipers were positioned, only that there were three of them, and they had set up hours ago, well before Jimmy was supposed to have arrived. I was wired under my sweatshirt and had a safe word, and they were supposed to be watching and listening to my every move.

Of course, my overactive and terrified imagination informed me that there was always the possibility that Jimmy had ambushed the snipers, and the three of them were hanging from trees right now, gutted like deer, their steaming blood staining the snow red.

I forced myself to ignore that image and took another half-step backward.

"Your family is the only family I ever had, Bobby. Being with you and Katy and Grant is the only time I ever felt safe or happy in my entire, miserable life."

Jimmy walked closer.

"That's what makes this so damn difficult..."

He pulled something long and white from his pocket.

I HAD SPENT the second half of Friday and all of Saturday wrestling with my decision: tell Detective Anderson about the note or keep it to myself.

By dinnertime Saturday—an early goodbye dinner at the house for Anne and her family—I had decided to keep the note to myself and not go to meet Jimmy. I didn't know if it was the right decision, only that it felt like the safest and least complicated decision for my family.

And I was at peace with that choice—

—until the phone call.

Detective Anderson had rung the house phone just as dinner was winding down, and I'd hurried upstairs to take the call in the bedroom.

"I'm sorry to interrupt your dinner, Mr. Howard. This won't take very long."

I paced back and forth in front of the bed, suddenly nervous that she had somehow discovered the note—and my failure to disclose it. "It's okay."

"Just two questions and you can get back to eating. Does a woman named Janie Loughlin work for you?"

"Janie? Umm, yeah, but technically she works *with* me, not for me."

"Is Ms. Loughlin an acquaintance of Mr. Wilkinson's?"

I stopped pacing. "Not really. I mean, they've met a couple times. At cook-outs here at the house. And Jimmy came to our office Christmas party once or twice over the years."

"Do you know if they had stayed in any kind of contact with each other?"

"I don't think so. I think Jimmy would have said something if they had, and I *know* Janie would have. Why are you asking me this?"

There was a short moment of silence on the phone, then: "I told you about the videotapes Mr. Wilkinson had made of some of his victims. The most recent tapes we discovered included nearly three hours of footage of Janie Loughlin doing everything from grocery shopping to gardening in her yard to walking across the parking lot into your office building."

I sat down on the edge of the bed.

"I think it's safe to say that Ms. Loughlin is a very fortunate woman this Christmas."

I leaned over and rested my face in my hands.

"Mr. Howard? Are you still there, Mr. Howard?"

I sat up. "There's something I need to tell you, detective, but you have to promise not to tell Katy…"

DEAD BRANCHES CRUNCHING beneath his feet, Jimmy walked closer in the dark woods, and I knew I had maybe two seconds to make a choice. I felt my legs tense, but remained frozen in place.

"I'm so sorry, Bobby." He reached out with a shaking hand—and I saw that he was holding a crumpled, white envelope.

He pushed it toward me—*He likes to play games, Mr. Howard.*—and I took it, backing up again once I held it in my hand.

The envelope was sealed. I shook it, and something heavy rattled inside. "What is it?"

"It's…something that belongs to you."

I didn't want to open the envelope.

I knew that whatever secrets it held inside would change my life forever, and I didn't want to open it.

But, of course, I did.

I turned the envelope over in my hand and tore it open along the top. I tilted the envelope and something metal slid out into my open palm. I held it up in front of my face—and suddenly I couldn't remember how to breathe.

It was a miniature lightning bolt pendant hanging on a faded, silver chain. The one my brother had been wearing on the day he disappeared.

AS I'D GROWN older, I had learned to tell people that my brother, Jimmy, had drowned for two simple reasons: first, because that was the most likely explanation for his disappearance. The lake was dark and deep, and people—kids and adults—drowned in its waters at the rate of one every three or four years. It wasn't a terribly rare occurrence, merely a tragic one.

The second reason was because it was simply easier. I could have explained that the body had never been found, and that the police had also conducted a missing person's investigation, and that the investigation had turned up no evidence of foul play; but that would have just led to even more questions and extended a conversation I loathed to take part in in the first place. If there was one thing I'd learned growing up, it was this: people couldn't shut up and mind their own business when it came to a real life mystery. They all turned into amateur detectives.

So, as the years passed, it had become the official explanation: James Alvin Howard had drowned in the lake at the age of thirteen.

Only now I knew better.

"YOU…" MY LEGS felt like they might give out. I staggered back a step, regained my balance. "You killed him?"

Jimmy nodded and lowered his head.

"Answer the fucking question. You killed him?"

"Yes." Barely audible above the wind.

I felt like I was going to faint. "How? That was…almost forty years ago."

Jimmy looked up at me, and this time I could see his eyes. I wish I could say that they looked dead or empty, like a shark's eyes; I wish I could say that they didn't even look human; that they looked like a monster's eyes.

But that wouldn't have been the truth.

He looked very much like my old friend right then, standing there in front of me in the snowy woods, his eyes sadder and more tired than I had ever seen a person's eyes look before or since.

He cleared his throat and started talking:

"I had just turned twenty the month before and was on a two-week leave from the Army. Most of my buddies had gone home or to the beach for some R&R and women, but I had taken off on a solo road trip instead. Mom was dead by then, so I had nobody, and nowhere to go.

"I'd driven south, and that's how I ended up at your lake on my second day out. At first, I'd just laid there and read a book on the beach and gotten some sun, drank some beers from a cooler I'd brought along; but then I saw your brother splashing around in the lake...and he looked so young and alive...and I felt something."

"*Something?*"

He flexed his hands in front of him. "An urge...an itch...down in the deepest part of my brain. I knew what I was feeling, and I fought it. I even packed up my stuff in the car and left. But a few miles down the road, I turned around."

"He was...the first one?"

"No." He shook his head. "The second."

"Who was the—"

"My sister didn't die from cancer, Bobby. She was real sick and she probably would have died anyway...but she didn't die from cancer."

It was too much; I felt something breaking open inside of me. "So all these years..."

"I followed the story in the news and the papers. I learned all about the sweet single mom who had lost her older son to the lake, and I learned all about the younger son still with her. The guilt and regret ate away at me. I tried to think of ways to make it up to the two of you..."

"Make it up to us?" I asked, incredulous.

"I was sick, Bobby. My brain wasn't working right. Even, years later, when I couldn't fight it anymore and I started killing again, I still thought about you and felt guilty about what I'd done. I did my best to keep track of you as you grew up. I kept a scrapbook. Newspaper clippings from back in high school about your baseball games and your business scholarship. Some of the guest editorials you wrote for your college newspaper. An interview you did for the alumni newsletter when you were working your first job. Even your wedding announcement to Katy.

"A lot of time passed, but I never forgot you, Bobby. I couldn't. And then one night, maybe ten years ago, not long after my wife passed away, I was living in New Jersey, and I had an idea. I knew it was a crazy idea, but I couldn't stop thinking about it: what if I found out where you were living and became a part of your neighborhood; a part of your *life?*"

"All this time…"

Jimmy nodded. "All this time…I didn't know what I'd thought would happen, even after I moved in right next door to you. But I never dreamed it would turn out like this. I never dreamed I would learn to love you and trust you. Like a brother."

"Don't you fucking say that!"

He put his hands up. "I'm sorry. I didn't mean to—"

"Why tell me all this now?"

"I *always* wanted to tell you, Bobby. Not a single day passed that I didn't think about it. I wrote about it in my journal all the time. But when all this happened and I had to take off…I knew that if I didn't tell you now, if I didn't find a way to return the necklace to you, you would probably never find out." He almost seemed to shrink in size in front of me. "I just thought you should know…no matter how much it made you hate me."

I took a step closer to him.

"What happened to my brother, Jimmy?"

He glanced at the ground. "When I got back to the lake, I watched and waited until he went to the restroom alone, and then I tricked him into helping me with my car in the parking lot. The whole thing took maybe three minutes, and we were gone."

My brain felt like it was on fire. "What…did you do to him?"

He looked at me. "I'm not going to tell you that, Bobby. I can't."

"Where's my brother, Jimmy? What'd you do with his body?"

"I buried what was left of…" He caught himself, quickly looked away from me again. "I buried him deep in the forest, up past Lake Codorus."

What was left of him…what was left of him…what was…

Whatever control I had left abandoned me then—and I pulled the wrench I had snuck out of Grant's Subaru from my coat pocket and smashed Jimmy across his face with it.

I felt his cheek and nose explode, and he collapsed hard to the ground, blood spurting.

It was hard to move with the bulletproof vest Detective Anderson had insisted I wear, but I lunged forward and was on top of Jimmy before he could get up.

Hitting him…again and again and again…until he wasn't moving anymore, and the wrench was slick with blood and hair.

He likes to play games, Mr. Howard.

But, even then, I didn't stop, I couldn't stop smashing what was left of his face, over and over again—

—until suddenly Detective Anderson and the other cops were there next to me, barking orders in my face and pulling me off of him.

And then the woods all around me were alive with voices and footsteps, and there was nothing left for me to do but lay there sprawled on my back in the trampled snow, staring up at the uncaring December sky, as one cop read Jimmy his rights—*"I don't think he's gonna need those, Dan."*—and another cop radioed in for an ambulance; and then a helicopter buzzed the treetops overhead, its spotlight cutting through the skeletal branches, bathing us in its circle of golden light, the snow falling harder now all around us, looking like angel tears sifting down through the heavenly glow; and then my shattered mind had just enough time to think—*Isn't it so beautiful? Like we're inside one of Katy's snow globes.*—before Detective Anderson was kneeling at my side, taking me into her arms—*"Hurry, he's going into shock!"*—and even then I couldn't stop, I couldn't stop sobbing his name, "JIMMYYYY!"

Over and over again.

Only to be drowned out by the roar of the helicopter overhead.

For Steve King

STORY NOTES

MANY READERS ENJOY LEARNING about "the story behind the story." They may be curious about where the idea for the story came from; or what the writing process was like; or, perhaps, when and where the story was written. I, myself, am one of those curious readers. For me, it feels a little like sitting alone in a dark corner with the author and listening to him tell me all his secrets. I like that.

Still, plenty of other readers could care less; and some, in fact, would prefer the writer just keep his big mouth shut and tell his stories and be done with it. I certainly understand that point of view, too.

Regardless of which camp you fall into, I ask that you please wait to read these Story Notes until *after* you have read the stories themselves. There are spoilers lurking ahead.

BLOOD BROTHERS—This one was originally published as a nifty little chapbook from Subterranean Press. When it was first released, I heard from several longtime friends who had just read and enjoyed it—and were completely convinced that the story was about them and their respective brothers.

And no matter what I said, or how many times I said it, they refused to believe otherwise. I grew up with some weird friends.

So, here it is, after all these years, my final, in-print denial: "Blood Brothers" came from the dark basement of my imagination, and nowhere else.

As proof of this, I offer the following argument: "Blood Brothers" focuses on two themes which often pop up in my fiction—the unsettling certainty that no matter who you are, no matter how happy or secure or safe you feel, your life can change in a heartbeat, and there is nothing you can do to stop it from happening; and the idea that sometimes life forces you to make hard choices and to do whatever is necessary to protect the ones you love, no matter the cost.

These are themes you will encounter time and time again in my fiction—a direct result, I'm sure, of my longtime wariness of this world we live in—and "Blood Brothers" is just one more example.

One other aside: "Hanson Creek" plays a pivotal role in "Blood Brothers" and many of my other short stories. I actually had no idea this was the case until I sat down and started assembling the nearly three-dozen stories that make up this collection.

But it makes sense.

I grew up and spent my entire childhood in a two-story, corner house on Hanson Road in Edgewood, Maryland. And, while there was no real-life Hanson Creek in Edgewood, there *was* a twisting little stretch of muddy water called Winter's Run located about a mile from my house. My friends and I spent countless summer days there, fishing and swimming in the creek, and exploring and shooting our BB guns in the surrounding woods.

Winter's Run was one of those magical childhood playgrounds that only us kids seemed to be aware of—picture The Barrens in Stephen King's *IT*, and you'll get an idea of what I'm talking about—and it pleases me very much to look back now and realize just how many times this cherished place of my youth has snuck into my make-believe stories.

THE MAN WITH X-RAY EYES—Most days, I sit down and write to entertain myself, and this story succeeds on that level. I had a great time writing it, and I think the end result is a whole lot of fun.

On one hand, it's clearly a throwback to the days of *The X-Files* or maybe even *The Twilight Zone.*

On the other hand, it reads like a pretty decent character study of an ordinary, small town guy who may—or may not—possess superhuman powers.

I like that the answer is never crystal clear.

Or is it?

And, yes, while I do primarily write for myself, I also admit that it tickled me to no end when author Rick McCammon took the time last summer to email me and enthusiastically praise "The Man with X-Ray Eyes." His kind and generous words fueled my writing for weeks to come, and still make me smile today when I think about it.

If you haven't read McCammon's coming-of-age masterpiece, *Boy's Life*, run out and buy it right now; I promise you will thank me later.

THE BOX—A lot of readers were shocked—and disturbed—by the ending/final reveal of this story.

I'll tell you a secret: *I was, too.*

When I sat down and wrote the first sentence of "The Box," Charlie was my killer. When I hit the halfway point of the story, Charlie was my killer.

But, somewhere in that second half, the story flip-flopped on me. The characters flip-flopped on me.

And I suddenly realized that it was Bailey who was keeping the darkest of secrets from her family. I realized something else, too—I was scared of that little girl, and with good reason.

HEROES—"Heroes" is one of my most popular and reprinted short stories. It's also one of my earliest efforts, first published way back in 1991.

Originally written for a paperback anthology of vampire tales, I still remember receiving the invitation from the book's editor and feeling determined to do something different with the vampire mythology.

While I loved the scary, bloodsucking vampires of *Dracula* and *'Salem's Lot* and *I Am Legend*, I figured that most of the anthology's writers would wind up following that familiar dark path—and I wanted to try something else. Something focused on the lore-based concept of vampires being able to grant eternal life with a bite to the neck—but in an uplifting manner, instead of a menacing one.

Somehow, from all those admittedly jumbled thoughts, I ended up with "Heroes"—a story about love and hope and redemption. Not in the romantic sense, mind you, but instead a father and son love story.

A love letter, as it turned out, to my own father, who was doing quite fine at the time, still out there in his mid-60's, mowing the lawn and tinkering with his car most evenings in the garage.

I wrote the story longhand, sitting in my junker of a Datsun in a college parking lot somewhere in Delaware, waiting for Kara, my then-fiancée, to finish a graduate school interview. I remember the story surprised me. It came fast and furious, and when I finished scribbling the final sentence, I had a lump in my throat.

The story wasn't scary, and it never once utilized the word "vampire"—but it was powerful and true, and most of all, it was *me*.

My voice. My heart. My fears.

It was the first time I'd felt that I had written a truly "honest" story—and it felt like magic.

Many years later, my childhood friend and successful actor and director, John Schaech, would fall in love with the short story, and we would combine forces to write and produce a short movie based on "Heroes."

The experience would lead to a successful writing and producing partnership with John and many other film projects. It also led to my first visit to Los Angeles for the filming of "Heroes."

Filming took place over two very long and chilly nights at John's house in the Hollywood Hills, and while I have many wonderful memories from the set, there are two in particular that stand out to me:

The first moment occurred during a break in filming, when I found myself sitting alone with actor Djimon Hounsou. Djimon is a kind and talented actor, whose work has appeared in blockbusters such as *Guardians of the Galaxy* and *Blood Diamond*. At the time, he'd been recently nominated for an Academy Award for Best Supporting Actor for Ridley Scott's epic *Gladiator*, and I often wondered what the heck he was doing playing the role of a vampire (or "Mystery Man," as he was referred to in the script) in our little movie.

Well, I was about to find out the answer.

Because Djimon spent the next twenty minutes or so pouring his heart out to me—explaining with sweet sincerity how touching and unique he had found the story of "Heroes," and asking me questions about my father and telling me stories about his own father. In the course of the conversation, Djimon also shared with me that his father was in his final days in Africa, and that he hoped to get home soon after filming to be with him one final time.

After a bit, John came over, and the three of us sat there, swapping stories about our fathers, and celebrating how blessed we were to have them in our lives. It was a beautiful and poignant conversation, and something I will never forget.

The second moment came during the final hours of filming—and it blindsided me.

There is a flashback sequence in the story where the son talks about how his father is losing his race against time and age. Growing more and more confused and slow and lost as each day passes.

One way we decided to show this decline visually in the film was by having the actor who played the father sit at a kitchen counter, staring off into space, while slowly eating a bowl of cereal, hand shaking as he lifted a spoon to his mouth, milk dribbling down his chin.

It was a subtle, but powerful moment in the movie—and I thought I was prepared for it.

I was wrong.

The camera started rolling, the actor started doing his thing, and I immediately began to hear the words I had written—as a private voice-over inside my head:

I don't watch my father anymore. It hurts too much. Ten months ago, on a Friday night, he forgot my name.

I lasted two takes, and then I had to get out of there. It was too much. It felt like the monitor I was watching was a porthole into the future, my future, and it was no longer an actor I was watching; it was my own father.

I walked outside and sat on the front porch until the scene was finished. I didn't talk to anyone. I didn't look at anyone. I couldn't.

Later, I found out that John had experienced the exact same emotions.

DITCH TREASURES—I'm blessed to call Stephen King my friend. If you know any background history at all about my magazine and publishing company, you know that if it weren't for King's books and short stories, neither the magazine nor the book company would exist. His work inspired me and gave me direction at a very early age.

So, to find out firsthand many years later, that the guy behind the books is not only kind and generous and still insanely talented, but also down-to-earth and just flat-out cool? Well, that's been the cherry on top of the sundae for me.

Steve and I rarely get a chance to see each other these days—our schedules are jammed—but we email or text frequently. Books. Movies. Sports. Pop culture. Our dogs. Family. We cover a lot of ground, including the occasional off-the-wall topic, which I guess should be expected with guys like us.

I take full responsibility for this one:

My oldest son, Billy, and I were hanging out together at the beach, talking about the wild and wonderful internet, and it occurred to me—completely out of the blue; no, Mom, we were not talking about porn, I swear—that kids nowadays would probably never get a chance to experience the juvenile wonder and joy of stumbling upon a rain-swollen, puffy-paged girlie magazine on the side of the road or in a Dumpster or tucked away in someone else's hiding place.

I explained to my son that every tree house or fort we'd ever occupied as kids had boasted a stash of just such magazines. It was as much a part of growing up in the 1970s as firecrackers or slingshots or BB guns. Billy was momentarily fascinated, and then he was on to the next thing.

But, for some reason, I couldn't stop thinking about it. My God, it brought back so many memories.

I immediately emailed several friends—including Steve—and expressed my dismay at this sudden revelation.

Several of my childhood friends soon emailed back, and while I cannot, in good taste, tell you what they wrote—*did I mention that I grew up with some weird guys?*—I can tell you that they possess wonderful memories and haven't grown up nearly as much as their wives would prefer.

Thankfully, Steve's response was much more measured and mature. He told me that he understood exactly what I was describing, and that he and his friends had always called such findings "ditch treasures" back when they were kids.

Ditch treasures—it was perfect.

A month later, I emailed Steve the first page of this short story and thanked him for the title.

THE SILENCE OF SORROW—I've written about this story a couple times before and discussed my own surreal experiences with "cleaning up after the dead."

Fortunately, I've never lived the nightmare of finding the sort of thing described in this story, but as the main character explains in heartbreaking detail:

> "Even then, while he struggled with the cardboard boxes and the packing tape, he'd clearly known that the details of the day would haunt him forever; he would never be able to forget what kind of plates and utensils the woman had in her kitchen, the titles of the books on her shelves, the simple prints and paintings on the walls, her favorite color of shoes, the style of dress she preferred, what her handwriting looked like on a grocery list magneted to the refrigerator door. And so many other little things he had no right to possess knowledge of."

And he was right; those memories have never left me. They remain etched inside my soul, a permanent scar.

Reviewers have been very kind to "The Silence of Sorrow"—calling it everything from "devastating" to "emotionally complex and powerful" to "an understated masterpiece" (*Publisher's Weekly*).

I usually couldn't care less about reviews, but I've always felt relieved and gratified that readers have understood and accepted this story.

It's the most difficult story I've ever written.

AFTER THE BOMBS—I adored the story of Robin Hood when I was a boy. Not so much the green tights and frilly outfit, but the idea of shooting arrows and hiding in trees and robbing from the rich to give to the poor was right down my alley. I still remember running through the woods near my elementary school, pretending it was Sherwood Forest and the sheriff's men were in hot pursuit. They never caught me back then. Not even once.

So, when Joshua Allen Mercier tracked me down last year and asked me to write a story for his anthology of reimagined fairy tales and folklore—cleverly titled *Twice Upon a Time*—you better believe I jumped at the opportunity to revisit my childhood hero.

My initial plan was to set my story in a war-ravaged, post-apocalyptic world and go very dark with it. Plenty of violence and blood and radioactive monsters—a completely modern take on the Robin Hood myth.

But that didn't happen.

Instead, "After the Bombs" turned into a story within a story—one about the perseverance of the human spirit and love passed down from generation to generation.

There was some violence and there was some blood, but no monsters—and for that, I apologize.

Joshua told me that he cried at the end of "After the Bombs." I hope you did, too.

LAST WORDS—When I was young, I would often bury foreign coins (from my father's Air Force travels) in my yard and draw a map leading to the treasure. I would do my best to make the map appear worn with age, wrinkling it and often charring the edges, and then I'd present it to my friend, Jimmy Cavanaugh, as an authentic pirate treasure map discovered in my garage or attic.

Common sense rarely applies to ten-year-old boys, and we were no exception.

Jimmy got wise after the first three or four expeditions turned up the same old, dirt-crusted coins (which I, of course, tried to pass off as pirate doubloons), so I soon gave up on these treasure hunts and turned my attention to more profitable ventures such as lemonade stands and magic shows.

But I never forgot about those treasure hunts.

And either did Jimmy. He now swears that he knew from the start that I was behind the treasure hunts and only followed along to be a good friend. That's only half true, folks; Jimmy may be the very best of friends, but he's also a big fat liar when it comes to my treasure hunts. And he knows it.

Okay, a quick admission before we move on:

Not many people realize that I took off almost a full decade from writing and publishing new fiction. I still had plenty of reprints appearing in books and magazines. Countless interviews saw print and my name appeared on the covers of more than a dozen anthologies as an editor. I also co-wrote a number of feature films, as well as episodes of Showtime's *Masters of Horror* and NBC's *Fear Itself.*

But, brand new short fiction? Nada. Not a thing.

The reasons (excuses) were many: I was busy helping to raise two young boys; I was busy coaching a dozen sports teams for those two young boys; I was busy traveling and writing movies; I was busy running the book publishing business. You get the point.

But the truth of the matter was this: writing short stories had simply stopped being fun somewhere along the way. I didn't have writer's block, the ideas were still bubbling, but the joy of writing them down and shaping them into a story had vanished for some reason. So, I just stopped—and got busy doing other things.

Written in the late summer of 2014, "Last Call" was my first new short story in nearly a decade—and it was both a personal triumph and a relief. A triumph because it was a brand new story, written very much in my familiar voice. And a relief, because, to be perfectly honest, I was terrified that I had forgotten how to write a short story.

I'm grateful to editor Greg Kishbaugh (also a fine writer) for pulling the story out of me. I still don't know how he did it, and that's just fine with me.

NIGHT CALL—I still remember the frenzy surrounding the Millennium with head-shaking clarity. Don't you?

Perfectly sensible folks lost their minds, and the crazy ones…well, they took center stage and seemed to relish every minute they spent in the limelight.

"Night Call" was my way of trying to make sense of that period of time; my way of trying to make sense of something that made no sense at all to me.

I really like the two cops in this story. They're my kind of guys. And if I ever have to experience that madness again, I think I'd like to do it riding shotgun with Frank and Ben.

"Night Call" ends with what is probably my favorite closing sentence of all my stories.

THE LAKE IS LIFE—I grew up with three older sisters, so I had plenty of early and prolonged exposure to the mysteries of the opposite sex. I learned a lot about mood swings and hairbrushes and waiting in line for the upstairs bathroom and how you should never ever look in a girl's purse without asking first. I even learned to like Bee Gees music.

My favorite activity was entertaining my sisters' dates while they sat on the living room sofa waiting for my sisters to finish getting ready. I would usually do this by sledding down our stairs on an inflatable Hershey Park pillow, skimming across the living room floor, and casually informing the date that my sister would be down soon, she just had a bad case of diarrhea. True story.

Anyway, despite their best efforts, I can't claim that I learned much in the way of wisdom when it came to preparing me to be a better boyfriend or husband—I can hear my sisters laughing now—but the experiences did probably help when it came time to write "The Lake Is Life."

I was pleasantly surprised by how much I enjoyed writing a story where almost all the characters were female. It was a first for me, and I look forward to revisiting it sometime soon.

It occurred to me later that the story of Becca and her mom and Grandma could've almost transitioned into a mainstream tale of a loving family in crisis.

Almost.

Becca probably deserved a better fate than the one I gave her.

THE GOOD OLD DAYS—For some reason, I've always enjoyed writing about elderly characters. I've also enjoyed reading about them, which explains why *Insomnia* is one of my Top 10 Stephen King novels.

Sure, old folks can be just as evil and despicable as their younger kin, but I think there's an innate grace and dignity to many old-timers that really comes across on the page.

That's exactly how I felt about The Three Horsemen in "The Good Old Days."

GRAND FINALE—This is another very early story, as evidenced by the frequent references to VCRs and videocassette tapes, and the occasional (ahem) clunky sentence or two.

I've included it here because it's the sexiest story I've ever written—which might not be saying much—and because I think "Grand Finale" would make a pretty nifty and frightening half-hour of television in the hands of the right people.

(For the record, I'm still thinking about Frank and Ben, the two cops from "Night Call," a few stories back. I'm going to have to write a new story featuring those two. I miss them.)

THE ARTIST—My father served in the Air Force during World War II. He saw action in both Europe and the Pacific, and his stories of that war were a huge part of my life growing up.

When I was very young, he converted hundreds of photos—from the war and his later travels in the Air Force—into slides, and our family would gather once or twice a year in the living room for a slideshow on our old-fashioned, pull-up screen. It was always a special night, and I would often invite neighborhood friends over to join my mom and my sisters and me.

I can still remember the sound and the smell of the projector; feeling almost hypnotized watching the dust motes floating through the thin beam of light; and the comforting sound of my father's voice as he described each slide to us.

I also remember going to sleep on those slideshow nights wondering how those young soldiers could have been so brave and unafraid. Many years later, I would remember those night thoughts when I first watched *Band of Brothers* on HBO—still, for my money, the finest hours of television I have ever watched.

My father's experiences also inspired my own fictional war stories at an early age. When I was eight or nine, I would often pretend I was John Boy from *The Waltons*—don't laugh; I was eight—and I would sit at my little desk in the corner of my bedroom and scribble war stories in a spiral notebook. After awhile, I started writing monster stories, too. Each time I finished a new story, I would illustrate it, and then show it to my mother (she was my first and kindest audience). She encouraged me to write more stories, so that's what I did.

Originally written for a tribute anthology honoring Richard Matheson's classic novel, *The Beardless Warriors*, "The Artist" is my first war story in close to forty years. It also might be the scariest story in this entire collection. It's certainly the saddest.

I was nervous when I emailed my story to the editors. I so badly wanted to honor Mr. Matheson and my father with my words. So, I was extremely relieved and thrilled when Richard Christian emailed the following response: "...a poignant story I think my father (as a young writer, himself, during the war) would appreciate. You did something very rare; conveying idealism of your soldiers and broken hearts of war in so subtle a way."

I'm immensely grateful to R.C. Matheson and Barry Hoffman for the invitation and kind reaction to "The Artist," and I'm honored to have appeared in *Brothers in Arms*.

FAMILY TIES—I don't remember whether this story was first written for a straight crime anthology or maybe one of the Cat Crime collections that were very popular at the time. I do know I had a great time writing it with Barry Hoffman, and that it very much reads like a homage to the supremely-talented Ed Gorman, especially that dark ending.

Looking back at the story many years later, I'll be damned if I can pick out which sections were written by Barry and which parts are mine. I like that; I think that's how all successful collaborations should be.

MISTER PARKER—I set out to write a simple Halloween story that involved a guy answering his door throughout the night to repeatedly find no one there. I wanted to make it spooky and atmospheric and a throwback to the days of Ray Bradbury and Richard Matheson and Charles Beaumont.

As is often the case with best made writing plans, that didn't happen.

Instead, "Mister Parker" turned into a deeply layered character sketch of a very decent man with a troubled past. I could have probably written a lot more about old Bulldog Parker—I liked him that much—but I knew the story didn't require it.

I truly wish "Mister Parker" had a happier ending, but it wasn't meant to be.

MONSTERS—I've always loved The Legend of the Hook. I can't tell you how many times I've told that story myself, trying to scare my friends or dates when we were parked out in the middle of nowhere. I always wished I had a fake hook with a stump of realistic-looking, bloody, torn flesh to hang on my outside passenger door handle, so I could take the prank one step further. Someone really should sell those, by the way.

"Monsters" tries to turn the Hook legend inside out, or should I say outside in. Umm, that was bad, but you get my point. I've always had a warm spot in my heart for this little tale, thought it was clever and fun. I'm not so sure readers agree with me on that—the story has usually generated a resounding silence—but that's okay. Even ugly babies are loved by their daddies.

LIKE FATHER, LIKE SON—When I was a teenager, I had two favorite bookstores in Edgewood. The first was Carol's Used Books, which was housed in a couple of trailers, sandwiched between a Dunkin' Donuts and a pawn shop. I spent hours in that place, and I can still remember the exact layout (horror and mystery straight ahead and to the right), the sagging, carpeted floors, and the comforting smell of old books. Carol's closed a long time ago. A used car lot stands in its place now. But I still have dozens of paperbacks on my bookshelves with the *Carol Used Books* stamp on the inside front cover, and that's good enough for me.

The second store was called Maxine's Books and Cards, and as luck would have it, Maxine's was located right next door to Frank's Pizza, the best pizza shop in the entire world. Maxine's is where I first discovered Dean Koontz's backlist—books like *Darkfall* and *Shattered* and *Night Chills*. It's where I bought my first Charlie Grant paperback and my first horror anthologies. It's also where I picked up new issues each month of *Fangoria* and *Ellery Queen's Mystery Magazine* (with the occasional Archie's Comics digest thrown in for good measure).

I always dreamed of seeing one of my stories in *Ellery Queen's*. It felt like such a "grown up" magazine to me—the kind of magazine my father read. Mostly straight crime and mystery, but dark stuff snuck in there too from time to time. The best genre writers contributing their best work; you never got the feeling *EQ* published any trunk stories.

My dream came true when "Like Father, Like Son" appeared in the March 1997 issue of *Ellery Queen's Mystery Magazine*.

I was so excited on publication day, I couldn't wait for my contributor copies to arrive in the mail. Maxine's was long closed by then, so I drove to the next town over and picked up a couple copies from a magazine shop. I stopped at my parents' house on the way home and gave a copy to my father. That was a good night.

THE TOWER—One of two recent stories—along with "The Lake Is Life"—that feel very much to me like old-fashioned, campfire tales. The kind of stories best told in the middle of the dark woods, around a blazing fire, with owls hooting in the background, and unseen creatures rustling in the brush. I've always had a particular fondness for this type of story. They remind me of the old radio programs my parents liked so much.

The water tower in this story exists in the town I grew up in. It overlooks my old elementary school, and I never completely trusted it. The tower looked too much like one of H.G. Wells' spindly aliens, and in the back of my over-imaginative head, I think I was always waiting for it to wake up and come to life.

Hanson Creek also makes another appearance in "The Tower," but that's about it for real-life references. The rest is just make-believe. I hope.

I really like the old man narrator of "The Tower." I wish he hadn't done the things he did.

BROTHERS—The second story in this collection about a bad seed brother. This one, written with my literary hero and all around great guy, Ed Gorman, was first published in England as a gorgeous paperback edition by Paul Fry, of SST Publications (look him up, folks; they do good work). This marks its first U.S. appearance.

Before all of you start thinking, *Poor Rich, he must have grown up with one holy terror of a brother,* here is an excerpt from the Afterword I contributed to the SST Publications' edition of "Brothers":

> I myself have one older brother, and I love him dearly. He's a fine, upstanding citizen. Father. Husband. Retired soldier. A good man and role model in every way.
>
> He's also a wonderful brother. Never tortured me growing up. Never locked me out of the house naked or shaved my head or tickled me until I peed my pants.
>
> So, I'm at a loss when it comes to explaining why I'm so drawn to the darker bonds of brotherhood.
>
> As with most of my short fiction, it's just how I *see* the world around me, how I see it and *feel* it.
>
> I'm a pretty cheerful guy, living an extremely fortunate life, but when it comes to my writing I definitely tend to ignore the sunshine and explore the dark shadows and dirty corners instead.
>
> I guess it's just where I feel the most at home, and where my vision is the sharpest.
>
> "Brothers"—and "Blood Brothers," for that matter—are stories about family and responsibility and how the past informs the present and very often leads to difficult choices. Sometimes, deadly choices.
>
> It's a dark story. An honest story.

So, there you have it. I dearly love my big brother, John. He taught me how to fish and watched Abbott and Costello movies with me. He even named his only son Richard—after me. It doesn't get much better than that.

CEMETERY DANCE—I've written about this one a lot, so I'll just give the short version for newer readers.

"Cemetery Dance" was one of the first short stories I ever wrote, and was the second story I ever sold.

But the magazine that bought it went out of business before they were able to publish it.

So did the second magazine.

And the third.

I was starting to fear the story was cursed when Pete Crowther finally published it three years later in his acclaimed anthology of superstitions, *Narrow Houses*.

Each of the editors who bought "Cemetery Dance" had commented at length about the tale's unique title. In fact, I have a sneaking suspicion several of them were trying to gracefully tell me that they thought the title was actually better than the story itself. Looking back, they may have been right about that.

When it came time to decide on a title for my own fledgling magazine, I remembered their enthusiasm and chose *Cemetery Dance* as the name. And despite some strange looks at my bank and local Kinko's, I've never once regretted that decision.

The story itself is a fairly minor one. An exercise in mood and atmosphere—a fly-on-the-wall view of one man's descent into madness and obsession.

The imagery in "Cemetery Dance" came from my childhood. As I wrote in my introduction to the story in *Narrow Houses*: "When we were around nine or ten, my friends and I used to believe that when the sun went down and the shadows emerged for night, the cemetery would come to life. Not the decaying corpses, mind you, but the cemetery itself... breathing for the dead."

BLUE—Not a whole lot to say about this one. I wrote "Blue" for Alan Clark and one of his amazing *Imagination Fully Dilated* anthologies, wherein he assigned each author a different painting of his to write a story about; a clever reverse-twist on the usual illustrative process.

The artwork I was assigned correlates with the nightmare scene from the story:

> *...when she finally turns away from the window and glimpses herself in the fancy gold mirror hanging on the opposite stone wall, there is nothing left of her but a bag of bones—a parched skeleton— grinning an awful grin and smelling of wet, graveyard dirt, and her*

hair is limp clumps of rotting string, her dress nothing but tatters of faded yellow cloth…

I like the characters I created in "Blue" quite a bit, especially my sweet Momma narrator. As usual, she probably deserved better. I have a nasty habit of doing that to my people.

A CRIME OF PASSION—This early story marked a lot of firsts for me.

First time one of my stories ever appeared in hardcover (the Borderlands Press edition of the censorship journal, *Gauntlet*).

First time one of my stories appeared alongside work from childhood heroes, Stephen King, Ray Bradbury, and Harlan Ellison.

First time one of my stories appeared in a signed, limited edition.

First time a story of mine was ever reprinted (less than a year later in Martin Greenberg and Ed Gorman's *Women on the Edge*).

It was also one of the first stories where I found myself paying as much attention to plot and story structure as I did characterization.

Years later, when Ed Gorman wrote this about "A Crime of Passion"—"The structure of the story is so brilliant, and the telling so polished, that I've been trying to do my own version of the story for the past three years"—I knew that I was slowly getting better at this writing gig, and it inspired me to work that much harder at it.

"A Crime of Passion" stretches the boundaries of good sense from time to time, but as a cautionary pulp tale of suspense and adventure, I think it does a decent enough job. Sometimes, that's the best we can hope for.

HOMESICK—This short story arrived in one furious burst of writing— an hour or so from start to finish. Written in 1996, it was published in a Marty Greenberg anthology called *White House Horrors*.

If you were a reader or writer of dark fiction in the 1980s/1990s and beyond, you were very familiar with the name Martin H. Greenberg. He was responsible for publishing thousands of stories in hundreds of unique anthologies in a wide variety of genres: horror, mystery, crime, science fiction, fantasy, even western.

Marty was a prince of a man, generous and kind and thoughtful, and I owe him a huge debt for treating me so well.

More than a dozen of the stories in *A Long December* also appeared in Greenberg anthologies. Thanks, Marty; you are missed.

DEVIL'S NIGHT—The second of a pair of Halloween stories in *A Long December*, "Devil's Night" reminds me in a way of "Heroes," in that both stories contain autobiographical moments and feelings—yet each was written well before those moments ever occurred in my life.

Let me explain. In "Heroes" I wrote about a grown son who is losing his father to the ravages of old age, and how he will stop at nothing to prevent that from happening. At the time of its writing, my father was in grand shape. Mid-60s and healthy and active. But I knew it wouldn't always be that way. I knew things would eventually change, and like the son in the story, I also knew "that there was nothing sadder, nothing more heart-breaking than watching your hero die." So, that's how and why "Heroes" was born; I wrote it to help myself deal with something that was still some twenty years in the future.

With "Devil's Night" it was very much the same sort of thinking. In 1996—when the story was written and first published—I was not yet a father. Nor was Kara pregnant. In fact, due to extensive treatments for cancer, there was great uncertainty as to whether I could ever produce a child naturally.

But I knew I wanted to be a father one day—more than anything. And I knew that if I were ever blessed with children, I would worry about those children. A lot. It's just how I'm made.

And that's where "Devil's Night" came in. Those long night drives to think and relax were taken from real life, as were many of the details about the small town in which the story takes place. The layout of the high school in the story was the layout of the old Edgewood High School, before it was torn down to make room for a new one. The old post office really existed. And the narrator's feelings of love and concern for his wife and newborn children were my own personal feelings and fears—only 3-4 years ahead of time.

That's right, several years after the story was published, Kara gave birth to a baby boy named Billy. Four years after that, Noah came along. Miracles, both.

Even now, all these years later, I still worry about my boys—especially now that they are both teenagers. And, yes, I still take the occasional late night drive to think and relax—and dream.

BRIDE OF FRANKENSTEIN: A LOVE STORY—This is another one of those "ugly baby" stories I have a feeling I like a whole lot more than some readers. And, hey, I'm okay with that.

But, seriously, how can you not like a story that features an insane, grieving doctor with a Norman Bates complex, a makeshift basement laboratory, and midnight grave-robbing?

And the guy's name is Francis Einstein. Frank Einstein. Frankenstein! Get it?!

Crickets.

THE SEASON OF GIVING—I'm a big kid in many ways, so I'm naturally a huge fan of Christmas. Always have been. But I've also always had a kind of innate understanding that the holiday season isn't necessarily a time of joy and celebration for many folks.

Even as a child, I noticed that for every happy person I saw sitting in church or strolling the mall, there seemed to be two or three others who looked lost and lonely and sad. Sometimes, even angry. I worried about these people quite a bit, and they were a frequent topic of conversation with my very patient parents.

Once I got older, I learned about all the statistics regarding suicide rates spiking during the holidays, and the reasons why, and it all made sense to me.

So, when I got a surprise, last minute invite to write for *Santa Clues*, a collection of crime stories based around Christmas, I knew (despite the silly title) that the holiday theme was ripe for a story of real substance.

The only problem was I couldn't think of one, and I was staring at a tight deadline.

I had my opening line of the story, which I really liked, and I knew my main character was a down-on-his-luck department store security guard dressed as Santa, and I knew he was going to help an abused little girl and her mother get out of a bad place—but that's all I had.

I wrote the first half of the story, and got no further.

And time was running out.

Fortunately, Norman Partridge (go buy Norm's Halloween classic, *Dark Harvest*, right this very minute; it's *that* good) swooped in and saved the day by finishing the story for me. He worked his magic for a day or two, snail-mailed me his version (that's right; this was before email, believe it or not), I gave the story one final writing pass, and we had "The Season of Giving." Just in time for Christmas.

A CAPITAL CAT CRIME—Written for Marty Greenberg's (remember him?) *Cat Crimes* series, this story was first published in *Danger in DC: Cat Crimes in our Nation's Capital.* I've never been a big fan of the cozy mysteries where the cat helps the heroine solve a crime, so I chose to go dark with my kitty story. Of course. I guess you can't get much darker than the end of the world.

THE SINNER KING—I'm not much of a fantasy reader or writer. My taste in fiction runs more to the dark stuff: mystery, crime, suspense, horror, adventure. Stories with an edge. So, when I was presented with the opportunity to write for *Grails*, an award-winning collection of fantasy tales, I decided to tiptoe around the book's theme and stay in the shadows. (P.S. I lifted this Story Note directly from a previous appearance of the "The Sinner King." Just to see if any longtime readers were paying attention.)

A SEASON OF CHANGE—Another one of those early stories (1996) that made me feel like I was maybe getting the hang of this writing thing. Decently plotted. A believable, mildly sympathetic lead. Hard-boiled and tough, but with a pretty tender heart beating inside.

I set out to write about loss and grief and the hidden dark side that lurks within even the best of us…and that's what I ended up with. Sort of. Somehow I also ended up with a story that culminates with a strong sense of hope and rediscovery. A rare happy ending for a very unhappy tale.

MIDNIGHT PROMISES—I wrote this story when I was thirty years old. At the time, I didn't have a hair on my body, and I weighed 150 pounds—the direct result of nine weeks of chemotherapy.

Fortunately, the other direct result of those nine weeks of chemotherapy was my cancer was gone.

Earlier in the year, extensive tests had revealed that I had cancer in both lungs, my liver, my lymph nodes, and my stomach.

The doctors told me I had a 50/50 change of surviving (which I knew, at the time, was bullshit; I was in rough shape).

I'll save the story of my battle with cancer for another place and time, but suffice to say I was a very lucky guy.

I still am.

There's obviously a fair amount of autobiographical detail in "Midnight Promises." A lot of the hospital stuff, and the apple tree/tumor dream from the story was an actual reoccurring nightmare from that period of my life, as was the nightmare that didn't make it into the story—the one where I was a corpse-conductor on a huge, shiny black train of death that roared across a ruined, radioactive and charred countryside, thick black smoke billowing from its immense exhaust pipes.

It was an interesting time for me—and my loved ones.

I didn't let anyone read "Midnight Promises" ahead of time. Late that year, when it first saw print as the title story in my debut collection, it caught a lot of people by surprise—and it made some of those people pretty upset. Some of them friends, some of them family.

I remember when Kara finished reading the story, she threw the book across the room where it crashed into a wall and fell to the floor.

A good story is supposed to elicit a reaction, right?

THE NIGHT SHIFT—One of two dialogue-only experiments in the collection, and a return to Frank and Ben, my favorite two police detectives from "Night Call." An absolutely perfect example of a story that was written, first and foremost, to entertain myself...and then, hopefully, others. Broken record, I know, but I really need to revisit these guys soon.

ONLY THE STRONG SURVIVE—*Fangoria* called this one "intense" and a newspaper reviewer praised it as "an unrelentingly dark vision of the werewolf myth." Both descriptions are accurate, maybe a little too accurate.

Looking back on "Only the Strong Survive," I wish Barry and I had sprinkled in a little black humor. I think the story is ripe for it, and I think it would have helped the characters be a little more dynamic and interesting.

THE INTERVIEW—I miss Richard Laymon—his voice and his laughter and his unique talent. I miss our phone chats and his books and stories. Dick was one of the good guys, and the genre is a much less interesting place without him in it.

When Dick asked me to write a story for his first-ever anthology, *Bad News*, I knew I had to come up with something special to mark the occasion.

I had an image stuck in my head of an old man sitting on his front porch in the middle of the night, just rocking away on his rocking chair and watching the neighborhood sleep. He looked like a friendly enough guy—but I sensed there was more to him. Something troubling, maybe even dangerous.

I decided to write the story using only dialogue, something I had never attempted before. It was a challenge, but I enjoyed every word of it—and my guy on the porch turned out to be a very sweet old man who had just…*snapped*.

I still have Dick's letter telling me how much he loved the story in a desk drawer in my home office.

THE POETRY OF LIFE—One of a handful of stories in this collection that was inspired by a dream. I've always been a big dreamer, my entire life, and I remember quite a few of them. But this one was…*different*.

I didn't just dream *about* this middle-aged music teacher—I dreamt that I *was* her.

Everything I thought and felt and observed and did in this dream came directly from her/my point of view. I actually walked in this woman's shoes, and when I woke up in the morning, the last two lines of the story were echoing in my head—"I had to walk slow. The guns were heavy."

The dream bothered me for days. Those two sentences bothered me for days.

So, I wrote "The Poetry of Life."

A LONG DECEMBER—I've always wondered what it would feel like to wake up one morning and find out that your best friend was not who you believed them to be—that they were leading a double life.

I don't mean the clichéd double life involving a mistress or a second family stashed away in a nearby town. Or the timid housewife moonlighting as a call girl stripper.

I'm talking Ted Bundy or Robert Yates or the BTK serial killer Dennis Rader.

What would it feel like to wake up and turn on the news and see your best friend's picture underneath a banner headline that read: SERIAL KILLER?

The emotions that would come rushing at you—shock, disbelief, denial, confusion, anger, guilt, fear.

I can't even begin to imagine what it would feel like.

But I've always wondered.

"A Long December" was my answer.

ONE FINAL NOTE—The stories included in *A Long December* were written over a period of almost thirty years—the earliest story ("Cemetery Dance") penned when I was just a wide-eyed twenty-year-old college student and the most recent ("A Long December") completed a week before my fiftieth birthday.

Many years ago, acclaimed crime writer, Ed Gorman, blessed me with the following praise: "Rich writes gracefully but without pretense. He knows all about the double-whammy, the device wherein the last few paragraphs of a story are able to raise hard cold goosebumps along the arms, and force the body to shudder.

"But what Rich does best of all is tell us about himself and by this I don't mean the egotistical ramblings of a Thomas Wolfe (or sometimes) a Norman Mailer...I mean, he is able to convey through his fiction the joys, sorrows, fears, and aspirations of a very decent and very talented young man who is very much a child of his age. Most good novelists, I think, are also good journalists—they are able to tell you honestly about their particular moment on this planet, and what went on during it, and what it amounted to, and how it felt to live through it. There is this same journalistic quality in virtually all of Rich's fiction. He takes great snapshots of America in the 1990s."

I hope Ed is right, folks. That's all I've ever tried to do in my stories—take something meaningful to me (a person, a place, a moment in time) and tell a good and interesting story about it. An honest story.

All the stories in A Long December might not be good and interesting (that's up to you, and I do hope the majority of them pleased you in some way), but they *are* honest. They are my truth, and the best I could do each time I sat down and put pen to paper.

It's fascinating to think back to where I was in my life when each story was written: a college apartment, a parking lot, a library, a grassy hill, a hospital room, a lot of different desks in a lot of different rooms.

Some of these stories were first published at a time when cell phones and DVDs and compact discs didn't exist, when payphones appeared on most street corners, and the Internet was just a burgeoning dream.

Many were written before I was married, before my wife and I had our two boys, before both my mother and father passed away. Others before my cancer, and still others before the expansion of my publishing company.

It's all a little dizzying—and humbling—to think about.

As usual, Ed found better words than I ever could have: these stories are some of my favorite snapshots from those almost thirty years; A Long December, my personal photo album of the many people and places and moments I wanted to tell you about.

Thirty years…I'm amazed and grateful to still be here, still telling my stories, and I'm especially thankful to all of you for listening.

COPYRIGHT
INFORMATION

AUTHOR BIO

RICHARD CHIZMAR IS THE founder/publisher of Cemetery Dance magazine and the Cemetery Dance Publications book imprint. He has edited more than 20 anthologies and his fiction has appeared in dozens of publications, including *Ellery Queen's Mystery Magazine* and *The Year's 25 Finest Crime and Mystery Stories*. He has won two World Fantasy awards, four International Horror Guild awards, and the HWA's Board of Trustees' award.

Chizmar (in collaboration with Johnathon Schaech) has also written screenplays and teleplays for United Artists, Sony Screen Gems, Lions Gate, Showtime, NBC, and many other companies.

Chizmar is the creator/writer of *Stephen King Revisited*, and his next short story collection, *A Long December*, is due in 2016 from Subterranean Press.

Chizmar's work has been translated into many languages throughout the world, and he has appeared at numerous conferences as a writing instructor, guest speaker, panelist, and guest of honor.

You can follow Richard Chizmar on both Facebook and Twitter.